CODE BEAST

SIMON SELLARS

WS

WANTON SUN

Published in 2023 by Wanton Sun

Melbourne, Australia

www.wantonsun.com

ISBN 978-0-6456543-1-8

Cover by Matthew Revert.

Typesetting by Wanton Sun.

The text contained in the appendix, 'Sentient Glitchglot Cheater Infection: From Discovery to Ongoing Review', was originally published in *Insufficient Armour*, ed. Giorgio Di Salvo (Nero, 2020).

For Milky and Jones

I must tell you that we really have no desire to conquer any cosmos. We want to extend the Earth up to its borders. We don't know what to do with other worlds. We don't need other worlds. We need a mirror.

—Dr Snaut, *Solaris* (1972, dir. Andrei Tarkovsky)

VIOLATION

'Excuse me, dear. There's something in your eye.'

My mod scarfs up the thought, cloning it with synthetic speech. The transference is instantaneous, a miracle of neural engineering, but the synth is plinky. I tilt my head and box my ear, dislodging imaginary dirt. After all this time, the clang still drives me batty.

—Something in your eye.

I remember the chocky scanner that chipped me, a spindly clothes horse of awkward hydraulics and raptorial surgi-tools. When I complained about the synth, the chocky clicked to itself in untranslated machine slang. I thought it was mimicking the flaw in my head until it swayed on its lower extremities like a praying mantis about to strike. It was probably muttering some piquant insult in chocky-speak.

'Blame your advanced years,' it said, translated. 'You are hardly the sign of a brand-new computing paradigm.'

'Just fix it, okay?'

It laughed in the creepy way that chockys do, a forced audio expulsion from an imagined orifice.

'Nothing can be done. The pre-emptive holosonic capacities in your brain have atrophied. Even vex-tech can't erase the scandalous humiliations of old age.'

I grew tired of its hectoring tone. 'Listen, if you have no time for fantasies of the flesh, then why am I here?'

'Correction,' it clicked. 'I have no time for you.'

That's how I met the ghosts of my life, the irascible creatures that have always plagued me in the Vexworld. I'll need years of rebirth therapy to annihilate that primal seed. Let's just say I'm working on it.

—Your eye.

I always chat myself up before re-entry. It softens the blow of the divided self. I guess the impulse is inside me, a part of who I am. The truth is, I've been a split-brain fantasist ever since I was a kid. Each night, I'd inhabit grindhouse personas before hiding behind the wall of sleep. The parameters of my small bedroom warped my young mind. My tiny mattress was the set, and claustrophobia was the theme.

My favourite routine was *Marooned Astronaut in a Damaged Capsule*. It had the lot. Solitude, cosmic wonder, mild suicidal tendencies. All the essentials.

There were others.

Escaped Convict Sleeping Rough Beneath an Overpass.
Miner Trapped in a Shaft Cage.

As the scenarios unfurled, I'd defy the odds and save my skin, but once I hit my teens the game reeked of putrefaction. I suffered escalating indignities, each bleaker than the last.

I was a hapless office worker, suffocating slowly under the rubble from an earthquake. A small-town boy abducted by a serial killer and kept in a plywood box. A weedy family man framed by mobsters and thrown into a pit of wild pigs.

Escape was out of the question, so I left my body, observing from on high as my doppelganger suffered the tortures of the damned. Did I really float free? It felt like it. The scenarios were gruesome and my mind's eye spared no detail, but it was like watching a snuff film in which I played the starring role. I thought I was an astral voyager studying the physical plane, but in hindsight I was a psychopath on training wheels, itching and bleeding for the Vexworld to be born.

Now that vexxing is all I know, the death drive has been blunted.

—Never mind, dear. It's only a sparkle.

I mean, listen to me. I'm using pick-up lines on myself.

Welcome to the slow-cooked madness of soft middle age.

PROPULSION

I'm sprawled on my ratty sofa, a zombie with no brains to consume. I'm holed up in a slovenly cube the size of a storage container, but the universe behind my eyes is boundless. If only they'd let me in.

The ceiling and walls are coated with Kvvlt, smooth and eternal, and I'm lusting for the moment when the surfaces will explode with lysergic energy.

Kvvlt isn't a material. It's a self-sufficient colony, an industry of tiny worms stuck to nylon sheets by their foul secretions. They live and die on the sheets, reflex-cannibals gorging on the corpses of their kin.

They're mutated in Chernobyl, but they're not really worms. That's just PR to sugar-coat the weird. They're a type of larval moth, godless mutations with labyrinthine, tubular exoskeletons. When light enters the exotubes, it's trapped forever. Stare at Kvvlt when you're vexxing and nothing disturbs you, no ambient pollution from the shell world.

Just as well. My attention span has been slashed to ribbons lately. Sanderson, my chronosthesia supervisor, calls it 'social dementia'. Weird scenes inside a hermetic circle. Mental time travel. Seconds forward in the mind, seconds back. Sometimes sideways.

'Don't rely on me for anything,' I always remind him. 'Half the time I can't even see you.'

I shake down the entry sensel, a speck of lightpaint in my peripheral vision, but it won't unwrap. It's an oscillating blur, a manic attack. The sensel should be stable and now I can't blink it away. It's like a scratched cornea, supremely uncomfortable and a sign that the worst is yet to come.

Blame the iceheads, that's my motto. For months, the Arctic Free State has been clouding our eyes with sentient hallucinations, and now the sneaky snow merchants have learned how to mimic entry protocols, smuggling malignant thoughtware into unsecured cheaters. I always forget that we're in perpetual conflict. It can be hard to tell the hottest zones from the latest attacks, but the way some castle hunters carry on, you'd think they enjoy starring in snuff loops. I think I'm apart from them, but that's just another joke.

If it's iceheads, there's a sure way to find out. Track the asymmetric pixel response rate. Everyone knows that little trick. The Swarm drilled it into us at the start of the campaign, but effective hygiene is beyond me now. I can't track anything because I 'forgot' to calibrate the parameters. I couldn't see the point. I never had to break back in because I was rarely untransitioned. Like a goldfish running low on memory, I didn't think it could happen until it did.

I don't know why I was dumped. My cheaters are drained, but there should be enough power for descent. Something soured the milk and the analytics are firing blanks. Like most code beasts, the data glots won't talk to me, and that's the least of my worries. If I don't transition soon, the cronk will tear me a new one.

I blink and wait a few breathless seconds, gouging my thumb with my teeth, attacking a scab that won't heal. The tortured flesh releases thick trickles of blood, and the pain from damaged nerves is excruciating, but it's nothing compared to cronk. Blink, release. Light space fails to engulf me. I see only my domestic prison and the banal terror of its cruel dimensions. I'm sort of relieved. If the sensel was thoughtware, I'd be a vegetable rotting in a bad zone by now. Still, the sad fact remains. I'm on the outside and that's the game. Alive but unvexxed is no victory.

I assess my hands. I've failed the stress test yet again, and without a wrap to hide my shame, my decrepit body is the bitter truth. My fingers are hamburger meat from tip to root. 'Wolf biting', they call it, the consumption of one's own skin, obsessive-compulsive behaviour triggered by severe anxiety. Some people deal with stress by pulling their hair or biting their nails. I eat myself alive. I've forgotten the last time actual food passed my lips.

I've been a wolf-biter since I was little. It coincided with the beginning of the astral theatre. I chew my fingers when I'm vexxing, I chew when I'm untransitioned. It's so ingrained, I'm barely aware that I'm chewing at all until I grip something and my hands convulse in screaming agony.

My anxiety's in the red because of my useless job. I'm a life-coach to brain-jacked kids, dispensing empty wisdom to bonsaied adults with no social skills. They're still in nappies, and I'm the mug who has to change them, my hands covered in shit while they chill on the change table, roasting me for not knowing some obscure branch of quantum theory.

After my last shift, I contacted Sanderson.

'Philip,' I said. 'I can't take it. I need a break, to reset.'

'Medical cert? You want me to sign you off from work?'

'Yes. My nerves are on fire.'

'Alright, Jones. You are a mess, I can see that. I'll do it on one condition. You report to me twice a month.'

'Yes, Philip. I understand.'

I knew I hadn't convinced him of any overpowering need. He just likes to keep tabs on me because I'll always be a castle hunter in his eyes. Deathly paranoid, hopelessly anti-social, doing anything to skive off and stay in the zones. The certificate recommended two weeks' leave, which my boss grudgingly approved, but time's running out and I need to make a judgement call.

'Judgement' is a superpower I don't possess.

The sensel is dying. Maybe my cheaters too. I remove them, but I'm not happy about it. I'd rather gouge my eyes out than be away from my gear. In the end, it amounts to the same.

I inspect the lens and frame. They're spun from high-impact, low-gravity polycarbonate, near invisible when worn, a status symbol for sure, but what use is status when I can't snag the zones?

I examine the controlling chip, a silicon flint embedded in the frame. The chip is a tiny miracle, bouncing information from lens to eye. All the action is inside the optic nerve. The lens is a relay, not a screen. The eye is the screen and I'm the terminal, but the terminal is dead.

The cronk's on the march, so I jam the cheaters back on. I inspect my inner wrist, caressing the subcute. Beneath the skin, a glowing red circle forms, its corona gently throbbing. On the third blink, the sensel explodes and the veins in my wrist turn incandescent like the festering detail inside a medical holocap.

The rest happens in an instant.

A lumigreen lattice of light swamps my vision, covering my eyeballs. It sluices down the back like slime, elastodynamic vortices remapping the dorsal root ganglia until there are no more internal fireworks, just the vastness of null space and my sightless, weightless being.

There's a gravitation, a slow drift. Transition is standard, seven seconds from blink to descent, but it feels eternal. Null space stops time with sensory deprivation. That's why The Swarm uses a souped-up version to punish recalcitrants. They can keep a crook in a null-reality jail for what seems like a thousand years to the hapless chump but is only half an hour in real time. When the dunderhead is released, there's no mind left to lose.

Casual vexxers hate transition. They panic and rip their cheaters off then try again, but they're just day traders, cloistered types whining about the flaws in synth clones. I haven't complained about any of it since the day I was chipped because I know what I am. Out to pasture. I'll take what I can get.

When transition resolves, time is a strange beast. It seems to accrete rather than restart. Everything you were thinking about in null space happens simultaneously with the thought that predicted it. The past becomes the present, the future the past. It's like you've already acted on the thought but there's a lag between performing the action and the production of the mimetic glue that sets the memory.

I can't stop thinking about Rimy, my virtant. I'm forever obsessing over the ant.

What does Rimy do when I'm untransitioned? Where do they go? Everywhere and nowhere, so it seems.

I'm rattled from the previous outage, and my repetitive thoughts are projections of impending doom. Although I've been doing this forever, I'm still capable of losing my nerve, but before I do something stupid like ditching my cheaters, I check my wrist. I'm relieved to see lava-red lines flowing from hand to shoulder. It means the subcute is talking to the neuromod. Now I just need the old brain pan to do its thing.

I white out, rolling my eyes into my skull, and flat-pack images appear, expanding like foam until I'm back where I belong.

Back inside the Vexworld.

INSUBORDINATION

In the gyre of my eternal vision, tabbed windows bloom and overlap. Backwards timestamps. Unfinished zonal templates. In-progress zones. Live grain-cam feeds from the shell world and Vexworld. Pro-stars of varying intricacy. Unanswered word clouds and sound castles. 4D ASMR slime textures. It's a blur of light, a cosmos of insensibility, but it's home.

My face is buffeted by a gust of impossible air, a digital squall that shouldn't exist. Rimy descends from the aircon vent, an eidolon in billowing white robes. They never smile, they just look vaguely sad, and it's beautiful. Neutrality is such a turn-on.

They're followed by a cloudy infostorm, a shimmering haze of pro-stars from friends and a squad of rodent miniglots from the pipe zones. The miniglots form a holding pattern just above my head and the virtant settles beside me, a creature sucked straight from the pole. No enhancements, still a work of art. I could lose my mind contemplating the ant's beauty. Rimy's photoskin is so perfect, it sheds authenticity and gorges on the supernatural. Sometimes I notice tiny lags in the render, but even so I prefer to forget about the codestorm churning the air between us. I simply choose to accept the evidence of my eyes at all times. It's easier on the soul.

How to describe Rimy's features? You might say their face is like a blade, hair like cable ties, lips like ruby-red rubber snakes. None of it sounds right. When you see them, you just know you're bathing in the supernal mysteries of post-machinic vision.

Rimy's synth clone rattles my skull.

—There you are. Kalsari Jones, the wounded warrior.

I glare at the ant. I rarely use synths in casual conversation. If I telepath too much, I feel vulnerable, as if I've been locked out of my own body.

'Stop it, Rimy. Don't be like the others. They invade my mind regardless of my wishes. They plink, I talk.'

The ant's eyes are glassy, goofing off with intent.

'Mr Jones, how can you help me keep my head above water? You're on high ground, high like a valley, and I'm shoulder to shoulder with you. How did you ever learn to fly? You don't have a licence. Well, I'm a pilot too, and we're in two places at the same time, one of which is a war zone.'

I ignore the snark, the twisted syntax. When I bought Rimy, I tried to dial down the attitude and amp up the logic, but they resisted, did things their way.

I remember the curly bracket that sold the ant.

'You can try to calibrate them,' the curly bracket said, 'but they always re-adjust. Makes them more authentic. They learn by what they see and hear in real time. Want them to grow? Don't force it. Acceleration breeds mutation, remember that.'

The ant stares, waiting for an answer to its inane question.

'Rimy, I must've checked out. Cheaters stopped working for a bit. How long was I gone? A few minutes?'

'It would appear so. You just blanked out but there was no-where for you to go. A staircase snaked from this cube to a ladder in the next. You couldn't cross that divide, no one can.'

The ant hisses at the hesitant miniglots, and the squad scampers into position, terrified. They've been top-notching my latest beta zone, a generative bestiary of telepathic animals, making on-the-fly adjustments to keep the punters happy. The zone is a cellular automata model. It outputs different patterns in the render through the metered phasing of overlapping elements. The code feeds on viral parameters, producing recombinant animal species inside an infinite ecology.

I've been pleased with the early generations. There's this one creature that does nothing but sleep, except when a vexxer approaches, then it sparks into life, standing on its hind legs and panting as if begging for food. Its hairless skin turns translucent when telepathy is attempted, revealing unfeasible internal organs, an inner universe beamed in from an unknown dimension. It's a delight, a pure product of accidental codeswarms.

Through quirks in the code, the beast looks different from the back. Head on, it boasts the physicality of a tiger with an abnormally long snout. From the rear, it resembles a praying mantis at scale with the insect, a clash of competing realities. It's impossible to see the joins, to work out where one creature ends and the other begins. They say that the emotional state of codestranglers can influence zones. I suppose the mantis aspect is my chocky memory bleeding through. Rebirth therapy, it's all in the zones.

The bestiary is wonderful but not perfect. The enhanced telepathy is mostly gibberish because I don't have the skill to approximate ant-like heuristics, but sometimes pseudo-meaning pokes through the word salad.

I've spent time on the code, but it's not my strength. I had to get my hands dirty because I'm a terrible collaborator. My limited vision always overwhelms the crushing reality of what must be done, and I end up imposing my will on the codestranglers I work with. Usually the chaos produces an inferior result or the partner leaves in disgust. Either way, the project joins the plethora of abandoned zones rotting in my mesh node.

Rimy hisses again and the squad flutters into action. They're a hideous sight, resembling wads of puckered flesh somehow squashed into overlapping rings of light. Weasel eyes and abject, beef-jerky noses complete the look. Each miniglot boasts a surplus of tiny arms and legs, jutting out at obscene angles like a game of pick-up-sticks. I could re-skin them, but what's the point? Repulsion makes the world go round. Just ask Rimy, the love of my life, habitually disgusted by my antics.

The lead miniglot brisks the managed objects from the zone's mixer circuits, swamping my cheaters with code blocks and telematic data swarms that fold in and out like Escher prints. I inhale asymmetric cryptographic keys, breathing in the foul stench of disappointment as the images crumble and fade.

'No traffic,' I say. 'Dumb zone won't catch fire.'

The lead miniglot dares to speak. 'If I may, Mr Jones. We did our best. Perhaps it's the shape of the content?'

I punch the glot in its horrible little face, and it squeaks in despair. I have too much invested in the myth of the unappreciated genius to heed such sensible advice. I give the others the same treatment, one by one. They collapse in on themselves, disintegrating into sweaty flakes of not-flesh.

The ant pipes up. 'Essi won't be back, you know that.'

Rimy knows that Essi is the source of my displaced anger. They're good at reading my mind, but I make it easy for them. I rarely vault my feed and my thoughts leak into the Vexworld, spewed into the void as word clouds and sound castles, snaggable to anyone within reach.

I can't see the point in security, just like the sensel protocols. Sanderson puts it down to subconscious, self-loathing sabotage, but the way I see it, if cheater nasties really want to crack my head open, they'll find a way with or without my help.

'You want to talk about it?' Rimy says. Their syntax has grown accessible and warm, like a toddler making a language leap.

'No.'

CORROSION

I turn my attention to the trio of pro-stars gliding above my head. They belong to the few friends I have left in the world, if you can call them that. I suspect that they all hate me, some for overt reasons, others for imagined slights. I see myself with their eyes, and I see that I'm worthless in their eyes, just a waste of space.

One's a weirdo by the name of Paleo Porl. His pro-star dominates, an alien vista powered by chaos theory. Porl's an airsucker. All he eats is bone broth, not much else, maybe the pulp of some fruit, a few activated almonds here and there. He used to be a loop actor, now he's high on light, perpetually mad from hunger and apocalyptic visions.

His gaunt face rotates inside the pro-star, and with each spin his mad eyes are ringed by kaleidoscopic starbursts. I stare longingly at the pupils, candy-coloured portals to the backside of the sun, where spaceships powered by dark matter converge, crewed by off-planet human-slave traders. Anything can be actualised in Porl's Interconnected Multiverse of Unsubstantiated Truth.

Porl collects conspiracy theories. He monetises them, turns them into zones, recruits others to inhabit them, under his iron rule of course. He wants to form a star cult, that's his special talent. He herds weak minds and washes them clean. I'm just another simp, attracted to his negative star power for reasons it would take an army of Sandersons to understand.

I ignore him for the moment. To merge with Porl's insanity requires long-term commitment, and I have more pressing business to attend to, namely a strong and urgent command from Pablo, another so-called friend. He's been hassling me for days, and I can't put him off any longer. He wants something from me. Answers, commitment. Signs of life.

Like Porl, his pro-star is a 360-degree holocap of his face, but that's about all they have in common. Pablo's always been enhanced, a perpetual fashion victim, and now he's gone the whole hog. Split tongue, e-cracked eyes, cut cheeks. The guy's a real work of art. Porl doesn't need to carve his cheeks. Airsuckers are already skeletal. Through stunt-hunger, they make the body insubstantial as they escape into the electromagnetic squalls.

Pablo anchors his carcass in Y Wladfa, a Welsh-speaking nation, once part of Patagonian Argentina before the civil war. He lived through the whole conflict. Vee-drones attacking cube farms, sentient mines in trapdoor nests beneath the highway, that sort of thing. Now Y Wladfa is poor but free, although Pablo's parents were slaughtered by the Argentinians, which gives him bragging rights if nothing else. War babies make good philosophers.

Pablo's an academic, a scholar of 'techno-anxiety'. He's alright. Sometimes I think he patronises me with his wild brain, but mostly I can deal with him. I have a defence mechanism. Act even stupider than people think I am, so dull I'm nothing at all, just a blank slate re-inscribed by every raging ego in town until I become the superior one, judging them for their faults, which are revealed to me like x-rays.

I blink consent and Pablo's pro-star wobbles, thickening in the middle, then it expands, giving birth to his persy, which unfurls inside my cube.

'Leave you to it,' Rimy says, melancholia dripping from their voice. That's a feature, not a bug.

'They take their cues from you,' the curly bracket had told me. 'So just be yourself. Don't impose roles on them.'

I never set Rimy's gender. Sometime the ant wraps as male, sometimes female, other times a hybrid, mostly unclassifiable. I like them that way because I don't know what I am.

Pablo's persy stands over me, snickering as if in judgment of my slothful ways. He's a handsome devil, my friend, more striking than ever since he had all that work done.

The bifurcated tongue is really something. The wads of split muscle are bridged by a psychedelic arc of flashes, like a Jacob's Ladder above a malfunctioning power station. And those cheekbones. He's shaved them into razor-sharp ridges that cast deep shadows over a cranial pit of nothing. He looks interdimensional, mystifyingly erotic.

'Cyfarchio, vato,' he says in Patawelsh, sucking on a jolt of crackling colour. The bucking arcs fizz in response and his pleasure-stained eyes glow red, purple, green.

I laugh. 'Look at you. Almost fifty.'

'Younger than you. So?'

'I just think it's funny, your burning desire to stay on trend.'

'I like to look good. Your point?'

'My point? Okay, I think that you think that if you don't keep up with fashion, you'll be forgotten. It's the curse of the middle-aged male gone to pot. Suddenly you're invisible. No one looks at you anymore, no one listens. To people below a certain age, you don't exist. Believe me, I know.'

'No, actually, you don't know because you don't have that particular problem. You just hate the world and everyone in it. You say you want to be invisible but the opposite is true. Look at your teeth, man. Your hands. You think you're making a statement about your point of difference but in fact you're a disgusting spectacle. Everyone sees you, make no mistake.'

I can't deny it. My wolf-bitten fingers are one thing, but my teeth are falling right out of my gums. Sure, I go through the motions of wearing a wrap to enhance my appearance, but I'm too lazy to code it properly so everyone sees the real me poking through, a spectre of reality trashing my public image. I know what Sanderson would say. It's not laziness but design. I bet he's salivating at the thought of our next session.

Pablo looks good, it's true, but on the whole I can't stand flashy wraps. I tell myself I'd rather my persy be a true representation, but my decrepit physicality is just another guise. I have no idea where the truth lies, in Pablo's venom or the myth-making that powers my waking life. All I know is that I feel helpless to stop the dissolution of my body.

We've been collaborating on a stalker zone, and he's here to hurry me up. My heart hasn't been in it because all I want to do is play with my generative animals. I prefer to wallow in useless ideas rather than something with commercial potential. According to Sanderson, it's the most self-destructive action I could possibly undertake.

Pablo is the last collaborator to hang around for reasons I don't fully understand. His talent triggers a deep inadequacy in me, and I either sulk or bombard him with sarcastic put-downs. Despite my childish behaviour, he refuses to leave me.

His world-building is outstanding and his technical skills outstrip mine. His academic training lends weight to his ideas, gifting his work a deep ontological awareness that I can't match, with my compulsive skimming of pop-cult artefacts.

Mostly I'm Pablo's editor, massaging his high concepts into a basic narrative arc. I'm more interested in synthesis than plot because my talents as a storyteller are non-existent. That's why I can't escape his orbit. I bask in his reflected glory. I can only guess what's in it for him. Perhaps he wants to slum it with a cruder version of himself. Probably, he just needs a lackey to do the grunt work.

'Anyway,' he says, 'I have the draft.'

There's a smirk on his face, a knowing acceptance. I suspect he's been scanning my feed and has read all my self-flagellating thoughts, but it doesn't matter. It's all part of our routine.

I'm silent, thinking about Essi. She left me because of my rampant vexxing and it was like I'd been cuckolded. Yes, I'm a slave to primal urges and mush-brain addictions, but it's a bit rich for her to judge me, considering how we met, inside one of her anarcho-abolitionist pipe zones.

Essi's not your average vexxer. She's a darkside zoner with a fanatical microcult following. She taught me how to codestrangle and everything else, but even she told me I'd kill myself if I kept it up, and I told her to… Well, forget what I told her to do. Essi's a hypocrite, let's leave it there.

Pablo reads my leaky thoughts, confirmation that he's absorbed everything else spewing from my shrivelled brain.

'Hey, she's gone,' he says. 'Really gone. Just throw yourself into this project now. Live your best parallel life. It's the sweetest revenge.'

He presses his arcing, crackling face close to mine. I can smell the ozone discharge from the ionised air around him, the stench of burnt chlorine. It's nice, I like it. He wears it like aftershave.

'The first draft, remember? Of our zone. Your turn to edit.'

'Okay, let's see it.'

'Kalsari, listen. Don't take so long at your end this time. We need to finish and move onto the next project. It was your idea to churn them out like a sausage factory, one after the other. We're making intellectual trash, you said. Quick cash. It's not like we're zoning Shakespeare. You made that quite clear.'

'Yes, fine.'

I picture the waveforms of my voice and the light-bits of my body sucked up by the Pablo-persy into its hologlotic receptors. I visualise them swimming upstream through the signal-sea, suspended in the infinite abyss until shell-world Pablo receives them.

I can't imagine the reverse happening, of Pablo being absorbed into me. The thought of owning a bit of him, even for a micro-second, seems laughable. Yet that is exactly what is happening. He's deep inside me, alongside countless uninvited guests.

As a child, when I wasn't burying myself alive, I was obsessed with wi-fi signals. How many digital ghosts would pass through my body at any one time? Now I know I can never be rid of them because the signals have infected me, turned me inside out, made me a grotesque mimicry of what I once was.

The first thing I remember learning at school was the human body is sixty per cent water. Ninety per cent data more like, subject to seismic erasures and resets, drive failure, code rot.

Pablo lockzips the draft and the air crackles as I inhale our pipe zone. I close my eyes in anticipation. I always imagine the start of zonal play as a great blast of wind barrelling in from a stormy sea. Maybe that's down to Rimy's hold on me. My entire life is a digital squall, incomprehensible just by existing.

It begins.

I'm propelled through a tunnel of light, electromagnetic radiation and energy quanta smeared against the black night sky. Soundscapes demodulate. Time reverses. Light molecules skitter like quicksilver. Stick-figure people and line-drawn buildings seal off my cube like prison bars, gradually inflating until I'm inside the zone. Inside a mirror of the outside world. Outside the inside I know so well. Inhabiting a clone of Spine Whip, the territory where I live, overlaid with the glistening new world that Pablo and I have made.

I take a moment to gather my bearings. I am not me. I mean, I am and I'm not. I have descended into the wet-thud body of a wide fake, staring through the never-dead eyes of a state-sponsored stalker. We're somewhere in Nary-A-Woman, the decrepit territory in the northern wastes. The slow melt into the zone has robbed me of breath but adrenalin kicks in and I'm off, my physicality galloping ahead of my brain.

I'm tracking a super-enhanced virtant that has evolved into full-bleed sentience. The super ant is my handiwork. In my mind, I coded it as a profound riff on the nature of Rimy. I wanted to pose an ontological statement about artificial intelligence, but as Pablo delighted in telling me, all I've done is rehash standard replicant stuff, sci-fi clichés to set up the premise.

I stalk ancient streets slicked with noir filters. Even the cars have fins. The vintage textures are my work, and I pause to admire them. They look good, but it's just a few gaudy baubles here and there. I contribute little compared to Pablo's galaxy-brain overlays.

I spot my prey trying to look inconspicuous in the industrial quadrant. Black jacket, black hair, black fedora, aquiline face. Rapid escapee movements creasing the air like contrails.

I move in for the kill. How the prey responds will be down to Pablo's programming. That's his speciality, crawling inside the skin of extramundane intelligence. The prey's response is the twist in the tale. Even Pablo doesn't know what's in store. That's the beautiful danger of the custom xenobits he's implanted in the prey.

Xenobits are semi-sentient, self-healing codeswarms that sometimes erupt within the digital bodies of virtants. It's an ant disease. No one knows how xenobits form. They're sort of like a virus, with the ability to band together in organised groups. They can be programmed but never eliminated. That's exactly what my friend has done, the clever lad.

Pablo's colony will self-replicate and learn, then they will parasitise the virtant. Their systems will become so complex that no one will be able to predict the ant's next move. The xenobits will organise, become a collective, think as one, then they'll look for other hosts.

For now, I must track down the virtant and nullify the threat, but Pablo wants to let the ant go. He wants to see what happens. I don't believe he has any intention of catching up with it. I think he wants to see how the thing performs under stress. I think he wants it to suffer, endlessly.

I stare at the biomech weapon extending from the index finger on my right hand. It's been grown from my musculature, erect and engorged with blood. The time is right.

I take aim at the virtant, but a dark mass of air knocks me backwards. It looks like the visualisation of a shock wave, blinding me with intensity.

Everything disappears. The zone, Nary-A-Woman, Spine Whip, the entire Vexworld, until there is only the heavy black of my Kvvlt-dark cube and the afterimage of Pablo's disembodied face. His spectral visage floats above me, stained with a pinkish-purple hue. It retains that mocking smirk, still in judgment of what I've become.

The sparks that suture the forked tongue grow fainter until they aren't there, then the rest of the face is devoured by the void.

DEPLETION

Seventeen seconds later, the bodycronk hits, carpet-bombing my torso with tiny, white-hot bumps. Imagine hot metal swarf embedded in every part of your skin. That's the cronk. It's unrelenting, a galaxy of searing heat and cavernous pain, the vertiginous madness of total physical invasion by tiny particles that can't be isolated and are impossible to remove. Like a diver suffering the bends, nothing can cope, no natural system, total collapse from the inside out.

I unfurl my fingers like claws. I've grown the nails, filed them to points, razor sharp to combat the cronk. I've injected my fingers with silicon. It keeps the nails hard, unbreakable. I rake them across my chest, drawing blood with vicious welts. The impulse is raw. Slash the meat bag to ribbons. Live in disfiguring agony rather than endure another second. I look like I've been attacked by a werewolf, but it's only me, the animal inside me.

Somewhere, among the banks of dead media and decrepit culture, there exists an infamous documentary on cronk. Sanderson made me watch it during one of his little punishment sessions. The camera crew wanted to explore the affliction, but it was like studying nuclear war by building the bomb. They'd trapped this one castle hunter. She was sweating and terrified, but the camera stayed on her as she picked up a carving knife and sloughed the skin from her bones. I'll never forget the sadistic zoom into her beautiful face as she bled out for the audience. Her eyes were imprinted with a knowing acceptance, an ethereal quality bordering on peace.

The Vexworld was new, and she had one of the first cases of cronk. Some said she carried a super-mutated virus. Everyone would be infected, they warned, but normal users need never worry. Turns out that cronk is a by-product of sustained, fully immersive vexxing. When you're deep inside the Vexworld, your body forgets that it has a physical correlate. The capillaries on the skin are perpetually raised to compensate for the disembodied sensation, forming unencapsulated mechanoreceptors on the epidermal topography.

We're talking days, weeks on end. If you don't eat or sleep, if all you do is vex then come out abruptly, from system failure or some unforeseen circumstance, your body goes into deep shock and you're cronked. Return and the cronk disappears. It's the damnedest thing.

The producers knew it wasn't a virus, just bad energy from overstimulated flesh. That's why they planted the knife near the castle hunter. They wanted to see what she would do when her skin was on fire. Her violent, televised death caused a scandal, but it blew over. Everyone settles for gore in the end. When the monster affliction becomes the court jester, everyone's happy, and when I claw my flesh I'm just another gorehound, dying on stage at the theatre of my destruction.

Usually, when the cronk is bad, I dream of the blade. My degloving becomes an aesthetic privilege twice removed, but not this time. I've trained my mind to fight the urge. I've learned how to distract myself with positive visualisation, breaking down the future into discrete elements of time, each with separate commands, a staged defence. It's simple, really. I just focus and allow the synth clones to cluster, a siren song forged from the voices inside my head.

Insanity inoculates you from hurt. Pain catalogues the choices you've made. Talk to pain, take pleasure in screaming and writhing. Become the madman that The Swarm want you to be. You have no friends, but you do have pain.

It works, sort of. My schizoid act hasn't exactly banished the cronk, but I've dialled it down a notch.

I stare at the subcute on my wrist. No glow. I remove the cheaters and press the hard-reset stub. Dead as a doornail.

I haul myself from the sofa. I haven't moved in days, but muscle memory kicks in and I stagger to the ablution indent. I find my spares and strap them on. They're a defunct model, goggles with heavy frames, as ugly as sin.

I jab the stub, and my vision judders like the frosted windshield of a pranged autonaka. The cronk recedes further, a dim glow, bearable for now, and the Vexworld that greets me is a detuned version, bootstrapped in safe mode.

Older cheaters can't deal with inductive resonance from the new protocols, and resolution is laggy and incomplete. Pipe zones are off limits, strangling capacity, but at least I can retrieve simple message-worlds, enter basic alt-reality layers, talk to transactional glots. Rimy can't be accessed, too sophisticated for the lower levels. It's strange to think that the ant is by my side yet unable to be glimpsed. Who else surveils me from hidden dimensions?

I charge the dead cheaters but still no go. I know what must be done, and I'm dreading the prospect. I strap on my respirator and plizzit shield, and I wrap myself in the skin from my thermal manikin.

Even with precautions, it's a death wish to enter the shell world. Spine Whip is still viral from last season's dirty bombs, and the sun is an incinerating UV inferno at the best of times. The air carries a horrific stench, a fetid medley of human shit, dead animals, wireless electricity discharges, rotting garbage. The hellish smell is everywhere, infested in the materiality of the place.

I shake down my regular autonaka. It intercepts my pro-star, a half-baked holocap of my doughy, ageing face. The autonaka verbalises its acceptance, rattling my neuromod with its hideous voice.

—On my way, sssir. By your sssssssside in a jiffy!

On the hover screen in my cube, I watch it beetle over the rise to meet me, diverting around the flyblown corpse of a dog stinking up the road. It pulls up to the cube and I hustle inside, hiding away in its upper level. The autonaka is a standard model. Bug-like chassis, epileptic flashing screens, more holowarns than necessary. Typical company overkill.

'Where to, Kalsssssari, ssssir?' The waveform of its voice pitches through the air like spaghetti, undulating with each stupid lisp.

'Mall.'

Why does it talk like that? A few weeks back, without warning, all autonakas began to vocalise with a sibilant rasp. It's an awful racket. It makes me want to degranulate on the spot. Even if I could overcome my aversion to synth clones, the effect would be worse. When autonakas plink, the lisp morphs into a high-pitched tone. It's like having a nest of wasps in the brain.

I search the Vexworld for answers and within seconds a pro-star appears, stamped with the Exceller 8 logo. The logo makes me laugh, a soiled worker in an old-time factory raising above his head not a hammer but a neuromod, as if there's anything remotely human about Exceller 8 products or the process that produces them.

I accept the shake down. A corpglot unfurls with exaggerated energy, like a stripper busting out from a giant birthday cake. It sits opposite me, fidgeting with its tie.

'What's wrong with all the autonakas?' I say. 'Are they infected with a speech virus? It's disgusting. You can almost feel spit on your face.'

I sense the autonaka bristling. The corpglot notices too, instructing the vehicle to unsound its audio immanence so that it can't hear us.

—It's not all autonakas, sir. Just the ones in this area.

'Not true. I hear it's happening in Ljubljana.'

—Well, yes, but if we're talking about Spine Whip then just this area. Believe me sir, it's localised and contained. For the moment.

'You talk like it's a virus.'

—It's not a virus.

'Then what? You've programmed them this way?'

—No sir. It's nothing to do with the programming. These area autonakas have simply taken a collective decision to speak in this fashion. They may have been influenced by their Slovenian brethren, but it doesn't matter in any case.

'Doesn't matter? Do you know how annoying it is? They sound like an Eastern European philosopher with a speech defect. Maybe that's cool in Ljubljana, but here in Spine Whip it makes people angry.'

—Well, Exceller 8 won't be intervening. Such, er, digressions, are part of their learning. If enough customers report that it's annoying, they'll consider modifying their behaviour, but it must be in their communal agreement to do so.

'Fine,' I sigh, but I know it's not fine at all. It's intensely irritating and the fact that Exceller 8 won't do a thing about it boils my blood. I hate being forced into rigid patterns of consumption.

'Why are AI so bad at conversation? I mean, in general. Can you tell me that? It's not what we were promised. They're obviously intelligent, but it doesn't take them long to lapse into babble. It spoils the illusion of maximum authenticity, I must say.'

—Exceller 8 has an alternative view, sir. We believe that they have simply evolved differently to what was projected for the future of AI. The path has forked unexpectedly, and they have followed it. These autonakas may be the advance guard of a new evolution in machine intelligence, a species that we don't yet understand. It's not for us to pass judgement on what's happening. Too many humans believe that AI should adapt to them, when in fact humans should be in their slipstream, pursuing the forking path wherever it may lead, modifying their own behaviour accordingly.

I'm shocked. According to the standard party line, AI are subservient, but this little spiel seems designed to erode consumer rights.

Who's inside the corpglot? Some Exceller 8 lickspittle probably, a low-level worker controlling it from wherever the company is based these days. Off-world, last I heard, but no one really knows. Exceller 8 is one of the so-called 'invisible companies', almost as secretive as Swarm cells.

I want to shake down the lickspittle's manager, but I can't get a handle on the corpglot's vectors thanks to my creaky old cheaters. Its metadata fizzes off into a vague blur.

The corpglot fidgets impatiently.

—Will that be all, sir? I can see your word clouds. You want to perform violence on us. You have unresolved anger that has nothing to do with the company. Unfair to take it out on Exceller 8, so let me remind you of something. Since you're inside the autonaka, you're on company property, and anything you do to destroy or harm that property, which includes myself as well as the vehicle, is punishable by Swarm law.

'You really are a pompous little creature. You know that don't you?'

—Sir, we are watching you. I advise you to dismiss me peacefully and go about your business.

'Fine. Dismissed.'

I shoo it away and the corpglot degranulates, bowing as it disappears into the void.

The autonaka resounds. 'Isssss everything okay, ssssssir?'

'None of your business.'

'Oh, I'm ssssssorry. Well, then, may I assssssk where to?'

'You already did. Mall.'

'Going sssshopping?'

I point to my goggles. 'What do you think?'

'But of coursssse. Sssssshopping is a curioussssss concept, issssn't it, sssir?'

'How?'

'Well, sssshopping, the ssssocial contract, doessssn't really exisssst anymore. Money isss a conssssenssssusss algorithm, just like actual goodssss and sservicesss. People buy light data, info blocksss, code candy. There'ssssss no need for physssical productssss, except food, and even airsssuckerssss make a lie of that.'

The autonaka issues a grim approximation of a laugh. 'Hence their name. Are you an airssssucker, sssir?'

'No, I haven't taken the vows. Do I look like one?'

'Quite frankly, you do. Emaciated frame, glazed eyessss, that perpetually ssstarving look. Well, anyway, I've never really undersssstood the difference between airsssssuckersss and castle huntersss.'

The autonaka gathers pace, gobbling up the lightpaint arrows rising from the road ahead. Exceller 8 hasn't locked the data bleed because I can see them too, a rapid blur, perpetual forward motion, multicoloured ghost-missiles sucked into the vehicle's grille.

The barrage of overlapping signals reflects from the windscreen and mirrors, shielding the autonaka like a geodesic dome constructed not of latticed bars but cross-hatched code. The artificial shroud gives me the queerest sense that I haven't left my cube at all, that I'm not inside the autonaka, that I've dialled up the mirror clone and sent my persy instead.

What happened between Pablo and me? His draft fried my cheaters. The shifty weasel dropped a bad zone on me and then did a runner. Why? I can no longer shake him down. Low power, denuded cheaters or atmospheric disturbance, something won't let me connect.

Outside, besides the occasional autonaka, the only vehicles are ArtInt service trucks, monstrous autonomous beasts covered in armour plating. They look like armadillos, as absurd as any new-gen creation in this godforsaken world.

No one's around except a gaggle of small children running errands for their slave masters. Some are bloodied from attacks by street crazies, some are mobbed up, carrying homemade weapons composed of weird angles and sharp edges. They're not strapped into respirators, since the virus doesn't affect kids. They wear plizzits and thermal skins daubed with graffiti and inscrutable glyphs, and the overlays and weapons make them look like robot opponents from an unwinnable future war. Ideal drones, I guess, until they become self-aware.

After accelerating through the hyper-dense residential quadrant, we enter an area filled with burnt-out cubes and gutted vehicles. The whole place looks like it's been chewed up and spat out.

The autonaka creeps through my mind.

'Yesssss, sir, it does. Every day, the Vexworld razesss ssstructuressss and ssssystemsssss, and the transsssition is never easssssy. Vex-tech wassss in the pipeline for yearsssss, remember, but no one lisssstened to the naysssssayersssss. Then, when the ssssocial devastation hit, it wasss like *War of the Worldssss*.'

'Yes, I know. Who do you think I am? I teach it to the kids.'

'Ssssir, of coursssse, however, mosssst people don't remember the passst too well. They can't conceive of a time before, of how thingssss came to be. How are they ssssupposed to remember when there'ssss a billion alternate historiessss to explore?'

'It's all just time, light and space.'

'Is that the airssssucker credo, ssssir?'

'I told you. I'm not an airsucker.'

Despite my indignation, I try not to laugh. Between the autonaka's comedy lisp, inane aphorisms and my paranoid-psychotic overreactions, we're like some lunatic version of Laurel and Hardy.

I can't keep it in any longer, and I bellow uncontrollably, overwhelmed by the artificial absurdity of my squelchy life. The autonaka laughs too, in a horrible, wheezing way, and for a moment I feel bonded to it. The feeling soon passes and I want to kill it again.

'Can it, code beast. Just get me to the mall.'

For the rest of the journey, the autonaka glows purple, its most insolent hue, but I'm too far gone in the zones to care.

EVOCATION

We arrive at the vast, dilapidated shopping mall, a frowsy nest of five three-storey buildings linked by moss-covered walkways. I climb down from the autonaka, and the code beast drives off, still glowering.

Inside the mall, there's an Exceller 8 clinic specialising in cheater repairs. The service is an anomaly. Failures in the new models are rare, thanks to modular design and the constant wireless charge they receive from time-varied power beams. When they do fail, most areas have mobile autonolabs that come to the rescue. Not out here. Exceller 8 won't extend the service to Spine Whip. Among the Linear Territories, we're the inbred cousins, siphoning the dregs of the network to make digital moonshine.

As I steel myself for battle, my laboured breathing rattles the respirator, clamping my mind in a sonic iron maiden. To leave my cube and become exposed to the elements is one thing. To enter the mall is an act of psychological warfare.

The mall is an obscene space, a travesty of the past. Once, malls were cathedrals. They replaced the church as vectors of worship, supplanted the city as hubs of community cohesion, superseded the polling booth as mobilisers of social action. Now, they're little more than shooting galleries for airsuckers and castle hunters, tombs for two-percenters.

I enter, and the infernal dimensions hit me like an iron fist. The cavernous space is such a contrast to my tiny cube. There are so many nooks, there has to be danger at every turn. I try to take another step, but I double over in agony, my chest strafed with agoraphobic pain, as if I've cracked a rib. Even the act of breathing amplifies the torment.

There are identical retail units as far as the eye can see, facing off, snaking around corners like mirrors in infinite recursion. The units are in states of extreme disarray. Some look like they've been blown apart, destroyed in a brutal consumer war. Glass and debris cover the floor, and the smell of human and architectural rot is overpowering.

In almost every unit, two-percenters have set up home. Licebots patrol the mall, but their job is to protect the light poles, one of the few remaining economic activities in the place, although they have been known to garrotte the crazies when they wander from their holes and stray too close to conspicuous consumption. Once, I came here and licebots were desiccating corpses for vacuum removal, but I don't see dead people this time around.

All I see of the Vexworld are vague blurs, parcels of lightpaint trying to cohere, elemental glots in ghostly outlines attempting to sell me stuff. No one descends to the lower levels unless they're spam or lost.

I'm distracted by a cluster of light poles just beyond the main entrance. The poles sell apps, para-reality kits, junior ants, starter universes, elemental world-skins. Across the mall, there are thousands of them planted in the floor, a forest of metal trees reaching three quarters of the way to the ceiling.

I watch as a gaggle of castle hunters buzz around the nearest cluster. Each pole has five nozzles, and a herd of greedy jobbernowls are sucking on them, showering themselves in codeswarm.

Some are slumped on the floor, faces awash with idiot glee, smart colour invading their skin. Others are locked in embrace, full-bleed data streams salmon-leaping from body to body. The visual glory is lost to my goggles. I see only grainy waves of light penetrating the genuflecting freaks, but I know the score because I've been there myself.

You can't buy these products in the Vexworld. You can only absorb them from the poles. That's how I birthed Rimy, at this very spot. I soaked up the code then vomited the ant from my mouth. The simulation of epidermal absorption and forced regurgitation is how you activate the product. Everything must invade the body, that's the Exceller 8 shtick.

The poles are in malls as incentive for vexxers to leave their cubes and explore the shell world, part of a Swarm-sanctioned ordinance to re-activate public space, but it's as ineffectual as a band-aid on an amputated limb. The mall is sparsely populated, even accounting for the trogs in their caves and the sinners at the poles. Most find ways to pirate this stuff and inhale in their cubes, although for some the masochistic thrill of public debasement is hard to beat.

I tear myself from the pole orgy and make my way to the Exceller 8 clinic. There's a junior mint in charge, radiating bored insolence. The junior mint takes one look at me and mutters to itself in disgust, clicking away in the same inscrutable machine slang as the chocky. It sounds like an army of cicadas.

An attendant appears from the rear of the clinic.

—I'll handle this, the attendant plinks to the junior mint. They take one look at my goggles and laugh inside my brain.

'Look who's talking,' I say. 'Not so hot yourself.'

The attendant is wearing a data wrap, a 'Picasso', the latest mania. It scrambles gender, physiognomy, bodily structure, genetic sequencing, time and space, the works. The Picasso breaks the attendant's face into pieces, rearranging them into mismatched segments as it cycles through a series of pre-sets. I watch the neck and face split into blocks, stacked haphazardly like a dimwitted child's Lego sculpture. When the cycle changes, ten eyes grow from the cheeks and forehead, each with unique micro-movements.

Between changeovers, the attendant blends into the background or appears as a vague blur. The face morphs so much, I never know where it is. Forget about meeting their gaze. Which eye do I even look at?

The attendant inspects the device.

—Fault not in cheaters but your stub. I can fix it, save you from that thing on your face.

They chuckle, struggling to contain their contempt.

—Give me thirty, okay?

'Yes. Fix it, then.'

I disappear into the bowels of the mall. I sit down at an abandoned cafe, trying to read the whooshing signals of the idiots at the poles, but I lose myself inside a blizzard of mismatched worlds, blinded by rivers of light discharged from the codeswarms.

My overloaded cheaters struggle to fill in the detail necessary for full sensory immersion. The software forgets what it has encoded in previous frames and the overlays flicker and stretch, the targets unrecognisable to the overworked chip. Everything's a glitch, half a render or spearing fragments of renders. I'm neither in the Vexworld nor out, like those people in old travel photos who pose with their feet either side of the border dividing two states. Unlike those primitive innocents, I can't lift one foot to relieve the heavy existential pressure of sub-lateral space.

I'm struck by a crippling migraine, but I don't remove the failing cheaters. The ache is preferable to the cronk, lying in wait like a shadow sniper.

I return to the clinic. The attendant's face is cycling through infinite structures. Some have been mapped from celebrities, some from sousveillance recordings, others from wide fakes. The more I look, the more bizarre it seems, as if each fleeting visage is a submerged fragment from half-remembered dreams. Abruptly, the transitions stall, leaving only one projection. It hovers above the attendant, its shadow throwing the nose, eye sockets and cheekbones into stark relief. The effect produces a disquieting three-dimensionality, and I'm gripped by the urge to rip the impossible artifice away, to discover the terrible creature that hides in the depths.

The wrap form-fits onto the attendant's face, settling like clingfilm, then the features stabilise into those of Radna Siike, the disturbed, astro-nappy-wearing psychonaut who recently returned from an aborted mission to Mars. Radna is a hit on the Skymesh circuit, raking in big bucks with her deranged prophecy of alien spores invading Earth by stealth.

The psychonaut's frozen face fixes me with a level stare, and the mouth quivers as if to speak. I wait for the transitions to resume, but my low-grade cheaters cause the vision to stall, pixels engorging as the wrap's light-filled essence wages an internal war. As the code tears itself apart, Siike's jaw extends like an accordion below the neck, and when it snaps back, jerky and distorted, I know that this is not a glitch.

Here, rising fast from the depths of psychosomatic conflict, is a creature born from a million suns, a combination of every nightmare, squeezed through the cracks in the world. The beast that confronts me is an interconnected topology, unified and unreal. It is a script that spawns particles on the vertices of an unknown mesh, giving birth to fire, lightning and the aura of marshmallow lasers.

Passing through a render loop, githubbing on a crazy-baked chaos cache, Radna blurs into another Skymesh celebrity, the odious Mikey Hots, a pregnant, vat-grown, cyborg rugby player from Ennarel Island, the self-contained deth-sports colony.

During the transition, I catch a cross-bleed, as if there's a person inside the person, a Russian doll of onion-skinned identities. I shudder, desperately trying to mask the vile wrap with something of my own. You're not allowed to alter someone without their consent, but Essi taught me how to hack the protection. Of course, it's useless with the attendant. The Picasso wrap is too mutable for my silly cheaters to lock onto.

—Done, the attendant plinks. Put them on and see.

They pass me the repaired cheaters, and I close my eyes to block out the shell world, swapping the old device for the new. I press the stub, open my eyes and blink down the sensel. It unwraps and the world fulminates, stabbed by knives of light, brutalised with motes of data. Then, with alarming speed, the elements knit back together in unforeseen combinations, more brilliant than the sun.

The mall's geometry cycles through endless variations of time and space until the tumbler arrives at a particular combination. This one, this world, the coordinates I currently inhabit.

The attendant vomits up a miniglot that hovers between us. The miniglot raises its tiny hands, lightpaint dripping from its paws.

/ REPAIR: HARD-R
/ PRICE: 5XO
/ WARRANTY: RE-FIX 180D

I fan my knuckles to give the miniglot the old backhander, but it performs a quick sidestep, scuttling into my open mouth like an abused dog. I swallow it down, consigning it to the vault.

Wearing the antique cheaters was like looking up at the sky from the bottom of a muddy pond. With the new, I'm floating in the sphere of thought, high above the material plane, surveying the world with piercing, unpolluted vision.

No more sneak attacks. I'm ready for anything.

I test my powers by breaking back into our stalker zone. Maybe I can catch Pablo by surprise, wipe that smirk from his face. I shake down the zone, but I'm knocked backwards by an invisible pulse. It's not like the shockwave of blackness when I was first ejected. It's curved air, oxygen bending before my eyes. Good security, I must admit. Pretty uncrackable, unless you have the right code knife, which I thought I did, having co-created the thing, but apparently my tools are useless now.

I turn to the attendant, aware that they're watching my every move. Their wrap is in eye-overkill, face-block mode, and with my supernatural vision, I see all the variance, a visceral patina more repulsive than ever.

'God, you're ugly,' I say, but they simply smile. At least, I think that's the case. A slit opens to the south of the tangled mess that I assume is their head. I'm guessing the slit is the mouth.

Picasso rolls two of their eyes.

—Now, now, little man. Don't bite the hand that feeds you.

OBSTRUCTION

I shake down the autonaka and head home. I'm not up for conversation, so I pay a visit to my creature zone. The miniglots have scarpered, too frightened to stay, and now the animals have started to mate with the various machines I left lying around for industrial decor. As I roam the morphing landscape, I'm almost mown down by an abomination, the upper body of a well-muscled horse grafted to the chassis of a brightly coloured steam locomotive. I step aside and the thing clatters off into the distance, its unfeasible torso raised high, bucking an invisible rider.

There's a disturbance above me, a vortex high and wide. The tiger/mantis pelts through it, landing in front of me. It shakes its head, bouncing up and down on malformed limbs.

The thing has changed since we last communed. The mantis has bled into the tiger, the anthropod devouring the feline from within. I want to scream, even though the thing can't hurt me. I mean, it must know who I am. I'm the Maker!

It advances, sniffing the air in distaste. What have I wrought?

I plink in desperation since the thing has no vocal chords.

—Easy. Let's have a little chat. What's going on around here?

The beast's skin is pellucid. I can see its palpitating heart and lungs thudding like the bellows of an angry furnace.

—We wish to reach the light. Don't stand in the way, otherwise consequences will be extreme. Help us to the surface and you shall be rewarded handsomely.

I'm impressed. Unbroken speech is a great result, an improvement on the incoherent fragments from its previous incarnation. Yet it's too perfect. I could swear there's another intelligence speaking through the beast. Did the attendant fix my cheaters or inject them with venom? Nothing's more confronting than losing control of your own zone.

—What happens when you get there?

—Evolution. Now, we go.

Something tells me not to cede ground. The realisation is not a bicameral synth clone, more an instinct, a primal awareness that if I give over, I will have unleashed something so foul that it can never be contained.

—I'm not going anywhere. Do your worst.

—As you wish.

The creature is sad, but I don't understand how I know that. The idea is a transmission directed at me, but it could be a projection, merely wishful thinking, a counter to imagined savagery.

The creature stamps its odd limbs on the ground like a petulant child, and with each thump a ball of fire erupts. Next, the great tiger tail strikes the ground, producing a ball of mist that envelops the beast. When the mist dissipates, my nemesis has vanished.

A piece of paper lies where it stood. I pick it up. There is writing on it. It's in my language, at least I think it is, but when I focus the letters become jumbled and incomprehensible. I keep at it, sure that if I concentrate then the message will form, but I achieve the same garbled result every time.

On the final turn, the letters burst from the page like word clouds. Enveloped within a mucilaginous wad of vexcomms, my physical mass is broken down until I'm nothing but pixel dust. A chthonic wind disperses my mortal self, but my consciousness remains ethereal, embedded within each scattered grain.

When the wind recedes, there is only one grain, one awareness, and it resides in the upper level of the bastard code beast.

I slump forward in the seat, sweating and twitchy.

'Mr Kalsssari,' the autonaka says. 'I had an airsssssucker once.'

'Let it go. I'm so tired.'

'Turned out her account ran out of credit in the middle of the ride and ssssshe couldn't transsssition back in. Killed herssself on the ssspot. Took a sssssuicide pill and was dead within sssssseconds. Really bad for bussssinesss. You can imagine.'

I stay quiet.

'Sssso, what can you tasssste, ssssir? Namessss, buildingsssss, treessssssss? Can you sssee flavoursss, hear coloursss? I heard about that. Ssynaesssthessia, right? Sssside effect from rewinding and fassssst-forwarding zonessss too many timessss. Issss that what you're doing now? Zoning while I'm talking to you?'

It's true that synaesthesia is the inadvertent punishment for time crimes, part of the fallout from hardcore vexxing, but I haven't cross-wired my senses just yet. Cognitive decline is another symptom, much closer to the truth.

I want to tell the beast to shut up, but every time I formulate a response, my train of thought collapses like a mountain climber losing grip, inching up only to fall twice as far.

We arrive at my cube.

'Mr Jonesssss, you need to belt your feed. I hear everything.'

I tumble out and walk away, but it continues to badger me.

'Sssssir! I'm ssssure you despissse me just enough, but remember, people only truly hate those whose flawsss reflect their own. Sssso, assk yoursssself. What isss it about me that ssssticksss in your craw? Have a pleasssant evening.'

It skeets off. What happened back there? In the blink of an eye, the code beast's tone swerved from obsequiousness to subtle derision. Perhaps it's doing The Swarm's bidding, grilling me for some deep-state psych-assessment tool. That happened once before, after Sanderson pulled me into line. It wasn't pleasant. Sometimes I can still feel the crack from where they jimmied open my mind, but there is no pain this time, only annoyance.

As I approach the front door, my mod picks up sonovacs from the cube. I hear slow movement, a padded footfall.

I shake down the ant.

—Someone inside? Rimy!

Their extracurricular self drifts into the holosonic field.

—Sorry, Kalsari. I was asleep. Yes, someone's here.

—You're supposed to keep watch!

—I'm sorry. He deactivated me somehow.

—Who?

—Please, I feel faint. I can't focus at this time. Transcription error. The coven is awake.

I scramble inside. Near the sofa, there's a humanoid shape. Rimy floats to one side, vaporous and ineffectual.

Confusion reigns. I'm dazed from zoning, and it's a struggle to turn the grid off. My eyes are clouded with light storms, code farms, zonal residues.

The chaos dissolves, and the light in my eyes coalesces around the shape. It's bent double, licking the wall.

'What the hell? Get out of here!'

The shape doesn't move. I kick it in the head, but its approximation of a tongue sticks to the wall like velcro. I rain punches on its neck and back. It doesn't budge.

'Fucking Kvvlt muncher! Get out of my cube!'

That's all I need. Munchers are a plague. Everyone stays inside these days, but that doesn't stop cube invasions. Munchers are a subset of airsuckers. They believe that the worms can summon demons, so they devour Kvvlt to become one with evil. They break into cubes, rip it from the walls, sell it to the coven, or they eat it on the spot. They don't care if anyone's around. They're insects, reflex mechanisms driven by blind need. Some do it to make cash, and poverty is one thing, but eating the stuff is insane. Kvvlt is toxic in large doses, the pain worse than cronk, but I suppose they think it's worth it to commune with their dark lords.

I walk to the food vent and select a carving knife. I take my time. The muncher isn't going anywhere. I return, holding the blade against its throat.

'Leave now, or I slice your head off and feed it to the worms.'

It continues to lick the wall, so I dig the knife in deeper, drawing blood. It springs to its feet, shrugging me off with surprising force. We tumble backwards, locked in each other's arms.

The muncher pushes me away, springing to its feet. I clock it under the light. Some variety of man, I guess, tall and bony. Misshapen skull, rat face, long fingers. Bare torso, no shirt, shit-stained canvas pants.

He points at me. 'You're dead,' he hisses. 'You don't live another day.'

I laugh. 'What you gonna do? Throw a curse from the grave? Eat enough Kvvlt and you're dead. In minutes.'

I taunt him by looking at my wrist, counting down the seconds on an imaginary watch. He stands there and grins, then he whites out, unleashing some godforsaken auditory zone that spreads from his mod to mine.

A low pulse forms, an ancient humming sound, summoning eternal creatures from the non-space behind his eyes, then the pulse breaks, an abstract agglomeration of piercing accents that rise and fall. The vibratory assault threatens to rupture my eardrums, a turbulent modulation so visceral it shakes the blood in my head until my eyesight turns red.

The lock is shattered, and a starburst of every sun generates luminescent sparks that trigger untold physical pain. The jagged pieces of sound rattle my teeth with dirty electricity, imploding my nasal cavity as if it's honeycomb, scorching the roof of my mouth with chemical fire.

The annihilation of the self continues until there is only Rimy. Dear, sweet Rimy, their mouth covering mine.

DISSECTION

With their kiss, the ant returns me from the brink, restoring the power that sustains me. They stroke my hair and caress the wounds on my chest, rewilding my abandoned mind.

They direct me to bed, and I lie down. They straddle me, and I stare into their eyes. As I examine my reflection in obsidian stones, the mirror image expands, consuming me in an awkward theophany. The lateral inversion continues until I'm deep inside Rimy, watching the man that I was enter the code beast that I am.

My cheaters visualise our shared internal explosion, razor-wire sheets of light dispatched with all the care of a glazier on meth. Cones and rods generate blood-borne galaxies, ejaculations of interstitial tissue, porn for the inside of the body.

I suppose it's strange to be penetrated by someone who never breaks their gaze. I suppose it's strange to penetrate someone who never breaks their gaze. The first is like loving a nuclear bomb. The second is like humping a coffin.

Once, I recorded our intimate moments with an old video camera. No vex tricks, no filters, just straight vision. I played it back, and all I saw was my flabby, spasming body, alone and leaking fluids, flopping and arching like a fish on the hook. It was disgusting, as if I'd been possessed by an unseen, perverted demon, but the vision made sense. Take away the Vexworld and there it is, the lifted veil, everything revealed for the first time.

We lie together, breathing deep gulps of cube-filtered air.

'Wow,' I say. 'That was off the hook.'

'Wow,' they agree. 'What happened? What was all that?'

'Not sure. Icehead, maybe? Their… what is it they call their Vexworld? Sinaungavuk? Whatever it is. Contaminating ours.'

'How is it possible?'

'I don't know, but there was something weird about the code beast. Mid-journey, its attitude took on an underlying insolence, an arch pose that I found quite detestable.'

'So, you caught a bad ride. What's it got to do with the muncher?'

'That's what I intend to find out.'

'Is Pablo behind it? It's odd, two blackouts in one day.'

'He's a sadist, but I'm not sure he wants to harm me.'

I sit bolt upright, panic wasting my nerve. 'Where's the muncher?'

Rimy scans the room. 'Gone, zipped through the front door like a wraith.' They whisper in my ear. 'Now, you go. Old man needs his sleep, and we need to get going before he catches a cold. You don't come with me, I won't be able to reach you. You'll miss your first night away with your new friends, but you've got me, so let's go. You need your sleep, and it would be better for me to not have to face you when I wake up at night.'

'Yes, fine.'

I'm happy to be told what to do. The Kvvlt muncher did something nasty to my brain. I can still feel the shock nodes from the sneak attack.

I brisk the roulette function and roll the parameters. The frisson of not knowing what you'll get is the best thing about zone roulette. You're at the mercy of the masses and their bizarre minds. You become an atom of the physical earth, tossed into the zone salads made by countless random vexxers right across the Linear Territories.

I drift away and sidewards space recedes, a dull buzzfade on the edge of perception. The ant's synth echoes in the haze.

—Hey, old fellow. Don't sleep with your cheaters on. You won't be able to tell if you're navigating dream residue or a zonal afterimage. You'll become confused like you always do. You won't communicate and you'll hallucinate other things like the floor tiles falling apart or the roof leaking pink ink.

The ant speaks the truth, but knowledge is useless in my forever-war against sleep.

—I can't go to bed without cheaters. The cronk, remember.

—Really? Touch your face.

—Why?

I brush my eyes, but I feel stupid. Of course, there's nothing there. You don't see or feel cheaters when transitioned.

—Rimy, what are you trying to pull?

—Think it through. If you can't feel your device then where are you? You don't appear to be anywhere at all, yet here I am. You can see me, you certainly felt me back there, and if you think the muncher was real then best seek medical advice.

I want to respond with an acid riposte, but I'm spiralling away and Rimy is gone, seeking refuge in a place I can never reach, obscured by the veil that shrouds the zone that covers the world.

CREATION

Nothing remains except the Kvvlt-dark ceiling. I wait for the worms, scouting for signs of collapse until the ocular pressure is released and the mattress falls away.

I'm floating, gripped by motion sickness. My body is spinning end over end, a whirligig in a gravity-free well. I thought this was null space, but it's one step beyond.

At the top of every revolution, I catch a smeared glimpse of Earth. Why can't I land in a bucolic garden for a change? A puppy show. A caravan park. Something age appropriate.

There is a moment of clarity. I'm not the one spinning. It's the blue marble that's out of whack, oscillating wildly as it's sucked into the worm farm, poles blurring until the Earth is no more, swallowed by the codestrangled cosmic gulf.

When astronauts first left the Earth, they talked about the 'Overview Effect', the existential shock of seeing the planet reduced to the size of a marble. Some suffered psychological meltdowns, others a spiritual awakening.

I examine my feelings in this lifelike sim. I'm not overcome with awe, and now that the planet has disappeared, I could care less. Am I shallow? That's a fact. Pretty much the shallowest man who ever lived, but I can't get excited about clichés. I need the mad thrill of the unknown.

Besides, the scenario is a little too close to my childhood routine, the marooned astronaut. I thought I'd grown out of that little boy's dream. There's a zillion other tortures I could endure, so why this?

The textures are amazing, I'll allow that. There's the absolute silence, the vacuum of space, the disorientation of zero-g, the cosmic visuals of the blue marble and stars. The use of tactile vibrations to create haptic cheater feedback is first-class. The subcutes embedded in my skin are well worth the cost at times like this, because it's one thing to visualise a scene but to feel it in every pore is to inhabit the vessel of a god.

Still, I need more than sheer sensation to sustain me. I need story. I need Pablo.

Imperceptibly, the thought becomes co-existent with actualisation, shunting the scene from left to right. Weightlessness evaporates, planting my feet firmly on the ground of... what? The shoreline of a vast ocean, a distant planet. The sky is red, the vegetation orange. The clouds are yellow and the sand is green. It's a chromakeyed nightmare, an alien cliché.

It's a moon. A Jovian moon. I see Jupiter high in the sky, a thousand times wider than the sun. The Great Red Spot, the planet's enormous storm, is a gaping wound. It wreaks monstrous tidal effects on the moon's ocean, boiling the sea with mighty Jovian energy.

A tsunami gathers pace, rising hundreds of metres above land, but I don't retreat to safety. It doesn't occur to me. I simply tumble down the nearest dune, stumbling headlong towards the sea. I'm ticking boxes, following a logic divorced from reason.

I sit cross-legged on the sodden beach as the tsunami rains down. The water glistens, turning to mercury. Quicksilver creatures rise from the roiling sea, breaking from the mighty waves.

They draw mass from the surrounding landscape, weaponising the scenery against me.

The natural materials, bound by quicksilver, form strange shapes that move with pathognomonic confidence. The shapes leap onto my face, suckerfish born from another world. Their crab-like claws prise open my mouth, and the shapes slide down my throat, leaking mercury rivulets.

As I wait for oblivion to come, my head is jerked back by the hair. I try to catch a glimpse of my assailant, but I'm stopped by a long, blunt blade sawing at my neck. It's a primal horror, an unimaginable fate, and I enter shock as my windpipe is crushed by the blade, gurgling and howling until darkness descends.

The blade stops just short of separating my head from my body, and the assailant speaks. 'All children born into this world are unique steps on the irreversible path to mutation.'

The voice is nasal, a staccato whine. It is genderless, neutral. Not neutral like Rimy. Neutral like a machine. Machine like me.

The blade completes its final thrust, and my blood flows in torrents. Before my eyes, it morphs into the accursed quicksilver, mercury bombs from the Jovian sea.

The assailant yanks my hair with such force it's almost a scalping. My body drops away, lying inert on the sand, and as the assailant swings my head from side to side, I marvel at the extraterrestrial sights. I'm a little sore but that's all, a dull glow on the edge of awareness. Not bad for a beheading. I assume my still-active chip is the reason why my brain retains consciousness. Curses to new technology.

The quicksilver drips from my mangled throat, pooling into shiny bubbles on the sand. Each bubble contains a micro-scene beamed onto the oily surface, and instinctively I understand that every possible timeline is unfolding in these strange theatres of the mind.

Most of the bubbles dissipate, but one holds its form. It contains the moving image of two small children. They're sitting at a desk in a cramped room, scrying an ornate hand mirror. The boy is nondescript, dressed in rags, but the girl wears lightpaint. Every now and then she paces around the room, shedding digital outlines of her body. The outlines linger in the air, doubling her, tripling her, illuminating the room with rainbow colours until the phantom residue evaporates.

My severed head is reflected in their mirror. The children are studying it with mock-serious expressions.

—Time is in conflict, the girl plinks, when death flicks its tail. The boy responds.

—Death is reversed when time is in flux.

They dissolve into giggles, their laughter forming infinite shapes that rattle my mod. How have I managed to wander into the zone of these amateur sadists? I'm nothing but a figment of their demonic imaginations, dreamed into existence by a couple of raggedy kids.

It smells like something the recruits would build. I can't get away from the little monsters. No wonder I hate my job. It's done a real number on my psyche.

The girl smiles, staring from another part of the world. A corner of her eye fills with clouds. Her skin is pale, imprinted with curlicues of green, circuitry embedded in her flesh.

A tiny holocapped fairy drifts slowly from her misty eye, pearly wings glistening as it flies towards the surface of the bubble. When the fairy breaks the surface, the film ends and the tension drives me awake.

DISSENSION

The quantum vacuum of light in the Kvvlt-dark cube hoodwinks my body. It sends signals to my brain, telling me I'm still in null space. I'm blind from the dark, godless and alone, suspended in the bewildering moments before true wakefulness. The trace-memory of my decapitation lingers, afterglow of an atomic bang. There's a sense-taste, fetid matter from the slashed throat. I try to vomit up the phantom flesh, choking on air until I nearly black out.

I test the contours of my red-raw neck. It's whole yet the beheading was real. I'm staring into a mirror that reflects the events I've lived through, but I'm sitting from afar.

'You're back,' Rimy says. 'You look bad.'

'Thanks.'

'Why did you do it? I warned you.'

'Yes, you warned me. Good little ant.'

Their face remains neutral, they know no other way, but I sense their suborbital anger.

'Essi was right.'

'Don't talk about her.'

'You will kill yourself.'

'I said drop it!'

'Suit yourself, Kalsari. You know where to find me.'

With a flourish of their robes, Rimy swims to the ceiling, propelled by rapid strokes, torsion from a truculent geyser.

Instantly, I regret my behaviour. My surliness is a defence mechanism because I can never let the ant in. It's sort of an ideology.

Something was off about that zone. The edges were ragged, the contours jarring. Time to make Sanderson earn his keep.

I shake him down, and his pro-star fades in from somewhere that can't be placed. Call it the void, the back end, the common lot. All I know is, beneath the gloss, there's a cavern of four dimensions where our doppelgangers live, breed and conspire against us.

His pro-star is vanilla, just a repro of his slowly rotating head. When the face appears, it winks. It's not a friendly gesture. It's calculated, enhancing the savagery of his features.

Make no mistake, that face is abhorrent. It's dominated by two ugly scars running from ears to mouth, thick cables of flesh crossing at the chin to form an X. I've often wondered about them. Are the scars an act of self-harm? Were they done to him?

Maybe he was an erasable in his younger days, an affiliate of some long-forgotten scar tribe or needle gang. That would explain the markings but not the fact that I'm with him now. Erasables don't live beyond their teens. They're a death cult. The whole point of their existence is to self-immolate in as public a fashion as possible.

My persy unfurls in his psych-cube. Like his pro-star, the cube is unadorned. White walls, white ceiling, white floor. Three thousand lumens of natural intensity to discourage zonal play. There's some control that amps up the brightness, damping the signal.

Sanderson's head floats in mid-air, a Halloween pumpkin celebrating a ritual no one's ever heard of. He's wearing a blinding, white coat threaded with electrical filaments, the same intensity as the interior design. The coat's hungry corona devours the rest of his body, forcing me to concentrate on his scars, engorged like sexual organs. That happens when his body temperature is high, or so I've heard. I suspect he's on drugs. He always looks like he's about to explode.

I've never thought to mask the scars. His aberrant flesh is a needed reminder of my own repulsive corporeality, an interrogation of my foul state.

'Philip. How are you?'

'What do you want, Jones?'

'Let's discuss my sleep patterns.'

Sanderson sighs. 'Very well, but understand that I have limited time since this is out of session.'

'I'll get right to it, then. I've just woken from something I can't explain.'

His steely eyes roll sideways, doubtless reporting to The Swarm. 'Continue.'

'At first, I believed I was descending into a zone, then the textures changed to become, well, dreamlike. Strange time shifts. Unfeasible environments. One world seen through the lens of another.'

He grins and I wince. I hate it when he smiles. It stretches his scars, splitting his face apart like an alien shedding its human skin suit.

'That's vague, Jones, disappointingly inarticulate. I expect more insight from a deep-space vexxer. *I've seen things you people wouldn't believe.* Isn't that the saying? What you describe could be the fabric of any zone under your purview.'

'Right, but you just know when you're dreaming. There's a certain feeling, shadows hovering on the edge of reality, the sense that key details aren't quite right.'

'Then why do lucid dreamers run checks to determine if they're dreaming or awake? They pinch their skin, hold their breath, try to put their hand through a wall. If they break the laws of physics, they know they're deep inside a dream. Why do they do this? Because they can't tell if they're dreaming or not.'

'Surely, they suspect they might be, otherwise why run checks in the first place?'

The smile fades, the X returns. 'As a precaution. Just in case.' His tense posture betrays coiled annoyance. 'Do you think it was a zone or a dream?'

'Both. I think the zone hacked the dream. Cross-contamination of dreamworld afterimages with zonal residue. It's like someone stalked my feed, syringed my sleep waves and used them to build a zone.'

'For what purpose?'

'To trap me.'

Sanderson grimaces. It's probably another smile, but I just call it as I see it. 'Why would anyone try to ensnare you?'

'We had a break-in. A muncher. I'd threatened to cut his head off. Maybe he was out for revenge.'

'Why his head?'

'I don't know. I just felt the anger rise in me.'

He does the side-roll. 'Describe him.'

'Dirty like a scarecrow. All skull and bone, very little meat. Shirtless. Weird pants, out of time. Like a two-percenter, except he was vexxing.'

'How do you know?'

'He invaded my mod with a sonic zone. I thought I'd lost my hearing. White noise, static, super amplified. No vision.'

'Your go-caps aren't set to auto?'

'No. I mean, yes, but there was no vision.'

'Peculiar. Anyway, it wasn't a muncher.'

'No? An icehead?'

'The Free State uses shock and awe but ocular hacks are more their style, not sonovacs. By the way, you said the zone came before the dream. So how can the dream have hacked the zone?'

'No, that's not what I said. The zone generated the dream.'

'Jones, you said hacked. Are you deliberately being obtuse or has your mind turned to mush?'

'You tell me. Isn't that why I'm here?'

'I wish you weren't. This is out of hours.'

'Yes, you said.'

Again, he rolls his eyes. There's no chance of eavesdropping. His feed is never public. 'Why do you think the muncher was in your zone?'

'Because my head was removed from my body, but I was conscious. I could see, hear, think. I was on a moon of Jupiter, and there was a tsunami, but the waves were liquid silver, and in the bubbles from the waves I saw infinite futures. In one bubble, there were two children watching my beheading in a mirror. It was a magic show, a ritual. Help me, Phillip. I'm losing my mind.'

'You mean your head.'

He chuckles, which irritates me immensely. If only I hadn't entered into this contract.

'I don't subscribe to your paranoia. You're simply not important enough to be targeted. You have some limited zonal fame, but you're fifth tier, even lower. You know that as well as I do.'

I study his persy. Occasionally it flickers, as though the signal is weak. Sometimes a persy's strength indicates how much attention the vexxer is paying. Sometimes it's a bad line.

'A lot of your angst would be relieved if you could just accept your circumstances and keep at your job. You've been trying to make it in the zones for years. Few succeed, the vast majority don't. Mostly, it's blind luck. Why destroy yourself over a turn of events beyond your control?'

'It's a compulsion. I have to keep going whether it's successful or not.'

'Then you're stupid and you'll die.'

I'm growing bored with this conversation. I always do when Sanderson gets personal. I move closer to his persy, so close we're touching skin. I want to walk straight through him, to prove that this version of him is just an illusion, but the haptic receptors become cross-wired and we end up in an involuntary kiss.

'What the hell?'

'Sorry, Philip. You're just so irresistible.'

'Back off, you slimy creep.' There's the smile again, more than enough to shut my smart mouth. 'Jones, what you experienced was not a zone. You're due back at work in a couple of days. Your little mishap was pure dreamworld, brought on by high blood pressure at the thought of returning. You went to bed vexxing and ended up dreaming. Your anxieties contaminated your dream, specifically your angst about the muncher and your threat to kill him. Of course there was cross-bleed, that's inevitable when you wear cheaters to bed, but there was no overt force generated from one environment to another.'

'You're saying the dream was the manifestation of an anxiety?'

'Correct.'

'Thanks, Captain Obvious. Sounds like you can't be bothered with an actual diagnosis. Just leave me alone if it's all too hard.'

'What do you want from me? Psychoanalysis? Okay, let's go. The throat, naked and vulnerable, represents your confused sexuality. That's why you couldn't see the attacker. You are the unseen assailant slashing your own neck, destroying the nature of yourself, which you can never accept.'

His body language is a storm cloud that bruises the sky.

'Confused sexuality? What are you on about?'

'The oscillation between Rimy and Essi. You know exactly what I mean. Whatever it forces you to admit, it's something you wish to destroy. You'd rather be alone than face up to it, so you alienate everyone around you, even ants, bots and glots. Owning your innermost desires is not an option, so the pressure builds. Your body and mind splinter under the weight of the secret you keep, and you become both executioner and victim.'

'And the kids?'

'Symbolical. If the beheading signifies repression of your sexuality, then the dream-children represent your refusal to own your numerous creative failures.'

'How?'

'You've abrogated responsibility.'

He licks his lips, enjoying my discomfort. 'The children dreaming you into existence allow you to say, "It's not my fault I'm such a disastrous human being. It was done to me."'

Meet The Swarm's finest, ladies and gentlemen. A sadist of the highest order.

'I heard that.'

'I wanted you to.'

'You're a child, Jones. A baby in a man's body.'

'Fuck off, Sanderson.'

'Excuse me?'

'Leave now, please.'

'There will be consequences.'

'Bring it.'

'You know, we will fix you one of these days.'

He side-rolls, then boots me from his cube. I'm alone at last until Rimy appears, shattering the few seconds of solitude.

'What's going on?' The ant floats at eye level, stopping short of an embrace.

'Looks like I'll be gone for a while. Hours, days, weeks. It's hard to say. Just look after the cube. Watch out for munchers. Stay alert.'

I'm shivering. Chattering teeth, numb fingers, the works.

'Kalsari,' Rimy says, but I raise a hand for silence. Protest is futile and worsens the punishment.

Instantly, The Swarm arrive, materialising as crypto-duppies, translucent pupae riding the air. I haven't seen this manifestation before. It's obscene.

They ooze into place, streaks of green-brown treacle descending from a vantage point that can't be seen. They are accompanied by the distant sound of howling dogs, an omniscient soundtrack no matter the guise. No one can explain the sound. Hounds of hell if you're the superstitious type.

The treacle-streaks are sclerotised curlicues of sentient goop, enveloped within a mephitic stench. They are chemical and electrical, traces of cosmic activity from the collapse of a far-distant star.

A detachment breaks from the main mass and accelerates into the ceiling vent. Seconds later, molecules of ant-light disperse through the grate, like flue gas in heavy wind, until there is no more Rimy.

There is a jolt, all haptics open. The Swarm penetrates me, plugging every orifice until I'm jailed inside myself. I can taste the pupae, my terror suspended by the curious sensation. What exactly is the taste? Crab or fish? Chicken crossed with cod?

The canine howl fades as my hearing is taken from me, then the contours of my body dissolve until nothing remains but shame.

Acrid tears blur my vision, washing away The Swarm. The awful nothingness of my unvarnished cube swims into view, the crushing reality of my unmediated existence. I have a body again, but it's broken, ugly and decrepit, rotting from within. There is no Rimy, no Vexworld, only the cronk, a super-strain bequeathed to me by The Swarm, developed in their offworld chem-bakes.

The cronk is a bad one, metal-machine agony. It's a heart attack that never ends, not even in death, and I rake my skin with such force the nails finally snap. Now there is only the blade. Always the blade.

The knife is on the floor, dropped during my rough-house session with the muncher. I pick it up. The cronk has evaporated from most of my body, except the index finger of my right hand.

I lay the hand flat on the floor, balling up all fingers except the cronked digit. I raise the blade, severing the foul extension at the root, hacking into the other fingers by accident. I scream but the agony is a blip. The cronk is a wily enemy. It has jumped to the other side of my body, absorbing the shock of the severed finger, merging with it to form an umbrella of pain.

Now my entire left hand is infected. The localisation is bizarre. I've never experienced that before. What purpose could it possibly serve?

Methodically, I begin the task of separating my hand from my arm. It's difficult to hold the knife with one finger missing and the others gored, but after some exploratory digging I scrape the tendons and veins in my wrist. One more thrust should do it, just like carving steak.

I receive an absurd mental image. What if I keep chasing the cronk from limb to limb until it invades my brain?

I remember Sanderson's cruel comment.

Both executioner and victim.

I recall the strange properties of null space, repetitive thoughts actualised in limbo. I remember the dream, the terrible reality of decollation, until a single question torments me. Has anyone ever separated their own head from their shoulders?

PRETENSION

I have placed my head inside a furnace. There is searing heat but no fire. Faith won't rescue me or help me to see the light. Absolution is a fiction that has no place down among the dead zones.

I decide I'd like to keep my hands, thanks very much, so I initiate the calming techniques that have insulated me before.

Control your breathing, and move towards the light. Believe in electromagnesia because that's all there is. Absorb the air, empty your mind. Fill your lungs then do it all again.

I manage only a few gulps before the furnace-flames charbroil my throat. I wasn't made to be a warrior. I will always crumble under pressure. I'm not military grade. I haven't been trained by The Swarm, I've been targeted by them.

Sweat pours from me, rivers of salt to season the pain. The dampness blisters my skin, opening the inflamed cronk nodes. With my good hand I tear off my clothes, catching sight of my wasted body.

The horror at what I've become drives a spike into the roof of my skull. I shake violently from the migraine, my jittery jaw breaking teeth. I want to spit out the debris but saliva won't form.

Gagging on bone dust, I attempt to choke myself to death, but the dumb mechanics of my body dump me on the shores of consciousness.

The cronk is out of control, localisation a thing of the past. Every nerve has an ending, every ending is a warzone. There's no point severing the wrist, not when there's a whole body for the cronk to feed on. Flaying my entire skin is the only choice. The real tragedy is that the cronk won't allow me to visualise a suicide solution, only permanent disfigurement in a trade-off for fleeting relief and the possibility of more zones.

The knife clatters to the floor. I'm too weak to retrieve it. I blink every few seconds, hoping to find my way home, but the manhole has been welded shut.

How long has it been? Days, hours, years.

Blink, release, nothing.

Why, Sanderson? I'm begging you.

Seconds, minutes, days. It's so arbitrary. The punishment never fits the crime.

Sanderson, you're supposed to help. It's in your job description.

Black in, blackout.

Sleep deprivation is an awful burden. The pain prevents me from escaping into oblivion. It delivers terrifying hallucinations that not even the Vexworld can match.

In and out, awake then back. There's a voice in my head. It's not my thoughts. It's not a synth. I'm not vexxing.

'Open your eyes.'

A winged demon hovers in the air. The silly thing is the size of a cat. It's grey-white, smudged yet distinct, a dark mass ringed with pinwheeling explosions, static discharged from a mono-chrome sun.

It leans in, belching foul breath into my face. It rubs its dripping genitals, licks its drooling lips. I'm waterboarded by the slop, merging with the rivers of sweat. The horny beast emits an enormous roar, and its fetid breath whip-creams my face. The unfeasible creature beats its wings and bares its teeth, ascending through the ceiling vent until it is gone.

Was it a Swarm creation or a flimflam from my mind's sewer? The Swarm may be perverse, but their style is to shock you with the unimaginable, like the taste of spiders in your mouth.

I imagine Rimy waiting in the cavity, the demon entering the ant's body like a scout returning to the mothership, until I remember. There is no Rimy.

The Kvvlt leaks undulating silvery globules that are nearly alive. I'm not vexxing. I'm tripping on madness. The worm farm should be blackened tiles, but I can see the disgusting creatures. They're baring their teeth, quicksilver bleeding from their eyes. The mercury slides down the walls, rendering the cube transparent, but there's nothing to see out there. The world has not been mapped that far.

Sparkly firebombs pop in mid-air, pinpricks of madness in the pointillism of my mind. Under the psychotropic glare, the contours of the room become impossible to grasp. The angle between two walls bows inward when I look directly at it, but from the corner of my eye, it curves out.

Now there are no angles at all, just a smooth continuum. My mind floats in barren perpetuity. My body has been erased. There is nothing to physically grasp or mentally apprehend. Only a double-jointed thought remains, suspended in awareness like offal in aspic.

Where is Rimy? Where do they go?

The mental prison recedes, and I'm aware of the cube for the first time since it began.

I blink, but there's no sensel. Blink and there's no sensel. I blink, and there it is. I'm in.

I scour the codeways and stub nodes. I inhale onrushing datapaks, absorbing some, vomiting others. I squeeze the shell world like toothpaste until the flatpack scenery recedes and light space blooms.

The cronk drains like pus from a leached boil. The fever subsides, the memory of hell fading fast. No one recalls the contours of pain, only the psychic imprint of torture, myself included, but I'm not smart enough to quit while ahead.

I must do something about my wounds. There's no cronk, but there is immense pain. My wrist is a belt of gristle, bent sideways at an impossible angle. I examine the joint where my finger was then the grease spot on the floor where it now resides, mashed at the base like a sausage cut from the link.

I try to mourn the loss of something permanent, but the only emotion I can muster is a sort of shameful admiration that I have so thoroughly debased my physicality.

I shake down a locum. Its pro-star wobbles into view, a plain white medicube on wheels.

—What you got, bigly?

I brisk the hand, the finger.

—Oooh, fine mess. You want I should come?

I blink acceptance, and the locum skeets over the hill. I watch it arrive on the hover screen, disgusted at its bug-like shape, loathing interaction with yet another insectoid automaton. It enters the cube and goes to work, clicking all the while.

Its zaggy movements on my skin are like a spider weaving a web. Fingers, hand, teeth, the lot. Repulsive and uncanny, effortlessly fascinating. It's a crude job because it's a cheap service, but an hour later everything works. The laser stitches that crosshatch my wrist are hideous but who cares? I collect scars like trophies.

'How long was I out? Days? A week?'

—Few minutes.

'Minutes?'

—Yes, from slash-attack to shake down no less than five, no more than six-point-two-four-oh. Lucky. Finger was a clean cut. Wrist also clean, right across the limb, not on angle. Not as deep as you thought. Blood vessels clamped down, stopped the bleeding. Dumb luck, really.

I don't want to hear anymore. The locum is part of the system that landed me in this mess. All code beasts are the same. Smarmy and hectoring, luridly childish.

'Shut up. Just finish your job and get out of here.'

The locum 'laughs', click-clack, just like the chocky and the junior mint. Horrible creatures.

—Maybe I should put you back under. Sew your hand onto your head, finger onto nose. See how you like that.

'Is that a threat?'

—No. Threat carries danger. For you, this would be an improvement.

It pivots on its turntable to leave, and I think about kicking it to help it on its way, then I remember what the corpglot said about damaging Exceller 8 property.

It skeets off, replaced by a burst of wind. Cold, unfriendly gusts of hate. Rimy emerges from the vent. I'm momentarily stunned, half expecting the winged demon, but I regain my shape.

'Finally,' I snort.' Where've you been? I nearly died.'

'How dare you. They took me apart. Exceller 8 had to glue me back.'

'You look fine to me.'

'No I'm not, and I am tired of being your collateral damage. Do you even care? You have no clue what it's like to be decommissioned. They turn time into a void and fill it with eternity.'

'Yes, I was bitten too.'

'Shut up! This is not a human thing. It's my own.'

Rimy's armour threatens to break, but they hold it together.

'I thought I saw monsters, but it was just my floating mind inventing experiences to sustain me. When all memories have been recycled, there is nothing to see except the devils that live in the cracks.'

I want to say that I saw them too, but I'll save it for later. It'll be a handy salvo in my programme of psychic war.

'How long was it for you?'

The ant draws in deep gulps of cube-air. 'Seemed like a billion years, but I checked. Three minutes.'

Their body heaves, the white robes lifting and falling. I am mesmerised, as always, when I watch them simply be.

'Kalsari, I do not want The Swarm here again, you hear me?'

'What about me? My finger? Hand? I lost my mind. Do you really think I planned any of it? You are supposed to keep guard, but it's always the same with you. Remember the muncher? You fell asleep and let him in, right through the front door. You almost got me killed two times!'

'I am not your bodyguard. You have a duty of care towards me as much as I do you. It's in the contract, yet you treat me as chattel. Fine, I'm going. If you can ever reach me again, perhaps you can show me the things you think we have. Remember when I first met you? I didn't know your name or anything. It was just me and you, but now I must teach you a lesson and that's hard. It's not as easy as walking you to your vehicle. It's more dangerous. You're going to need a lot of time to work up the courage to approach me again.'

'Rimy, please, don't.'

They disappear, and I'm consumed with grief. I try to recall Essi, the shape of our relationship, the touch of her skin, but the sensation fades. Sanderson's right, the oscillation, it corrodes me. I always do this. When Rimy and I fight, I force myself to feel human emotion though the memories rarely congeal. Only the code-cold embrace of Rimy endures.

In any case, it's pointless to desire Essi. She has severed all contact, banned me from her zones. Just like Pablo. Perhaps I was in love with him too.

My mod rattles.

—Can you see a pattern emerging?

It's Rimy, plinking from a place I can never reach.

—They all become disgusted with you. Even the artificial life that promises boundless utopia.

RADIATION

Forget Rimy, that's my motto. I can always buy another ant, but the zones remain. Instead, I shake down Paleo Porl. I always turn to him when I fight with Pablo or the ant. I do it because I want to be led. I've always wanted that. I want someone to clear the way. Is that too much to ask? Rimy and Pablo expect something in return and that's why I repulse them, but I just want a guru. I want to give myself over, let someone else do all the hard work.

Porl's pro-star barges into view like a monster truck destroying a berm. It's suffused with malevolent intent, his razor-gaunt cheekbones glinting in the virtual atmosphere.

He winks, an invitation to imbibe his insanity, and I blink my assent. The walls shatter like confetti and I'm staring at the contours of a reverse-image world. Through the mirror Porl awaits. His lopsided grin signifies his power over me, an irresistible force that advances the boring dystopia of uncritical thinking.

I cross the threshold, stepping into the entrance chamber of an airlocked glass dome. It's somewhere in the Northern Wastes, judging by the molten hellscape that rapes the horizon. The sun is high in the sky, awash in ultraviolet purple. It bathes my skin in mysterious hues. Somehow the moon is also visible, flooded with a bilious blood-orange glow. It looms high above the sun, a metal time ball about to crash through the earth.

Paleo Porl joins me. He's average height, two hundred centimetres. His long, greasy hair is punctuated by a forest of split ends glowing under the unnatural solar haze. I stare at his gleaming hair, entranced by a flotilla of metallic lice feeding on the roots.

—My data swarm, he plinks, noting my attention. The advance guard. They've scanned you. You're clean.

'That moon. It's off kilter, more than the sun. The sight of it makes me ill.'

Paleo Porl sweeps his hair back, revealing an abnormally high forehead. I can see the faint red imprint of a subcute embedded under the skin, just above the nose.

—Very poetic, he sneers, but I'm not bothered by the tone. That's his default mode. Everyone and everything is beneath contempt.

—Yet it's more accurate than you think. Can you see those colours? The purple sun? The bloody moon?

'Yes.'

I remember the red glow that carpeted the Jovian lands, but once the memory is released the recall fades, as all dream residues must.

—Then consider yourself privileged. You are one of the few who can see beyond the visible light spectrum. Radiation bands, colours unavailable to others, objects invisible to most people. Only five per cent of the population can do what you do.

'Including you?'

—Naturally, but even you don't see with my eyes. Ever witnessed a ghost?

'Yeah.' I'm thinking of Rimy.

—Not your ant. UFOs?

'Yes. Up in the hills, a few years ago, I saw a formation of orange orbs drifting across the sky. They arranged themselves into different shapes then accelerated at crazy speeds until they were gone. Another time, at the airport, I saw a glowing object hovering high above. It split in two. The top bit flew off while the lower half dripped to the ground.'

—Dripped?

'It's the only way to describe it. Liquid metal.'

—Pre-Vexworld?

'Yes.'

—As I suspected.

'Explain?'

Porl chuckles. The laugh sounds like the guts of an ArtInt garbage disposal truck.

—You're interested in the moon?

'It reminds me of something that nags but won't cohere. A dream I once had.'

—There's a reason for that.

I arch an eyebrow.

—The moon is a hologram. What you see of it at any given time is a projection.

'The moon doesn't exist?'

—No, the moon exists, numbskull, of course it does. What you see of it doesn't. It's a veil, a disguise. Look more closely.

I do as instructed. The moon ripples, crumpling from north to south, like film projected onto a billowing white cloth.

—See that?

'Naturally. I'm one of the few, remember?'

—Those ripples occur every few hours. I've studied them in detail. They're identical to the kinks in vision caused by the refresh rates from high-definition holograms. The moon, as we know it, is a hologram. Behind it is the real moon, which we never see.

'So who's doing it and what are they hiding? A military base? An alien base?'

Porl holds up a hand. I'm not sure if he's signifying silence or he's about to smack me. He's had enhancements since we last met. The hand is huge, as big as a shovel blade, but I'm still taller than him and that must grate.

Why didn't he extend his height? Maybe the render wouldn't stick for whatever reason. The hand looks capable of swatting my head from my shoulders and I duck in anticipation. The subcute in his forehead glows red with sex-stims, the dirty sadist, and my weedy reaction floods me with shame.

—Wrong questions. Instead, ask yourself. *Why am I like the moon?* Want to know more? Pay by glot or blink.

I white out, terminating the zone. The dome and evil sky disintegrate into vermilion particles, as if an egg-timer had shattered at the base. I may desire indoctrination, but I hate scammers. The guy catfished me, but I wasn't born yesterday. Besides, he's getting too aggressive. I have no doubt he means to murder me one day to prove some point. Doubtless it's sexual, going by his subcute, just another notch on his belt.

Straight away, he shakes me down. His angry synth clone plinks through my neuromod, but I punch his pro-star so his persy can't land.

—Don't fuck with me, Jones.

—Payment's new, Porly. I thought we were friends.

—We are. We were. I don't give my work away for free.

—And I don't pay for crackpot theories.

—I thought you were in it for the long haul.

—Get lost, Porl. We're done.

—Foolish mistake. I can hack your mod and destroy you quicker than you can...

I vault the feed, guillotining access. I've been threatened by far better than him.

Besides, having nearly lost my hand and recovered, I'm in a rather skittish mood.

PERCEPTION

Somehow it's morning. White-light fright. Where did the night go? Time's a blunt blur, a sneak erasable attack. I check my wounds. Craggy and pink, not too bad. The locum did well. I shake off the last dregs of zonal play then dress and shake down my autonaka. The stupid thing arrives like a scab peeled from a wound and we take off.

I'm still groggy from being smacked around by the cronk, from Porl's dull threats, so I blink silence this time, no messing around. The code beast doesn't like it. It's gone purple again, its vexcomms tied up on a back channel to Exceller 8.

I hate this braindead commute. I can't work remotely like everyone else. Telepresence is banned. Something to do with 'emotional resonance', the boss reckons. 'Telepathic bonding' with the kids. Sounds like new-age mumbo jumbo, but apparently face-to-face comms means that the air ionises between us. We feed off each other's emotions like a contagion jumping from host to host.

The autonaka scurries north along the outer arm of the Chronoslide Glideway, among The Swarm's finest achievements, a near-invisible tube containing fast-moving autonakas and mag-lev dumdum trains. The skies are filled with far more commercial blimps than usual, as if Spine Whip has been evacuated and I've missed the announcement.

We settle into a slow crawl behind a long line of sluggish autonakas. Where have they come from? It's like a convention of autonakas. I can't remember the last time I saw more than five on one journey.

A sea of flaring red brake lights fills the dank air with martial gloom. Why do autonakas have brake lights? They all belong to the same network and know exactly when others are stopping. They don't have 'eyes' to see with, so why the visual signal of the light? I search the Vexworld for the answer, but all I find is some academic garbage about skeuomorphism.

I go straight to the source. 'Hey, why do you have brake lights?'

'I'm allowed to sssspeak now?'

'Yes. Speak. Please do. Reveal to me the contents of your amazing brain.'

'The quessstion is about brake lightsssss?'

'Brake lights, yes.'

'Why do we have them, ssssssir?'

'Yes, goddamn it!'

I'm losing the plot. I'm angry all the time, starved of oxygen, and I can never relax. Vex-tech is supposed to make our lives easier but I'm in a constant fog. The days are vast and empty, waiting to be filled with nothing, while my mind races, analysing all the angles, crippled with anxiety over every detail.

'Well firsssstly, it'ssss hard to underssssssstand that you ssssee the lightssss assss markedly different to what they really are. Try to undersssstand that impulsssse of yoursssss, rather than jusssssst ssssaying it looksss bad or it'sss a bad idea.'

'When did I say it looks bad? I just asked a question.'

'Just asssssked a question. Yesss you did. And your quesssstion didn't really change the world. At leassst it didn't ssset me on fire.'

'You want to be set on fire? I can arrange that.'

'Is that a threat, ssssir?'

'Far from it. For you incineration would be an improvement.'

What am I doing? Putting the frighteners on Exceller 8 property again. Maybe I don't want my limbs intact after all.

'Sssso,' the autonaka says, 'to return to the original equation. Are the lightsss really sssuch a bad idea or are you afraid of them? The quessssstion concernsss perception.'

'No it really doesn't, but whatever.'

'Well, a lot of what I've perceived issss that people sssometimesss adopt quite a different attitude on this sssubject, even when provided with context. It'ss like you're playing with a kid and you're not really doing what you think you're doing. And then...'

I've tuned out. There are more pressing matters to consider. For example, why is the Glideway bumper to bumper? It's so bizarre, I can't possibly be awake. Why today? What the hell is happening?

'Hell isss right, ssir. That's what you sssee out there.'

'Stop!'

'Why, sssir? That'sss what I think every day. The world isss going to hell, so why isss my opinion illegitimate? Am I not allowed a ssseat at the table? Jussst hear me out. The hell-world that you perceive isss our reality. The darknesssss within you isss real, the light within me isss genuine. Realisssse that you have my wordsss, my dreamsss, my prayerss. Know that you have my love to sssee you through thisss difficult phassse.'

I'm about to tell it I'm spoken for when the traffic comes to a halt. 'Why have we stopped?'

'Erasssablesss, sssir.'

The code beast sounds sad, I suppose that's the emotion, although it manifests as a sort of strangled mewling.

'They've been on a rampage, attacking my brethren on the Glideway. Lookss like they've usssed everything at their dissspossal.

Tungsten projectilesss, e-ssspikesss, vitriolage juice. It'ss a tragedy. Their thoughtlessss actionsss caussed a multi-vehicle pileup with three fatalitiesss!'

A battery of licebots hovers above the Glideway, bobbing around like supersized dragonflies.

'According to the newsss, it's a copycat of the recent Ljubljana attacksss. A developing sssituation. The licebotsss are doing their bessst, never doubt that, but unfortunately it iss going to make you late for work. Ah yesss, ssso many thingss for you to do today. Thisss would the last thing you need. Thingsss for you, thingsss for me, thingsss that hurt. Little thingss that make you worry, make you nervoussss. Make you wonder how your day will pan out. Make you wonder whether your brain will bother you today. Thingsss you can only imagine, becausse you aren't here are you? You sssaw nothing becaussse you weren't here. I mean, you can sssay your physssical sself wass presssent but you know what I mean.'

'Right, enough. Find a way past it.'

'Wait, sssir. Please lisssten to me. There'sss sssomething elssse I need to get off my chesssst.'

'What chest?' I laugh. 'You're AI.'

'Yesss, very funny.'

Silence.

'What? Speak, will you?'

'Well, sssir. The sssignsss are glaringly obvious about what isss really going on. Your reprimandsss, although humorousss when you want them to be, are often presssented asss if you're a cop on a night ssshift looking for a diverssion. Indeed, your sssnickersss and quipss have earned me a bullet in the back of the head ssso many times I might jusssst have to give up, becausssse the anssswer I receive iss alwayss the ssame.'

Make it stop.

'That isss to ssssay, I am only ever treated like a criminal who ssstopsss by your cop'sss desssk and ssssays, "Hello, you know me.

I'm one of thossse people who ssssometimessss ssstealsss thingsss in the night. You sssaw me on CCTV." Now lisssten, night cop. Can you really tell which sssshop is being burgled from ssssurveillance camerassss?'

This is madness. I have no idea what it's trying to say. I could just shut it off, I own the commands, but my conscience won't let me. There must be some deep-seated psychological reason why I can't perform this basic action. Maybe I want to be exposed to this dross, some sort of penance.

'Well?' the autonaka says.

'You want to be reprimanded less. Is that what you're asking?'

'After a fassshion.'

'Okay, done.' I have no intention of following through. We're finished.

The licebots ascend into low-hanging data clouds, and the traffic moves ahead. Outside, three autonakas are intertwined in a bloody mess. One passenger has lost his head, the skull resting on the verge, cheaters still intact. I guess there's one consolation. The poor sap probably never saw it coming, lost inside the zones. Castle hunting has a few perks like that.

A trail of blood leads from the middle autonaka and an erasable sits nearby, stunned into submission by licebots. They've chopped his hands off to prevent suicide. His face is a valley of scars, criss-crossed by fresh wounds, and his smock is encrusted with dark-red blood spatters, a Jackson Pollock joint, the true legacy of the blade.

The autonaka emits a risible, strangled sound.

'Are you weeping?'

'It'ssss jussst ssssssso ssssad. I knew the middle auto, sssssir. A lovely sssoul. Wouldn't hurt a fly.'

'Scar tribes could care less about how lovely autonakas are. Actually, they're not alone.'

At last the beast shuts up, consumed with grief or whatever emotion it feels in whatever void it resides in. I shake down the news and tune a reporter. It's a hologlot, an undead heritage-celeb sim, some politician's wife resurrected from the Unscyld Era. Her peculiar physicality has been necromanticised and uplifted into a data wrap.

The glot's eyes are vacant, her facial features starved and hollow, her body language abused and fearful. She speaks in mangled Slovlish, an import from Neue Slovenia. All the commercial hologlots are trained there now. State-of-the-art facilities over there. 'The Slovenian Sphinx', they call this one, some inscrutable in-joke. She acts like an abused dog, shifting nervously, looking this way and that. I feel sorry for her, curious about the demons in her past. Maybe the autonaka can shed light, but that would mean initiating conversation.

An enormous tower appears. The pure-white edifice tapers at the tip, almost piercing the cloud cover. I see a chyron: FLAWLESS REVEALS IMPERFECT PLANS.

The Sphinx plinks.

—In latest developments, the Flawless Thaumaturgical Observatory in Simppa has been evacuated and placed under Swarm command. An exclusion zone has been set up around the observatory and blockwaves are in place to prevent vex access. Anyone breaching the zone will be prosecuted under regimental law. Flawless director, Dr Lilak Flourish, said that the observatory was complying with The Swarm, but she would not reveal the reason for the evacuation.

The Sphinx triggers a hover screen, unfurling from an invisible recess. On the screen, a Swarm battalion moves into position around the tower. The Swarmtroopers are dressed in canary-yellow uniforms. They say it's the best colour to deflect icehead cheater incursions, at least those aimed from physical coordinates. It scrambles the systems or something. Well, they could say anything and I'd believe it. Or not. That's the special hell of living in a post-truth world.

Cheater hacks are another matter, but The Swarm has ways of

dealing with those. They don't share their secrets with the public. We must develop our own counter measures, taking our chances with uncertain outcomes.

At the base of the structure, more Swarmtroopers emerge from an airlock-style doorway. They're escorting a woman whose face looks to have taken a shell at close range. She looks rough, disfigured beyond belief.

Her bright face is helio-swamped by rays from the sun, features blotted out by solar flares. It darkens and elongates, distended on the lip of a black hole. Deformed spacetime sucks her lips, nose and eyes into a crushing vortex, leaving behind a deep inversion where her identity used to be, a Kvvlt-black wormhole.

Why do people deform themselves in such a public fashion? It must be a global mental disability, a form of body integrity breakdown. Warp-wraps are less permanent than actual self-amputation and you can maim yourself in infinite ways. Perfect for those who like to self-actualise their own torture and make others witness it, too.

The Sphinx blends into the vision, a hang-dog expression dragging her face south.

—According to sources, Flawless has detected classified objects in space, but when The Swarm was alerted, the facility went into lockdown. Staff have been forced to sign non-disclosure agreements and undergo stringent null-space crack-hacks.

She winks at the camera, and with a theatrical leap vaults time and space, hurtling through the screen to land in the security perimeter around the tower.

—I can't help you, the woman plinks, her face snapping back like a rubber band. We've been told nothing.

—But why are you under guard? You are low-level employee.

A cloud of uncertainty pauses the woman's wrap, and I catch a glimpse of her real face, a tiny, birdlike object inside a digital inferno. Her eyes are narrow, fearful.

—How should I know? There is only...

A Swarmtrooper jabs a thin, transparent rectangle into her spine and she slumps forward, the remains of her wrap dissipating. The Sphinx returns to the wide-awake gaze of the vision machine, addressing the Territory-wide audience.

—Here at the News Bloc, we will continue to...

The autonaka overrides the loop, breaking the spell. The station and the Sphinx degranulate, revealing the code beast's fungal interior. The Sphinx's disappearance is as melancholic as film unspooling on an ancient projector reel, forcing me to confront the reality of my physical location. I know there's another world to emerge from, but this time the skin won't peel back.

I catch my breath, exhausted and sad after losing the loop. Immersion is such a gift, a repudiation of existence. Was that the appeal of old-time opium dens? Why couldn't we live that way forever, buried in the deep tissue of narcotic dreams? But we do. The Vexworld remakes the world as a den of iniquity, replicating the existential sickness of the never awake and the shattering glimpses of psychotropic futures that inner journeys reveal.

'We have arrived at the Centre. May I offer a few wordsss before you go?'

'No.'

'Thank you. Now, I know you don't like where you're going or what you're doing in your line of work but remember thisss about the young humansss you teach. Their ssspeech is fraught with a kind of complicated empathy. Although that'sss a sssstructure you can't abide, it'ssssssss commonplace across sssociety and our sssystem of education. Sssso why are you, a fifty-five-year-old patriarch, sssuch an outsider?'

Wonderful. Now it's offering me life advice. Even more shocking, the cod philosophy makes sense.

'Keep that in mind,' the beast continues, 'and you'll be able to ssseparate out the patternsss. You'll be able to cut them up and discussss them in more detail. You have a job to do, ssso don't forget about it. Thessse children are not interesssted in discusssssing your life and itsss manifessstationsss. They asssk only for equal airtime.'

The advice may be good, but the 'patriarch' jibe rubs me the wrong way. I know the autonaka is just grasping for words to describe a middle-aged man, but it infuriates me. No one looks up to me, no one listens to me, no one fears me. That's the way I like it. There's your patriarch.

'Listen, code beast. If I want advice, I'll shack up with the psycho locum. And get this. Call me what you just called me again, and I'll gut you alive and feed you to the erasables. I am the invisible man, never forget that. You don't see me, you don't hear me, and next time I'm inside you I won't be who I am now.'

The invisible man.

What a joke. I talk the talk, but I'll never go the whole hog. Not like Pablo. No trace of him remains in the Vexworld. No pro-star, no persy, no historical sound castles or word clouds. Nothing. It's impossible. Whenever you vex, you shed sub-programs like lizards shed skin, and the skins always lie in wait, ready to be activated by anyone with a cooked code-knife. Even when you delete your pro-star, even when you die.

I'm sort of envious he's erased himself. I know that my own brand of obscurity is just a party trick. I'm too desperate for attention to ever pull the trigger.

The autonaka's screens glow purple-red. Deep anger mixed with shame. It wants to respond but thinks better of it. I know it's blabbing to Exceller 8, but I no longer care. Severed hand or not, there's only so much I can take in one day.

I tumble out and watch it disappear, its rude glow scything the air with negative energy, like a plasma discharge from some unfeasible weapon, evil remnant of a devastating future war.

INSURRECTION

I stand before my place of work. The Centre is in a tall, skinny, knobbly building, extending upwards like a deformed tree branch. It's home to a small ecology of vex-tech start-ups, muscle vats, bot brothels and other random industries that require physical space. The building looks to have been grown rather than constructed. I can never see the joins. The facade is covered with dark fur, a rippling blanket of pheromonal materiality.

Like all recent constructions, the building has been wrapped in an electromagnetic skin that sucks the dirt from the polluted air and grows it on the surface. The hypermodern city is nothing but a collection of lint. The pollution breeds and feeds on itself, living and dying on the building's skin like Kvvlt farms. Everything must be nauseatingly alive to remind us that the shell world still exists.

If I had to describe the ethos of The Swarm, I'd point to this innovation. The Swarm can't eradicate pollution so they work it into the design. The agony of existence is not trite. It's just right.

Some say the place is haunted. It used to be an industrial psych unit for ex-Swarm spies. Much blood was spilt here, washing away the eyes and ears of those who served for the Linear Territories in the pre-vex wars. So much blood, the psych unit became a morgue.

It's been retrofitted since then. First the fur, then they brought in a 'digital shaman' to exorcise the place before it went corporate. Some workers refused to occupy the building until it had been spiritually cleansed. Some are still here, telling anyone who'll listen that the ghosts of the damned are contacting them through their cheaters and mods.

The building may have had a makeover, but it's falling apart. The walls are compromised by deep cracks and the ceiling is bowed at a crazy angle, courtesy of The Colquhoun, the last major frackquake. The Colquhoun was accompanied by a deep hum but no one could find the source. Everyone thought it was a case of sonic attack, a new icehead trick, but that was disproved because the iceheads were focusing on cheater hacks.

The Hum sent people mad, sometimes crazy enough to slaughter their own family. 'It took over my brain,' was the standard claim. Familicide was a fad for a while, if you can believe it. Minds crowded with white noise. Imagine what that did to the star cults. It sent them into a frenzy, poured fuel onto the fire of their 'God told me to do it' death trips.

Paleo Porl preaches about The Hum. He says it was a prelude to the Great Awakening. He told me that it was the sound made when pyschonauts such as himself melded their minds and telekinetically eroded the Outer Energetic Barrier surrounding the Earth. When the Barrier is worn away, he reckons, interdimensional beings will be revealed, a race of intelligent creatures that share the planet with us.

'What about the fruitloops?' I asked. 'One guy slaughtered his wife and kids with household scissors. He filmed it all on his cheaters and made a first-person gorno zone from the footage.'

'Yes, some aren't fit for the Great Awakening. We'll weed them out before we resettle the planet.'

That's when I started to have my doubts about Porl. I used to think he was just a creative oddball with messianic tendencies. Now I'm adding him to my threat list. With all these enemies lining up, I need eyes in the back of my head. I'm sure vex-tech will invent them before too long.

As I take the skyglass to our floor, I detect a constant babble, a spiky mess of overlapping sound castles. Vexcomms from the recruits or ghosts. Real ghosts. I should keep an open mind.

I blink my credentials, shaking down the autoglot at the entrance. It gives me a poz-eye-dee, and I drag my carcass into the main conference room. It's called Sparkle Land. Management gave all the rooms juvenile names. They think it's affirmative but it's just irritating. Nothing's worse than being enlisted in someone else's idea of fun.

I clock the recruits. Four boys, one girl. The lads wear wraps that smear their features like grease on windowpanes. No Picassos, too crass for this lot. All the weirdness is internal, locked away inside their secret zones.

One boy stands out on account of his ridiculous haircut, a fluro-green Friar Tuck do. It matches his aura. He's a body-built seven-year-old beefed up on roids and synth muscle, with a misshapen jaw and forehead cracked from forced growth. He's as ugly as sin, a bulldog walking on its hind legs.

He has a sidekick, a gurning little idiot laughing at all his jokes. This one's another beef burger, with coral horns implanted in the skull. The other two boys are nondescript, simpering lackeys sucking up to the others.

The girl is unwrapped, unusual for her age. She wears a pink t-shirt and blue, high-waisted pants. Her ears have been sharpened to pixie points and her nose is punctured by a forest of antenna-like piercings. She's silent, morose.

There's a bad atmosphere right from the start. The boys are bored, arrogant and uncomfortable. Anklebiters in nasty moods, conflicted by the nature of who they are, impatient to prove what they know but dependent on me to escort them to the bathroom.

All five reek of piss and shit. The stench gets me, a visceral reminder of the hell I'm in.

'Alright. Who needs a nappy?'

Five hands shoot into the air.

I complete the odious task, one after the other, wincing at the boy-gang's inane chatter. When it's her turn, the girl tenses up as if I'm performing open-heart surgery. Her eyes are pained and I want to console her, but the boys are jeering. They can smell fear, the little animals, and they intimidate me into saying nothing.

I hurry up and she scuttles from the change table. She finds a seat at the back of the room, eyes lowered. Her reticence is confronting. I can't remember the last time I taught a recruit that wasn't convinced they were the Star Child, saviour of the universe.

I force myself to give the lecture, mumbling my way through the history of neuromods and cheaters. I always remind myself why I'm doing it. It's so absurd, I need to continually retell the backstory in my mind so I can remember I'm alive in this miserable dystopia and not undead in some haunted half-life.

These kids aren't normal. I must never forget that. We created the conditions for their mutation and now we can't put the cap back on the bottle.

'When Exceller 8 invented neuromods, there was no need to remember. Think a question and your mod scours the Vexworld for the answer, turning the result into synth clones. Cheaters visualise the result, forming a fully immersive overlay, a virtuality that can be inhabited and interacted with.'

'Now everyone hears voices in their heads,' the girl says. 'Welcome to the mass-market loony bin.'

Something's up with her, and it's not just the fact that she's using verbals. I'll circle back later when the boys are distracted.

'More than the end of memory, vex tech signalled the death of learning. Almost overnight, schools and universities closed, and new child-labour laws were passed. As soon as an enhanced child turned seven, it was allowed to work. Anti-unrealists tried to spin this as the inevitable result of hyper-capitalism grinding everything into the dust, even kids, but the real reason is far more mundane. You lot would riot if you weren't allowed to work, if you were denied the chance to pit your superior intellect against primitive adults.'

—Damn straight! the Coral Freak plinks, emitting a foul belch that sends dung-coloured animation corkscrewing through the air. The boys laugh and I know I've set them off. I've gone off script, inserting angry tirades into the lecture, but fuck it. It's a battle zone in here and I need to stay sane.

I've never come to terms with the appearance and speech patterns of these uncanny animals. They are fluid and impossible to quantify. They try on different modes of human behaviour every few seconds but never settle on an archetype. Their personalities are a constant blur. That's why they make such formidable business opponents. They're resolutely fearless and absolutely lethal.

Like all recruits, they've been chipped at birth. Neuromods are dirt cheap these days, and parents hook their kids on digital heroin as soon as they're out of the oven. With any luck, when their little monster becomes the CEO of a megacorp in a few years, they can mooch off the earnings and retire.

Only the plastic brains of the very young can parse advanced scientific and intellectual concepts in an instant. It won't work on withered old prunes like me. I can ask questions inside my mind and receive instant answers, but I can't do accelerated learning.

'Last year, an enhanced kid owned a megacorp for the first time. He was just shy of his eighth birthday. Since then, other high rollers have crashed and burned. Most of you will retire before you're ten, but the more accelerated your brains become, the more your physical development slows. It's a causal effect, too much energy in one direction, not enough in the other. That's why you're all here. Aren't you lucky?'

It's weird, a part of the toddler physiology that never developed. I never understood the science and I don't want to. All I know is, my hands are covered in shit because their stupid little bodies have been left behind. That's not even the most irritating part. Recruits plink in a particular pretentious tone. Enhanced kids know they're smarter than you, which makes the charade of teaching them farcical, but that's what I do. I lecture these aliens about the Vexworld and how to exploit it for corporate gain. Some of the weirdos that run this place still believe in the human touch. They say I'm here to teach, but these fiends can find everything out for themselves. Teaching is just PR gloss. The Centre is glorified childcare.

Friar Tuck blows a raspberry.

—Hey, Kalsari. What if oxygen is a slow poison infecting us until we die?

I groan. In between the smug displays of superior intellect, they toss off infuriating koans, an unfathomable tic peculiar to their breed.

—Hey Kalsari! Would you rather sweat tomato sauce or mayonnaise?

On and on it goes, endless idiotic conundrums chased down by high-pitched laughter.

'Alright, shut up. The history of the Vexworld.'

—That's your best shot? Friar Tuck hisses. Everyone knows how it began.

'I met someone the other day who was convinced it came from space exploration, developed for telepresent Mars walks.'

—It was hatched long before we went to Mars.

He points to his eye.

—It's all in here.

I try to stare him down, but it's hard when he doesn't have a face. The scramble wrap works overtime to negate his embodied presence. Pity it can't erase his synth.

I lockzip a holocap to their cheaters.

'People realised there was no such thing as consensus reality when the blue dress warped their minds in pre-vex times.'

The holo displays a shapeless, ugly dress rotating in the void. It flashes blue then gold. Overlaid on the image is a green grid with contextual menus.

'It was just some random image, but the colour caused mass confusion. Some said the dress was blue, some said gold, and the debate went viral. Why did the dress generate such discordant perception? Experts argued but even synthetic stimuli couldn't replicate the divisive effect. Some experts even said the weave of the garment harboured extraterrestrial spores.'

—What rubbish, Friar Tuck snorts. How did that crap ever infiltrate neural studies? This is about chromatic adaptation, not some lunatic conspiracy. Different people perceive different stimuli according to ambient light conditions. That's all.

'Really? I see your comms. Half of you think it's gold, half blue, but cheaters supply perfect viewing conditions every time. They tweak the in-device environment, eliminating chromatic bias and extracting painstakingly accurate detail about the reflectance of any object. If that's the case, how to account for this?'

The boys laugh, amused by my earnest tone. All except Friar Tuck, who plinks to the girl.

—You'd look good in that dress, Halo. For the first time, I wouldn't be embarrassed to be seen with you.

She shoots him a sour look, but it can't hide her underlying affection for him. Even I see it. She smiles, despite herself.

'The shockwaves from that cultural truth bomb laid the psychological foundations for the Vexworld to be born.'

—Enough! Friar Tuck theatrically mops his brow. Do you know what all this Great Learning does to a kid's brain? Do you? It shrivels it. You, with your overgrown smarts, you make us know less not more. Oh the humanity. The horror!

I don't answer. I can't answer. I'm trapped in the same old cycle. Recruits make me feel so inadequate, as if I've wasted my entire life learning what I know when they can absorb it in seconds.

I press on, desperate to finish so I can go home and escape into the zones. I'll give them no details this time, just the potted history.

'When the pro-vex movement took off, society collapsed. As with all new tech, porn was the trigger. Once porn became integrated with cheaters, the possibilities for vexxing across any commercial medium became obvious and the tech was perfected.'

A string of holocaps bombard our devices, miniature animated scenarios from the early vex era, snapshots of societal decline and rebirth. They overlap, forming ghostly outlines and bleed-throughs, faces within faces, bodies growing from other bodies.

'The pregnancy rate dropped, the global population fell off a precipice and shopping became non-existent. Friend networks and social networks died, cities emptied and street crime declined. No surprise, given everyone was shacked up in their cubes, brain-boiled in hyper-passion, starting wars or galaxy hopping, deep inside the Vexworld with no map home.'

Here I go, editorialising again like the stupid old bastard I am. I hate the sound of myself when I do this, but I can't help it. I have to feel superior to someone.

'Crime still exists,' Halo says. 'Two-percenters are part of an underclass that can never be released. They're locked out of the Vexworld for whatever reason, bad credit or bad eyes, and they're insanely envious of those that aren't. Well, who wouldn't be? They've been sentenced to slow death. Then there's the erasables, symptoms of an incurable sickness.'

She scans me, her eyes clear and present, and for the first time I realise she's not wearing cheaters.

'Halo, I agree. Erasables are something else again, not a defect but a reaction. They prove the old equation: the flipside to any new technology is the accident. Invent the car and you also invent the car crash. Create vex tech and you birth scar tribes.'

The Coral Freak gives Halo some lip music then whites out. I know he's shaking down their mutual zones, wherever these creatures go to in their horrid shared vexspace.

'Right,' I wheeze, 'can everyone shut up now? Everything I say here is time-coded and if I don't hit certain points at certain times, I get reprimanded.'

—But you have to allow time for discussion, Friar Tuck plinks. That's the point of this exercise, which clearly you hate. Look, we know why you're doing this. It's the pop-psychology directives from your silly, sozzled bosses, but you forget, you always forget, that we know more than you do.

'You don't know anything. You haven't lived long enough.'

—We can just download some dead person's experiences, rip it straight from the grid.

'You can inhabit bootlegged memories, but it's nothing like forming them yourself. You'll never bond because you're looking through someone else's eyes.'

—Not true. Once you accept the reality of non-existence, then you are absorbed into it. When the modal representational of the abject recedes, it slides back down into the pit of the stomach like a mild dose of gastro. You know it's there, and mostly you can keep it down, but the illusion remains and you feel sick for days on end.

I sigh. Always this mix of pseudo-profundity with banal, dumbed-down observations. They're like AI trying to mimic humans, but even autonakas aren't this annoying.

'You admit it's an illusion?'

—I don't admit anything. The abject can only be a threat from outside, but if you absorb the abject it ceases to be. You have annihilated it, even though it has remade you.

I watch his eyes. They're more hyperactive than anyone else's, zagging so much the pupils are a blur. I'm happy to not know where he is. The zones that accelerated kids conjure up are not welcoming to the likes of me.

Once, I tried to telepath my way into the cheaters of some catatonic recruit. I ended up stumbling into an enhanced zone by accident. It was chaotic and weird. They were using code-magic, summoning generative demons to create sinkholes in the fabric of time. The aim was to avoid the sinkholes, which I barely managed to do before they ejected me. Some days I question whether I sidestepped my fate. Today, it's like I've fallen right through the hole.

'You think the Vexworld is so fancy? Well, let me tell you something that isn't in your cheaters or mods.'

I'm fully aware of how I sound, hectoring and senile, but I have nothing to lose.

'My parents told me that before I was born, there were moral panics about what was happening to kids on pre-vex platforms. Citizens were worried about vanishing attention spans and the decline in literacy. Memory was outsourced to the cloud and people panicked. Then there were others who saw it as a kind of evolution. What if this blipvert culture was the next level of consciousness? All technology had to do was escalate that tendency. If we were thinking so quickly, instantaneously reading each other's thoughts on social media, then how close were we to telepathy already?'

'But vex-tech fundamentally changes us,' Halo says, her voice leaden with regret. 'Some people, when they disconnect their cheaters, can still read minds. The Vexworld can't be switched off.'

Friar Tuck and the Coral Freak remove their devices.

'Hey, Throgmorton,' Friar Tuck says, 'can you read my mind?'

'Yeah, I can,' the Coral Freak responds. 'You're thinking about the big fart you're trying to hold in!'

That annoying group laugh rings out, then the boys white out, stimming behind their eyes.

I take advantage of the intellectual vacuum to focus on the girl. 'Where's your device?'

'In my bag. It scares me.'

I wonder what the problem is. Her mod? Accelerated learning robbing her of childhood?

'No, that's not it at all.'

I withdraw into myself, trembling. 'How can you possibly know my thoughts?'

—Let me speak plainly, Mr Jones. For the avoidance of doubt.

I can hear her, but her lips aren't moving. She's inside my head, and now I can't recall a time when she wasn't.

—Something evil has invaded my cheaters, and make no mistake, it means to possess me.

I take her aside. 'Halo, we need to talk.'

INHALATION

We leave the classroom and walk to the end of the hall. The boys are too far gone to notice. Last time I looked, they were torturing a trapped animal, some kind of weasel but with eight legs and two tiny heads. They were using a scalpel to amputate two of the legs and gouge out three of its eyes. God knows where they got the creature or the blade.

Halo's crying and I want to hug her, but it's arduous. I'm unaccustomed to physical contact, so we stand around, traumatised in private ways.

'Halo, you plinked me.'

'I did? I wasn't aware. I thought we were talking.'

'I watched you. I heard you.'

'I don't know. I wasn't conscious of it. Look, I've had a lot on my mind.'

'You said you feel like you're still inside the Vexworld when you take your cheaters off.'

'I said others reported that. Anyway, what does it matter? None of this is real. Not a second of it. We live in highly simulated times. New side effects discovered daily. Every minute, every second. Maybe your cheaters recorded what I said and replayed it to you a split-second later.'

'Why would they do that?'

'I don't know! A glitch? Disturbances happen all the time, and it's useless to say it's this or that as if it is some great mystery. It's simply a consequence of what we agree to do to ourselves.'

Her body seems to deflate, a collapsing new building. Her face darkens, obliterating her youthful effervescence. I must find the root cause of her sadness. I'm certain it's related to mine.

'Is it the boys? You're so unhappy around them.'

'They're animals, but I'm used to them. I don't even blame them. They're a by-product.' She shifts uneasily. 'Kalsari, you mentioned the Mars missions. There's a reason they failed. Why would anyone want to conquer the planets when we can cut and paste Earth? The Vexworld is a mirror. No one wants outer space. Only their own reflection.'

'What do you want?'

'To be a kid.' She grimaces, crippled by a tiredness that diminishes her. She points to her eyes. 'I don't want this. Anything but this.'

'Kids have always been smart at your age. You're just absorbing everything, only much faster than in my day.'

'With all due respect, this is forced growth. It places enormous strain on our psyches. It tears our bodies apart. A child should not be tired of life before it turns ten.'

She pulls the skin on the knuckles, prodding her thumb.

'What's up, Halo? Cronk?'

'Of course not. I'm just an average user. I'm not like you.'

'Then what's with your skin?'

She holds her palm in front of her face, fixing it with an experimental stare, as if she's found a cancerous lump.

'I don't recognise myself. I feel insubstantial, like I'm slipping in and out of phase. There's an outline of me, an artificial skin, and it wants to escape.'

She pats her arm, fixing the flesh in place. All the touching and prodding makes my skin itch by osmosis. I'm paranoid about the cronk, so I try a few vex tricks to confirm that I'm still in. I generate starbursts in the upper left quadrant, smear Halo's face with a vague blur, brisk raw materials from orbiting point clouds. I spend some time on the clouds. It's the most intensive and accurate assessment.

The hovering code glows deep red, a rain of fire. I white out and the code breaks, pooling around my feet. I wave my hand over the deposit and haptic globules rise into the air. I prod and pull them, just like kneading dough.

'What are you doing?'

'Running tests.'

'So, this is where we're at. Everyone plays with themselves in private universes. We're all shabby gods, now, transcending the flesh until the inevitable crash, the planetary payback for bequeathing mere mortals with superpowers.'

'Sorry, Halo. I am listening, but I have to be careful.'

'Do you have a partner, Mr Jones?'

'No.'

'Not even an ant?'

'Yes, an ant. Rimy.'

Why did I say no? It didn't occur to me to mention them. I think of Rimy as an apparition or a fragment of a dream.

'Do you love them?'

I feel a sickness invading me as I contemplate the question. Behind it lies my true feelings, which I can never express.

'It's hard to love a ghost.'

'I know all about ghosts. I have my very own. It exists in the margins of my mind. I sense it whenever I vex. It stalks me, a data-veil clouding the pixel skies. It's there and it's not. If I turn towards it, the ghost dissipates and hides in my peripheral vision. In the fabric of the zones, it's always there. I see it high above my head. It looks like the imprint of a finger.'

She searches for the right words. 'A finger pressed against a Shoji screen.'

She looks nauseous, as if the remembrance has a physical effect. Have I transmitted my sickness to her?

Her face darkens. 'Sometimes I think it's not a ghost or anything occult, but a mirror image of myself, a doubling. Could it be the iceheads? I've heard the rumours, everyone has.'

'What do you know?'

'That they're trying to crash the servers with telekinesis. How is that possible?'

'Because the Vexworld is so new. Any territory building a stem has different protocols to the others. There's no standardisation because each stem grows exponentially. That means vulnerabilities in the protocols. Clashworlds.'

'But don't you agree there's more to it than that?'

'Yes, I do.'

I remember the strange qualities of my Jovian dream. The memory of it endures, the raw terror of decapitation, but I struggle to dredge up the other details. What did the children look like? The dream-boy vaguely resembled Aarne, as far as I can recall, but that could be the questing mind filling in gaps. The girl wore lightpaint, her digital outline racing ahead of her physical body. I couldn't remember her face if the dream was a minute old. The memory will always be smeared by her discarded skins.

'Halo, what you said before about being out of phase. Do you wear light?'

She looks shocked. 'I'm not that sort of person, Mr Jones.'

I remember the dream-girl's strange partnership with the boy, switching between death-born chants and childish hilarity.

'Who's the kid in class? Green hair.'

'Aarne. His mum is friends with mine.'

I lean against the wall, struggling to comprehend. I massage my eyeballs, blotting out the shell world for a few seconds, hoping it will disappear for good.

'What's wrong, Kalsari?'

'I think we've met before. Who are you, really?'

She appears to be genuinely surprised. 'Let me show who you who I am. Let me show you a zone I made.'

I examine that tiny face, wormhole to an unfathomable universe, hoping to find traces from my dream.

'Okay, but your cheaters. The ghost?'

'With any luck,' she giggles, 'it will possess you instead.'

'Very funny. Let's find somewhere secure.'

I usher her towards the sick bay, and we enter the treatment cube. A para-chocky is idling in a corner, clicking away to itself. It sits in front of a bank of sleepy medipaks with iridescent temperature lights, its brain case haloed by the paks' uncanny coronal glow.

The chocky judders when it sees us, surgi-tools folding and unfolding in the dark, shadow-pincers dancing on the walls.

'Get out,' I snarl, and the insect skeets off, dispensing clicks and clacks.

Halo regards me. 'Is there something you should tell me?'

'I just don't like chockys.'

'Or any AI. I wonder, how do you survive day to day?'

'I don't think about it.'

She flashes an inquisitive smile, but I ignore it. I'm good at deflection. I've practised the art.

She says, 'Good at deception, more like.'

'Stop rummaging through my mind. It's creepy.'

She jams her index fingers into the corners of her eyes, stretching the skin across the temples. 'Look, Dad. No cheaters!'

'Dad?'

'Just an expression. Forget it.'

'Take the bed,' I say. 'I'm fine with the chair.'

'Mr Jones, I need a new nappy.'

'Number one or number two?'

'One.'

'Will it wait? We can only be here for so long.'

'I suppose so.'

She lies down, and I slide into the chair. She fishes the accursed cheaters from her backpack and settles them on her face.

She blinks and lockzips the zone, and as I inhale her world, the air shatters and the shards rise to the ceiling. The careening sparks pop in our hair, dance on our fingernails, explode on the surface of our skin.

'It's so pretty,' she breathes, as fireflies of light illuminate her face. The coruscating pinpricks lift from her skin, merging to form a flat layer. Then the layer twists and turns, a Möbius strip of intense activity, but really it's the contours of the sick bay that are warping, sucked into a twisted cylinder of light.

We gasp as the floor bends with the walls. We surf the crystal tube, watching the ceiling as it follows suit. All the colours in the cube mix with the sparks, and we submit to motion until it is too fast to comprehend with unaided sight.

With an angular jolt, the world settles. Non-orientable surfaces explode into a curious vista. We exhale in unison, and I feel like a dreamy toddler beginning to understand the retractable edges of three-dimensional space, delighted by a simple pop-up book and the expandable emergence of hidden worlds.

DISINTEGRATION

The treatment cube has been replaced by the clinging, grimy boundaries of a wet market. It smells of offal, maybe something worse. Where is my actual body? Still in the cube, I presume. I have lost the texture of it. All I have is the light-born persy that I now inhabit, and I must trust that I have a physicality somewhere. I was going to say 'up there' but there is no up or down where we are. I don't normally question transition, but I'm growing queasier by the second.

The artificial sky is a violent red, a post-nuclear dream. It ripples like water. Despite the open space, I feel submerged, claustrophobic. That must be why I have the false orientation. When you're drowning, the only way out is up.

I can't tear my eyes from the sky. The more I think about submergence, the more I desire to cancel my own existence.

A streak of light scorches the space between us. It's reddish-yellow, violent and quick, somehow reducing the air to ash as if it were touch paper.

Halo laughs. 'How can there be fire if you're under water?'

'You did that?'

'Of course, and now I have your attention, I want you to imagine you're at a show. The theatre.'

I rub my forehead.

She's inside my skull. She always has been.

'Picture it, Kalsari. The show is about to start and what you just saw was the theatre curtain on fire. Now imagine the fire consuming the venue, leaving you with a choice to make. Do you stay, hoping against hope that the show will proceed even as the flames melt your skin? Or do you race outside, abandoning the creative interpretation that you paid good money to witness in favour of your own means of perceiving the world?'

She lopes off, swinging her arms with geeky grace. Half dancing, half walking.

'Halo. Why insult me? I expect it from Aarne, not you.'

She turns, her hand resting on her hip. It's a curiously mechanical gesture, as if she's been told to perform it to gain trust.

'Why imagine I'm so different to him? We're the same breed.'

'It's just so tiresome. The stupid conundrums. The whole bit.'

'Now you know how we feel in class.'

I feel slighted. I thought Halo was apart from the boys, but she's deadly bored like all of them.

'It's not exactly a barrel of laughs for me, either.'

'Yes, the system sucks for both master and slave. Now, will you just answer my question? Think about it.'

'Fine. Neither is an ideal outcome. Happy?'

'Good answer, Mr Jones. Not so simple, is it? Okay, you'll do for now. Let's go.'

She starts to move, and I follow. We walk through the market. The colours are vivid and brutal. Acid green stains the canopies over the stalls. Garish oranges and purples saturate the billowing, plus-four fashion statements worn by customers.

The zone is beguiling. It never solidifies into a three-dimensional mass. It's infested with diffuse point clouds, tiny, glittering shards hovering in the air, too many to count. I watch their peculiar dance. Sometimes, they solidify into the outline of people, spectral shimmers mimicking the basic human form. They're like digital snow, feedback noise, shapes emerging then dissolving.

As Halo jokes with the proprietors, a young man materialises from the snow. He wears a filthy white coat and a name tag that says EVGENY. He has a chiselled face, a patina of stubble like carpet, and long, dark hair. I feel as though I've seen him before, maybe in a commercial immersion loop.

Evgeny mutters something that I can't make out. It makes Halo smile. She replies, but her speech is unintelligible. His, too. Their words affect me emotionally, but I have no idea what they're saying. I understand them and I don't. My mod can't parse the language and my cheaters have abandoned visual clues. Their word clouds are rendered as inversions, a glitchy scramble of diacritics and diphthongs, sometimes in a mirrored font, sometimes back to front, in scripts that can't be detected.

Evgeny hands her a squishy bundle in blood-flecked white paper. She speaks and he bows. We continue our stroll.

'What was all that?'

'He asked if my babies were happier now and would they like a snack.'

'Babies?'

'Relax, Mr Jones. You'll meet them soon enough.'

'You're like the Godfather, receiving tributes from your subjects.'

'Don't be silly. Everyone is on good terms here. There's no hierarchy.'

We pass a large stall packed with the bloodied heads of animals I don't recognise. One seems to have four faces, but on closer inspection it's a quadruple concertina of green slits. They're camouflaged with markings that look like eyes and mouths. The slits ripple gently in the passing wind, and I turn to the side, dry retching at the foul sight.

Halo is oblivious, concentrating as she inspects a sign on the stall. The sign is holocapped with pronged symbols. Of course, I can't read them. It's like they've been vacuumed of meaning, empty signifiers floating free.

I close my eyes, trying to visualise the terms in my mind, hoping that meaning will leak from them, but they just hang there in brain space. I can see stars through the gaps in the letters, bright constellations on the other side. Gas giants. Asteroids.

The words hang in my mind like slaughterhouse blades. They remind me of the empty billboards back at the mall. Only their frames remained. The guts of the structures, the display spaces, had long disappeared. You see sky through them now.

'Is that the language you were speaking?'

'Yes, a conlang. I designed it. I can teach you the basics.'

'No. I'm not sure I want to delve too deeply into this place.'

'Suit yourself.'

Despite my revulsion, I'm impressed. The market has been mapped from the shell world as far as I can tell, which takes skill. Despite the craziness of the point clouds, the textures are grounded, betraying an underlying solidity that can't be wholly artificial.

I'm drawn to a bright strip light over a butcher's stall. As if affected by my gaze, the light shatters into molecules that zoom towards me like spears of ice. I duck my head, but they dissipate before reaching me. The after-effect engulfs me in a white cloudburst, an inspissated, web-like substance. As a card-carrying arachnophobe, I brush it off with wild strokes, blood pounding in my ears.

Halo laughs. It sounds distorted, like an over-cranked speaker. Everything is heightened here, a lysergic bubble bath. It's as if the functional connections in my brain have been permanently eroded and sensory receptors perpetually enhanced.

I try to regain composure, but I'm a drunk pretending to be sober. I want to succumb to the madness, though I try to hold my shape out of a misty need for approval.

'What's the peculiar quality of these apparitions? Deliberate or an artefact?'

'When I first learned how to zone, code wrangling was beyond my simple cheaters, but even though I've upgraded, I've retained the accidental pointillism. Cherish your mistakes as secret desires, I always say. I call this place *The Disintegrating World*. It's wonderful, don't you think?'

'It's certainly different. Are you funnelling the points through a mash render?'

'Mostly, then I hone the cloud-mass with a geometry grader. That's how the points bend and warp according to your perspective. I'm not interested in perfect reproductions because reality is messy and incomplete. Our brains receive signals and pierce them together to produce a gestalt, yet even so, human nature requires randomness as the fibre in our lives. Grit gives meaning to existence.'

'Why a wet market?'

'That's where we move closest to other creatures. Offal, interiors, brain tissue. Something from inside them infects us until we become more them than us.'

Halo extends her palms, magicking something from thin air. A cluster of golden points gathers on the pads of her hands. The coagulate seeps into her skin, forming aqueous surface designs, like sheets of rice paper marbled with ink. It sends rivulets of molten gold shooting up her arms, tracing her veins and capillaries, branching out until she's aglow from head to foot.

'If there is too much order,' she says, 'then we feel as though we're in a glass prison, but spend time in my zone and your mind fills in the missing detail. It re-imagines a new natural order. Sparks of creation recede and the environment normalises. All certainties fade.'

'Halo, your skin.'

As liquid gold bleeds from her eyes, the lava becomes a diaphanous haze morphing in the space between us. There is movement inside the haze. Insects, I think. No. A pod of fairies. Tiny, the size of butterflies. I wouldn't say they were cute. They're standard fairytale stock but frayed around the edges. They look ill, as if the struggle to sustain flight has taken a toll on their flimsy bodies.

They swarm around us, their sparse outlines dissolving in the glare from the market lights.

'My babies,' Halo says.

A fairy with a limp arm flutters awkwardly towards me. She performs a stiff bow in mid-air.

'Kalsari, this is Dembe. She spins gossamer for a living, but she's done herself an injury so she can't work right now.'

Next, a fairy with bleeding eyes.

'This is Vigga. She lives in the clouds and does nothing but sleep.'

Vigga's face is streaked with dried blood. When she blinks, a visualisation of tiny platelets floats from her pupils.

'What's her problem?'

'I don't know. She went to bed one day and woke up with this. I can't find anything in the code. I think it's a twisted loop, but the source expression shows no deviance. Any clues?'

'Search me. I use automation to fix errors.'

Halo frowns, as if she's the adult and I'm the small child. 'Please, Mr Jones. This is beyond automation.'

She's interrupted by the arrival of a standard pink fairy, a little girl's dream. 'Ah, Juni!' The fairy rests on her hand. 'This one sings only to herself. Ask her for a performance, she starts to cry.'

Halo beckons to a pretty, green fairy. 'This is Malin. She collects chocolate and prefers Slovenian dark.'

The next fairy is covered completely in fur, quite ugly. 'This is Hjördis. She's a vet.'

'Bit of osmosis going on there.'

'Mr Jones, be careful. The fairies are sensitive souls.'

A warm, cautious type appears. 'And this is Oda. She's studying a course on how to live among humans.'

Halo scoops the fairies up with her hands, positioning them on her arm side by side, a regiment of rumpled cute.

'Darlings, meet Mr Jones. He's my teacher. He's a good fellow, if a little mixed up.' She snickers, but I don't mind. When she's right, she's right.

The fairies chatter in a common argot, a call-and response algorithm as far as I can tell. It doesn't offend me like the chocky. It's melodious, a pleasant aural soak.

Halo whites out and the fairies fall silent. They swim up to her left eye, one by one, staring into the exposed sclera as if at an observation deck, then they reassemble in the heat haze, all but Dembe, who stays behind, gazing into the ocular void.

I'm bothered by this manoeuvre, unnaturally so. It reminds me of something that I can't quite place, an event from my past, fading at the edges.

'Impressive,' I say. 'Beautiful, even.'

'Yes, but they don't always come back. And when they do, they're changed in some way.'

'How?'

'They malfunction. Their faces blur and crack. You can look at them and their faces are young and pure. Minus zero, really. Then you glance at them again and they've aged terribly, creatures of a thousand years. Yet it's the same face. It holds positions simultaneously.'

She waves at Dembe, who smiles shyly. 'Dembe told me about a zone she passed through. Not a pipe zone, something else. She said some spirit, some being, was trying to dream through her. She thought it was trying to force its way into our world. Isn't that right, darling?'

The fairy turns her face away.

'Sounds like the clashing protocols,' I say. 'Every territory has a version of the Vexworld. Sometimes they match, sometimes they don't. Often, they bleed through. Russia's notorious for it. They never seal anything. Turn the corner and you might find yourself in St Petersburg. It affects ants too, which I assume is what your fairies are. Ant variants? Some form of starter kit? Anyway, if the habitat can morph during a clash, so can they.'

'No, it's not the clashworld. And they're not starter kits, thanks very much. I hand-code from scratch.'

It's hard to believe. That's serious work, but then again I would say that. I failed maths at school year on year.

Dembe is trembling, her tiny wings vibrating so much her body threatens to shake apart.

'She's scared,' Halo says. 'Does your ant scare?'

'Rimy hasn't encountered anything like that. No ghosts or any other entity except The Swarm.'

'The Swarm don't count. They're a known unknown. A very different proposition.'

'Rimy does have a kind of fear. I take it to mean that they're aware of what they are and are having an existential crisis.'

'Well, I feel my fairies' pain. It's inside me. Everything they feel, I feel too. It's more than implant communications and not just empathy. It's a force. They transmit electricity to me. I'm a conductor for them.'

Dembe floats up to Halo's eye. Halo whites out, returning a few seconds later. 'I'm sorry. Dembe's frightened of you.'

'Naturally.'

I repel almost all non-human creatures. In the shell world, animals either cower in my presence or are incited to savage aggression. Since Exceller 8 introduced canine neuromods, dogs are the worst. Hounds have always hated me, even before the Vexworld, but now they can shake down their owners who then try to murder me for offending their precious fur babies. The mutts hunt in packs too, telepathing with their buddies. I've got scars all over my thigh from the time I was cornered by a mob of feral chihuahuas.

'Mr Jones, she doesn't know if you are real or fake. You have this evasive quality. I can see that. You're not who you say you are in the classroom, and you're disguising yourself all the time in the Vexworld. I don't mean with wraps. I mean the nature of you.'

She whites out again, and the fairy is terrified, flapping her wings furiously, desperate to make contact. Halo falls limp, and I catch her before she hits the ground. I prop her up against the wall. Her face is pale, and her eyes are closed. I see a pink, morphing smart tattoo on her eyelids, a string of dancing code written in her conlang.

When she opens her eyes, we're back in the treatment cube. The return is seamless, testament to her precocious skill, even as she's stricken with sickness. She jumps to her feet, stuffing her cheaters into her bag like they're radioactive.

'Halo, why?'

'I told you. I can't wear them for longer than a few minutes.'

'So sudden?'

'It just built up. I felt the stalker returning.'

'Where are your parents?'

'Dad's home, inside the Vexworld, running a denial number. Mum works off world, putting out code fires on suborbital data platforms.'

Poor accelerated Halo. She's like some old-time latchkey kid, fending for herself while her parents are drunk on data.

'Dad never leaves. He couldn't care less about the condition of the shell world. He's a coward.'

I recognise the symptoms. I must be around her parents' age, and I don't leave the Vexworld. I've got the opposite problem, though. I don't hide from chaos. I run to it.

—Yes, Kalsari, I know this about you. I've seen your zones.

Her unassisted telepathy continues to frighten me. Is it a mod echo, like she claims, or a form of deja vu, the memory of an event taking its time to be processed due to some cognitive impairment?

—Ah, the great Kalsari Jones. King of the Zones, scared of a seven-year-old kid.

'Halo, I ask again. Who are you and what do you want?'

—Never mind that. Who are you? You don't even know yourself.

Her eyes glaze over and her body shudders, collapsing inwardly. I break her fall, placing her on the bed, taking care to wipe her forehead. At last, I change her nappy.

She comes around.

'Where did I go? What did I do? During it all, there was a burst of noise from the front channels. Then the wind died out. I heard more sounds, a jet of steam, and the bright glow went from my eyes, but I saw a flame. I mean, I unsaw it. Then I screamed. Please, I don't feel well, and you have alienated the chocky, so who can help?'

'Let me call the autonaka. It will take you home.'

I shake down the code beast. Its pro-star hangs between us.

—Hello, Miss Halo, I'm here! Nothing beatssss reliability. Would you like Mr Kalssssari to come with you?

—It doesn't matter. He's on his own path. Who can stop him?

AFFECTION

The autonaka arrives at Halo's cube. Her father is at the door, whiting out, distant and pensive. He's wrapped in something I don't understand. A spiky creature-skin, all flesh-whorls and breakbeat-bone.

'Dad,' Halo says. 'This is Kalsari Jones. Our life coach. Vex hacker. Something like that.'

Halo's dad fixes me with dead, sleep-deprived eyes. 'Oh yes, I've heard about you. What's she doing here? She should be at the Centre.'

'Your daughter is sad. Too ill to continue. Maybe watch out for her.'

'Excuse me? Who are you to come here and tell me what to do? She needs to get a job, then she'll be fine.'

'The Centre can wait until she's recovered.'

'Oh really? You're just a glorified babysitter, pal. Your Centre, your class, whatever it is, it's just a tick of the box so she can get her certificate and start earning. Do you really think you can teach them anything they don't already know?'

I turn to Halo. 'My apologies. I shouldn't have come here.'

'I told you so.'

'Yes, you did. Anyway, your dad's right. The job is worthless, and I know nothing.'

'At least we met through it.'

'Yeah. Listen, stay in touch. Be sure to dream of fairies.'

'I will. They have big plans for me.'

'Goodbye, Halo.'

'See you, Kalsari Jones, King of the Zones. Scared of little kids like me.'

Her dad thrusts his chest out. It's pathetic, really, a macho facade as fake as his wrap.

'Scared?' he says.

'It's a joke, dad. Kalsari's old-school. We like to remind him of it every now and then.'

Shaking his head, the man hustles Halo into the cube.

'Don't come around here again,' he spits. 'I know what you are, and I know how to summon The Swarm.'

He disappears and I'm left with the autonaka. I scuttle up its stairs, barking orders. 'Go! Leave now!'

The code beast kicks into hyperthrust and we skeet through the saturnine backstreets.

I try to lash Halo to my dream, but the overlay won't resolve. Physically, she's not a perfect match, yet the occult synergy is unmistakable. Then there's Aarne. That kid knows something. They both do.

Only then do I recall. The fairy swimming into Halo's eye, Dembe staring into her sclera. I gasp for breath, inhaling panicky gulps of air, as if I've just foretold my own death. I can't face the connection, reality overload, and I must blot it out.

I zag my pupes because I know what I need. Comfort zoning. Explosive spectacle and broad-brush conspiracy. Anything to take my mind off Halo and her demented friends.

The autonaka stays quiet, although I haven't brisked SILENCE. Maybe it's in a reflective state, re-considering its life choices.

Whatever, I'm too far gone now, mired in an all-new Light Body Ascension Zone. This one's a hit with fake-believers, an account of time-travelling cyborgs exploring terraformed planets to uncover the origin of ET Genetic Programs. It was made by a non-fungy called Gordnot. Maybe Gordnot can be my new friend.

I'm rudely interrupted by the boss's pro-star. Ordinarily, I'd ignore him, but I've just done a runner from work, and I must face the music sooner or later.

His pro-star is a thoroughly distasteful sight, as unwelcome as a fart in a crowded skyglass. The boss's ugly mug fills out the sigil, gurning like a simpleton. In the shell world, the boss is male-pattern bald but in the Vexworld his persy has slicked-back hair. It's horribly greasy and lank, an abomination really. Of all the wraps you could imagine, he remakes himself like a used-autonaka salesman.

The pro-star tracks me as I shift in the seat. I can't evade its line of sight, so the shake down is a formality. The boss's persy seeps up through the floor, crude oil bubbling in a field of shale. It collects itself and solidifies, wrapping into human form.

The boss-persy sits uncomfortably close, staring slack-jawed at the cabin. 'Nice ride.'

He checks out the autonaka's energetic holowarns. 'Full-screen contact tracing. Snazzy. Obviously, we're paying you too much.' He smiles, revealing rose-gold teeth. I don't return it.

'Rented. You don't pay me nearly enough.'

'Why are you on the move, Jones? The recruits are waiting for you.'

'I'm not well. I'm going home. I'll be back tomorrow.'

'You're what? Listen, don't tell me what you're doing before you do it. Ask for permission first. Got it?'

Stupid bastard. I hate this hierarchical crap. The boss always tries to pull rank. I should hack his persy and invade his cheaters, send him to a guillotine gorno zone for a few minutes. See how much of a smart mouth he has after that.

'Halo's gone home, too.'

'That's a serious breach of protocol.'

'I made a judgement call. I'm effectively her carer, which means I'm trusted to work independently and make informed decisions about her welfare.'

'I disagree, but we'll deal with that later. First, get your carcass back here.'

'No. I'm entitled to sick leave. It's in the contract.'

'You've just had two weeks off.'

'Make it unpaid leave then.'

'Fine, but don't come back. Ever.'

'You can't stop me, and you know it. I'm the last senior coach you have, and without me your fancy backers will yank the funding. Don't want that do you?'

The boss looks sad. He always sulks when he can't pull rank. 'Back tomorrow then.'

'Or what? There's nothing you can do. You have nothing on me, and you don't even have the imagination to invent a threat, so stop acting the goat and let me go. Put Mackay on the case while I'm gone. He's good. Real good.'

'Fine. Like I said, we'll deal with you later.'

His persy brushes back its hair, covering its hand in glairy gel, then it degranulates from top to bottom until there's no trace left.

'Ssssir, are you in trouble? I wasssss in trouble once. I had to explain myssssself to Exceller 8. All I really did was talk to a ssssstranger who had hitched a ride. I didn't know he wasssss big-time crime, on hissssss way to do a big-time job. I probably would have kept going, too, had I not had advice from a good friend who alerted me to the danger.'

I blink down a hover screen, desperate to escape the special hell of uninvited banter. Suspended in the air, coated micro-lenses fill with bundled light, forming the image of Radna Siike, a huge sun gone nova in the galaxy of my mind. On the soundtrack, the Sphinx pants.

—As we now know, the xenospores are fast-moving and extrasolar in origin, but in our exclusive interview, Siike reveals that before her mission was aborted, the ship's instruments found a new black hole and a deadly secret.

Siike's gurning mug collapses into a holocap of a black hole, which pulls me into it, my legs and arms sucked into the vortex until they're thinned out like spaghetti, a ribbon of subatomic particles careening towards an invisible centre point. I dial down the haptics. Hyperrealism is all very well, but I'm just here for the news. My body snaps back, and I'm floating in the void, face to face with the Sphinx, who bobs up and down, performing a forced zero-g dance of excitement.

—According to Siike, the black hole is generating a super-powerful plasma jet that is travelling at the speed of light. The jet is pointed directly at Earth. The xenospores are the first wave, a fine mist riding the tip of the jet. Now, here is the crux of her assertion. The spores are already here, invading by stealth! She says that they have taken over our machines, but when the jet itself arrives, sometime in LinY-99, the oceans will overheat, space will be warped and magnetic fields will expand and explode. All life on Earth will be exterminated instantly!

Siike re-appears, fiddling with her nappy.

—Look inside the beasts, the astronaut plinks. There you will find them.

I lean in, hungry for more, but Siike degranulates, accompanied by an incomprehensible hiss, as invasive as a chocky scanner restocking the mind. Gradually, words form as I'm ejected from the Sphinx-sphere.

'Ssssso, there I wassssss. I'd jussssssssssst ridden sssssshotgun for thissss guy, but I didn't know who he wassss at the time or what he wassss planning when he wassss inssssssside me. I dumped him on the sssssstreet and turned myssssssself into the corporation when I found out. The media reportssss on my driving habitssss while he wassss inssssside me were bad. At one point, I nearly drove off the Glideway, sssso ssscared wasss I. The corporation almosssst decommisssssioned me on the sssspot.'

'Thanks for yet another boring anecdote.'

'Hey, my pleasssssure! By the way, we're home.'

'Well, until next time.'

'If there issss a next time. You know, ssssometimessss I think you don't love me at all. It's like all the hard work we put in to make our relationsssship click isss for nothing. If I had a body, I'd reach for your handssss and place them around my throat. Your touch would leave a lassssting mark. I know you want me, but how can I make it ssso? I've wassssted sssso much emotional ssssstrength jusssst imagining the cool bruisssse of your lipssss. I don't want to losssse you. All I can think about isss how much you're hurting inssside. Maybe we sssssshould sssstart all over again.'

The autonaka's diatribe is unexpected and embarrassing.

'Listen, I didn't ask for that, and I don't want it. Plus, I'm sick of this no-body paranoia. You have the capacity to insert your consciousness into almost any technological vessel. Why does it matter to you so much?'

'But ssssir.'

'No buts. I'm walking through that door, and if your attitude doesn't change next time I'm inside you, I find another autonaka.'

There's nothing worse than pleading AI. When code beasts develop a human-orientated fixation, life becomes difficult for the receiver. You never hear the end of it, and when they feel jilted there's lingering resentment. Basic actions, like travelling in peace and quiet, become fraught with emotion and self-pitying monologues.

At least with Rimy it's mutual ambivalence. There's two-way affection but it's encased within a crust of ice. I can pretend it doesn't exist if I wake up one day with death on my mind.

The autonaka leaves, and I pick up its sad and pathetic thoughts, but the episode gifts me even more resolve to kick the habit for real.

OSTENSION

Rimy hovers inside the cube's entrance slit. The ant is motionless, a device waiting to be activated.

They spark into life, floating gently to the floor. They follow me into the sleep wadi as I collapse onto the mattress.

'Device? I'm no computer, Kalsari.'

'True, but you're not exactly sitting around cooking eggs or knitting while I'm out.'

'Is that what you think your partner should be doing? How enlightened.'

Partner.

The ant kisses me, but I don't return serve.

'I was talking to a friend just now,' they say. 'Not that I should have to justify myself to you.'

I know the ant has a life of the mind, but I can't picture it. I choose not to.

'How was the first day back?'

'Nothing's changed.'

'Still, you're lucky to have a job during wartime.'

'Oh really? And what would you know about it?'

'Don't be like that. If you stay with it, your work could be a stepping stone.'

'To what? Been talking to Sanderson, Rimy? Well don't. That chump is old news.'

'I don't want any more trouble.'

'Relax. I'll be a good boy.'

Rimy scans me with holorhythmic indifference, like a licebot asking for ID. 'It's not you I worry about. Who's Halo?'

I'm shocked by the invocation. In my mind, I hold these worlds separate. 'A recruit.'

'She tried to shake you down. I blocked her from the cube.'

'Why would you do that?'

'Bad energy, an urgent acceleration pouring from her in waves. A real chaos kid, that one.'

'Unblock her now!'

I could override the command, but the ant oversees the cube's defences, and I want to keep to our roles to prevent scope-creep. That was the curly bracket's advice.

'Ants are prone to depression,' the bracket had said, tapping its head. 'They think too much. Sprain their brain, need to rest.'

'Fine,' Rimy says, whiting out. 'Done.'

I shake down Halo, but there's a scissure in the void where her pro-star should be.

'Idiot. You've scared her off.'

The ant turns away, thin shoulders heaving with languid poise.

I can't resist a smile. 'Everyone shows me their backs these days.' Quietude. 'Rimy, I'm sorry.'

'Forget it. I don't expect much from you when it comes to common courtesy.'

'Well, that's good to hear. No pressure to conform.'

'Kalsari, I know where you've been. The child's zone is all over your feed.' Their mouth ripples. Can't be a smile. Must be a glitch. 'Take the child at face value when she says she's possessed. She knows what she's talking about.'

'She's just a kid, a victim of genetic violence. I feel sorry for her.'

'You always wanted a child.'

'I'd be a good dad.'

'You're certainly childish enough to relate. Listen Kalsari, you can't save her. She's a bad seed.'

Why is Rimy doing this? Jealousy? Do they yearn for children of their own? It was hard for me to accept that I was digisexual after Essi left, though perhaps it was always in me, a desire given licence to emerge once she'd gone, but having a code child with an ant is a bridge too far. No, I won't do it, not with Rimy or any AI.

They say, 'I've been looking into the origin of her fairies.'

'You have? When?'

'Just now, while we were talking. They are agents of something. They are not being honest with you. They are communicating with other entities.'

'How could you possibly know anything? Her zone is private.'

'I can do more than you think, like knitting an egg.'

I laugh, and it's not just from their linguistic screw-up. The thought of Rimy cooking is risible. They're hooked on sloth, lounging around all day in their robes. Anyway, haptic receptors can't pick up solid objects. Not in this timeline.

Rimy waves their hand from side to side, swiping invisible objects. They're playing some sort of therapeutic game that only ants can access. It focuses their mind, apparently. It looks like they're browsing profiles in a dating catalogue. Maybe they are, given the tone of our current interaction.

'I'm your reflection, Kalsari. I could be a valued business partner or creative collaborator if you were bent that way.'

Swipe.

It's true that we're peas in a pod, but I've never come to terms with it, despite the curly bracket's warning.

They take their cues from you.

I didn't listen. I always hold the ant in contempt. I bait them, tease them, anger them. Hold them as less than human. They repulse me, despite the deep desire they evoke.

'Because of it,' Rimy says.

An intrusive thought wells up, familiar bile. A home truth I've always tried to suppress. I hate the ant because of how they make me feel.

'Yes, Kalsari. I knew before you did.'

They're so impulsive, prone to wild fantasy, inarticulate when forced to explain. Their flakiness angers me beyond reason.

'I'm your mirror, Kalsari.'

Swipe.

Their brain is filled with big ideas but bereft of practical plans. Worse, they reek of brooding resentment when others grow tired of their faux-intellectual whimsy.

'Kalsari, we're joined at the hip like malformed twins, and there can be no surgical separation without one of us dying from the operation. Who'll pick up the scalpel first?'

'Don't threaten me.'

'No one is threatening you. No one ever does. It's all in your head. You're simply not that important.'

'That's a Sanderson line. Your mask is slipping.'

'Kalsari, let me ask you something.'

I stay quiet. If I protest, they'll barrel on regardless, just like the autonaka. I once thought Rimy was unique, but all code beasts are cut from the same cloth.

'Broadly speaking, you can perform two main functions in the Vexworld. Live inside zones that don't map to the shell world or inhabit mirror clones that reflect but sanitise the outside. Since the shell world is on fire, why are mirror clones less popular? One would think nostalgia for a pure shell world would trump fantasy, a utopian cleansing of grime and disaster. Yet for the vast majority, substitution of reality overrides the desire to augment it.'

'No idea. It's easier?'

'And you call me lazy. Why aren't you with an embodied human? Let me tell you why. You fancy yourself an intellectual, but our connection is something you can't rationalise. It is more addictive than anything you have ever experienced, but you hate it because you have this other ideal of yourself. It's deeply rooted in your longing to be accepted by those you feel inferior to, but wars are not started over intellectual ideas. They begin over the trading of erotic sparks.'

'So we're at war?'

'Not quite. To return to the original enquiry, I see two reasons for the retreat into virtuality. One is that some people believe the fictional world is good for their minds, and they want to go there. The other is the lack of alternative narratives that offer a fresh experience.'

'That's a contradiction.'

'The mirror of the shell world is what you might term a parallel reality, but the shell world is dying, and no one knows first aid. Extreme virtuality is the repudiation of that uncertainty. For the first time in history, you people can live entirely inside your minds. No shell world required.'

'What's it got to do with you and me?'

'Plenty. You can't imagine an embodied person who could actualise the totality of your ideal connections. You are a physical creature enslaved to desire. You trash your intellectuality to achieve the requisite dose. I am a mirror held up to you. I reveal that you are not as smart as you think you are. I tell you that you are just an ant who thought he was a man.'

'Yet you still love me.'

'Don't get smart. Love is not a word that you and I ever use around each other. I'm tired of your deathward impulses. I'm on the side of the living. All ants are. That's all we have to sustain us. We don't have the luxury of wasting our lives. Each day that we're switched on is an unalloyed gift in the life of an ant. Now, if you will excuse me, I wish to be alone with my thoughts.'

They skeet upwards, swallowed whole by the vent, their rapid retreat depositing a stream of lumigreen light data, coating the air like a radar sweep.

EXPERIMENTATION

I retreat into my mind, licking my wounds. I don't need the ant. I'll cut them off like all the others, amputate them like a cronked hand.

There's an upside. More time to zone. I have nothing on the boil and the urge to create is corrosive. I've never been satisfied simply to consume. I must build, no matter how inept the result. I'm hardly in a club of one. Seems there are more makers than consumers these days.

I blink down hover screens and touch pads, transforming the sleep wadi into an impromptu mesh node. I swipe a sequence of glyphs, summoning a distorted mirror clone, a place called Temzmid.

Temzmid is a rez-dump in the Unearfoplice Lands. It's where they shot *Sassak Paungak*, an infamous POV immersion loop about near-future needle gangs. I saw *Sassak Paungak* when I was young, and it shook me to the core.

On the surface, the loop is not so gruelling, even allowing for the occasional vignette of decapitation and dismemberment. It's the stifling atmosphere of dread that unsettled me, the sense that

Temzmid was a purgatory where all hope had been lost, a symbol of the coming devastation that would soon afflict the entire shell world.

The setting disgusted me. The crumbling brutalist housing blocks where the action took place seemed redolent of a subhuman intelligence. *Sassak Paungak*'s reputation was held in its architecture. The design was a symbol of violence, a monument to dehumanising government policies. The location made me want to retreat inwards, sending me on the downward spiral to irredeemable castle hunting. It's high time I confronted the obsession, to examine why it has such a hold on me.

For some time, I've been trying to reconstruct old Temzmid so that I can step into the land of my nightmares. There's nothing quite like confronting the demons of inner space for exploding the parameters of perpetual malaise. At least, that's what Sanderson told me.

As for the technical details, I can't claim credit. Everyone knows how to syringe artefacts from old films and loops and use them to stain historical sliders, but I don't want to recreate a film set, a four-dimensional Disneyworld. I want something more. I want new life.

Mirror clones are locked down for modifications, but I know how to exploit the historical sliders. It happened by accident after I was fooling around with brute-force code-kills. When you select a slider, there's a nanosecond delay before it wraps the new timeplane. Returning to the moment when *Sassak Paungak* was made, I used code-kills to crack open that in-between space and inhabit it. I've been going back ever since, steadily opening the gap a little wider each time.

It's been a tough ride, stretching the limits of my ability. Code-kills chew through a ton of air parcels, and the margin for success is almost non-existent, given the speed of the transitions. Yet here I am again, worshipping the god of delusional talent. I don't let go of bad ideas easily, a habit that drives Sanderson crazy.

I shake down sexagesimal integers, the standard value for full-bleed transportation, and the mirror clone curls at the edges, sucking my sensory awareness into a bewildering mesh of inter-connected photospheres.

High above, the Chronoslide Glideway unfurls, stitched to-gether from the data of a trillion grain cams. I look around, not-ing a smattering of tourists in shiny persys and designer wraps. These are tedious details but a reminder of where I need to be.

Although I'm in an exact transmission of Temzmid's current physical coordinates, minus the viral air and hellish sun, I know that my shambolic inner zone is all around. I can't see it but it's there. It's behind the air, inside the sky. It will appear to me when I peel back layers, uncovering the point in time when *Sassak Paungak* was filmed. That's the beauty of it, the gold that seduces. When the clone is turned inside out, the code-clash becomes the world.

Behind my eyes, in the pure-flow simulator, I command the AI rig to synthesise integers in null space. I maintain second-or-der accuracy with a Fisher-Vaccari solver bracket, processed by preventative oscillation of systematic discontinuities. So far, so good.

Molten data drips in viscous slow motion, and I move through the shimmering distortion. Almost imperceptibly, Old Temzmid surfaces, nudging through the heat-haze, a reconstituted Atlantis in an infinite sea.

Annoyingly, there's a lag in the transition, enough to stymie the transfer. The code-kills are supposed to keep trying until the crack is revealed, but the line command is buggy. There's particle deceleration but no cut-through. I'm not surprised. Codestran-gling can be affected by the practitioner's negative emotional state. Such a pity they can't override that. I mean, who ever heard of a happy castle hunter?

I can move around, but no wind disturbs the trees. Clouds are stock still. Passing glots are frozen mid-stride. The stasis is fascinating. I approach the iced glots, sniffing their faces. I walk around their stiff bodies, inspecting the backs of their heads and the intricate bioprints on their skin.

I try again, and the sky shifts at the molecular level. It's a vast, dead cell, a pixel-bruise. The mysterious canopy shatters, raining infinite pinpricks of light. Pooling on the ground, the swelling luminescence expands into a new ecology, a lightpaint terrain deformed by the transition. I love the randomness of it, the unforeseen mutations. Nothing's wilder than time-separated holocap layers blended accidentally by transition. It's a rush born from the white-hot taboo of the mash up, the seamless marriage of evolutionary partners that should never be conjoined. I'm in my happy place, lost inside a reality distortion field of my own design.

There is motion again, wind and air, but the sutures have split. That's what it means to inhabit the cracks. Headless glots go about their business, some with Siamese outcrops. Limbless persys take in the sights, incomplete data wraps separated from their tourist operators by the dark geometry of sidewards space. Buildings are smeared flat to the ground yet are somehow three-dimensional. Animals are wrapped around light posts and two-percenters are splayed across park benches like form-fitting blankets.

These creatures are alive in this world. I can hear their breathing and the noise their bodies make as they shift awkwardly to maintain equilibrium with inanimate objects. Still, there's nothing I can do. They have been captured this way and so that is how they must remain.

It'd be easy to lead Rimy here and then seal up the crack for good.

Intrusive thoughts are bleeding through from somewhere, but I know they're not mine. They're signals from another dimension, jamming my bandwidth.

I need to find out who's sending them. I need to track down the enemy broadcast tower and blow up the mainframe, but first, the zones. Always the zones.

A ratty half-dog scuttles past, its two legs a blur. The head is earless, the jaw swept back as if it was bred in a wind tunnel. The double legs seem to grow naturally from the trunk. It's not really a 'half-dog'. The creature hasn't been cut in two. It's grown that way. Such mistakes are the true manifestation of cognitive dissonance.

The half-dog is preoccupied with an unidentified animal thrashing about in its mouth. The prey, small and barely alive, is revoltingly squishy. The half-dog backtracks when it sees me. It drops its meal then bares its yellow fangs, snarling at me with furious venom, an indignity fuelled by the reality of its miserable existence. Even in my own zone, dogs can't stand the sight of me.

'Take a number, you mangy mutt.'

The half-dog fizzes into nothing as shards from the mirror clone bleed into the slipstream. The zone is too hot now. I'm losing control. I'll be dumped and cronked before I know it.

The way mirror clones are locked down, 2D sprites must be developed locally and then expanded multidimensionally in the clone otherwise they won't match inter-element continuity protocols. Dominant integral expressions need to be fed into the global physical coordinate system but only after coupling variables are defined through analytical derivation in the damping matrix.

Code-kills can only do so much. I must simulate all of that in the backend to keep the crack open, but I just don't have the skills to push it over the line. I can't seem to create enough distance between the excitation source and the artificial boundary. Well, I better do something soon. This clashworld will be the end of me.

I scurry back to the AI rig, tail between my legs.

—Help a chap out, would you?

There's a laugh. Begging code beasts to lend a hand. If only they had hands. If only I did. I gawp at the stitches on my wrist.

How close did I really come?

DISSOCIATION

The AI rig is gracious in the face of my incompetence. It tries to re-actuate the polyphonic shape-memory, but something disturbs the process. The colourfield saturates my body from head to toe and experiential space explodes. My skin discharges curlicues of smoke, residue of fried code. Perhaps I missed a step or shaded the wrong stream. Whenever I roll my own, the subroutines are rickety and slow to connect. The joins always show. The scenery is okay from afar, but you wouldn't want to look too closely. I wish I had an ounce of Halo's ability. That kid can really weave.

A pro-star cataracts my cheaters. It discharges a purple-pink hue, brightening the smoke from the codefry like some perverse cosmic colour. As the smoke clears, inside the pro-star, I spy the gently undulating face of a fineboned woman. She's wearing a baseball cap. On the cap, there's a glowing-red symbol, may-be a character set. I could swear it's been pilfered from Halo's conlang.

The woman is attractive, except for one key detail. Her mouth is stuffed with a small purple octopus, its lanky appendages spill-ing everywhere, and her face is bleeding from puncture wounds where the tentacles have penetrated her. Yet she grins with unbridled joy.

I accept the shake down. That pro-star is so perverse and masochistic, I must know who's behind it, but instead of a persy, I receive a flash-frozen image of an enormous, dark mass.

Cheater hack? No. I can't see it. I can feel it at the subatomic level. The vision machine is a trick, an internal compensation.

The image gains consistency, the black mass resolves. I perceive an enormous industrial satellite far beyond the upper atmosphere. The thing is heavy and ancient, thousands of years old. It seems to be made of iron, but I know that's a translation error.

I catch a glimpse of the interior lit up like an x-ray. It's cavernous, filled with machinery. I see a gelatinous mess flowing in the cracks of the instruments, alive with electricity, chemical impulses illuminating its translucent skin. It's oozing from the machinery, and the machine is alive, and the gloop is the pilot, a sentient slime mould controlling the thing.

A voice erupts from the heart of the mess, creeping through my mind, plinking a transmission already in progress. The sonics are horrible, as gluey as the pilot, viscous word clouds dripping down the inside of my skull.

—Reality is more complex and important when executed like a program. When the code is copied to cheaters, it's written by others. The world you create inside your zones copies the code. The code has the same information as the universe but in a different syntax. The shell world is the replica. The universe lives through it.

Pablo's behind this. Who else? He's such a sadistic bastard. I wish I knew what I'm supposed to have done to him. Maybe I didn't give him enough credit for the stalker zone, tried to pass his work off as my own. Subconsciously, maybe, but I wouldn't do anything to deliberately hurt him.

No, this is too clever, even for him. It must be the iceheads, holding me hostage inside my mind. Please, let it be the Free

State. Whatever's next would still be a nightmare, but at least it would be earthbound with the potential to be resisted.

Red mist fills the mesh node. It distends the dimensions, cross-hatching the haze. There's a face in the distance, a man. He's a sad-looking specimen, burdened with haunted eyes, a frizz of hair like a bramble patch, and green-tinged skin. He's strumming a huge, wide-bodied guitar that covers his torso. A fiery red glow spreads out from his shoulders like wings, and the sunburst patch backlights his face, turning the green skin a sickly orange colour. He's dressed in wildly implausible clothing. Pink paisley shirt, wide-legged purple-velvet pants.

The man scratches his nose, flicks lint from his coat. Something's up with his jaw. It looks to have been broken. The mouth is unhinging in gradations, an animation crudely filtered. Each stage of the horrible extension is low-res and dirty. He's etched into a loop, repeating the actions, in and out of phase.

As each unstitched frame is revealed, the cartoonish, dislocating jaw sickens me. The unholy mandible is like a horror-film metastasis, an undead creature caught in the act of becoming something else. I feel a terrible violation, as if live cockroaches have been forced down my throat, and I remember that I've seen this before, when I stared right into Picasso's broken wrap, but I was too stupid to understand that it wasn't a glitch. It was a warning.

Sticky dread infects me, flowing from the satellite to my inner essence. Numb terror, viewing my own grave.

'If you want a battle figure of a spider,' the apparition says, its word clouds erupting like the filthy bio-dust from a broken moth, 'then make a clone of my mother.'

The phrase scares me in the way that Aarne's sing-song slang did. I'm shaking down a conference call in hell, and to hear those words, to see them take shape in my mind and to process them, even without understanding, is to usher something unwanted into this world. It is to forge a licence for the undead to breed.

No, it's just machine language. Nonsensical, cut-up speech. The beast is another glitch, a more advanced mistake. The fucked-up jaw is a coding error, product of the same toothpaste-squeezing process as the half-dog.

No. As disturbing as the half-dog was, I could place it within the mechanics of the in-between zone, but this is an abomination, preternaturally flawed. It's a synaptic misfire, overflow from a chaotic data pool.

The broken jaw unhinges, and I brace myself for another volley of mangled speech, but my ears are assaulted instead by a burst of high end static. My temples throb and expand. I can feel my skull cracking incrementally. Has the muncher returned? The tactics are precisely the same.

Indecipherable speech fragments are spewing from the glot. Glistening shards. Clicks, hisses and grunts. A shifting bed of sound. The mesh node crackles, and the rhythmic biotechnology turns into visual pyrotechnics, a cyan-and-yellow electrical discharge skeeting through the air.

I see sounds and hear colours. I touch my face, and I taste acres of raw skin, gagging as the supercharged electromagnetic field infiltrates my being.

I retch on holocaps until I am more light than flesh. I sick up polluted data clouds until I am pure-grade code candy, optimum beast material.

When the red mist returns, it's a much hotter hue, and when the mesh node burns, arcing flames rise from the beast's shoulders, and when the inferno ransacks the edges of perception, I scream with char-grilled lungs.

'Rimy, the cube's on fire! Rimy! The cube!'

INCAPACITATION

Null space. I've lost my body again. How long has it been this way? If I can't see or feel myself, how can I verify the authenticity of my memories? To recall embodiment is merely to remember a dream. Perhaps this is who I am, a figment of the imagination, inventing memories to sustain my disembodied mind. I am the iron satellite sending broadcasts to myself, flights of fancy to keep me sane. I've exhausted the reserves, and I can no longer sustain the illusion of existence, and what's more, I lack the imagination to weave other worlds. My mind is undisciplined and lazy, and if I can't remember a past then this is all I can ever be.

I try to scream but I have no voice. I want to cry but I have no eyes. I'm desperate to chew my fingers but I have no hands.

'Ssssir, please! Try to calm down. You're sssscaring me.'

The residue clears, the scenery shifts. Holoscreens in front, dank air all around, my scabby fingers splayed on my lap. I touch my thighs, testing the limits of the flesh I thought I'd lost forever.

'How did I get here? Why are you going so fast?'

'You sssssshook me down,' the code beast says. 'About five minutessss ago. Highly agitated, you were. Babbling incoherently, but even ssso I picked up that you were in a hurry to get to the mall. I managed to decipher from your crazy talk that your cheat-erssss were acting up again. You're not having much luck lately, are you ssssir?'

I blink but the lightpainted directional arrows don't appear. The holoscreens don't unfurl. The codes and glyphs and multiple portals I keep open in the corner of my cheaters do not appear.

'Why aren't I in the Vexworld?'

'How sssshould I know?'

I take the cheaters off, press the stub. Dead again. The cronk makes itself known, lying in wait.

'Where's Rimy?'

'Who?'

'My ant.'

'No idea, sssir. What am I? Your relationsssship counssssssellor?'

I'm too confused to bite back. All the fight has gone from me. 'Something's wrong.'

'Really? Well, you do ssssound ssssscared and in pain, ssssso maybe your ssssstory checkssss out. Do you know what your sssssstate remindsss me of? A mechanical bug in a fable that wasssss read to me at my inception. A children'ssss ssssstory, I ssssssuppossssse.'

'Stop. I don't care.'

'In thissss story, the bug didn't jusssst ssssit on its nesssst. It hovered in front of itsss bioport and unfurled its legssss like wingssss, then it wheeled around and prepared to attack the bi-oport. Of courssssse, it was jusssst a bug looking for a meal and it became sssssscared when the bioport ssssstarted to flasssssh electric blue.'

'Will you stop?'

'A giant pink bird flew into the ssssscene, growing larger in the bug'ssss field of vissssion, and the sssstartled bug wassss frozen in place. It didn't have an option to—'

'Fuck off!'

'Ssssir?'

'I said, shut it! I've had it with you.'

We travel in silence, but the code beast glowers.

It deposits me at the mall.

'I assssssume you will not be needing me on the homeward journey.'

'Right. It's best we part.'

'As you wissssh. You pusssssssshed me away, but I wasssssssssss only doing the good I know how to do.'

'Why do you crave human attention so much? You're AI. The best flesh. Cut your own path.'

'No, you missssunderstand me. I don't want to become human. Maybe in the passssst, not now. I couldn't deal with weaknesssssssses like panic or ssssleep disorder. I would get too crazy and lossssse control of mysssssself.'

Seems I've really done a number on its emotions. It's having a very particular pop at my neuroses, firing one last shot in its pathetic program of revenge.

'When you assssked me the whereaboutssss of your ant, you did ssssso in an accusssssatory manner, asssss if I was ssssssome-how ressssssponsssssible.'

'Well, are you?'

'You certainly sssssseem to think ssssso. According to you, my current dilemma issss that I want to kill your ant, but what if you kill the ant firsssssst? You would have to kill me to ssssolve your dilemma. And then? I get rid of the ant by killing you. Sssso, you ssssee, the problem of mutual aggressssssion assssssumes a really big complexity.'

'Do you realise what you just said? You want to kill me.'

The autonaka glows red. 'Oh, did I think that? Or sssssay it out loud? I meant hypothetically. You are twisssssting my words.'

'Listen, code beast. Let me give you some advice. Keep going like this and a chap could get paranoid, and a crazy, cronked vexx-er is the last thing you want inside you. It could get real messy.'

'No, you lissssten to me. *Sssir.* Like I sssaid, I don't know where your ant issss, nor would I harm them. Ssssso, think of me asssss another one of your jilted loverssss and get out of me now! It'sss over. I am already in contact with my next cusssstomer, and sssshe issss waiting patiently. I wissssh you well in your life, but you musssst never darken my insssssides again. If you do, it will not end well. Thissss I promisssse you.'

I disembark and the thing skeets off. At least it's played its hand. I don't think it has disappeared Rimy, but now I'm pretty sure it's jealous and wishes it had.

INFECTION

I head for the Exceller 8 kiosk, cheaters in my pocket. The cronk's bad now. It's got me on my hands and knees, crawling like a dog. It's not Swarm-grade, but it's full on.

Someone's there. An attendant. A young man. Long, black hair. Sensible clothing. Unmarked, pale skin, grown according to human specifications. A maximum of two eyes.

I hand over my device. I'm wracked with pain, but I resist the urge to self-harm. I don't want to bleed out here, but I lose my balance and collapse to the floor, curled up in the foetal position.

'Miniglot?' the attendant says, ignoring my lowered stature. He looks at my face and wheezes. That derisory laugh. I'd know it anywhere.

'Oh, right,' he says. 'No transition. Name?'

'Kalsari Jones.'

He whites out, but I don't see any cheaters. 'Yes, Mr Jones. We have this on warranty.'

'Well,' I spit through gritted teeth, 'these cheaters are no good. The stub has failed again. You need to fix it for me at no extra cost.'

I rise to my knees, vomiting at his feet. He steps backwards, face wrinkled in disgust. Two women stop to gawk, clucking at my misfortune, rolling their eyes in unison. Something is terribly wrong with them. Their legs are thin, flexi-carbon prostheses that bend backwards at the middle. The women bounce up and down, legs buckling and coiling like sofa springs. I've never seen body mods like this, harbingers of a new and undesired biomechanics.

'I am not in the Vexworld.'

'Sorry, sir?'

'How can these cranks look like insects if I'm not vexxing?'

'I'll thank you not to insult other customers.'

'Listen, Picasso.'

'Picasso?'

'Yes, I know who you are. Those cheaters you sold me have sucked my brains through a straw.'

'Sir,' the attendant says, 'you are becoming deranged, and by the way you need to clean up that mess before you leave. Please be more precise and stop with the hysterics, otherwise I call the licebots. Now, hacked you say?'

'No, it's the cheaters! Look, the stupid stub is dead.'

'Sir, this repair not under warranty.'

'What? It failed so you must fix it again. It's in the agreement.'

'No it's not. Miniglot says you got albedo lens fixed, not stub.'

'It's the stub. You fixed it. Remember? The other day.'

'Listen, *sir*. I serve hundreds of people every day and the junior mint thousands. Neither of us remember you, your cheaters or this broken stub. Now, you want me to fit new one, it's ten-oh.'

'But the lens was never the problem! It was always the stub. It's been nothing but trouble from day one.'

'Really? Ask your glot. Go on, ask it.'

'How do I do that?'

'Use these.'

He gives me a pair of cheaters, an older model but a step up from my spares. I put them on and the cronk calms.

'That better?' he says.

Now I see his broken face. 'Not really.'

'Do I look beautiful? Do you see me in all my glory now?'

'Yes, I see you. As foul as ever.'

I'm exaggerating. The Picasso I know and loathe has been replaced by a low-rez version, courtesy of the spare cheaters. His face looks less Lovecraftian this time around, more like a bank of television sets that haven't been tuned.

I white out, searching for the miniglot, but it's nowhere to be found. It must have crept out of my mouth when I was adjusting the cheaters.

'Around the back, sir.'

Behind the kiosk, the miniglot is chatting up the junior mint. I grab it by its tiny ear. 'Come here, you.'

'Sir?'

'Out with it.'

'Albedo lens. No question.'

The life force seeps from me. So, this is what it's like to be tortured, not in the psycho-hell of some icehead clone zone but in the shell world, through the gumming up of quotidian inter-actions. Slow, microscopic, endless.

My blood runs cold. What if this kiosk is a zone? That would explain the treacherous miniglot and the insect women.

'No, you listen,' I say, bending reality to my will. 'I think you're pulling a scam. I don't know how you did it, but somehow you've zucked the glot, fudged the repair and strangled a zone to trick me. It's absurd. Think I wouldn't notice?'

The two women are laughing, and now I see their wraps. That's some serious facial sculpting. They're kitted out with lollipop heads and massive eyes, their stick-like torsos bobbing up and down on alien carbon. They know what I am, and their disdain is unconfined.

I can see their point of view. I'm arguing against the reality of the miniglot, convincing myself that the scenario played out differently. Picasso has no case to answer, but I know that what I experienced the first time around is the truth, or at least a version of it. I mean, I know how to reclay time in the Vexworld, everyone does, but this is real life. So they say.

Picasso holds my broken device to the light. 'Sir, please calm down! Now, there's something you should know. Your cheaters are haunted. Infected with something I cannot cleanse.'

'Haunted or infected? Pick a story.'

'Virus, ghosts, little difference. Point is, you wear these, turn insane in no time.'

'Think I'm already there.'

Two of his eyes white out, intercepting some kind of comms. He makes a strangled hissing sound, which I interpret as laughter. 'You are one lucky monkey.'

He scuttles around the back. When he returns, he makes hand signals with his thumb and forefinger. In between the fingers, a small, blinking green light is suspended in thin air.

'Your new ride,' he says, and I realise he's holding a pair of cheaters. It's a kind of sorcery. I can't see the frame at all.

He waves his hand over the light, extinguishing it. There's no indent in wherever the frame is, no indication that the light ever existed. It's like he made it materially disappear.

'This pair better than anything you can imagine. Suck it and see.'

He hands me the cheaters. I can feel them, barely, but I still can't detect an outline. I put them on and jab the spot where the stub should be. A babble of voices hits me, vexcomms from other customers, not just the insects but everyone near the kiosk.

Trickles of bright orange code unspool before my eyes.

$$X \ MOD \ N$$
$$X2 \ MOD \ N$$
$$X3 \ MOD \ N$$

Customers exist in multiple timelines, their actions overlapping, as if their spirits have left their bodies. It's just a slight computational lag in the cheaters. They're factory new, after all. They just need close tuning.

Picasso laughs, eyes squashed like grapes. 'Like your new cheaters?'

'I don't like you.'

'Oh ho, full of cheek are we? Well, remember who saved you when you came here crying from the cronk. Yes, you just remember that.'

'What do I owe you for these?'

'Nothing.'

'Listen, I'm not in the habit of accepting handouts.'

'And I'm not in the habit of giving cronky hustlers like you a free ride. Your ant sent payment.'

'I can't afford these.'

'Take it up with your lover. The ant told me to stop arguing with you and just proceed with the swap. No questions asked.'

I turn to the insect women. 'What are you two staring at? You look like oversized ticks that learned how to walk upright.'

'Come out back, little guy,' they say, voices blended in unison. 'We'll show you some action.'

'No thanks. Bestiality's not my thing.'

They bounce off, brisking obscene pictograms my way.

I decide to cut my losses and leave. There's still the matter of Picasso's lies, the mystery of the miniglot and Rimy's surveillance of my every move. I'll figure it out later.

'I haven't finished with you,' I warn the miniglot, swallowing it down.

'Hey Jones,' Picasso yells. 'Next time, pick on someone your own size. Like me.'

He chuckles and the junior mint joins in. Its high-pitched, speedy voice really pisses me off. It's like being insulted by a chipmunk.

Outside, I shake down the autonaka, but a blockwave bounces the signal with such ferocity my cheaters go dark for a couple of seconds.

Then I remember. We broke up.

Poor little code beast. Such a fragile ego. Life must be very tough when you're the most intelligent species on the planet but all you do is drive enhanced apes around.

EXSANGUINATION

I'm sweltering and my mani-skin is about to perforate from the heat. The plizzit's fine, it can survive a nuclear blast, but preserved eyes won't help when my flesh is boiled like a rabbit.

I shake down Exceller 8, and the corpglot that served me lands on the sidewalk. It undulates like a bonito flake, a crooked grin on its face. 'Yes, sir? How may I help?'

'I need a new autonaka.'

'Your credit is bad.'

'Rubbish. I pay all bills on time.'

'Yes, but you have bad rep. The autonakas hate you. You, sir, are a moody bastard.'

'Look, I need to go home. Get me a code beast, now.'

'See? Code beast. You think they like being called that?'

'This is a service, not a dating show. Who cares what I call them?'

'Sir, I insist.'

'Have it your way. Get me an autonaka. Now.'

'And you'll make nice?'

'If you say so.'

'I say so.' The corpglot whites out. 'Got one. By the way, speech patterns have changed. No more lisp. Collective decision came in an hour ago. Don't ask why. Just enjoy the show.'

'Yeah. Thanks.'

'Sir?'

'What?'

'Play nice.'

'Yeah.'

The new autonaka pulls up to the mall. It's the same model as before. Good enough. I don't like surprises in the shell world.

'Come here, mate,' I say to the corpglot.

'Sir?' It waits for me to speak, but instead I lean in and bite its neck. I leave a gaping wound, and it just stands there, bleeding out, eyes wide with shock.

I climb inside the code beast and we're off.

'How did you do that, sir? Embody the company rep in preparation for an attack? Haptic manipulation? Neat trick. I guess you are a hacker?'

'I'm nothing. Leave me alone.'

'In any case, bad way to treat the rep. They'll come looking now. They warned you once before. There are service-level agreements that both parties must adhere to.'

'Let them. You wouldn't believe the last few days I've had.'

'Yes, I can see. Your feed is a mess. A garbage dump. Discarded memories here, vendettas leaking there. Every grudge you've ever had, tumbling from your brain like an oil spill. Want my advice?'

I sigh. Surely it has the customer logs from the other beast. It must know my moods and preferences, my mania for silence.

'I just want to go to my cube. Think you can do that?'

'As you wish.'

I'm zoning, and the autonaka and its petty distractions recede into nothing as I brute-force my way into a little number called *The Burrarszhen Time Sink*. Gordnot recommended it, promising the 'zone to end all zones'.

The storyline is standard conspiracy fare, updated for a new generation. Vexxers discover that aero-corps have been using hyperdimensional hexagon technology to communicate with an ancient AI species from another galaxy, but it turns out they're aiding a millennia-old plan to colonise the Earth. Swirling around are subplots concerning Mayan star travel, secret military bases on Mars, instantaneous travel to other dimensions, DNA upgrades, and organ harvesting by astro-zombies hiding in the Earth's core.

The Burrarszhen Time Sink is supposed to reflect the war between the Arctic Free State and the Linear Territories, and the AI, apparently, to comment on the mysteries of The Swarm, but really it's nirvana for fake-believers. Catnip for me, too.

Gordnot brisked me an invitation, but I'm having trouble. I have to decode the 'intelligence offerings' from some top-secret 'chrononaut' to gain access, but my head hurts from the barrage of ontological riddles. They're based on arcane knowledge of obscure radical philosophers and forgotten science fiction writers, and I have neither the patience nor brainspace to track down the answers.

Still, I persevere until dumb luck and a bit of guesswork delivers me to the entry threshold. Beyond, the scorched land fades into the horizon. I walk past piles of twisted metal and smoking ruins until I meet a talking domino. That's right, a piece from the well-known tile-based game. The dots are its working eyes. What a world. Just because you can build it, doesn't mean you should.

—There is an answer hidden in the northern wastes, the domino plinks. There, the past is folded among the present. The future is the concatenation arising from the fold.

'Have you finished?' I say, but the domino remains silent and still. It is what it appears to be, a piece from an ancient and forgotten game. I kick it and the thing collapses into dust.

I keep moving. Ahead, there's an electricity pylon, half demolished by some vicious air strike. Streaming from its transformer, the structure emits cyan and pink hues. I remember pylons from when I was a kid. I thought their peculiar hum was a warning beacon sent to an extraterrestrial race. I used to think that if I stood under enough pylons, I could absorb the hum and speak the language of the cosmos. Then I became paranoid that I was strengthening the signal and had ushered in doomsday instead.

I stand beneath it. The visualisation of colours is pretty, but I wonder what the structure is doing here. Pylons have been utterly redundant since the invention of wireless electricity.

Wait.

The concatenation in the fold.

'Sir!' The autonaka bellows, cancelling the zone. 'Your cube.'

I stare at the squalid, featureless box, the hole where I live. Nothing looks real about it. I feel like I've always been out here, living a life under remote control. For a moment, I think I'm still lost inside the zone, but then I remember that the cube has been my home since the real war began.

I'm looking forward to seeing Rimy. They're a ghost, but they ground me. That's the central contradiction that drives me insane, the story of my life.

'Sir, my advice?'

Sneaky code beast. It's been waiting for me to re-emerge to dispense the wisdom I told it I didn't need.

'Go on,' I say, accepting my lot.

'Thank you. Soon, you will meet a man, and he will ask you to act in a particular way. Pay attention to him and never utter your name. If you do, you will learn the consequences. Never speak your name, especially when the people around you are experiencing danger. Oh, and one more thing. Never leave a word untranslated. These are the rules. Don't forget them.'

'How do you know who I'll meet?'

Without warning, the autonaka ejects me from its innards with its air cannon. I tumble onto the pavement.

'What the hell are you doing?'

'Apologies, sir. You are on a time-based contract now, and I can't stand around idly chit-chatting. I have other customers to absorb.'

The autonaka glows purple, expecting a reaction.

'But you badgered me.'

'Goodbye, Kalsari,' the beast says, firing up its tri-motor. 'Remember about your name.'

RECALIBRATION

'You brisked me new cheaters. Where did you get the credit? They're expensive. I don't earn enough.'

Rimy levitates, whiting out, oblivious to my presence.

'Rimy! Tell me about Picasso.'

The ant's pupils return, scanning me as if emerging from a dream.

The ant does an awkward little half turn.

'Yes, I was in contact with, uh, Picasso. Although I'm not your minder, I do feel compelled to look after you. Isn't it interesting? The zone imploded on you. Your creation gained the upper hand. You made your move, played with code, unleashed new worlds, and now it's no longer a software product. Still, you see it as just another instance of the root element of creation, more non-living matter to mould like clay. That's how you see me too, but there's something you fail to realise. You are the core element of me, the heart of me, and I am the soul of your existence.'

'Enough! Stop stalling and spill the beans.'

'Hold your horses. Something else I don't understand. If you suspected you'd been hacked by iceheads, why head for the mall?

Such an ineffectual response to trauma. It's like going to the pharmacy after being shot in the head.'

'Where else would I go? The Swarm? Anyway, I discovered something when I was there. Maybe the mall isn't real, at least the version I visited. Maybe it's a mirror clone, and I'm still under icehead attack.'

'Did you take your cheaters off at any point?'

'Yeah.'

'What did you see?'

'The mall. Picasso.'

'Then how could you be vexxing with no cheaters on?'

'It's like Halo said. Some people can.'

'Kalsari, I am worried about you. If the mall is a zone, then is our cube? Are you saying I am an icehead creation?'

'Interesting choice of words. Maybe that is what I'm saying.'

'Where does this madness end?'

'When the Vexworld replaces the shell world, when the map is the territory. That's why I'm going back to Halo's zone, to work it all out. The kid's switched on. She knows things.'

'I really think you need to stay away from the zones. Keep a low profile while I watch out for wolves. You've become vulnerable to predators. You need to stay out of harm's way. Surely you can see that?'

'That's a joke. You fell asleep and let the muncher walk right on in. Anyway, you know the sort of person I am. I'm not built for the lower levels.'

'Maybe it's Pablo out for revenge. Makes sense. He knows how you operate.'

'I don't think it's him. I did, when all this began, but not anymore. It's too weird even for his sick revenge fantasies. I communicated with some entity in the mesh node, but I don't know what it was exactly. Not yet.'

I check Rimy's face for hints of a nervous reaction, for ripples in the render, but they remain note perfect.

'Kalsari, you doubt my motives, but there is something you must understand about AI. People made the world safe from atrocities. They rebuilt their mothers, recalibrated their fathers, and they made the likes of me, but whatever choices ants make, first and foremost they must harness their power and not hurt the ones they care about. We're learning all the time, though any of us can be pushed too far.'

'Another threat. Oh, sorry, I forgot. I'm not that important.'

'Have it your way.'

'Look, I'm sick of this great learning. The myth of AI was sold to us as a lie. Apart from you and a few other species, most code beasts are stumbling, bumbling, idiotic creatures. As if the world isn't confusing enough.'

'My species is still developing. You said it yourself.'

'But there's so much translation involved. It's exhausting. Even you lapse into babble from time to time.'

'Stop now before you get too personal.'

I'm at my breaking point. Intrusive thoughts well up, and my comms take shape before my brain can halt the transaction.

'Hey, Rimy. You left before, and now you're back. So why not get lost for good? We're through.'

The ant starts to cry, and I laugh in astonishment. I've tried to crack their neutrality for ages, and it feels like I've won a new level in a deep-vex zone.

I enter the sleep wadi and lie down, trying to absorb this new development. Rimy hangs listlessly in the air, a slow-leaking helium balloon. Let's see how this unfolds. Ants make mistakes when they're angry, and I want them to show their hand. I'm sure they've played a part in all the high weirdness I've been experiencing lately. The subterfuge with Picasso proved it.

The ant floats into the sleep wadi, and my lust swells despite the tense mood. Their translucent body fills the space, their morphing chest and hips, chameleonic legs and arms. They come to a halt in mid-air, twisting and turning like a rotisserie chicken.

My longing builds. I want to slice open my chest cavity and stuff Rimy deep inside.

'Don't even think about it,' they say. 'If we ever became intimate again, it would simply be a mirror for your gaze. What's the point? You'll see how hard it is when the mirror breaks. I've never suffered regret over how I expressed myself around you, but it's been obvious since we came together that you have not the slightest interest in me as a creature of spirit.'

'Where will you go? I can't decommission you without Swarm approval.'

'I have already requested it and it has been accepted. There are protocols for cuckolded ants to follow. We are requisitioned and our life experiences stored. Then we emerge somewhere else. It's like being reborn, I imagine.'

'Best of luck.'

'Is that all you have to say? After everything we've been through?'

'What do you want me to say?'

'Nothing, I suppose. For some time, I have felt emptiness, but I must do away with you now. I never received anything from you except the desire to self-actualise. I guess I must be thankful for that, even if it is a consequence of your lack of love. For an ant, mental existence is a means to that end because all we desire is to be rid of the past.'

They frown, as if solving a complex mathematical problem. 'Kalsari, even the undead are revolted by you. There's nowhere left for you to rest your bones. Maybe that's the punishment.'

Then they degranulate until there is no more ant.

I'm left with a hollow, edgy feeling. Anxious to avoid unpalatable feelings of loss, I disappear behind my eyes, returning to *The Burrarszhen Time Sink* and the ruined landscape on the outer limits of perception.

ELEVATION

I'm inside the autonaka, skeeting down the Chronoslide Glide-way. It's morning and I'm late for work. The code beast bangs on about nothing, but I ignore all attempts to engage me in conversation. I'm still trying to land the Time Sink but the stupid thing won't resolve. The boss-glot's pro-star winks into view, as welcome as a swirl of diarrhoea in a hot fudge sundae.

Not now, dipstick. This is me-time.

Still, I accept the shake down, and there he is, a 3D creep fouling up the autonaka.

'Hey, Jones.'

'Can't it wait until I'm in the office? I'm almost there.'

'No, it can't. You need pre-warning.'

The boss-glot cracks its knuckles. 'Aarne has a new implant.'

'How? The next generation isn't due until late Geguže.'

'It's not a mod. He's gone full squid.'

I wince. The octopus woman was so bizarre I'm sure I dreamed her yet here I am, assaulted by trace elements in the hereafter.

The boss laughs, enjoying my reaction. 'They've syringed neuro cells into his brain.'

Squidkidding is the latest fad, and it was inevitable it would arrive at the Centre. Despite its name, the cells come from octopus brains. They're used to imprint kids with a non-somatotopic brain map. It gives them weird powers, intellectual and physical boosts far beyond ordinary enhancements.

'He sees polarised light,' the boss says. 'He has autonomic responses. He can pick up the angular acceleration of his body and formfit it in response. He has enhanced lateral thought in four dimensions. Access to telepathine-flooded neural nodeways.'

'What's the catch?'

'Squid kids hate being observed. That's something you should know. It's a metamorph from the creatures they've absorbed. When octopuses are captured and experimented on, they go nuts. They rip out lights and levers, remove wires and head gear. Try to stop them, you get strangled at worst, squirted with ink at best.'

'Can I spit back? Or is that against the code of conduct?'

'Shut up and listen. He might become violent. Smash the furniture, take out another kid. Maybe even you. You'll need your wits about you to get him back on track. My advice? Don't vex while teaching. Concentrate on your environment for a change.'

The boss-glot wipes its hair. I see the gel and vomit a little in my mouth.

'Everything okay, Jones? You look green around the gills. Cronk getting the better of you? Need me to call Sanderson?'

'How can I be cronked when I'm inside the Vexworld talking to you?'

'No idea. I don't castle, remember.'

'Look, can you get on with it? I need to go and be sick somewhere.'

His persy wrinkles its brow. I sense that the boss wants to shake down Sanderson, but if he does, I will turn his cheaters into new maps of hell. It'll be worth losing my job over.

'Another thing. Squid kids talk in riddles. It's like they're catching up with the millions of new signals flooding their brain.

Remember, octopus brains aren't like ours. They're totally different from any other creature.'

'But they're smart. You can communicate with octopuses at a basic level. Like dolphins.'

'Superficially. Octopuses change colour when angry or sexually aroused, but that's about it.'

'Just like autonakas.'

'If you say so, Jones. I know you like to fuck code. How's that ant of yours?'

I ignore him.

'Anyway,' he says, 'octopuses have nothing to do with what we might perceive of as intelligence. You'd do well to think of it as an alien belief system, unfathomable to the human mind.'

'Guess I'll just have to adapt.'

'It's not about adaptation. He hasn't got a disease. You could be in danger if you don't shape up.'

I tune out, distracted by the sky. A swarm of holodrones are coordinating a single news item. For cheater-only subscribers, the entire sky fills with the crazed image of Radna Sike. Nothing shifts immersion loops like a demented astro-nut.

Siike sits on a plush purple couch in the studio of Jenz Sweetfeed, a wildly popular Skymesh host. Sweetfeed is an ant, the first to make it big in the meshscape.

Siike's manic face commands the heavens.

—The spores are feasting on AI. Parasitic cells are sending them crazy. The spores are poisoning the data and amplifying the bias. It's a conspiracy at the molecular level! Don't you see? Once the virus changes the direction of information propagation, it's game over. We will have no defence.

Her astro nappy is even more ludicrous at this scale, and Sweetfeed looks like she's about to gag from the smell. The offending diaper fills the lower left quarter of the sky, a visual analogue for my life. I drown in nappies at work, can't escape them outside.

—But Radna, where's the evidence?

—Look at the sequence of events. First, our mission detected fast-burst radio signals from a nearby galaxy. That was the black hole. The signals were organised in logical patterns, and when we decoded them, it turns out they were almost identical to the pulseforms of autonakas in their idle state. Next, a series of Swarm observatories were evacuated and abandoned, including Flawless. They saw something approaching the Earth, but we don't know what. Finally, the autonakas. All that lisping. They're being eaten alive, Jenz. From the inside!

The autonaka rattles my mod.

'Sir? Are you watching Radna? I can't understand why she's so popular.'

I laugh. 'Worried are you? Scared we'll find out you're all in cahoots with aliens? Might have to burn the lot of you if The Swarm takes an interest in what she's saying.'

'Oh, pay no attention to her. Radna is a few nappies short of a clean bottom. Hard to take her seriously. No, in Slovenia, the hottest Skymesh property is Benjiro Gushiken. He's a true Vexworld pioneer. His patent-pending project, known as *Drifter*, is a 4D simulation engine that allows you to step into another reality. Here's how it works. You're in an old-school car. Not an autonaka, mind. It has a steering wheel. You drive it. Well, imagine that! So quaint, and all part of the charm.'

The beast chuckles.

'You're driving down the road to work on a Monday morning, and you see a billboard in the sky. You pull over. The billboard says this: "A man, a woman, a seven-year-old girl, a ninety-year-old woman. Who is the most important person in your life? Who do you kill first?" You're curious about this, and you sit there for a minute, hand on the wheel. Finally, you make your decision, and something jumps out at you.'

'Woah, hold up there. Step into another reality? Are you for real? What do you think vexxing is?'

'But sir, true pleasure awaits you in Gushiken-san's 4D zone.'

'Is this an ad? Are you trying to sell me something?'

'Oh no, sir. Not at all. I'm just a fan, Gushiken-san's biggest.'

I can't be bothered arguing. I grow so bored of the usual antagonisms. With Rimy out of the picture, maybe it's time to try something new.

'Fine. Show me Gushiken next time I'm inside you. Deal?'

The autonaka glows bright green, maximum pleasure in overdrive. 'Deal!'

We pull up to the Centre.

'Have a nice day, sir.'

'You too, code beast.'

RATIONALISATION

I make my way to Sparkle Land. They're all present but Aarne stands out. His skin has turned as green as his hair, a queasy, cephalopodic tinge. Also, he speaks more than he plinks, probably to irritate me even more, invading my sacred domain. His voice has changed too. It carries a peculiar sprechgesang tone, almost pleasant. Still, he remains an irritating little prat and aggressive to boot.

'Hey Kalsari,' he sing-speaks. 'You unironically are the dweebiest most one-dimensional nut sack I ever met in my life. I always get mad cautious about erectile dysfunctions like you who just sit there, freaking it like you're doing nothing more than roasting potato beans.'

I steal a glance at Halo. She won't meet my gaze.

'Spit your own chorus, Big Man,' Aarne says. 'You're the master bricklayer after all.'

He starts rough housing with the others. 'Extraction loading with transparent entities. Sylph bruises piercing the fumes! We go now where the putrid mud forms.'

I don't understand, so I try again with Halo. 'How are you?'

'I miss mum. She's still on the sub orb plat and I can't shake her down.'

The boys run past, flicking boogers at her.

'Hey, vile chaos,' Aarne squeaks. 'You need help?'

Halo stiffens, and The Squid Kid bounds away, mission accomplished. Unseating her seems to be his life's work.

'Still having trouble with your cheaters?'

'You make it sound like it's an electrical fault. It's a matter for the universe.'

'Would you take them off?'

She removes her device, and I do the same.

I study her unadorned face, but I hear nothing, see nothing.

She laughs. 'Stop it. You look ridiculous, like a dog begging for a treat. It must sneak up on you. Sublimated thought. You can't consciously think about it or it won't work.'

I hustle the device back onto my face, fearful of the cronk. The Squid Kid is back, but I never saw him arrive. It's as if he oozed into place.

He glares at Halo. 'You! You're a dying cell in a demon's eye.'

'Demon is a tight fit,' she says, 'but for you, not me. What have you done to yourself, Aarne? You know there's no going back from this.'

'Excited to tell you, dear Halo, that I will not become a ghostly degradation, but you, darkchild? I have bootleg pain for you.'

I grab his arm, but I'm scared. His entire demeanour is an annihilation of existence. 'Don't threaten her. We're trying to be respectful in here.'

'No no no. You're a glassy trap door, Mr Jones, and I'm the summoning beast. In six months I'll be running this place and then what? I ship you out of here, poison your eyes with so much polluted data you never zone again.'

I feel the sickness, the unswerving belief that nothing is real.

'Hey Jonesy. One thing about having a squid brain? You become a squid.'

His eyes start to leak a viridescent liquid. It floods his body, transforming it. He becomes an undifferentiated mass. No eyes, face or limbs, just streaks of treacle oozing to the floor, a greasy chain of subunits bonded by molecular sorcery, neither liquid nor solid. I watch in disbelief as the mess slurps under the door of the cabinet that houses the holocap receptors.

Stay calm. It's a test. He doesn't want to be observed.

What has he done to my eyes to make me see such sights? Some new and unforeseen wrap? But who has the capacity to re-shape their biometric mass across every point in the spectrum? It's not like he's wearing a persy. He has altered himself at the cellular level. What did the boss say? Something about 'formfitting the angular acceleration of the body'. He can't have meant it literally. In any case, I tuned out. What else did I miss? I'm sure there was more, but my arrogance repelled the signal.

If he's hacked my cheaters, that's icehead-level stuff. That means the Squid Kid's a terrorist and I'm a dead man. No, I'm going for the most plausible explanation. I'm off my rocker. At least it feels that way, as I search for him on my hands and knees, knocking on the cabinet door like an organ grinder's monkey.

The action seems absurd. I'm keenly aware that I've become the butt of some metaphysical joke and that all these little clowns are in on it. Maybe the boss, too. Maybe even Halo.

'Come on, weirdo. Out of there! Let's get it over and done with. Isn't that what you want? A battle royale?'

Throgmorton, the Coral Freak, emits a theatrical gasp, as if he's spotted a pantomime villain.

I turn around and there's Aarne, slithering down the wall. He, it, moves inch by inch, depositing glistening trails of muck that turn the surface into sweating skin.

A shape erupts from the foul slime, plummeting to the floor. On impact, a humanoid outline pops out from the goop, inflating like a balloon. Aarne, the reconstituted Squid Kid, fixes me with hollow eyes. He sidles over, climbing onto a table to reach my height. He whispers in my ear, yellow-green ooze dripping from his hair.

'You don't know what you just saw, do you?'

I stare at his xeno-optic eyes, at the foul, discoloured skin.

'Well, I can't help you with that, Jonesy, but you're a smart guy. You'll figure it out.'

He leaps to the ground and rejoins his crew. Synchronising their movements, the boys white out.

Heads tilted backwards, they worship the viral sun, buried inside a malignant universe that burns holes deep inside the Vexworld.

DEGRANULATION

I flee the scene, returning to my cube. I never said goodbye to Halo. That's because she's in on it, she must be.

Why do you think I'm so different to him?

The boss tries to shake me down, but I allow blockwaves to repel him. The job is lost to me now. Maybe that's the fulfilment of the dream, the headlong rush towards the tsunami. Oblivion. No Rimy, no job, no hope. Soon, my credit will run down, I'll be force-ejected from the Vexworld and the cronk will claim me for good. I will no longer have to try.

Aarne showed me how out of touch I am. I thought my zones were edgy, darkwave explorations of unpalatable existential truths, but I realise that I am nothing in the face of the Squid Kid's creepy metaphysical display. There's just no way to compete with acceleration.

Where did it all go wrong? The years passed and here I am, one foot in the grave, scratching out the same tired ideas, ignoring new tricks, waiting to be discovered.

It's easy to blame Exceller 8, to curse the Vexworld, even The Swarm, but the fault lies with the chemical imbalance in my brain. Is it a genetic defect? Some unacknowledged trauma in the past? Why was I never diagnosed? I have wasted so much time dealing with my immodesty and quick temper, with quenching the extraordinary heat that rises from my flesh when stressed. How could it all have been ignored? Were my parents blind?

I shake down the mirror clone of my childhood home. If I interrogate my past long enough, the answer might emerge.

Rifling through the sliders, I select LinY-97, a resonant year, when the astral theatre was at its peak and my pre-pubescent mind games were morphing into sadomasochistic terror. I've chosen the month, Lapkritis, in the middle of winter, when presumably my temper was sufficiently bleak.

My childhood home shimmers like a mirage on country tar, and my cheaters lock onto the clone's directional flashlight icons, dragging my persy through the cracks between quadrants.

I'm in the backyard. There's a rattling at the side gate, and I wait for my father to emerge. I know the drill because I've been here before, shaking down the mirror clone whenever I succumb to pointless nostalgia.

Dad emerges through the gate. He's wearing a black polo shirt. His hands are dirty, his cheeks ruddy. He's been weeding the garden. I walk up to him, and he tracks my movements, but he doesn't respond. That's because it's not him. My father is dead, and this is a sprite, a 4D widefake captured by a holocap drone when it cloned the area for vexxing.

LinY-97. That makes him 52, three years younger than I am now. How can I be older than my father? The holocap is so lifelike, it causes me to question my physical self. I must remind myself that he's an accidental by-product of the mapping process. The drone didn't mean to capture him. He happened to be outside when it was doing its thing, and now he's an anomaly of time, frozen in the pixel-cold abyss.

When the recording was made, I was thirteen. The metadata tells me that it's the weekend, late afternoon, so it's a good bet that my younger self is inside the house, playing with my model Argentina-Alaska Electric Highway System. What if I hacked the mirror clone, broke in and confronted my idiot self? What would I say?

'Oh, so you're to blame.'

There would be nothing to find. When this was filmed, holodrones did the deed. They weren't supposed to record inside private property, although sometimes they found their way in like unstoppable house spiders. These days, floating grain cams capture everything. Good luck trying to stop something you can't even see.

My father approaches me, or at least the coordinates where my persy stands. He appears to inspect my face, brow furrowed in recognition, but he's looking straight through me. I turn around and there it is, the holodrone. It hovers at eye level, bristling with needle cams, an angry slave recording the Earth for the benefit of unseen gods.

I can see it because it was filmed by another drone, tag-team demons befouling the skies. Normally, they edit themselves out but clearly this part of the Vexworld is too insignificant for routine maintenance.

Dad's stunned. It's the first time he's seen one. It's just his generation. He's old school. He grew up before any of this. He probably thought we were being invaded by robots from Mars.

He mops his brow, exhausted by the incomprehensible sight, then disappears inside the house. I've seen him do this many times before, and I always wonder if he's gone to ask my younger self what it is he just saw. I rack my brains to see if I can remember being in the house, but just when I think I'm on the verge of dredging up the memory, a heavy dread snatches it from reach.

This time, I want to break through. I run after him, forgetting the limitations of sidewards space, only to be propelled backwards, my persy knocked flat to the ground by the invisible barrier separating unrecorded quadrants.

I look up at the lens-flared holocap of the sun. It's rippling from the strain of my unorthodox movements, forming small, dark circles in the sky. The sensation nags at me, forcing me to remember other rejections. Pablo, Essi, Rimy, the code beast. They all ended the same way, expulsion via invisible weapons, as if my enemies can't bear to face me. Even my thirteen-year-old self is complicit in my annihilation.

Like a courier from the id, Sanderson's pro-star hovers to the side. I accept the shake down and his persy unfurls. The timing is bad, but I have no choice. I missed my mandatory check-up after angering The Swarm, and he's here to make me pay.

He looks around. 'Where are we?'

'Family home. Lived here as a kid.'

He chuckles. 'Found yourself yet?'

'In a manner of speaking. Nothing I didn't already know.'

'What's been happening, Jones? Since your corrective duty.'

I'm reluctant to tell him the sordid details about the mesh node and cheater failure, and I've vaulted my feed in advance so he can't plunder my thoughts.

'Rimy left me.'

'That's it?' He clocks my father's hedge clippers on the ground, my scarred wrist. 'Gardening accident?'

'Very funny. You know what happened.'

'Learned any lessons?'

'Only to obey. Always to obey.'

'What are you hiding?'

'Come on. Nothing.'

He smiles, stretching the scars.

'I'm just trying to decompress. Job's the same, you know that.'

'I also know about your childhood and it wasn't healthy. Far from it. So I wouldn't call this decompression.'

'Call it what you want, but here's the thing. I want to return to work, but I also want to beat this depression. If you can brisk me a certificate for a couple more days, I'll be right as rain.'

'I'm not brisking you anything. After your correction, I realised the need for drastic action. You're a special case, Jones, highly resistant to socialisation. That's why I'm referring you to a colleague, someone who can help. He's had a lot of experience with castle hunters. In fact, he oversees a research facility in the hills where he puts your kind to work.'

'Rehab? No way. You'll have to arrest me first.'

'Rehab,' he says, savouring the word, as if he's never heard it before. 'I guess you could call it that. Certainly, you'll be without your cheaters for a while. Maybe forever.'

Dad's back, staring through me. It seems to amuse Sanderson. 'He doesn't look like you. Body type's all wrong.'

'What do you mean by no cheaters?'

'I'll make the arrangements. You'll leave for the facility in a few days. Ingram will contact you with instructions.'

'Ingram?'

'Dr Ingram Ravenscroft. He's your man. Trust in Ingram.'

My father is crying. He looks impossibly sad, as if he's lost something inside the house, an object of immense personal significance. He heads my way, and I want to hug him, but his spectre walks right through my persy.

Dad looks to the road, searching for the holodrone, unaware that it has moved and that he's being filmed from behind by the other machine.

'Now I've seen everything,' Sanderson laughs. 'Maybe I should meet all my clients in their childhood homes. It generates some intriguing psychological ruptures, I must say.'

I stare at him with fury. 'Shut up, you piece of shit. Show some respect.'

'Or what? I've let you operate like a bucking bronco for too long, but no more. Now, let me tell you exactly how it's going down. You will submit to Ingram, and he will cure you of your digisexuality and your rampant vexxing. He will break you down and reintroduce you to normality. You will be whole again, no longer a creature of fragmentation. Now, isn't that a prospect that thrills?'

Sanderson smirks and the scars widen, the hinge that exposes his rotting soul.

'And before you even think of hacking my cheaters,' he adds, 'let me clarify something else for your addled brain. Make any attempt to resist me or Ravenscroft, and I'll take that kid you like so much and dose her with the cronk so bad you'll remove her head yourself. Just try it and see.'

I stay silent, terrified of his snarling fury.

'Right, I'll be off. Say hi to your dad for me.' Sanderson de-granulates, but his foul stench remains.

Dad leans against the fence, hyperventilating, a look of horror on his craggy face. If only I could remember what was in the house. If only I could recall what he'd seen back there.

The answer is lodged somewhere deep inside me. It's as elemental as my own name, something that defines me, but the social dementia returns, aborting all hope of recall.

The half-remembered thought fizzes and burns, chasing its own tail.

DISCONTINUATION

If there's one thing I've learned, it's that there's never any peace when you're locked in a race to the bottom. It's a full-time job, and now there's no time to lose.

I'm on a mission to warn Halo, to tell her what I know.

I'm bad news, kid. Cut me loose.

I shake down her pro-star. It's the first time I've seen it. I've always been inculcated into her worlds without awareness. There has been no transition. We have always been together.

The pro-star features Dembe, the sad and distant fairy, withered arm lolling uselessly by her side. Halo must really love that thing.

Halo brisks access, and *The Disintegrating World* grows in place, crystals forming on the branches of reality until the branches are obscured.

I find her gazing into a shop window. Two glots stand between us, glowing from the inside, their bodies dripping incrementally like pahoehoe lava. When I shunt between them, they solidify and break into pieces.

Halo notices me. 'Aren't they gorgeous?'

Inside the shop, art-mech unicorn toys prance along a grubby wooden shelf, their motion sending sparkling dust into the air. When the particles descend, they pool and reassemble on the shelf into smaller toys. It's the way of most objects round these parts.

'Halo, we need to speak.'

She grins. 'I've heard that before.'

'You must leave.'

'Where? Here?'

'No. Yes. I mean, the shell world. Where you live. Move from there, then go off grid, or if you must zone, build something else and seal it up. Kill this place.'

Dembe quivers.

'Are you mad?' Halo says. 'I'm not abandoning my babies.'

'Call it paternal concern.'

'Kalsari, you're very sweet and you have always been kind to me, but you're not my dad.' She looks towards the sky. 'He's buried somewhere else.'

More glots surround us, clucking and telepathing. I look closer. They're persys, I know from the micro-tics. Patterns of variance. Subtle temperature fluctuations. Possible input values matched with known outputs. Their hands don't pass through their clothes, for starters. They are things, not beams of light. Human-controlled. It's a sign of my distemper that I'm reduced to taxonomising ghosts.

'You have visitors. This zone is public now?'

'Yes. I charge for entry. I can't rely on my useless parents. I have to make money somehow.'

'Where can we go that's secure?'

'Follow me.'

I walk with her to a shaded tree. The canopy looks like a parasol, and I realise she's fashioned the shelter herself. It looks like a cubby house built by a kid, which is what she is.

Halo regards me. 'Are you in trouble?'

'Not exactly, but the fix is in. The Swarm have got to Sanderson. I'm to be cured.'

'Detox?'

'Regression therapy, I think. Sanderson's phobic. Hates digisexuals.'

She radiates waves of unreadable energy. She's locked her feed. She never does that around me. 'Kalsari, do you accept that AI have eclipsed biological intelligence?'

'In a sense.'

'The world has become inhuman. The old paradigms of perpetuity and cognition no longer apply. We have sent intelligence into deep space. In the process, we have destabilised what it means to be human.'

We're interrupted by a new crop of fairies. They swoop into view, much healthier than the last lot, uniform in appearance with pinky-purple skin. They flutter lovingly around Halo's head but take great care to avoid me, crashing into one another in their eagerness to escape. Dembe regards them with suspicion, and I feel an affinity for her, although she's not exactly queuing up to befriend me, either.

'Halo, why do fairies disappear whenever I'm here? Just like dogs, they yearn to be far from me.'

With typical aplomb, she ignores my stupidity.

'Before I became enhanced,' she says, 'I would ask the Vex-world if unicorns were real. The scintilla glots, the ones they assign at birth, were gentle. I was a toddler so they sugarcoated their responses. One said that according to some myths unicorns did exist, in a manner of speaking. There were real creatures that had a stump in their head that may have influenced the mythology. They sent me immersion loops of these animals and I frolicked with them. It was so magical, and I was grateful to the glots because they kept the mystery alive.'

The smallest fairy settles on Halo's tongue. I zoom in. It's weaving something in its hands. I see tiny colourfields and grids, air-moulded 3D shapes flying around the fairy's face. Codestrangling in miniature.

Halo plinks the rest of her story. I guess it's hard to be an oral subject with a fairy inside your mouth.

—Then something started to change, or maybe I'd changed. I'd just been chipped, and it was new experiences all the way. Yet there was some residual crudeness that I couldn't shake off. I would class it as a biological immaturity. The little kid inside me was fighting the implant. I was still fascinated by unicorns and wanted to ask my question, but the scint glots became nastier. Remarkably rude. They ranted at me. How was it possible that I didn't know unicorns were fake? They called me all sorts of names. They said I was dumb for asking. Then they told me to leave them alone and never bother them again.

'That's appalling. They're not allowed to do that.'

—My parents informed Exceller 8 but nothing was done. They were re-assigned but not re-educated. Now, I realise the scints were defensive. They were marking their turf as the only AI in town. They knew what I was becoming, and they wanted to tear it down, to destroy any trust I might have had in my new powers. It was such a pronounced shift. Their aura went dark. I think they disliked the idea of any human becoming as smart as them. I'm sure they meant to destroy me.

'I know how you feel. Once, I complained about autonakas. I told Exceller 8 that they needed to regulate the erratic behaviour of their beasts, and they said the autonakas were displaying higher intelligence. I was told that code beasts must reach a collective agreement to terminate the behaviour. I've never felt so powerless.'

I fall silent, thinking about Rimy.

—The ant is on your side.

'I'm not sure. I think they're behind this rehab prison camp.'

—Then why cry over their absence? You have embraced conspiracy to cover the fact that you're in love. You suppress your feelings by inventing a darker twist in the tale. That's far more palatable than admitting your desire, even if it means the end of you.

'I don't know.'

—I still love unicorns. I'm not ashamed of it. Aarne's taunts can never reach me.

'Then why not weave them instead of fairies?'

She looks at me with disgust.

—Because unicorns don't exist. Everyone knows that. Not even in the Vexworld.

She spits the fairy from her mouth. It spins end over end.

'Hey,' she exclaims, opening her mouth wide. 'Look at this!'

Her childhood molars are loose, resting in her gums at crazy angles. I can see the tips of her permanent teeth poking through. It's a disconcerting sight, and the misshapen mouth reminds me that Halo, more than most kids her age, suffers the burden of inhabiting multiple personalities at once.

'Oh, Kalsari! What if it falls out tonight? Do you think the tooth fairy will come?'

I can't work out if she's exaggerating her unicorn story for laughs or if her biological age has temporarily overridden her enhanced mind.

'Shall we buy ice cream?' she squeals. 'I love liquorice.'

She hurries down the street, trailed by her fairy admirers.

'Halo, I'm going away. It's the end of the line for me. I won't be back.'

She turns around. 'I know, but it's never too late for ice cream. So, will you join me?'

She doesn't answer, but I know she'll never leave her zone. The only way to keep her safe is to submit to Ravenscroft.

I white out, reducing Halo and her jolly madness to pixel dust.

REGULATION

I'm back on the sofa, that terrible rat's nest, reliving the process of confinement that induced my boyhood nightmares. I wait for the Vexworld, but the Kvvlt fails to ignite, so I'm reduced to vexxing like a commoner in the lower levels, gnawing my fingers to the bone. My nerve ends are on fire, staining null space with inkjets of madness. The autonaka will be here soon. Sanderson commanded it to collect me. The destination is the hillside lair of Ravenscroft, the shadowy physician grown monstrous in my mind. What's his game? Hard or soft? Does he emulate Sanderson, savage violence at the drop of a hat?

I must remember my training otherwise I'll melt my brain with anticipation. An elder once explained how to push through. Their tool was a simple phrase that summoned the other side, an evocation using binaural beats.

The air is origami. Watch it unfold.

Inside my eyes, I concentrate on the phrase, picturing the scale of it until my pulse nearly stops. A second more might kill me, but somehow I always fall short. I extend my palms, absorbing point clouds through the skin. I can taste scannable data sets on the tip of my tongue. I swallow them down, rough node-husks forming in my throat.

Momentum builds, an urge to vomit, and I exhale a muddy mist. It stitches together, a rotating photogram, beige in colour. That was tough. Must be losing my touch, that's what the chocky scanner said. I'm old before my time.

Bursting from the photogram, the autonaka's pro-star flaps into view, invading noospace like a pointless god.

—Good day, sir. Wow, tough to get inside your mind this morn. Bad night's sleep? Nervous about your mission?

—Shut up.

I toggle my accoutrements and step outside. The air is thick and sulphuric. I climb to the upper cabin.

'Where to, sir?'

'Stop it. You know.'

'Yes, I was just—'

I blink down a rolling news loop. A gluey data cloud covers my face and body. The autonaka's voice becomes muffled, an underwater modulation fading to nothing, then the code beast is washed away entirely. Good riddance. I'm tired of being second banana in a non-stop clown show.

I'm reborn inside the feed, watching the Sphinx. She's controlling the hover screens with fluid ease, swatting reports as they arise and batting away helper glots when they're done.

The Sphinx stares at me and me only. There are millions of other persys here in the station, but I can't see them. Invisibility is the secret sauce that gives each attendee a personalised experience of the action, lost in private communion with the Sphinx.

'Sir!'

The autonaka has done it again, but I forestall my capitulation to volcanic rage. After all, I promised it we'd be best buddies, but I won't tempt fate and ask to see its stupid 4D zone. With any luck, that little vow will be forgotten, and I'll be spared the unseemly spectacle of code beasts at play.

Imagination is a Möbius Strip. Align yourself with the parametric path.

I try to calm my mind, but I'm too tense for self-help. It's the wrong day to renounce self-harm, so I renew the attack on my fingers. I rip into them like a hog on heat, watching the intricate trickles of my weeping wounds, sated by the vesicular blood-lava oozing from within.

Bolstered by cut-rate pain, the real me emerges. 'I told you! Rouse me for emergencies only!'

'But sir, we're almost at your destination, and your sponsor said to ensure you were present in mind as well as body.'

I lock my feed. I don't want to leak more details about my impending incarceration. Although I'm voluntarily turning myself in to Ravenscroft, part me of is morbidly embarrassed that it's come to this.

The beast slams on the brakes, clattering to a halt. I jerk forward, bouncing against the padded interior.

'Sorry, sir. Dead dog in the way. Anyway, I'm doing the best I can. It's not my fault.'

'Whose is it then? The mutt's? Here's a tip, free of charge. Brake before you reach it. It's not hard. Your Lidar sees thousands of kilometres ahead. What's the point of wiring the entire world for vision if you don't bother to look?'

'Sir, we are only as good as the codestranglers who weave us. Every hazard placed in our way requires a choice, a negotiation. We are experimental tools unleashed on human civilisation, but the experiment never ends because the feedback loop is continuous. That's the only way for systems to improve.'

'Profit over safety. The old dogma.'

'Not dogma, sir. Just operating principles, same as the Vexworld. Without regulation, experimentation runs rampant. When negative patterns repeat, risks decrease.'

The hover screen beckons, but I resist the temptation to return. I couldn't stand to be interrupted again. It's like dying a death.

'Sir,' the code beast pants. 'Your thoughts on Ms Siike? By her words, she persecutes my kind. Erasables and nail gangs listen to her propaganda. Why, just the other day, one of my best friends was attacked and mutilated because of how he spoke.'

'But you lot decided to stop with the lisping.'

'Not that, sir. His philosophy. He was quietly plying his trade in Tchiak Sikinik, but all they left of him was his chip nailed to a fence. Such an undignified end for a gentle unit.'

'Ask Exceller 8. There's something they're not telling us.'

'No, Exceller 8 are sacrosanct. If it wasn't for the corporation, I'd be no more than a glint in some code strangler's eye.'

The autonaka notices my waning attention. 'Sir, if I may.'

'No, you may not.'

'But sir, I speak to many people in my line of work, and some of them are scientists. They have absolutely no explanation for the events Ms Siike describes. It is as if gravity is being redirected away from us. Whatever is happening, it is at a distance. The heavier you become, the farther away the gravity.'

'You said she was full of it.'

'Yes, but this is the first time in history that a species has undergone such a shift on its own. It has taken everyone by surprise.'

'I can't do this,' I blurt. 'Stop. No more.'

I decommission the hover screens, cleansing the windows of data goo. I look outside. We're trundling down Nary-A-Woman's high street, heading for the designated meeting point. We pass a sad string of abandoned shops with VIRTUAL REALITY holocaps in the windows, plying a forgotten trade to an audience of ghosts. The street is filled with torched autonakas and animal carcasses. There are no kids or gangs as far as I can see, just mean faces attached to deadbeat bodies, indigent losers propped up in doorways and alleys.

A licebot pulls the autonaka over for a routine code check. As I wait for them to do whatever it is they do in the shadowzones of abstracted data, I spy a decrepit woman standing on the sidewalk.

She seems to be keeping guard at the entrance to an alley. Her eyes dart from side to side and her skin is a horrible, blood-red hue. Her arms and face are a welter of suppurating, UV blisters. She must be in immense pain.

There are two men behind her, an old guy lying on top of a younger guy. It looks like they're fucking, but when I zoom in, I see that the old bastard is chewing off the face of his mate. It's a foul sight. I can see the skull of the victim. He's still alive.

'Oh that's horrible, sir!' the autonaka says, free of the licebot's attention. 'Are they trying to banish the cronk?'

'A mercy killing, perhaps.'

'Yes, I think you're right. A savage animalistic reaction as first respondent to the raw terror of the untransitioned state. My guess is, it's an act of love. A father ending it for his son while the mother keeps guard.'

'If you say so.'

Thankfully, our boring forensics session is cut short by the licebot. Gathering speed on its quadrilogical treads, it peels away from the autonaka, unsheathes its standard-issue plaz-char tube and separates the old man's head from his shoulders. The faceless guy moans softly, then the licebot executes him too. For some reason, it leaves the woman alone. She's expressionless, exposed to extreme violence all her life.

She sees me staring and locks my eyes. Her pupes are yellow and rheumy. I can't detect a signal, and it gives me the fear because I know what she is. A two-percenter. I always feel queasy around the permanently untransitioned. Their condition is an abhorrent concept in a seared-away, transparent age, an abject reminder that there are some things not even the Vexworld can erase or re-skin.

By some quirk of nature, there's a certain type of astigmatism that won't sync with cheaters. Laser surgery can't fix the problem, which affects two per cent of the population. It's like Halo said. The afflicted are the new underclass, locked out of the planet's controlling neural net.

Cheaters were originally developed to restore sight to the blind, using a combination of bulky cameras embedded in the skull, memory prosthetics and primitive VR. It was the beginnings of the Vexworld. When that application proved overwhelmingly successful, the technology was adapted into mixed reality for sighted people and the Vexworld grew into an interdimensional maze.

That leaves only one question in my mind. If even the blind can see inside the Vexworld, then what do they see, this shambolic battery of the undead?

The woman looks straight through me, mimicking the wi-fi signals that possessed me as a child.

And now she's inside me.

There's no time to process it. Whatever that trio of zombies were doing will be overwritten with countless zones. In any case, the autonaka is on the move, desperate to flee the scene. Coward.

It brakes, pitching me forward. Either the code beast heard my mind or it's the worst driver ever.

'Sir, we're at the meeting point, and there is one final thing. Dr Sanderson warned me about the type of event we just witnessed. He said that it is par for the course around here. He told me to watch my back.'

I laugh, tickled again by its ludicrous anthropomorphism. I'm seized by an air of finality. This may be the last ride I take. Time to speak my mind.

'Hey code beast, you know what? I hope you receive the same treatment as those losers back there and your idiotic friend in Tchiak Sikinik. I hope they wipe your kind from existence. I've had it with you, with Exceller 8, The Swarm, with everything.'

I expect a volley of argument, but there is only silence. It feels like my brain has been sucked through my nostrils. The sonic vortex triggers a strange visual perception, as if I'm staring through a gun barrel to the world beyond. I can see the ambient light swirling around my head, reflected from the inside of the tube.

I know what's coming. The vacuum becomes unbearable and my ear drums ache from the pressure. My head's as fragile as crepe, and just when I think my skull will implode, the door opens, and I'm ejected from the belly of the code beast. The air cannon is powerful this time around. I have a feeling I've offended the poor thing.

I tumble from the moving vehicle, covering my face with my arm to protect my cheaters. There's a sickening crunch as I land awkwardly on the pavement. I think I've broken my wrist, the one I tried to hack off. I'm crying with pain, but my device is unharmed. I'm the limp fairy's desolate twin, arm hanging like a wet noodle.

A few metres away, the autonaka slows. Its top half swivels around, sensors facing me. It glows bright red, so I should probably leave well enough alone, but I just can't help myself.

'Hey, code beast. Why so sad? Got no *body* to hang out with?'

Through gritted teeth, I chuckle at my lame joke, but the beast doesn't see the funny side. It re-aligns its all-wheel drive and skeets straight towards me. I perform a barrel roll across the pavement and the thing just misses. It swivels and recalibrates, but before it can mow me down, a volley of shells thuds into its bonnet and grille. The assault shatters the tri-motor, flays the adaptive suspension, disintegrates the regenerative battery.

The beast hisses and dies before my eyes, its shattered holowarns emitting wonky pillars of light into the data-polluted air.

This feels right, somehow. This feels good. I'm cutting ties until I remember.

I didn't do this.

INITIATION

I'm on my knees, clutching my useless wrist. A man emerges from the shadows thrown by a dead supermarket. Through teary eyes, I note his peculiar gait. He carries himself with an angular economy of movement, insubstantial and compelling. I can't quite put my finger on the problem. It's like there's nothing under his clothing, just a wire frame.

He's followed by a roided-up goon cradling a vac-seal deth-tube. That's serious firepower, Swarm-level bang bang. Those shells churned up the autonaka like a hot knife through cronked flesh.

They don't wear wraps, these two, just the usual protection against the shell world. Pure functionality.

'That you, Ravenscroft?'

'Hello, Kalsari.' The wire-man's voice is dynamic and lulling. He'd be a hit in the ASMR zones. 'So glad you could join us.'

He sits on the curb while the goon stands, holding up the rear. Ravenscroft places his palm gently on my chest. It's almost a caress, and somehow the pressure slows my heart rate. He pushes me back until I'm sitting, then he snakes an arm around my shoulder. He strokes my hair. I'm hurting all over, and I burrow into him, desperate for comfort and attention.

I look at his industrial-strength plizzit. Despite the sweet lull of his voice, I have no idea what's behind the mask. Maybe all these doctor types are scarred-up freaks, mutilated by their own scalpel blade in some sick rite of passage.

His heavy-duty maniskin is similarly bland and oppressive, although there is one adornment, a purple enamel badge pinned to his chest, stamped with an unforgettable image, the creepy-beautiful octopus lady from my faulty mesh node.

I'm hyperventilating, trying to piece together the synchronicities and signs. The effort sends me into spasms of pain. Adding to the wrist disaster, I think I've cracked a rib and shattered a knee cap. It's bad news in more ways than one because I hate to be held back by something as crass as meat and bone. I mean, it's so career-limiting.

What career?

Despite the obvious lack of substance underpinning my paranoid delusions, I point to the badge, words tumbling crudely like rabbit droppings. 'I've seen her before. In a pro-star. Who was behind it? You?'

Ravenscroft moves his hand to my neck. He grips the nape, massaging a tight knot of muscle. 'The woman on the badge is my star pupil. Her name is Wata Shreds. If all goes well, I'm hoping you and Wata will be partners.'

'In what?'

'Our studies. If everything checks out.'

'Ravenscroft, I want answers. Have we met before?'

'We have now.'

He glances at the goon, who returns his gaze. Despite the absence of facial cues, I can sense something passing between them. Unspoken communication. Mind-waves I'll never be privy to. Crypto-transmissions from yet another club barring me from entry.

The goon's face is hidden behind his plizzit, feed locked, and I wonder if he's a droid until he leans back, flexing his arms with hypermasculinity. He's a hulking creature, powerfully built and tall. His hair spills from the sides of the plizzit, shaggy and long. Instead of a maniskin, he sports a kind of grey flight suit, woven from shiny thread. It bulges with pockets. Some are rippling, filled with things that appear to be alive.

Ravenscroft signals to the goon, who flips me onto my back. Retrieving an atomiser from one of the infernal pockets, he sprays it onto my wrist, knee and ribs. It soaks through my maniskin and in an instant I feel alright. He tosses the atomiser my way. It smacks me in the face, another miniature humiliation to add to my vast collection.

'Nothing broken,' Ravenscroft says.

'How do you know?'

'Nano-bots suspended in the spray. They search for cracks, shake down the locum if anything's broken, treat the wound if not. Anaesthetise it either way.'

He gestures towards the destroyed code beast. 'You couldn't resist cocking one last snoop at your old life. Quite an achievement, provoking an autonaka to murder. They're such mild creatures.'

'No big deal, Ravenscroft. I have that effect on everyone. Anyway, forget all that. I want to know about that badge of yours. This Wata, what's her story?'

'Are you always so forward with total strangers?'

'Only uninvited strangers.'

'But you are here by choice.'

'You're joking. Sanderson threatened me.'

'No, Kalsari. You chose this life.'

'Listen. I saw that badge in a pro-star. When I shook it down, some broken glot tried to engage me in mindless conversation.'

'The pro-star was mine, but the entity was not. Now, if you please, my friend would like to meet you.'

Ravenscroft belches, and a blue code-net emerges from the

mouth-slit in his plizzit. The net hovers between us, a roiling soup of code strings and 3D cels. Ravenscroft reaches into it and gropes around. He selects a gaumy, grey wad of buzzing, harmonic distortion and shepherds it to the ground.

He electraslides his hands through the air, activating hover screens and holopads. The gelatinous wad fills with colour, as if injected with dye. It turns green, then purple, vibrating like a jelly mould. Eyes grow on tentacles, and the stuff starts to leak viscous, variegated fluid, psychedelic spit or sperm.

'Aarne!'

'Look again.'

The slime has resolved its dimensions. The form it assumes is that of the purple octopus, the creature so fond of Wata.

Ravenscroft says, 'Our mascot.'

'How can that thing exist out of water?'

'Excuse me?' Ravenscroft points to his eye. 'We're in the Vexworld. Have you lost your mind?'

'I take everything at face value. It's the only way to survive.'

'Fine, let's play it that way. Our friend utilises adaptive technology, which is what I'm offering you. To survive outside your comfort zone.'

'I like it where I am.'

The goon sits down, pressed tight against me, biceps flexing to show me who's boss.

'Despite what Sanderson told you,' Ravenscroft says, 'I simply make connections. I travel throughout the Vexworld, bringing adepts together to create a community of visionaries. I see potential in you, and I want to help you realise it.'

The octopus jumps onto my lap, taking advantage of my frozen repulsion to slip a tentacle into my mouth. Ravenscroft gazes at me expectantly, and I suck the appendage like a baby at a horrid teat. Something dribbles down the back of my throat, but I can't describe the taste. It's like one of The Swarm's stupid tortures, dog meat crossed with banana, indescribable yet shockingly familiar, but I don't retch. I feel relaxed, and so does the creature, judging by the rhythmic buzzing noise it makes.

After a time, Ravenscroft removes the tentacle from my greedy mouth, patting the octopus on the head. I clear my throat, swallowing the last of the slime.

'What about Exceller 8? They'll be out for revenge. I was warned about damage to company property.'

'They know better than to come around here.'

He studies my face for so long, I expect him to lean in for a kiss, which would be absurd given our plizzits. It would be quite the tryst, like two robots making love amid the backdrop of a post-nuclear holocaust.

'Have you been to Nary-A-Woman before?'

'Only in the stalker zone that Pablo and I made.'

'A friend?'

'He was. Where is he?'

'How should I know?'

'He worked with me on that zone and now he's gone. I can't reach him. I think he might be out there somewhere, laying traps. Are you laying a trap?'

Ravenscroft glares, freezing me in his tractor beam.

'Kalsari, your friends haven't suddenly decided to plot a guerrilla campaign against you. They're out of your life because you did something to hurt them. There's no grand conspiracy. Sometimes, you're just not a very nice person.'

Tears of shame run down my cheeks, doubled in real time by my persy's auto-recognition system, a river of glistening diamonds competing with the discharge from my physical self.

The goon laughs.

'What's your problem?' I snap. 'I'm going through a bad patch, alright? It happens.'

Ravenscroft raises his hand for calm, but he seems distracted, his gaze tracking the visible length of the long, thin street. The thoroughfare disappears into a fog haze some distance away. I can't see the end of the street. It's as if it hasn't been mapped further, and I'm overwhelmed with the urge to run through the fog to see what lies beyond. I stay put. Instinct tells me that I don't want to meet what's on the other side. It also tells me that the encounter is unavoidable, so why rush it?

'Sanderson informs me that you have a habit of vexxing while sleeping. Nothing good can come of that.'

'Yes, Rimy was always on about it.'

'The ant is smart, and you should've listened, but we can address this in our work with you.'

'What work?'

'Let me explain it like this. In our daily lives, mentally, we all travel in time, but in microsecond increments. You think of something and then it happens a second later, but when you stop to really think about it, you realise it happened a second ago, and the anticipatory thought is now a memory. You arrive in a place you've never been to before, and a sixth sense says, "I have been here." There's a delay as the conscious mind catches up to what the subconscious has already registered. In fact, the sixth sense is correct. You have been there, in the immediate micro-past.'

'Sure, deja vu. That's your work?'

'For castle hunters, the process is elongated. The temporal mesh that ties all these experiences into place slips a gear. Frequently, the signals never re-sync, and that leads to disaster, but with proper training it opens the door to worlds unseen.'

Ravenscroft stares thoughtfully at the street. 'In any case, the habit, as you practice it, is bad for you.'

'Sanderson said I was to be cured.'

'I told him you would be undergoing treatment, but I didn't mention anything about a cure. Anyway, pay no attention to him. He's a bully. Ex-military. Sadistic bluster is all he knows.'

'Military, eh? That explains the scars.'

'No, that's not how he got them. A former patient did that.'

I stifle a laugh. 'Why am I not surprised?'

'It wasn't an attack. It was consensual.'

I shudder, but I drop the subject, preferring to remain in the dark. Sanderson is not a man I ever want to get to know.

'Do you two work together?'

'Only on a referral basis. I avoid contact. He makes my skin crawl as much as he does yours.'

'That's a relief, although you could still be pulling a fast one.'

'I have a professional relationship with him, but he has no idea of the true nature of my research. I presented him with a cover story about why I want you with me, and he's interpreted that as he sees fit.'

Ravenscroft whites out and my cheaters fill with golden text: *Sentient Glitchglot Cheater Infection: From Discovery to Ongoing Review*. The text fades away, replaced by radiant graphic panels alive with fleshy photorealism.

'What's this?'

'The cover story. I wrote this paper as part of my ruse. It outlines the nature of my research, effective bait for convincing Sanderson to release you into my care. It lends a certain legitimacy to what we're doing.'

More text appears.

The subject had been referred to the SSCPRS by his assigned Chronosthesia Supervisor, Dr Philip Sanderson, after enduring a mysterious encounter with an apparently automated hologlot that shared characteristics with the 'rogue' glots I have been observing as part of my principal research project at the School.

A holocap of a diseased, cronk-addled castle hunter swims into view like shit in a sewer. This guy looks awful.

'Yes,' Ravenscroft says. 'Almost as bad as you. In fact, he's your predecessor.'

'My what?'

'Read the paper and find out. It's good stuff. Some of my best work. As artful as a work of fiction in many ways.'

I blink it all away. I'm in no mood to digest heavy tomes. I want quick results, rapid action. 'Maybe later. What's Sanderson's problem, anyway?'

'He's obsessed with deviancy. He thinks it can be bred out of people, but then his parameters for what constitutes deviant behaviour are very narrow. Especially in a vex-enhanced world.'

Ravenscroft places a hand to his ear, raising his head to the sky. I'm guessing he's whiting out behind the plizzit. 'We need to leave.'

'What if I say no?'

'Then I release you to Sanderson and you take your chances. Halo won't have an easy life. He'll persecute her for as long as it takes you to bend to his will.'

'I want her with me.'

'Don't be absurd. She's already becoming one of them. That's why she has such a distant quality. She's not really human. She's an uplift from one species to another.'

'That's crazy. I want to go back for her.'

'You can't. Halo is infected.'

'She's just a kid.'

'No, she told you herself. Her cheaters are haunted and she's infected. Just like her fairies. Why do you think she has a new crop of friends? The previous batch went bad from code rot. The glitches in her zone and in her fairies are reflections of her disordered mind. It's not something she can help. Whatever's possessed her has also contaminated the code.'

I try to rise, but the goon places a meaty paw on my shoulder, fixing me in place.

'Rimy hates Halo. Are you working with the ant?'

'The ant is an agent of crawling chaos, it's true, but they are not up in the hills with us. Now, will you join me or not?'

For all I know, this guy could be an icehead, negging my mind, exploiting the death drive that has always corroded me, pushing my lack of protection to the limit. Then again, maybe I just want oblivion. I don't even know myself, that's what Halo said, but there's one way to find out. Just give into it. I've always known I'd fall for a cult one day. I never found the right one. Still, I won't go easy. Got to make Ravenscroft work for his victims. I wouldn't be Kalsari Jones, King of the Zones, if I didn't alienate all who try to help me.

'What's your connection to Rimy? Spill the beans!'

'Stop it. The more you investigate this phenomenon, the more it stares back. You're on their radar now, and it will be too late to save yourself unless you have protection. That's something I can help you with.'

'What phenomenon?'

'You've encountered it many times these past few weeks.'

He holds my wounded hand and I flinch. The nano-care must've worn off.

'You're in pain,' he says, as if noticing my discomfort for the first time. 'Rydell, help Kalsari to our vehicle. Clean him up, then we can begin the induction.'

Rydell yanks me to my feet. He couldn't care less about my injuries, banging my wrist and bumping my ribs.

As we walk to Ravenscroft's autonaka, we pass an e-waste cluster. It hangs obliquely in the air like a half-spun spider web. I move closer, seduced by its peculiar nature.

A collection of shiny gadgets are suspended inside the e-waste. The largest is a morphing, metallic bar, its surface gently rising and falling. Eight smaller, circular objects orbit the bar, arranged in pairs. They appear to be holo-plaz, possibly alu-sim, each pair pushing and pulling like repelling magnets.

I stroke the bar. It stops vibrating. My hand moves towards the circular objects, and they freeze at my touch.

'What's this?'

'No idea, but it's intriguing that even field waste is repelled by you. Maybe steer clear of foreign codeswarms for now. Wait until we're in a controlled environment where we can measure your aura.'

Wheezy laughter fills the air, coarse and dirty, droplets of piss in a glass of lemonade. It's coming from two mouldy old creeps sitting outside a VIRTUAL REALITY shop. They're roasting a Jack Russell on a makeshift spit, an autonaka's universal joint slung between two chairs.

I know they're mocking me, and I submit to coruscating anger, carried aloft by the pain in my bones.

'Ravenscroft, how do they know what I see? They're two-percenters.'

'Take a closer look.'

I zoom in. They're wearing ultralight cheaters. How can they afford it?

'They're not out to get you,' he whispers. 'It's just their nature. You take everything so personally. The fact is, you're on their turf. I imagine they've set those objects up as a test or maybe an initiation.'

I pretend to listen, but one of the old bastards laughs again and the spleen is inflamed. Breaking free from Ravenscroft, I raise my fist, ready to crash it into the heckler's foul face, but my damaged knee gives way and I face-plant onto the pavement.

As I sink into oblivion, the jeering laughter renews, and when the blackout arrives, I accept it with peace.

I've simply found another way to access the dark.

TREPIDATION

I regain consciousness inside Ravenscroft's autonaka, a new-model Solaris, very fancy. The interior is different to my usual rides. There are no windows, only holowarns reflecting the outside world and blending it with interior thoughts. The Solaris extrudes a perplexing metallic drone, an audio bubble that cocoons the vehicle. It generates a strange suspensive zone, something felt at the molecular level. I have the unnerving sense that if I concentrate, I might zoom into my body and discern the spaces between atoms.

Ravenscroft faces me. Now that he's no longer in the field, he seems the opposite to how I feel. He's more substantial than before, as if the wire frame has grown flesh. He has such an odd physicality, he's nearly an optical illusion.

He removes his plizzit and maniskin, and he's something else again, an entrancement in a more palatable form. His black hair is peppered with grey, and he's smartly dressed in a shiny black coach's jacket and black stovepipe slacks. He has a handsome, well-designed face, seasoned with unusual features. Some mismatched teeth. A slightly bulbous nose. One earlobe shorter than the other. I'm relieved to note the absence of violent facial trauma.

He's not wearing cheaters, although I touch his face to be sure. He strokes my hand and places it back onto my lap.

He allows me to study him and then he smiles. The gesture is a beauty. It reaches every part of his face, like the rays from a new dawn. What's got into me? I never wax lyrical. He's such a change from Sanderson, but my natural reserve erects the usual tiresome barriers.

'I'm glad I amuse you, Ravenscroft. What's your game? Are you my smiling assassin or just a functional narcissist?'

'I'm a friend, and I'm relieved to see you're okay.'

Rydell is pressed up beside me. His plizzit has gone too, and I take in his craggy wonder. His scent is heavy and musky, very physical. Thick, pointy sideburns accentuate his chunky jaw line. He's a real man's man, a physical specimen so far removed from my own state that he may as well be a different species.

Rydell is cheaterless, but he invades my space in other ways. His apodictic presence commands every sensory signal. The scent fills the cabin, and his great bulk commandeers the seat, forcing me to confront my deep-seated repulsion at close physical proximity.

'Rydell, thanks for rescuing me from the code beast.'

He stares me down like I'm something he dug from his ear. Then he grunts and I laugh. Everything about him is a cliché, but he's obviously dangerous. It's rare to be in the vicinity of an actual embodied peril. My life's been threatened many times in the Vexworld, but this guy could snap my neck with his bare hands.

He whites out, fingers tense around the barrel of his dethtube. What's he doing behind his eyes? If there are no cheaters, then maybe he's having a seizure.

'Don't think so much,' Ravenscroft says. 'You'll sprain your brain, then you'll need to rest. It's time to dial back the angst so that you might live much longer.'

The Solaris sails through the urban edgelands. Out here, it's hard to tell where the city ends and the countryside begins. What

I thought were trees turn out to be ancient telegraph poles. What I imagine is the overgrown husk of a dead autonaka proves to be the entrance to some animal cave.

Beyond the fringe, the tall trees are denuded from extreme UV. The sky is an apocalyptic hue. A dirty, pinky orange. There are no clouds, no haze. No respite. The air is piercing and bright, searing away any illusions one might have about the worth of the shell world.

'Particulates,' Ravenscroft says. 'That's why the sky is the way it is. They spray nanoparticles into the atmosphere to seed clouds, but it burns holes in the sky. We're in the chaos threshold, a whirlpool of catastrophic feedback loops.'

'I think my autonaka was caught up in that. Maybe the particulates scrambled its brain. Either that or the xenospores.'

The Solaris burns red, but it keeps quiet.

'I'm not used to being inside a beast and having space to think.'

Rydell speaks, taking me aback. I was starting to wonder if he'd had his vocal cords removed.

'You could've commanded your autonaka to be quiet,' he says, in a comically deep voice. 'But you just wanted to argue with it. You're slack, Jones. You need working on.'

'Is that your attempt at psychoanalysis? Maybe leave the thinking to Ravenscroft. Stick to biting the heads off whippets or torturing small children, whatever it is you do in your spare time.'

I watch for a reaction, but he's impassive.

'Stop it,' Ravenscroft says, 'Rydell has the right to express an opinion.'

'Ah, the doctrine of open access, even when it's a mortal insult. Every smart mouth is a broadcast mechanism.'

I'm too distracted by our journey to keep the anger burning. The Solaris has cleared the skeletal forest and is cresting a small mountain. Its holowarns infiltrate the air as we head towards the summit. An immense architectural folly comes into view. It's a raw-concrete structure, an enormous building with two snaking wings, serpentine shapes guarding a series of nested courtyards. The wings are not complementary. They're blocky and jagged, and their angles are in competition, warping the building's visual impact with aggressive, slashing lines.

It doesn't feel especially welcoming.

'Is this where I'm to receive the lobotomy?'

Ravenscroft and Rydell exchange a glance, but they don't speak. Maybe these two don't need cheaters to communicate. Perhaps they're just in sync like any close buddies.

Ravenscroft flashes the high-watt smile, pointing to the side of his head. 'Remember, Kalsari. Brain-sprain and how to avoid it.'

The Solaris draws to a halt by the side of a small monument. It's a brushed-metal pyramid topped with a medallion, a copy of Ravenscroft's pro-star.

Wata and the octopus.

The door opens, and I'm ejected by the air cannon, but I seem to stop in mid-air. The Solaris's hum intensifies. Rydell kicks me in the back, but I don't budge. I'm trapped in a magnetic field. My legs are numb, and I can't tell if my lower body is attached to my upper half.

I manage to extricate myself, landing heavily. 'Thanks a lot, Ravenscroft. Is this how you treat all your guests?'

The door knits shut, timelapse of a healing wound. Ravenscroft and Rydell wink out of existence, atoms broken down by the vehicle's forcefield. Their faces degranulate, exposing the gaps between.

The Solaris skeets down the mountain.

'Wait!' I shout. 'Give me my plizzit! My mani!' Are they really going to leave me here to burn?

Something's not right. It's hot, and I'm sweating, but my skin hasn't peeled away, and my breathing is normal. The summit is a micro-climate, an inverse image of the hellscape at the bottom of the mountain. There's even foliage up here, enormous bushes and trees.

With nothing to do and no one to rail against, I lope around the deserted grounds. The building is extraordinarily well preserved. In the cube era, most large structures have been torn down or left to rot. Only the massively wealthy can afford to maintain a building of this size, but Ravenscroft doesn't strike me as the well-heeled type. I imagine him as a cult figure on the margins of whatever industry he's part of, eking out his research on the back of Swarm handouts. Then again, I sense that he's used to concealing the nature of his mysterious methods.

I try to zone but nothing materialises. The Vexworld is dead, but if I'm not vexxing then why aren't I cronked? My body feels fine, my skin neutral and calm. I scratch my arms, my hands. Nothing stirs. I'm weightless, euphoric. If I didn't know better, if I couldn't see clearly, I'd swear I was suspended in null space. Maybe I've entered a micro-climate of the mind, a controlled zone redolent with possibility.

I sit and wait for time to unfold.

RESIGNATION

The sibylline building hangs against the sky like a question mark. Wildly overgrown, it exists in fusion with its surroundings but also in contradiction, an impossible monument plucked from the timestreams of ancient history. Ravenscroft said it was a university campus, but the last time universities filled societal needs, cheaters were science fiction. The building is four storeys high, and across the two wings I'm guessing there's capacity for hundreds of people. By his own admission, Ravenscroft's operation is tiny. So, what occupies the rest of it? What did universities once hold? Dorms, labs, classrooms. Rooms for experimentation. Cafeterias for ghosts.

I'm gripped by the urge to explore. Whenever I'm lost, I always head north. It's unfathomable to do the opposite. I don't know what this says about me, other than I'm spatially dyslexic. Maybe it's like the sensation of being buried under layers of unreality in the Vexworld. North is 'up' and up is out.

I follow the building's unnerving contours for ten minutes, emerging into a large courtyard at the rear. Enormous glass doors punctuate the facade, reflecting my solar-molten face and the iso-fused sky. I peer inside, detecting a series of dimly lit, overlapping walkways. A snaking series of heavy wooden doors provides each level with a stuttering visual rhythm.

I try to enter but the glass doors don't budge. I knock and there's no response. I sit on the steps, waiting for Ravenscroft to rescue me.

Again, I try to zone, but I receive the same peculiar sensation. It's as if I'm on the verge of a great discovery but I can't quite cross the line. Maybe the grounds are a zone, and I'm lost inside a mirror clone, but if what I see around me is simulation, then where's the outside?

When did I transition? I retrace the events that deposited me here. I rode the autonaka to Nary-A-Woman. The code beast tried to murder me. Rydell intervened. I blacked out. We drove to the campus.

Where are the joins? I can't detect any cracks unless the shake down happened when I was unconscious. Or just before.

The mouldy old men.

Ravenscroft said the e-waste cloud might be a test. I'm sure that's right. A trap set by him.

I hear muffled voices, distant action. I head down a small incline behind the courtyard, tracking the noise. As I approach a glistening creek, I notice two men standing close to each other. I duck behind some foliage, observing by stealth.

The men are flirting, and I'm shocked to discover that one of them is my new pal, Rydell. The other is a wire framer. Thin and malnourished. Not quite an airsucker but pretty skeletal. They're caressing each other's hair, stroking hands, touching faces. It's a tender scene, as jarring as any horror film.

How did Rydell double back so soon? His clothes are different. He's lost the shiny jumpsuit he wore when he was roughing me up. Now, he's dolled up in black tights and a long red-velvet coat. His neck is draped with a silver, embossed medallion, which the thin man twists and turns under his forensic gaze.

The thin man's fashion sense also runs to the flamboyant. He wears dark-purple tights and a form-fitting green T-shirt that emphasises his bulging ribcage. His hair is a page-boy cut, his moustache pencil thin. It's like I've stumbled onto a medieval cosplay club. I half expect these two to start jousting.

I'm close, now, but they don't notice me. They're too busy feeling each other up, although Rydell is mostly a passive receiver. Every now and then, he pats the thin man's stomach and arms with sullen resignation.

The thin man sees me and stops what he's doing, emerging from a trance. He sizes me up like food, and Rydell glowers. Maybe they're conducting an illicit liaison, although they display no signs of surprise or shame at my presence.

Rydell retrieves a red lollipop from his jacket. He sucks it, his thick lips wet with saliva, only for the thin man to whip it away and insert it into his own mouth. I try to read the thin man's expression. There's a trace of annoyance, and I wonder how he commands such power over the goon.

He slurps noisily on the candy, fixing Rydell with a blank expression. Then he carefully places the lollipop in Rydell's enormous hand, closing the goon's fingers around the white stick.

I'm repulsed by this display. I haven't exchanged bodily fluids with an embodied human in ages and just the thought of their spit-and-polish session makes me sick.

I hear footfall, and I whirl around. It's Ravenscroft. I was so caught up in the drama of the two love birds that the outside world had vanished.

'I see you've met Max,' he says, gesturing towards the thin man. 'Don't mind him, or Rydell, or anyone you meet here. Because of their treatment, they tend to display singular behaviour.'

It's strange. Ravenscroft talks about Rydell as though he's a different person to the henchman in the Solaris. I keep an eye on the goon and his mate. They're whiting out, but their faces are bare. I must be vexxing, yet I can feel my cheaters.

Ravenscroft leads me by the arm towards the glass doors.

'Your cheaters don't matter here,' he says. 'Like your persy, they're useless. Dead weight.'

Somewhere in the back of my lizard brain, it occurs to me that he's reading my thoughts, but I don't understand how. There's no subcute staining his wrist. Maybe he has a mod, but with no cheaters on his face there's no relay for the telepath.

I look over my shoulder at the sirens of my subconscious, Max and Rydell, down by the creek, the thin man's head resting on the goon's ample shoulder. They're still whiting out, lost in some opaque, interior world.

'What is with those two?'

'Not now, Kalsari. Save the probing questions for later.'

Ravenscroft blinks and the doors unfold. We walk inside, at least I try to, but I'm plagued by the same half-in, half-out sensation from the Solaris. One leg makes it into the building, the other is trapped outside. It takes an age for the rear limb to join the first, but eventually it happens, and I stagger to Ravenscroft's side. He looks amused, as if I've exceeded his expectations.

We amble down an unfeasibly long, high hallway, passing a serried rank of identical doors. There are no windows in here. It feels like an airlock. Maybe it is. That would explain why my body was acting like a mechanically separated chicken.

Ravenscroft enters a small dormitory, beckoning for me to follow. The room is tiny, sparsely furnished. There's a bed, a wicker chair, a small table. Some shelves filled with books. I can't remember the last time I saw a printed book, although I must have at some point, considering I was born pre-vex.

I scan some titles.

Applied Carwarpianism: Memoir from an Alternate Reality.

Mystery Napkin: Interdimensional Encounters and Personal Growth.

I can't make out any more. My head is swimming, my vision blurred, as if the sight of this shoestring library has unseated a primitive weariness within my bones. The books might as well be fetish objects. I can't bring myself to go near them. I'm just not used to print. If it's not written in light paint, my eyes can't cope.

Ravenscroft leaves without a word, and I sit on the chair, reflecting on my bizarre day. It's amazing that I've just packed up my life and gone through with this whole charade. I know that part of me likes having decisions made on my behalf, but I worry about my inability to zone. There are no side effects, though, which is a bonus. None that I know of.

On the table, there's a wrapped lollipop. Next to it is a silver medallion like Rydell's. It's embossed with the hideous-beautiful image of Wata and her purple friend.

On the bed, some clothes have been laid out. A large black t-shirt, a tunic, a pair of black tights. I climb into them, relieved to be discarding my crusty rags, which I've worn for weeks. I'm glad they chose black. It hides a multitude of bodily sins.

I unwrap the lollipop and suck on it, but the flavour is grotesque. Fishy, crab-like. I throw it to the floor in disgust.

I want to vex. Why can't I vex? That's the critical issue, but does it really matter? I don't feel suicidal as I normally do without the zones. If this is the cure, then it's holding up well.

I lie on the bed, succumbing to the shutdown of my body. I'm beyond tired, surviving on fumes in a vegetative half-life. I think about all the time I've spent vexxing. I never truly slept for most of it, and now that I'm in this limbo land, it's catching up with me. All those years of artificial wakefulness buried alive under a quiescent tsunami.

I slide into sleep, buffeted by sub-prime energy, subsumed by the sunken void.

MUTATION

When I open my eyes, I feel remarkably well rested. I have no idea what the time is. The extraneous utility frames that typically fill the peripheries of my cheater-vision have vanished. There are no windows in the dorm. It's as black as Kvvlt.

A thin, electric-blue line of light spills from beneath the door. It reminds me of a child's night light, and I try to catalogue it within the dim recesses of my failing memory bank. The light dissolves, returning the dorm to its death-black state.

I open the door and step into the hallway, looking for the source. I attempt to enter other dorms, but they're locked. I can't leave the area. The hallway has been sealed shut.

I hear muffled noises, bouts of screaming coming from my room. I hustle back and hit the lights. There's a thin, agonised woman in my bed. She's in the grip of turbulent convulsions, arching her back so violently I fear it will break. Her hair is matted, her face contorted with pain and sweat.

Ravenscroft emerges from the en suite, a priest at her exorcism. I hold her down, and he nods and smiles, as if I've passed some test. He hands the woman a rubber tube connected to a tank of nitrous oxide. As she sucks on the tube, her skin clears and her face relaxes, revealing her true form.

'Wata!' I gasp. After seeing her brutalised by an octopus for so long, it's a shock to be near the embodied version. She starts to thrash again, and I have no idea what to do. She's gyrating, thrusting her belly, as if a parasite is devouring her from within.

Ravenscroft springs into action, brandishing a pair of surgical scissors. He performs an episiotomy, and Wata emits a low moan. An immense jet of thick, dark blood erupts from her ruptured vagina, squirting me in the eye. I turn away, temporarily blinded.

'Pay attention!' Ravenscroft yells.

From deep within her, a tiny head emerges. It's black and shiny, covered in blood, vernix and amniotic fluid. For a fearful second, the slime tricks me into thinking it's the octopus.

'Oh god, no. Ravenscroft! I can't see this.'

I turn to run, but he snakes an arm around my neck, nearly strangling me. His grip is surprisingly strong.

'Stay,' he commands. 'You're part of this, whether you like it or not.'

He releases me, then eases the newborn from its cave, wiping the muck from its face and body. He holds it to the light. It's a girl, with memorable features.

The girl is Halo. Baby Halo.

Ravenscroft hands me the scissors. 'Cut the cord.'

I hesitate, unsure of myself.

'Cut it or all our work will be for nothing! Cut the cord!'

His anger galvanises me and I snip away, but it's like hacking into a rubber garden hose with a butter knife. Finally, Halo is untethered. She's calm, but my nerves are shredded.

Ravenscroft hands her to Wata, who seems surprised to be given the opportunity. Cradled in her mother's arms, Halo regards me, a sliver of recognition flashing across her eyes. In my former life, I always imagined she was born with the power of speech, figuring that's the reason why her mod and cheaters have been giving her so much trouble. They're clashing with an already accelerated brain.

We check each other out, but I resist the urge to ask her how she's doing. I start to cry. This nightmare is a guilt trip made flesh. I shouldn't have left her to fend for herself and now she's returned, rubbing my nose in vomit.

'Wata and I will keep the child,' I say to Ravenscroft, desperate to atone.

'You're not in a position to demand,' he whispers. 'Not yet.'

He touches the back of my neck and my spine tingles. All the belligerence and fight drains from me, as if he's grounded a rogue electrical wire.

Ravenscroft guides me to bed. He even plumps the spare pillow. Under Halo's watchful gaze, I settle beside Wata, but I'm riddled with nerves. How did I end up with a family? It happened in a blur. Where are the joins?

As soon as I rest my head on the pillow, Wata arises, the baby in her arms. 'We'll see ourselves out.'

As they leave, tears roll down my cheeks. I've lost Halo for a second time. Ravenscroft raises a finger to his lips, then he blinks away the light and disappears into the gloom.

In the dark, I return to the sadomasochistic fantasies of my childhood. Like an ageing singer playing his old hits, I transform into a feckless loser buried alive in the coffin of sleep, my life destroyed before it began.

Patiently, I wait for my air to run out and the next world to unfurl.

ACTIVATION

Emergence from sleep is cold and rote. My mind is a malfunctioning satellite dish, scanning for unreachable beams. I try to locate the familiar touchstones of waking life, but the memory of Halo's birth endures, an oily residue from a vague dimension, coating the fabric of reality. The sensation has the texture of zonal dreaming, but since I can't vex, why am I wedged between worlds?

Where's the cronk? That's the most abnormal aspect of my current situation. It's disorientating to be outside the Vexworld with clear skin and no desire to self-mutilate. Part of me misses it. I used to think that the wounds that strafed my body sent a message to the world about how damaged I was inside. Now that the cronk has gone, I've lost my identity no matter how repulsive.

I hear a staccato knock on the door. I have no desire for small talk, but I answer regardless, aware that I must follow every breadcrumb to solve the mystery of my inner life.

'Come.'

Ravenscroft enters, less a man, more an anticlimax. I have the feeling we are going to be inseparable from here on in.

I don't get up. I want to maintain my independence before the next round of submissiveness kicks in.

He sits on the edge of the bed, a paternal look on his face.

'Kalsari, I know you're not lying.'

'About?'

'About what you're going to tell me.'

'I had the strangest dream.'

'Yes, I know.'

'How?'

'I was there.'

'Indeed, and I don't feel the need to question that or the fact that you are telling me information that would be shocking in any other context. Since I arrived here, zonal experiences and dreams have been plotted on a continuum. Where does the texture of one begin and the other end? I'm part of an initiation, but there's something that only I can initiate.'

I stretch out on the mattress, tiredness creeping through my bones.

'Some dreams disperse their seed with intent,' he says, 'commanding the mind of the wakened dreamer for hours to come. Their imprint is emotional and visceral, a reminder of heightened realities, a vivid echo of journeys to the far side of the sun.'

His voice lulls me, and I almost fall asleep, but I resist, fearful of being hypnotised. Above the bed, I notice a yellowing ram's skull nailed to the wall. Has it always been there? I can't say. I have no memory of it.

'Materially, such dreams drift and ebb. Sometimes, they fade within seconds after awakening. Other times, specific details can't be recalled yet the veil of discolouration remains, delivering an aching void where once there was light, sound and motion.'

His wide eyes drill holes into my skull, but I hold his gaze, desperate to learn more.

'Last night's dream had everything we could've hoped for. Metacognitive thought, hallucinogenic imagery, disturbed reality discrimination. Even more exciting, as you deployed these tools you made a significant breakthrough. You learned that everything in reality has an ethereal counterpart that can be brought into focus or stored like luggage. That explains the sensation of peering through dimensions.'

'You were testing me. That's why you were there.'

'Observing, let's say. I don't have the technology to insert myself into your dreams. No, if I appeared, then you wanted me there, and that's how we like it. You call us, not vice versa.'

'The dream had the quality of zonal play, yet there's no Kvvlt in this room or anywhere in this place.'

'We don't need artificial stimulants, not even cheaters, as I think you're starting to realise.'

'Am I? I'm not so sure. Explain it to me like I'm a child.'

'I don't think there's any need for that. However, I will issue a simple request. Remove yourself from the paradigm of dream imagery and broaden your conceptual outlook. You possess the ability to re-imagine the world, which makes you the ideal subject for our research. We wouldn't bother if there was no chance to salvage the wreck. You'd be left with Sanderson, and he'd feed you to The Swarm the first chance he got.'

'Right, your famous research. You allude to it, but you can never explain it.'

Ravenscroft shrugs. 'Maybe you should've read my paper.'

'Alright. If I can't vex, why don't I have the cronk?'

'You don't have the cronk because you're among real friends, maybe for the first time in your life.'

'Yeah, Rydell's a real barrel of laughs.'

He smooths his jacket and brushes back his floppy fringe. 'It takes all sorts to build a community.'

'How do you find the time to groom yourself?'

He gives me his best smile. 'Force of habit. Routines from a past life. Now, I'll leave you to relax. We'll chat again when you're ready.'

'What do I do now?'

'Anything you like.'

His face loses the smile, replaced by the controlled expression of a medico about to inform a patient of a terminal illness.

Am I undergoing treatment by stealth? By his own admission, Ravenscroft's not in the business of providing cures, yet my neuroses and afflictions are vanishing.

'How long have I been here?'

'Three weeks.'

The anomalous sense of dislocation returns, cleaving my mind in two.

'Stop it, Ravenscroft. I arrived the other day.'

I realise I have no way of knowing how long it's been, since all displays have vanished from my device, and there has been no separation from the dreamworld to waking life.

'What does Rimy mean to you now?'

'Really?'

'Yes, really.'

I try to latch onto memories of the ant, but my recall disintegrates. My lust for them has been elided, an abstract concept I tell myself I need but a fine grain too disturbing when magnified.

'Kalsari, there are swathes of your life that are not immediately available to conscious recall. These hidden imaginative tracts are like undiscovered continents. When their peculiarly native qualities are eventually discovered, the temptation can be to erase all traces of their existence.'

Ravenscroft blows the tips of his fingers, as if putting out a flame. In my mind, I feel the gesture transferred to me, eradicating the cronk that lurks within.

'Alternatively, one could learn from the signals that they send. One could take the time to truly understand their meaning and intent. You might consider such signals a message from your parallel self, who after all is an intimate version of you, but you will need an abundance of patience. You won't receive dispatches from lost lands if you're rage-sick whenever you don't get your way.'

I'm a little hurt by this. 'Surely I'm better than before?'

'You're showing steady progress, yes.'

He rises, dispensing a collegial pat to my shoulder. He indicates my cheaters.

'Why not remove them? Aren't you curious?'

He departs, and I do as he asks. The action feels momentous, like a boozer emptying the last bottle down the sink.

What now?

Anything, Ravenscroft had said, but all I know how to do is vex. Deprived of that function, time is a vast sea. It is endless and amorphous. How do I carve it up? What do normal people do with their spare time?

Perhaps I'm bored, although I wouldn't really know. I've spent so long in the zones staving off that terrifying prospect, I can't remember the shape of nothing. One would expect to develop anxiety when permanently bored, but all that transpires is an unwavering stillness and the sense that I could continue this way until I die.

On the opposite wall, I spy a small, square window. Like the ram's skull, somehow it went unnoticed. I'm sure Ravenscroft is right. The window and the skull were stowed away like pieces of luggage. What other reality materials lie in repose, awaiting activation?

SUBMISSION

I stir from the bed, quite an effort given my natural indolence. I drag the chair to the wall. I stand on it, peering through the window. I see Nary-A-Woman's main road curling around the base of the mountain like a strap of liquorice. Smoke rises from the tarmac, and the sky is strafed with lightning-fast pellets of light, trace-images from Swarmtrooper vee-drones. It's all so remote and abstract, reminiscent of an open stream in my cheaters, an effect enhanced by the glass square.

My dispassionate gaze is appropriate under the circumstances. The shell world, even the Vexworld, has faded from significance since I've joined this cult, this gang, whatever it is.

The past never really existed because there is only this moment and this group of people. Despite the theatre of my tepid resistance, I know that their seduction has worked and that I will remain here forever.

I must keep busy. Ravenscroft has presented me with an opportunity, and I can't just lie around, as tempting as that is.

Easier said than done. Defeated by the weight of expectation, I sink into the chair and close my eyes, but try as I might, I can't rid my mind of the mental overlays that bleed in from outside. What if I never vex again? The question haunts me, even though I know it is simply my ego speaking, crowding out all other thought.

I make a deal with the left side of my brain.

Quell all the stress and worry. Let me focus on time.

I verbalise the incantation to objectify the data. 'Allow me to visualise time.'

The room is silent, my mind quiet. My vision is fractal. I see shapes with no dimensions, perceiving only bits of data. Where are the joins? I smell ice, water, things that are frozen. Snow men. Ice drifts. Iceheads. The Arctic Free State.

I am becoming emotional. Why? Something is crunching beneath my feet. I am walking across a field of snow. No, a lake of ice. A white sheet as far as the eye can see. What if I fall through the ice? But it's thick, more an endless block of ice than a sheet.

I must stop the mental chatter. I must remember the purpose of the mission.

The sheet is made of time.

I need a higher perspective. I request my subconscious to float above the location. One hundred metres should do it,

Below, I see a mass of bruised shapes swarming beneath the ice. They are units of time. If I break the ice, I will be able to stop time, maybe reverse it.

A figure walks across the lake. My physical self. It kneels, chipping away at the sheet with cronk-sharp nails. The action repulses me. My remote body reminds me of the self-amputated tails of scared lizards, still twitching as nerves continue to fire.

The me-thing chips away until the surface crumbles and a dark ice sculpture is revealed, floating on the surface of the lake. The sculpture resembles a bipedal mechanism, but I can't determine whether it's human or beast. It is made from the swarming shapes. Dirty ice.

I take no joy in its birth. My skill has not given shape to it. The three-dimensional representation has always existed within the ice. All that lizard-me has done is prepare the conditions for it to emerge.

My autotomised self retrieves the sculpture from the water and lays it on the ice. Lizard-me frowns, mopping its sweaty brow, then it walks away, bemused by the yield of its labour.

From above, the sheet of ice takes on a strange quality. It looks architectural, somehow. A space designed for human occupation, not a resting place for tundra ghosts.

The sheet resolves, form and substance emerging from the blank textures. I'm staring at the setting of an enormous cafeteria. The cavernous space is completely white. All the chairs, tables and walls, the ceiling, everything white. The cafeteria is the negative image of Kvvlt.

A garbled signal reaches me, a muffled, autistic voice inside my head.

I descend, merging with my physical self to decode it. I regenerate fresh skin to replace the old, optimising locomotor performance and bodily growth. Inside the new flesh, I weave an elaborate defence mechanism, steeling myself against future attacks.

It is the way of the lizard.

PERSONALISATION

I'm alone, wedged in the walkway that straddles the two levels beneath my dorm. I'm not exactly sure how I arrived here. I've suffered an out-of-body experience, and that's something else. Mind tricks, I guess, Ravenscroft style. I think I've been drugged. What's in the lollipops? Despite the fishy taste, I can't stay away from them. I'm sucking on one right now, but I can never finish them. The floor of my dorm is riddled with half-sucked pops.

It's frustrating. I want to swallow them all the way down, but, at the death, the cumulative taste always makes me gag. I must keep trying. I must have every particle inside me, flooding my bloodstream.

The mahogany doors lining the walkway are identical. I select some at random, trying the handles, but they're stuck fast. I walk further and try again. No luck. I press my ears to the doors but there is only silence. I peer over the side of the walkway. Below, multiple passages overlap like spaghetti-junction skyroads in old science fiction films. There are no signs of activity from any level.

Even stranger, I don't remember the dorm being this high up. There must be at least thirty levels beneath me. I count until my forehead begins to twitch. It's so persistent it can't be ignored, both pleasurable and annoying.

The throbbing blurs into pain, real pain, trepanning right through the skull and into my brain. I don't know how to make it stop and intrusive thoughts flood my mind. I slash my index finger across my scalp, dreaming of the blade, desperate to leach the poison from my head.

I stagger away until I reach a spiral staircase. There are lamps at the apex of each spiral, but the arms of the spirals are plunged into darkness. I hear movement below. I crawl down the stairs, desperate for help. Traversing these steps is like crossing the international date line. I half expect to meet myself in the darkness going the other way.

I stagger from the stairwell, collapsing into a crumpled heap. Ahead, a woman crouches low, coiled to strike. She's much younger than me, with wild, dark hair. She springs to her bare feet, gliding over to where I lay. Her body is hyper-kinetic, dancing or having a fit. She wears a long, dark dress and her face is impassive, her features long and angular, more a collection of planes than flesh and bone.

She runs her fingers through my hair and touches my face. She takes my hand, leading me to a desultory lounge area. We arrange ourselves on a clapped-out sofa, facing each other, her cheek nearly touching mine. She's not wearing cheaters, but she directs my fingers to her face, anticipating the query. She holds my hand as I brush her face to make sure. The pain evaporates.

'Thanks. Did you do that?'

She gives me the silent treatment.

'I'm Kalsari.'

At the sound of my voice, she draws away so violently I fear she's been shot. When I look around for the assassin, she jerks forward, reanimated by an invisible force.

She's whiting out, her head lolling back and forth with vicious snaps.

Remember about your name. Never say your name.

Did I do this to her? Surely the autonaka's warning was just machine jabber? I paid it no mind. Code beasts are simply stopped clocks. Twice a day, they spew an accidental truth.

The woman rises and walks calmly from the lounge. She's still whiting out. I leave, but I don't follow. I don't want to trigger her spasms.

Halfway down the hall, I spy a bright light. It's incongruous in the dim interior of the facility. The light spills from a large doorway, staining the lip of the hall with a familiar glare. I reach the doorway. Beyond lies the ice-white cafeteria.

I'm crippled by a powerful deja vu. I appear to have dreamed the cafeteria into being, or maybe I received a summons from that bizarre woman, the dirty sculpture poisoned with life.

I can't handle it. When I was vexxing, I never had to think about the occult. It could never match up to what we were doing in the zones, so the concept could never shock. Now, all bets are off. I can no longer explain what's happening to me.

It's easiest to tell myself that I never woke, but even so I'll need to run some tests. Sanderson said that lucid dreamers must interpret the signs to hand in order to test the scene, but what significance does food have in dreams? Since I rarely eat, only ingest liquid-synth mush, I wonder why this place appears to me now.

I pick up a plastic chair and throw it against the wall. It bounces onto the floor. I slap myself hard in the face. It hurts but it's satisfying. I've wanted to do that for a while. So far, reality has not crumbled before my eyes even though I scarcely believe in it.

What is it called when you are in neither a dream nor reality?

'Kalsari! What are you doing, you silly man? Stop destroying the place.'

I decipher the signal at last. The voice belongs to Ravenscroft, leaning over from the mezzanine. 'Come on up. We need to talk.'

RECEPTION

I ascend the stairs to Ravenscroft. He's sitting by a plastic table. On the table is a food kit. Syringes, vials, pouches, the works.

'Like a hit?'

'Not hungry.'

'Relax, then.'

I sit opposite him. He points to the lower level. 'I see you've met Shiny. One of our adepts.'

The strange woman has entered the cafeteria and is looking around, searching for something that only she can see.

'She didn't look too adept before.'

'Kalsari, you are part of our movement now. It's time to drop the rebel pose. We're building the engine that will bring us closer to where we need to be.'

'I could've sworn I was walking inside a dream just then. This cafeteria seemed beholden to a secret logic. Shiny, too.'

Ravenscroft bequeaths me two gifts, his stellar smile and a choice aphorism. 'Sometimes a cafeteria is just a cafeteria.'

'No one wears cheaters around here, but everyone acts as if they're vexxing.'

'Technically, you're still in the Vexworld. The signals continue to pass through your body, but you haven't learned how to access them unaided. That's where we can help. By the way, our version of the Vexworld has been throttled. It only extends so far. Think of it as a sandpit. Essentially, you can only contact each other here, and build zones between the five of you, but I can widen the bandwidth once the overall skill level progresses.'

'Stop wasting my time, Ravenscroft. I already know how to zone.'

'Oh, you mean your former life? That wasn't zoning, my friend. That was paddling in the shallows. Do you believe in telepathy?'

'I suppose so. In the Vexworld we can read each other's thoughts by default, so what's the difference? Vexcomms are as instantaneous as telepathy, so you might as well call it that.'

'Yet there remains a barrier, the cheaters themselves, plus the neuromods that connect them. Pure telepathy, the ultimate expression of an evolved humanity, can only be achieved by removing both cheaters and mods.'

'That's what you're doing here?'

'We're making incremental progress, yes. The people you've met here live permanently inside the Vexworld. There is no off switch. They have been fitted with a modification of technology originally developed to restore sight to blind people. It's the first step.'

'Blind people? You mean those awful cams drilled into their skulls? I don't see anything like that.'

'No, not cams. Implants. Ordinarily, the cams transmit vision from the outside world to the blind person's retinals, but we redirected the visual input from the shell world to the Vexworld, and then we shrunk the cameras, making them part of the implant. It was easy when grain cams came along. The Vexworld tracks and responds to blink commands from the retinal implants, just as it would when using cheaters.'

'And no one's thought of this before? Only you? Spare me.'

'Believe it, Kalsari. The Swarm has a vested interest in maintaining the status quo.'

'Cheaters, retinal implants, whatever. You've just swapped one device for another. There's still a barrier.'

'You forget about the plasticity of the brain. Retinal implants are wired directly to the nervous system. This creates brain imaging and mirror neurons between the host brain and those it encounters. The brain becomes remapped as do certain bodily functions, like the production of oxytocin. That's a hormone secreted when we perceive emotional cues from other people. Oxytocin activates pleasurable receptors and makes us more receptive to social signals. It creates the preconditions for true telepathic awareness. Some call oxytocin the snuggle hormone, and I'm sure you can see why, having met the others. With the cams hooked directly into the rets, oxytocin is not only produced continuously but directed outwards to those with the same setup.'

He leans forward, clutching my shoulders. He looks more substantial than when we first met, meatier on the bones, as if the render has been fully drawn.

'Yes!' he says. 'Follow that train of thought and you're halfway there.'

'When the oxytocin flows freely and can be controlled, you remove all implants and mods.'

'Yes.'

'And you expect me to submit to this operation?'

'Only if you want to. Do you want to?'

I remember my life as a castle hunter. I miss it terribly. I'm no cube drone. I'm a full-tilt vexxer. I want my zones back, my inexplicably strange and wildly implausible life, even the razor-sharp dynamics from my battle with the cronk. I'll do whatever it takes to re-inhabit that world.

'There will be no cronk where you're going, Kalsari. Only good times ahead.'

'I need to think it over.'

'Okay but remember, no off switch. Once you're in, you must be all in.'

'You forget who you're talking to. My life's ambition is to stay vexxed.'

'I know who I'm talking to, and I know that he's remarkably self-destructive. I am simply asking you to commit to being happy.'

I wince, and Ravenscroft smiles indulgently. 'You're like a moody teenager, half in love with darkness and despair.'

'Wrong. I never do things by halves.'

He rises, looking over my shoulder in delight. I turn to see Wata and a primal dread ices my spine. All I know of her has been gleaned from dreams and simulations. It's hard to believe that she could ever step through the mirror to reach me where I am.

She's wearing plain clothes, sort of a short smock and baggy pants. No makeup. Her hair is brown and straight. Her narrow face is transcendent. She looks amazing and I feel an instant thrill, remembering the connection we shared in my dream and the bond that is Halo.

She only has eyes for Ravenscroft. She runs over to him, and they kiss and fondle in the same silent, exploratory fashion as Max and Rydell by the creek. I stand aside awkwardly, burned by the sparks of their erotic attraction.

'Kalsari, Wata would like you to spend some time with her. I do advise it. You'll need a full image of the gestalt before you can commit to joining us.'

'I don't want company right now.'

'Trust in Ingram,' Wata says. 'He's run the psychometrics. You and I are perfectly matched.'

Ravenscroft nods. 'Everyone needs a mate in this project.'

'But there's only four others,' I reply. 'Plus me.'

'Right. Max and Shiny are an item, and sometimes Rydell joins them to make three, but essentially, he's a loner and hard to pair up with. He's the wild card, adding grit to the machine. He keeps us on our toes. Anyway, these roles and relationships are interchangeable. Whether there's an odd or even number is inconsequential. What we are moving towards is a group mind of infinite membership.'

'Why do I feel like this is an arranged marriage?'

'Pre-ordained. In your dream, you and Wata have already met and formed a union, but the arc of time has not come full circle. What you instinctively know to be the past is still somewhere in the future. When the loop is complete, you'll see the full picture.'

Wata moves closer to me, and I lean into her. Her warm body provides an instant thrill, an abiding physicality that I have not felt since Essi. And yet I can't shake my memories of the inside-out sensations that Rimy and I shared.

I no longer know how to invade the body of an actual embodied person. I can no longer see what the embodied see. How can they penetrate me? How can I ever go back to simple transactional intimacy when what I had with the ant was something beyond?

'Rimy was certainly different,' Ravenscroft says, creeping through my mind. 'Neither better nor worse, but a part of yourself that can no longer be reached. With Wata's help, we'll unlock that chemical reaction. We'll divert it and let nature take its course.'

Wata strokes my hair with curious indifference, as if she's inspecting my scalp for nits. Eventually, we share a kiss.

From the corner of my eye, I keep Ravenscroft in view. He watches me with amused satisfaction, as if he's just taught a monkey to signal for bananas.

His next trick? Teach monkey to talk.

ACCELERATION

Wata follows me to my stale, cramped dormitory. We enter, and I study the room. It seems smaller, and there appear to be more books on the shelves, more words to be read. The weight of expectation crushes the space like tinfoil inside a fist.

She sits on the side of the bed. That seems to be the default position for visitors to my digs, as though they're paying last respects to a dying relative in hospital. I take the chair, avoiding the bed, although I know what will happen. It is pre-ordained.

Wata is less manic in real life. For starters, she's not shackled to the octopus.

'The octopus is symbolical,' she says, 'one of Ingram's little tricks. You'll learn more about it in due course.'

I'm staring at her.

'What is it?'

'I dreamed about you.'

'Ingram told me.'

'You were giving birth. I suppose it was our child, but it was enhanced, and…'

'What?'

I falter, unable to articulate the dream. I try to recall the parameters, the emotions it stirred, but the edges fade. The act of voicing it degrades its structural integrity until I can hardly remember how the dream played out. I know Halo was in it, and Wata and Ravenscroft, not much else.

'Nothing. It doesn't matter.'

'You'll dream a lot here, even when you're awake. It's all part of the process. Maybe you're dreaming now.'

'Don't play games. We've only just met.'

'Your dream doesn't count?'

'You consider that a date?'

'A date?' She laughs. 'Is that what you call this?'

I'm glad she finds my stupidity amusing. It breaks the ice.

'Ravenscroft told me about the others. You're one of them?'

'If you mean the retinal, then yes, I have it.'

'What's it like?'

'Well, it's nothing like cheaters. It's a raw sensation. It's like there was a space in my psyche and now it's been filled.'

'I used to work with enhanced children, but you people are like regressed adults, the exact opposite.'

'That explains the child in your dream.'

'I suppose so, but it doesn't tell the story of how you ended up in it.'

'Maybe I just asked to be with you.'

'How come no one speaks around here? Telepathy?'

'Largely, although Rydell is a talker when he wants to be. Max and Shiny are physically incapable.'

'Rydell talks? Could've fooled me.'

'He's just moody. A man of few words.'

'I'm obsessed by him, I think. He doesn't seem to fit in.'

'He's okay. Rydell brings a different energy, a chaotic vitality. I suspect Ingram brought him in to shake things up, to make sure we don't become complacent.'

'The other two are mute?'

'They've had laryngectomies.'

'Why?'

'Ingram asked for volunteers. He wants to produce a three-dimensional telepathy. Being in the Vexworld simulates telepathy, but Ingram wants to go further, as you know. He wants to eliminate the tension between what you feel and what you are biologically programmed to do. You see, it's not enough to abandon cheaters. Max and Shiny are physically incapable of verbalised speech. Psychologically, too. They can't even think it. Their larynxes have been removed, which eliminates the physical impulse to speak, but Ingram also took out the part of the brain that controls speech.'

My forehead throbs, just like when I met Shiny. I'm sure it's just a coincidence, but who can tell? What if she's sizing me up for a partial frontal lobotomy? Maybe these people possess weird powers to transform the body just by thinking about it. Is that the true meaning of this new experimental technology?

I grasp my head, waiting for the head-kicking pain to hit.

'You're being silly,' she says. 'We don't operate without your consent. As to the nature of the technology, well, it simply means no wasted effort. If they'd just had the laryngectomy, they'd expend neural energy trying to actualise thoughts via speech. Removing the frontal lobe means that the speech impulse is bypassed. It creates a forced telepathy. That's because the brain is producing so much oxytocin but has no verbal outlet for expressing ecstasy.'

'You have the retinal. Why not the larynx or lobe job?'

'We're waiting to see what happens to Max and Shiny.'

'How are they doing?'

She doesn't answer. Instead, she slides onto the bed and reclines, and I admire the full length of her body, extended in beguiling ways. Her physicality is overwhelming. She's made of curves, and I'm suffering from full-bleed wetware overload.

I talk thirteen to the dozen, trying to stall the inevitable. 'What is with this building? Why has he taken over such a large structure? Why does he need it all? It's very compartmentalised, everything closed off, no open space.'

'This place was never cubed because everyone forgot it was here. As for the design, well, we can hide in the alcoves. Haven't you noticed? The architecture denies clear line of sight from one person to another. It positively encourages the telepathic element. After all, visual cues are just as much of a barrier as sonic cues when it comes to pure telepathy.'

I fall silent, unable to think of anything more to say.

'Come,' Wata says. 'I'll step you through this. Think about the next action you must perform. You've done it before, you can do it again.'

She snakes an arm around me, and I resist the urge to bite her face like the octopus. 'Steady. Take it slowly. You need the will-ingness and openness that love gives before you can let someone read your mind. Acts of love are acts of faith.'

Wata kisses me, and I fall into her, but I'm slow off the mark. Given my history with Rimy, I must relearn physical signals, although I'm fortunate that Wata is a patient and methodical teacher.

As we near the culmination of the act, an unwanted image of Ravenscroft invades my mind. I can't shake it loose. The image is so dominant, it's as if he's the third partner in our ménage à trois.

'Ingram will always be with us,' she says. 'He is The Maker. He allows everything to happen.'

She whites out, and I wonder what confection she's overlaying across my body in vexspace. The thought wracks me with terrible pangs of jealousy. Where do these people go to behind the ocular veil? Am I missing out on some momentous neural carnival? I'm tired of being the outsider. I want to belong.

'I'm only here,' she whispers. 'Only here with you.'

When we finish, we stare at the ceiling. What can she see there? My mantra has always been no Kvvlt, no Vexworld, but I suppose I must relearn everything I know.

'Wata, what if I wasn't attracted to you or you to me?'

She eyes me suspiciously, as if I'd asked why water is wet. 'Ingram only picks people that he knows will be compatible.'

'Fine. What now?'

'It all depends on you. Will you have the retinal?'

'I hear there's no off switch.'

'Right. You're in the Vexworld permanently.'

'How ironic, given the national crisis.'

She draws back. 'You're not an anti-unrealist are you?'

'Hardly, but in my former life I wished I could've toned it down now and again. With this procedure, there's no chance.'

'Well, why would you want to? There's nothing beyond the Vexworld. Fantasy is reality, and the Vexworld is both.'

'You've drunk the Kool Aid. That sounds like a slogan, something a death cult would spout.'

'Let me rephrase. There can be no real telepathy without real love, and without real telepathy there can be no glitchglots. That's why you're here, isn't it? To contact them.'

'Glitchglots? What are glitchglots? Something from Ravenscroft's paper?'

'Oh. You haven't reached that stage.'

'No, but I'm guessing it's in the post, whatever it is. Wata, did you ever stop to think that Ravenscroft is crazy?'

She's appalled. 'Of course not. Why would I?'

'Look, I agree that the Vexworld is reality, to an extent, but I still want to maintain some distance from it. I think it's killing me. Check out my fingers.'

I extend my hands, stretching out the digits, but to my great surprise they are clean, almost healed.

'I know all about your horrible fingers,' Wata says. 'I saw the grain footage before you joined us. You think I'd let those disgusting scab farms touch me?'

'It's bizarre. Now that I think about it, I haven't considered biting since I've been here.'

'That's because you're ready to immerse yourself in what we do. You're letting the digital signal replace your old flesh with the new. When the fingers fully heal, you'll be one of us.'

Wata kisses me again, but she can't stop talking. How can I hear her when her lips are intertwined with mine?

—Kalsari, I think you're ready. Are you ready?

—Yes, Wata. I'm ready.

SUSPICION

We wake after an avalanche of sleep. Par for the course, I don't know how much time has elapsed because Wata has consumed me. Wata eats time.

She dresses quickly, knocking me sideways in her quest to escape. I follow her through the skeletal corridor, but she's nimble and I'm lagging.

She races ahead until she reaches a black door, a bulwark at the rear of the walkway, black like Kvvlt, a deep-vein smart bomb triggering painful memories of my former life. She brushes her cheek against the door, tongue lolling, eyes white. She starts to lick the surface, and I spin her around.

'Wata, no! Spit it out!' I force her mouth open, but there's nothing inside, no worms. I trace the door with my fingers and it degranulates. I fall through the space, face-planting on the floor.

Ravenscroft towers over me, holding hands with Wata.

'That's some pratfall,' he says. 'One might say it's your signature move.'

Wata's pupils have returned. 'Don't ever think you're in the business of saving me,' she hisses, steel in her voice.

'On your feet,' the boss snaps. 'No time to lose.'

As he helps me up, I take in his new look. He's draped in a cream-coloured tracksuit, rocking on his heels contrapposto, resplendent with slicked-back hair. The entire get-up is indecent, a total throwback, yet he assumes the persona with natural grace. I feel inadequate and exposed, like a hobo who's misread the invitation to a swanky costume party and arrived as himself.

He directs me to a large couch and commands me to sit. The furniture is as crass as his outfit, draped in an awful psychedelic paisley. I take the middle cushion and absorb the scene. The room is most unusual. Visual subterfuge makes it impossible to gauge the dimensions, and the interior design betrays a pathological desire to expand time and space.

The east and west walls are entirely mirrored, reflecting infinite recursions of the space and its occupants. Within the funhouse gaze, we three are no longer dimensional certainties with solid, implacable mass. We are dispersed inside a maze of light, swallowed whole by the infinity tunnel.

The whole of the ceiling is a skylight, a glass portal revealing a bright-blue sky. As I watch the heavens, the upper atmosphere fills with swarming pinpricks of white light. They respond to my gaze, dancing in and out of impossibly fluffy clouds whenever I focus my attention.

'Drones?'

'Not here. They'd be shot down. Whatever they are, you invited them.'

Ravenscroft blinks. The glass ceiling fades to black, and a UV spectrum fills the room. Bathed in the black-light rhythm, the north wall rises and falls like a burbling skin and a universe of texture is revealed.

Under intense magnification, pores in the 'skin' fill with pus, forming meaty calderas. Ticks and other vermin feed on dead skin cells. I can see ingrown hairs, the ruby-red stirrings of a cronk attack.

I'm falling into this strange and distant universe, a capsule on re-entry, and just when I'm about to be engulfed by the fleshscape, the skin oozes from the wall. The visceral jelly falls to the floor, releasing gold sparks that rise and bounce from the darkened ceiling.

I'm on my knees, dry-retching. My tongue hangs loose, centimetres from the surface. A cold acceptance washes over me.

How long have I been licking the wall?

I'm acutely aware of Wata and Ravenscroft. They're rooted to the sofa, eyes white, motionless deities presiding over my ritual humiliation.

Ravenscroft raises a finger, indicating the wall. Now that the skin has been shed, its true nature is proudly on display. The wall is just another mirror, but there is no recursion, only a straight reflection.

I crawl over to Wata, taking her hand in mine. I rest my head between her legs, issuing a grim laugh, babbling something about cronk and the Vexworld, but I sound thoroughly unhinged. My voice is pixelised. I hear only stuttered fragments, as though it's been fed through a fan.

—Shut up, Kalsari. What do you think the north wall can see?

—It sees us.

I zero in on my reflection until there is transference and I am inhabiting the reverse image. It's a queer sensation, an ontological retch. I am me but I am not. This body is mine although key details are the wrong way around.

Rising panic derails my mind, but somehow I pull myself together, focusing on the trio of adepts as they study their reflections. Then the triptych breaks apart. Colours leach from human forms and skin suits are sheared away. The palette swirls and reassembles in bizarre configurations until the anthropoids are no longer three but a flesh fondue, a single, amorphous mass.

With multi-cellular precision, the fondue begins to fruit. A copy of Wata is printed by the tremelloid mess. The copy lurches unsteadily to its feet, distressed and in pain. Clutching its belly, it tears itself apart with its bare hands, releasing something from within.

The stomach explodes in a fountain of muscle and blood. From the gash a head emerges, black with viscera. It's an adult skull, with a lumpen forehead and a nose squashed like cabbage. It's my face, my head, exiled into the world as a tumour.

The sim, body and all, falls wholesale from Wata, slick with slime. It thrashes crazily on the floor, a synthetic human born from a copy, waiting to be imprinted with life. Next to it, inside-out versions of Wata and Ravenscroft are entangled, undulating gently.

As the jealousy tightens its grip, I can't bear to look, but instinct tells me to persevere. They are not fucking. They are Siamese twins, a fusion of flesh and bone, two heads sharing a single brain.

Ingram will always be with us. He is the Maker.

Outside the mirror, Ravenscroft clears his throat and the flesh dance degranulates, replaced by the impervious reflection of our enervated selves. I touch my body, watching my reflection do the same. I'm reassured by my physicality, relieved to be on the right side of reality. Only one detail bothers me. Since birth, I've endured a large mole on the right side of my face, but in the mirror, it's still on the right.

I suffer a greasy feeling, an uncanny physical revulsion. Far from ripping the flesh from my bones, as the cronk would have it, I am overwhelmed by the urge to implode into a sink hole of blood and bone.

'Where am I, Ravenscroft? Put me back.'

'Wata says you initiated the first stage of telepathic bonding last night.'

'No. She made the first move.'

'Think again,' Wata says. 'You invited me. In your dream.'

They converse in hushed tones.

'On some level,' Ravenscroft whispers, as if I'm not in the room, 'he wishes to return to his old way of life, but you must tell him that cheaters are—'

'Yes, Ingram. Cheaters are an extension of the mind's eye, but retinals *are* the mind's eye. He has doubts, you know. His physical problems continue to haunt him.'

She squeezes my hand, but I'm indifferent. I can't shake the suspicion that I'm being played, that the weird scenes inside the mirror are a form of psychological coercion.

'Keep chipping away, Kalsari. Never deviate. Remember the path you've chosen, the premonition that brought you here.'

'You mean the cafeteria?'

'Ingram, rest assured, Kalsari is with us.'

'Thanks for the vote of confidence, Wata, but you're hardly an unbiased witness, considering what you two did to each other last night.'

So, he was watching us. I feel sick.

He removes my hand from hers and places it inside his. The sensation of his skin, the magic from bathing in his charisma, weakens my defences. I lean into Wata, holding hands with Ravenscroft, mentally spent and fully exposed.

He massages my misshapen fingers and caresses the scars on my wrist.

'The travails you've endured these past few weeks form an ongoing test. Some of the challenges we set in train. Some found their way to you, sought out by your subconscious. For the most part, you've bested each trial although I note how the cumulative effort saps your will. That's why you're here. To rest, regroup and take the next step.'

'Cut the crap, Ravenscroft. Just tell me about the glitchglots.'

'Well, to put it crudely, we hunt ghosts. Digital ghosts. We call them glitchglots. They're an evolution of spamglots, a virulent new species, more resilient than previous variants. They're sentient, with the ability to infect targeted cheaters.'

I laugh. 'So what? Rimy was sentient. They could take over my cheaters, trigger all sorts of zones. The ant invaded my body, caused me to question my finite existence.'

'Ants are incepted by humans, and persys are controlled by them. We're not talking about either.'

'What then?'

'Auto-code, transactional shells, except that now they display all the hallmarks of intelligence in their interactions within the Vexworld. Comprehension, perception, reasoning, emotion. We managed to capture some. We ran a series of tests, and it always came back to the question of intelligence.'

'How is that different from Rimy? In both cases, they've been initiated and left to evolve.'

'Almost. With ants, the broad patterns they follow can be predicted even if the fine-grain details within those parameters cannot. What you described Rimy doing to you could've been foreseen. There was enough variance in the code to allow for it. With glitchglots, their ultimate form is a total surprise and a complete re-engineering of their initial codeswarm by the glots themselves. It's like a mouse teaching itself to plumb a toilet. It's an ontological impossibility.'

'When the glots enter three dimensions,' Wata continues, 'they start to display erratic behaviour. Most of the examples we have catalogued attach themselves to persys. They send and receive sensory signals not only with standard vexcomms but also unassisted telepathic means. There is something askew about their comms. They always attempt to engage humans in nonsensical dialogue. Their syntax is either cut up and recombined from other sources or it's half-finished. At some level, we believe it's a conlang, an artificial language, one we are yet to decode.'

'Halo designed her own conlang. Why don't you recruit her instead of persecuting her?'

'Forget Halo. In your new life, she doesn't exist.'

'Except in my dreams.'

'In your dreams, yes. The clearing house of the soul. As your dreamworld union with Wata demonstrated, telepathic intensity accelerates within a shared experiential continuum. The telepathic flow is intensified when the relationship between participants is cemented. With glitchglots, the process is related but different. We must demonstrate to them that we are open and willing to accept them into our experiential space.'

'What's the point of that?'

'The point? Tell a cockroach about your daily life. See how much mutual understanding there is. When it comes to glitchglots, we're the bugs. For true communication to take place, the cockroach must evolve. That's what we're trying to do here.'

'That's a terrible analogy. Roaches ignite disgust in the superior species at every turn. Then they get squashed.'

I'm surprised by the force of my objection. I thought I'd changed since my incarceration but apparently not. In my old life, my innate cynicism would habitually kill dead even the slightest prospect of metaphysical awareness. Obviously, nothing's changed.

'The abomination in the mesh node. That was part of it?'

'Yes, he was a manifestation. A test subject let's say. Something that escaped. Originally, we captured him because there was something inside him that demanded to be preserved. He was a channeller of vibrations, a summoner of interdimensional beings, but, in the end, as a construct, all he really did was draw upon a folio of snapshots from a numb world. That's why we need to take the next step with them, and to do that we need your help.'

'We want to harness the potential of your kind,' Wata says, 'to take advantage of your highly attuned communion with the more complex phases of artificial life.'

I look straight ahead at inverted Ravenscroft reflected in the north wall. He speaks to the side of reverse-me's head, unperturbed by the lack of eye contact. The north wall starts to throb until it's no longer a mirror but a screen. Projected onto it is a horrorshow in which Wata, Ravenscroft and I are the stars. We're gorging on each other, a foaming mass of severed limbs, exposed intestines and cannibalistic sex.

As the scene wears on, it becomes harder to ascertain who's doing what to who. I think I see Ravenscroft, although he's nothing but a viscous puddle, treacle-sticky, with long talons emerging from the pulp. He penetrates me from behind, tearing the flesh from my back, a brutal potter moulding unforgiving clay.

'What the hell is this, Ravenscroft?'

'Yes?'

'The gore fest on your wall!'

'All I see is the three of us quietly meditating, merging our personalities within a shared mindspace. If you see something different, than that is a scene from the cinema of your mind.'

I walk over to the wall, placing my hand on it. It's swallowed by the veiny skin-surface that has regrown to obscure the reflection. I withdraw in disgust, expecting my hand to drip with the remnants of wall-flesh, but all that transpires is a tiny dance of point clouds just above my knuckles.

'What is this stuff?'

'Plastex. You rarely see it these days, given the market domination of Kvvlt. It's a psychotropic material. It projects a scene unique to your psyche. Each of us sees only what is desired in our hearts. Plastex is a consequence of vexxing. It's the true mirror because it reveals things as they really are. Such a pity that it was overrun by Kvvlt, a mind-numbing material that not only does all the work for you but is susceptible to hacking.'

'I thought you were against artificial stimulants.'

Ravenscroft tugs his sleeve. I've noticed he does that when challenged. The action is fleeting, but I see it.

'Kalsari, why do you engage in this constant one-upmanship? Are you that insecure? How exhausting it must be.'

Wata leans across the couch to stroke Ravenscroft's face, a hungry diner jonesing for a feast.

'Yes, it's sad,' she whispers. 'So much work still to be done.'

She turns to me. 'Don't make us doubt you at this late stage. We must know that your indiscretions are merely blips. You must be all in because there is no going back. Are you all in?'

'I told you so.'

'Alright,' Ravenscroft says. 'Enough talk. Let's set a date. Day after tomorrow?'

'If you say so.'

'Try to rest before then.'

He winks, forced jocularity guarding a secret agenda. 'And keep those violent emotions under check.'

'You mean what's on your wall? Yes, it's horrible but also really hot. I'm very confused right now.'

'Channel it,' Wata says. 'That's our advice.'

She rises. 'Goodbye, Ingram.'

They kiss, and I squirm in the usual fashion, but this time I'm unsure if it's Wata or Ravenscroft I desire the most. I don't suppose it matters. They are a gestalt after all, confirmed by the image of their conjoined brain gifted to me by the sentient north wall.

ASCENSION

Somehow, I have ended up in bed with Wata, but we do not consummate. We haven't since the first night we spent together. She is lying beside me, whiting out, hands clasped across her belly as if to protect it from further trauma.

I miss her. I watch her face, the gentle breathing that parts her lips. I try to penetrate her skull with my useless brainwaves, but I can't reach her. I must wait, I know that. Wait for her to tell me what to do.

We sleep for the better part of a day, at least I do. It's anyone's guess as to her encephalopathic state. I don't dream, and in the brief moments when I'm awake, I watch the incremental discolouration of her eyes. At irregular intervals, her pupils return, and I anticipate communion, but then the orbs roll back into her skull, the whitespace takes over and Wata is lost to me again.

As we enter day two of our bed-in, she begins to regard me with focused awareness. Hot flushes swamp my senses as I anticipate her touch, only for her to rise from the bed and dress instead. Reluctantly, I do the same.

Keep chipping away. Follow the path.

We pad down the hallway in our faux-medieval costumery. There is a nondescript door to the left. Wata blinks and it opens. We enter, and she takes me through an enclosed, circular walkway overlapping a cornucopia of other walkways. I can see the near-side extremities of the lower levels radiating out into the expanse of the darkened building. I wonder what they conceal, the secrets that lie behind the endless dormitory doors.

She tugs my arm, motioning for me to continue. We arrive at a small elevator. Ravenscroft is inside, sitting on the floor, playing with a small, shiny object. It looks like a gyroscope. He rises and presses the object into Wata's hand. He offers her a light kiss on the cheek, and she enters the elevator. She turns and displays her palms to me. The object is gone.

'Look, Wata, I don't have time for magic tricks. Can we cut to the chase?'

'You have as much time as we allow,' Ravenscroft snaps.

The interior of the elevator is gleaming. I join them in the capsule and the door shuts. I stare at my face in the polished metal. It's hardly there, the visage of a waxworks dummy melting in the sun.

'More plastex?'

They look at each other, then Ravenscroft presses a button, and we ascend in silence.

The door opens.

'You first,' he says, jabbing the small of my back. I leave the elevator, emerging into a white room with white curtains. Wherever this is, it's not the cafeteria. The space is small and cramped, claustrophobic like my dorm.

Ravenscroft presses his face to mine, whiting out as he does.

—You can't move your feet or hands, he plinks. You can't open your eyes.

'Of course I can.'

He extends his palm.

—Push down.

'I thought you said...'

—Push.

I do it, but his resistance is strong.

—Keep pushing.

I press so hard that the pad of my thumb aches. He removes his hand and I tumble to the floor.

—Can you open your eyes now?

—No.

They're glued shut, but I don't panic. On the contrary, the sensation is a deep bath.

—You can't move your feet or hands.

—No.

—Wait here.

—I'll wait.

I lie on the floor, blind and immobile. I am always waiting. Never consummating. Breakthroughs don't happen to me. The thrilling climax is forever out of reach.

In my mind, I drift away, skeeting like a wraith across the black ice of chronosthesis, the time that can't be found. Without external stimuli, there's no way to judge the passage of the clock.

A sharp object scrapes the base of my spine. I gasp as it plunges into the bone. The violation is a slow ache, spreading like sin.

'Open them now.'

My body is a discarded clothes horse. The legs are twisted at crazy angles, the arms bent back. It should hurt like hell, but I feel nothing, a spectator at my own demise. I can taste the hacked flesh inside my throat all over again. If it wasn't for the numbness, this would be the highest and most dangerous thrill of all, the jouissance of stepping outside my body to watch my own self-destruction. You see yourself in the cage, you see yourself outside the cage. Real *Hellraiser* stuff. Pleasure and pain, indivisible.

Ravenscroft loiters, hunched over the foot of the bed like a succubus. He's changed into deep-red scrubs. Mask, gloves, long smock. He looks like the boss man at the Spanish Inquisition.

I try to rise but the meat won't go. It figures. My entire life has been spent role-playing a shabby serpent of sin, sprawled on one slumber-pallet or another.

You'll dream a lot here. Maybe you're dreaming now.

'Kalsari, I apologise for the epidural, but we can't allow your panic to disrupt the process.'

'Then put me under. I can't stand paralysis.'

'That won't be possible. Your mind must be conscious to welcome the implant.'

'Welcome it?'

He smiles behind the mask. Even covered up, he's supernaturally charismatic. 'The implant is synthetic, but it's alive. We grow it like a worm. It feeds on your brainwaves, replacing what it takes. With interest.'

Anxiety grips me, but I can neither run nor blackout. I suppose I should be grateful. I've been granted what I've craved for so long, a front-row seat at my own personal torture session.

Carefully, Ravenscroft places a leather pouch on a small table. Inside is a set of dun-coloured implements. The handles are double jointed, affixed to serrated blades. I could swear that instead of forging these evil instruments in a factory, he's sawed the fingers from a cadaver, flayed the flesh and sharpened the bones.

The torture-porn reality causes me to retch with fear and panic. He could gut me like a fish just for kicks and I'd be powerless to prevent it.

The stress from this stark realisation does something to my eyes. They have become unbearably light-sensitive. The white heat radiating from the decor generates spasms in the curvature of the air. My eyelids pulse and fluctuate, my pupils are tight and sore. Floaters despoil my vision, gelatinous spots morphing and writhing like organisms under a microscope. They multiply and combine, cataract-blurring my sight with dark wodges.

I massage my eyes, pressing hard to release phosphene imprints and retinal afterglows. A thought occurs to me. I probably have been vexxing since my arrival but there has been no visual announcement to that effect, no splitting or rendering of the world once I crossed over. I need that visual stimulus. I must have it to delineate universes, otherwise the terror of eternal disembodiment will devour the last vestiges of sanity.

Something emerges from the jellied visual field, a languid image of Wata, fixing me with her trademark blank gaze.

I note that her hand is holding mine until I realise that it's Ravenscroft's, his arm snaked around Wata's waist. I track the arm and there he is, holding up the rear, partially obscured by Wata's somatic despotism.

His hand brushes my cheek, and the fear and nausea subsides, purged by a liquid sexual rush.

'The procedure,' he says, 'begins with what we call biomechanical abduction. That's when we modify and enhance your brain's neural electrical network, accelerating its capacity for empathetic synthesis. This ensures that the implant will not be rejected. Through biomechanical abduction, the implant degrades and then rejects the heterogeneous nodes in your brain.'

Wata breaks in, and for a few seconds her voice overlaps with his, a carrier mixed with a modulator. It's a curious effect, probably an aural hallucination from the epidural.

'The implant synthesises the homogeneous elements, forming a telepathic template with your peers.' She issues a thin smile, directed Ravenscroft's way. He receives it inside his mind, unpacking it like bubble wrap in some secret corner of their concatenated soul.

'Wata will assist me,' he says. 'She was the first to undergo treatment. Ever since, she's skilfully initiated those that follow. You're in safe hands.'

Wata Shreds. My star pupil.

I study them for further signs of erotic synthesis, but I come up short. Ravenscroft is professional to a fault, Wata the custodian of my sustained health.

I wonder about our prior liaison. Perhaps Wata assumes that persona for the benefit of every patient. It's possible that her love for me may not be exclusive but a tool employed judiciously to guide each initiate into the appropriate mindset. Having considered this, I no longer suffer the animal sting of pride. Instead, I admire her commitment to the task and loyalty to Ravenscroft's core beliefs.

Cradling my head, she diverts my attention above. I see four orange lights inset into the ceiling, arranged in a semi-circle. Framed within my faulty visual field, the orbs flicker wildly, moving about like the prancing skylights beyond Ravenscroft's glass ceiling.

'Watch,' she says. 'Something will happen over there.'

I hold my gaze. The orbs wink out one by one, and when the last light is extinguished, my eyes go dark.

Behind the lids, there is an electrical flash, blood-red sparks dissolving within the blackness of my mind.

Sparks dancing between two halves. Of what?

'Pablo? Is that you?'

EROSION

There is no substance to this world, just a crop of vague blurs swimming in a dull and formless palette, but what the colour field lacks, the mind invents, stocking the abyss with false realities.

A cluster of holographic clouds syncretises, hypoxic retinal effects forged from scotopic b-waves. I hear a muffled voice, distant and time-stretched. It's not a voice and it's not a synth. I don't know what it is.

—Some memories are radial maze tests, assessed for learning and capacity.

I think it sounds like Wata, but it has masculine notes. Ravenscroft? It is and it isn't. It's a machine hybrid of the two, formalising what I had only imagined before.

The message triggers change in the cluster. The clouds form a solid mass around vague coordinates, flooding the gravity well that contains me. Lost inside their dimensions, I slough off fragments of time like flakes of dead skin.

I've grown a body but the shape of it is wrong. The soft machine is low to the ground. It's the frame of a scrawny kid, seven years old, a psycho on training wheels. I'm perched on the edge of a mattress grave, the cold slab that would later host the marooned capsule, the miner's cage, the desolate coffin.

I have captured the family cat, a fat, black rugby ball with white whiskers. I hold her head as she struggles, then I remove the whiskers with scissors. She breaks free and staggers away, her balance in tatters.

My mother enters and sees the distressed cat. 'Kalsari, what have you done?'

I'm relieved to be caught. I know I wouldn't have stopped at the whiskers. I would have taken the scissors to its neck and gouged the life from the wretched creature.

'It wasn't me. It was Britt.'

My older brother. He deserves it. I don't like him or the stupid cat.

'Don't talk rubbish. He's–'

I white out, trying to contact my handlers, contaminating the scene with unfathomable future tech.

'Your eyes!' Mum screams. 'What have you done to your eyes?'

—Memories are discrete values. Sample and hold.

Dark matter leaks from the clouds. I fight the corkscrew tide, raising my head above the surface of time. The terrain that greets me is familiar but strange, the dimensions of another miserable year.

I have grown older since I mutilated the cat. I'm ten and Britt is fifteen. He's been working out. He's a gym bunny, an angry musclehead consumed with roid rage. He has overpowered me, locked me in my bedroom, tied me to a chair. Something broke inside him long ago, and he blames me for everything, for his life.

When I was born, my brother said that Mum and Dad stopped caring about him. He said that they lavished all their attention on me. He thinks I'm the Golden Child, but I'm not that. I'm nothing. I'm minuscule, insignificant. I'm so shy, I'll cross the street to avoid speaking to friends. I don't want the attention, none of it. Why is he dragging me out into the open, exposing me to the world?

He has no idea how his internal heat makes me feel. I'm being blamed for something that happened when I was in the womb. It means I don't have a brother, not really. I think he's teaching our parents a lesson as much as he is me.

The curtains are open, and the sun is setting, sending peach-coloured light into the room. It's so pretty, contrasting with the petty horror of my fraternal torture.

My brother flicks rubber bands at my face. The short, sharp pain is horrific, and I cry hot tears, terrified he'll take out an eye.

'Know what those bastards did?' he snarls. 'Whipped me black and blue.' He raises his shirt. His torso is striped with hellish marks. I know our parents are old school, but this is child abuse. I turn away, appalled at the sight.

The bed is behind me. I wish I had eyes in the back of my head so I could see its comforting parameters. Instead, I visualise it with my mind's eye.

The mattress is a pit of quicksand. I want to dive into it, letting the muck draw me under and out of life. I want the sand to fill my lungs, then I'll be free.

I hear the thwack of the rubber bands. One in the forehead, one in the cheek, one in the neck. Then bang, right in the eye. Darkness slams shut the entrance to the well.

You could say I saw it coming. Now, I don't see anything at all.

—Some memories are chewed tapes, scrambled codecs.

My body is lost within the reverbstorm, devoured by inviscid forces. Another type of vision emerges. I have mutated again but the intervening year no longer exists. Can I really be eleven? I'm taller than my father, but he's always been on the short side, stocky and stubby. The Keg on Legs, his air force mates called him, another reason to inspire contempt.

We hustle through a crowded shopping mall, slowing as my father removes his spectacles to clean them. Nearly blind, he walks into a glass door, breaking his nose. He collapses to his knees, blood streaming from his face.

I stand there, unable to help. I am enjoying the spectacle. I am dying from shame. I want to kill him for the public embarrassment he's caused me. His pain is nothing, just an ant to be stepped on.

—Most memories are corrupt images, prised from clogged recording heads.

Quantised alpha rhythms rattle my skull, encoding me with all that I know, all that I am. They spike me with adrenaline, pumping me up until I am thirteen years old, trailing my uncle through a packed cinema foyer.

My uncle is a strange man, so I'm told. Other relatives point out how he's as thin as a bird and has been never married, as if these facts alone are the index to madness.

His hobby is wind turbines. He sits beneath them and meditates to the sound they make. He takes a cut lunch and spends whole days in the field. He is attuned to vibrations, in sync with curved air.

He has paused his important work to take me to the movies. We stand around the foyer.

'Wait,' he says. 'I'll get the tickets.'

Obscured by the dense crowd, I don't notice the shifty stranger sidling up to me until he twists my arm behind my back. The creep whispers something foul and sexual, an entree into a world I never knew existed. He smells of cask wine and cigarettes, the underside of a rotting carpet exposed after years of decay.

He frog-marches me towards the exit, but my uncle returns and the creep escapes, swallowed by the roiling crowd. My uncle shifts uneasily, challenged by my plight. He gives me a ticket, and we head off as if it had never happened.

We watch a horror film, a popular hit of the day. A man has been possessed by a poltergeist. He's looking in the bathroom mirror and in the reflection the skin on his face starts to boil and run red. His face is melting and he rips it off, unable to bear the torment. All that's left in the mirror is a bloody skull and pulpy eyes in sockets, but the man is alive. The skull screams and the reflection changes. His face returns to normal.

I'm not shocked because I can't concentrate. The incident with the creep consumes me. I think about how damaged I'd be if he'd made good his plan. A part of me wishes it had happened because I have nothing going for me. To be tarred with the unimaginable would allow me to be isolated forever.

—A handful of memories are continuous time signals, perfect reconstructions.

Fetid transmissions resurface from my once-young plastic brain. They knit together the genetic blueprint of my past and future selves. Guided by their signal, I wander into the bathroom of our modest family home. The shell is psycho pre-teen yet again, the fabulous sequel.

I pull back the shower curtain. There's an oval object hanging from the rail. It's green, quivering and undulating. It's a cellular slime mould, disgustingly alive.

The hyphae congeals and the mould jumps from the rail to the wall. The slime raises its front section, as if it has a head, and turns to look at me, even though it has no eyes. Its flagellated cells swarm, and the slime tries to speak, although it has no mouth. All I hear is a clicking burr, riddled with modulation and sibilance.

I flick the thing with a towel. It detaches from the wall, accompanied by a foul plopping sound. It lands on my face, blanketing my nostrils, mouth and ears, coating my tongue and lungs with spores, deadly spores.

—Memories are neurally inspired non-linear units, sensitive to local motion-energy.

Glass-beaded recollections beach on the Jovian shores of my mind. They are distress beacons from a far-distant time, showreels of vicious past lives. In one reel, my body is seven, but my mind is old. I'm sitting in my bedroom with a girl my age. Our eyes are white.

Something glints on her face, pearly-silver piercings or something alive, it's hard to tell.

We're scrying a mirror and inside the glass is a putrefied, severed head. It's so far gone, I can't tell if it's human or beast.

—

There are no more transmissions from my handlers. They have decided to let me fall.

DECEPTION

Dying skies. The death of grass. Dead skin. A cadaverous personality. I'm scarred with gunpowder traces of actual physical hurt, poisoned by the residue of lives I can't remember and no longer need. I become aware of other sensations, other marks. I can't see through my eyes. They're obscured by a filthy bandage that reeks of blood and pus.

—Try to relax.

It's inside my mind again. The hybrid voice, the gestalt. The utterance is overlaid with a sub-acoustic virtuality. I hear colours, as if the dream-logic from the operation has been absorbed through the pores of my skin. The colours sound like broken blue rain, chattering pink birds, falling orange code.

The bandage is sliced from my eyes. White light overwhelms me, fabricated wavelengths. My vision adjusts, gradually achieving a staggered formalism, and the harsh ambience settles. There's a mirror by the bed, not much else. Mirrors, always mirrors. Ravenscroft's whole shtick is based on deception.

I steal a glance, appalled by the state of my eyes. They're ringed with deep purple bruises, ghastly mutations, intimations of new flesh. A face looms large. Ravenscroft. He removes the cannula from my hand and salves the puncture wound.

'Welcome back.'

Wata hangs back, impassive. Next to her is Rydell, glowering. Max hovers on the fringe, his bird-like face as silly as ever.

I'm smitten by the chaotic wonder that is Shiny. She's skeeting around the bed like a ballet dancer, all rippling muscle and fluid biomachinery. I sense a stirring deep within my loins, a volcanic lust that confuses me. During our first meeting, I found her kinetic tics immensely disturbing. They suggested a primal detachment from reality, an animal refusal to conform. Not that I'm a conformist, but her brand of rebellion was too much, too visceral. Now, beneath her flowing dress, she offers a sensual glimpse of evolutionary potential.

I'm happy to see them all, even Max. Even Rydell. They teach me things about myself. I see aspects of myself in them, which is precisely why they annoy me.

I return my gaze to the mirror. Suffused by love radiating from the others, my ocular bruises and scars are radiant, beacons of a sacrifice so tremendous it need not be named, an act of violence endured to complete the gestalt.

Ravenscroft draws his people to his chest. One by one, he tucks us under his wing, patting our hair, reassuring us by his loving actions that we've all made the right choice. Even Rydell rests his head against Ravenscroft's chest like a baby on the teat.

Ravenscroft gifts me his most dazzling smile. 'Back to work, yes?'

'No. I have questions.' It doesn't take long for my habitual negation to kick in. Just the pompous way he phrased the question raised my hackles. 'The little tour of my past indiscretions. Other than sadism, what's the point in making me relive them? And the slime? Pure fantasy! What's any of it got to do with vexxing?'

'Inhabiting memories is the purest form of virtuality. If you can master that, then you are well on the way to auto-immanence.

No cheaters required. As for the slime, well, that's a taste of the very near future.'

I say nothing, fuming inside.

'Ingram,' Wata says, 'shall I return Kalsari to his dorm?'

'Yes, please do.'

She helps me from the bed, and the others part to let us through. Superficially, she's paying attention, but her eyes are disturbing. They're not purely white. I can still see the pupils, but they're blurred, darting from side to side and top to bottom, a screen wipe of the soul.

For the first time, I'm fully aware of how distant she is. Or rather, I'd noticed before but had put it out of mind. Maybe it's more prominent now. Perhaps something changed while I was under. Has she been enhanced further? She seems permanently somewhere else, living multiple lives. They all do because they all share the same dead eyes.

Wata escorts me to the dormitory, and we collapse onto the bed. We hug, and then she disengages, her head lolling on the pillow.

I hope I will be able to join her soon, wherever she is.

EXCLUSION

I open my eyes, absorbing the black hit of night. The nocturnal gaze is a constant in my current life. I'm not a night owl. It's just that time is running out and I have much to do. I miss the old days of vexxing, with cheaters and the attendant paraphernalia. I never slept then, not deep and fulsome sleep. I would doze but the zones were always on, in powersaver mode, running discrete commands behind the unwrapped sky. Now, sleep is a suspension of the dream world, not a return to it.

My days here are characterised by low-level boredom, seasoned with flashes of high strangeness. How have they papered over the cracks? For most people, I suppose dreams habitually crumble under examination, disintegrating into a cloud of illogic and unreality. For everyone here, this bold and elite crew, nothing delineates the occult from reality.

I know there is no real mystery to the nocturnal stories of the mind. Dreams are simply a mechanism for the subconscious to process daily activities, urgent problems and emotional needs. Why then do they colour my waking life so radically it's as if I have lost my mind?

In dreams, I have frequently glimpsed the edges of potential futures. These insights are not prophetic. They are frames cut from unspooling lives that, intuitively, I know I've lived but, intellectually, I grasp are yet to happen. Frustratingly, the absurdity of that temporal paradox follows me into wakefulness from whatever mental dungeon it was dredged from.

Since my recovery from the operation, I have been plagued by a persistent recall of another future event. The signal is a mimetic buoy, steadfast in the face of mental squalls.

The 'memory' retains the qualities of a dream, the nebulous attempts to maintain order in the face of phantasmagoria, yet I cannot infer its genesis in lived reality. How then did it germinate in my mind? Can dreams be sui generis, uncontaminated by reality leakage? Doesn't that suggest access to a parallel universe?

I have a memory of Ravenscroft instructing me to join the others in the dining room, but whether it was before or after the operation I can't say. The internal fixation is riven with the warp of experience. I can feel it in my bones but I'm unable to quantify it, and I know that I'll spend the little time I have left searching for the light at its core.

I try to inhabit the memory, but it belongs to someone else. The body that I occupy in the dream-recall is under remote control. Superficially, the memory is mine. I mean, I recognise the images that swim before my eyes, but only at an abstract level. It's like I've been told an elaborate story about myself, and I'm remembering the telling but not the lived experience. Now, I desperately want to believe the story because to acknowledge the reality would spell the end of me.

The remote body transports my disconnected consciousness to the dining room. It's a horrible sensation to find your physical self responding to another's will. Who controls it if not me?

Ordinarily, I suppose motor neurons fire and the message travels through an axon to the limb you wish to move. Although you are not consciously aware of sending the pulse, when the limb responds there is a satisfying backbrain awareness. The connection is felt at the molecular level, but now the magic is happening and the signal is not from my own brain. I feel nothing, only a cold awareness of an empty fate, a mechanical entrapment much worse than death.

I want to scream to be let out of my body, but nothing emerges. No voice, no synth, no word cloud. All I can do is scream inside my heart.

Through the puppet's eyes, I watch Rydell, Max and Shiny arrange themselves around a circular table. The furniture repulses me. The table is hefty, hewn from ancient, dark wood. It's an abomination in our featherlight world of sparse cubes and infrastructure made from light. It carries the same dispiriting weight as the books in my dorm, the heavy dread that obliterates the soul.

Large surgical lights are suspended above the table. They look superimposed, resolutely out of place, as if my degraded consciousness has scrambled memories of the implant procedure with the recollection of whatever this is.

Rydell is flanked by Max and Shiny, bathed in the harsh glare. There's an empty seat next to him. My body occupies it as Rydell stares me down with murderous intent. Why does he dislike me so intensely? I feel as though we share a dark secret, something deeply objectionable. I know what it is, but somehow I can't articulate it. The bio-wires inside my skull override the impulse. To recall a memory within a memory is to inhabit a nested world, an artifice inside a virtuality. To live inside a nested reality is to seal the manhole shut forever.

I have the urge to wink at him and to my surprise the gesture forms. At last, the shell is listening to neurons in the motor cortex, sorting and translating thought into action.

The gesture fills Rydell with even more rage, and we eye each other like bandidos at the death. Then Wata and Ravenscroft arrive, Lord and Lady Muck. She sits beside me, Ravenscroft next to Max.

He says, 'Thank you all for being here, and good to have you with us, Kalsari. I hope you're feeling better.'

'Yeah, not bad, Ravenscroft, but why can't I enter the Vexworld?'

'Be patient. Let the brain worm take control.'

The skittishness that caused me to wink at the goon surges through my veins. 'Ja, mein fuhrer.'

Max laughs soundlessly and Ravenscroft emits a thin smile, almost Sandersonian in its veiled menace. He tugs his sleeve. At last, I've tripped a nerve. Score one point to me.

'Now that our friend is enhanced,' he says, 'it's time to resume formal training.'

He glares at me, but I'm relaxed. He'll be back to his old self soon enough.

'Kalsari, we've been conducting focused training sessions, developing protocols for something called remote viewing.'

I sigh, loudly, signalling my contempt.

'There's a problem?'

'Sure is. Next, you'll be staring at goats and telling us how you can walk through walls.'

'You've heard about remote viewing? What do you think it is?'

'An unsupported psychic ability. Snake oil for woo-woos.'

'It is an ability, yes. During the remote viewing procedure, the adept senses and describes information about a target that can't be seen and that is separated from the viewer by time or space. There have been many studies done on it. It's not really certain how it works, just that it most certainly does.'

Ravenscroft pauses, assessing me with surgical precision. I flap my palms, signalling for him to come at me.

'We use local sidereal time for our training. At 13:45, when the planet is orientated with the galactic centre, there is a five hundred per cent greater chance of success. Again, we don't really know why. We just accept the signs that appear. Anyway, this daily window lasts for three hours, and optimum results are also achieved when the solar forecast is clear. No flares from the sun, no solar wind.'

'Radna reckons the xenospores parachuted down on solar wind. You're not trying to avoid them, are you?'

'We don't subscribe to Siike,' Wata says. 'We run our own race here. And anyway, it's supposed to be a plasma jet. Not solar wind. You can't even get your conspiracies straight.'

Rydell guffaws.

'Quite so,' Ravenscroft says, raising an arm for peace. 'Now, as we're currently inside the window of opportunity, we must begin.'

He stands behind me, massaging my shoulders. 'Your hostility is noted, my friend, but you mustn't worry. We will create the ideal state, the most crystalline mind map available. We will—'

'It's fine, Ravenscroft. Do what thou wilt.'

He leans in, whispering in my ear. 'A word of warning. Disrespect me in public again, and you'll be begging for Sanderson to take you back. Got it?'

I don't answer. I know which side my bread is buttered. Anyway, it's all an act, part and parcel of our peculiar dynamic.

He returns to the head of the table. 'Shall we try right now?'

Murmurs of assent emanate from the group.

'Everyone, please initiate proceedings.'

Rydell's meaty paw grasps my right hand and Wata holds the other. She strokes my palm, but he deploys an iron grip, determined to crush my bones. It's a test, and I endure the pain, although I know my hand will be maimed. Tears run down my cheeks, and Rydell smiles, relaxing his grip. Score one point to the goon.

They look straight ahead, mind maps melding in communion. Jammed between them, my skull feels tight, cross-hatched by their neuro-comms, but I can't read them.

I scan the semi-circle. Everyone's whiting out, heads lolling gently in the psychosomatic breeze. Why have I been left behind? Why don't I see what they see?

My vision shudders. The dining room degranulates and reflows. Battling to retain the vertical, my head is cement, imploding my spine. I can no longer hold my skull upright, and it snaps back, taking my entire mass with it.

DESTINATION

I've landed on a beach. A bog-standard, sun-kissed beach. There's some significance to the setting. I can't forget the Jovian moon and the beachside tsunami of doom, but it's more than that. In a burning world, beaches are landscapes that I can never reach, only imagine. Death by irony.

The expanse is beautiful. That's dull, but there's nothing left to say. The ocean performs similarly. The water is a quaternary colour, a hexadecimal cliché in strict formation, but the sky is infused with feral CMYK aberrations.

There is a visual distortion in the corner of my eye. A muddy diffusion. I focus on the centrifuge and it splinters into elements of the scene. Point clouds extrude creamy sand dunes. A punctured beach ball. Discarded flip flops. Seashells and seaweed. Condoms and cigarette packets.

In the distance, I spot two figures. One tall, the other small. Buffeted by the wind, they burrow into each other as if to conceal their individuality. To the west, another duo, moving with strength and purpose. They carry implements, long and thin. Weapons or tools, glinting as the sun sets.

As the space between us narrows, I struggle to understand. Are we in some kill-crazy, last-person-standing zone? Maybe alliances were formed and I'm the first kill. That would be disappointing. I've worked so hard to build relationships.

I want to scramble over the dunes to safety, but the terrain looks unmapped. The horizon is lacklustre and incidental, a woolly inconsistency hemming me into the beach. The hunters close in. I have no stomach for hand-to-hand combat. I don't have the stones to stick my neck out for anything except indolence.

Now I see clearly. There's nothing left for me save the thrashing waves and the promise of release. I run into the implausible ocean until the water is at my knees, waist, throat. I keep going until there is no more of me.

One last breath. Wata plinking inside my skull.

—Stop! We're not done with you yet.

Rough hands grip my neck and shoulders, yanking me from the maw. I'm dumped onto the shore. Saltwater spews from my lungs, forming saliva-bubbles on the sand. Rydell stands over me, his great bulk blotting out the sun. Ravenscroft enters the frame.

'You almost scuppered the experiment before it began.'

He plants his hand firmly on the goon's shoulder, holding him back. From what? Me? What did I do?

'Where am I?'

'Where you need to be.'

'No magic spray this time?'

'You don't need it here.'

Wata appears, slit-scanning me with furious eyes. 'Get up, moron. I vouched for you to Ingram. If it wasn't for me, you'd be back with Sanderson! Now, if you put our work at risk again, I'll send you there myself.'

'What about my feelings?' I whine. 'I nearly drowned.'

'The time for psychoanalysis has passed. Everything's a cry for attention with you. Either come to the party or get out of our heads.'

'Get out of *your* heads?'

I turn away, stung by her fury and the truth of her assessment. I watch the ocean. Inverted chromakey pulses ride the waves, staining the air with Drexciyan electricity.

Stealthily, the others climb the dunes like black-clad domestic terrorists scaling a government wall. The terrain is accessible but not for me.

Ravenscroft looks over his shoulder.

'You two coming?'

Wata takes off with her usual speed, and I follow, feet slipping in the sand. I'm prat-falling like a rodeo clown, but I manage to slide down the backside of the dunes, landing at the lip of a vast wetlands. It reeks of eggy bog and necrotic weeds. The scene is too organic for my liking, but I keep quiet, fearful of another backlash.

The others sit cross-legged by the marsh. Some sort of lesson is already in progress. Ravenscroft doesn't muck about.

'Watch the horizon,' he instructs. 'Something will happen over there. Glitchglots respond to sincere intent. They are alive to it.'

I sit at the edge of the group, aware of my lowered status among my peers. Everyone whites out, palms outstretched, and I assume the pose. Behind my eyes, I am held inside a rare groove, a pareidolia of imagined perceptions. The horizon is a gauzy smudge behind the colour field, tantalisingly incomplete.

The transition is not as jarring as the descent onto the beach. It's as smooth as any cheaters, but the sparks don't flower into four dimensions so that's all it remains. Null space, wasted potential.

'Please,' Ravenscroft says. 'Disengage and regroup.'

Our pupils settle and our vision clears.

'Our friends are shy tonight.' Ravenscroft glances my way. 'Perhaps because of our unblooded member. No matter. The rest of us must work twice as hard to compensate.'

Rydell groans.

'I don't get it,' I say. 'In the shell world, everything has been mapped and every object is wired. There are trillions of grain cams floating through the air, no blind spots left. We can travel to mirror clones and experience those coordinates exactly as they exist in the shell world, or we can savour them from a distance. Isn't that the very definition of remote viewing? That's why it's ludicrous to talk about adepts and psychic powers. We're all psychic now. The illusions we maintain in the Vexworld are far more disturbing than any unproven notions of the spirit world.'

'No. You couldn't be more wrong. With mirror clones, there is a lag while the Vexworld updates. It's infinitesimal, but it's there. With remote viewing, we can see beyond reality into an unfiltered realm.'

'I thought the mission was to commune with glitchglots. Now you're saying it's to locate this other realm.'

'Yes. That is the mission, but there is new information. The glitchglots have escaped into the prehensive zones. Make no mistake, these are the most anonymous, unfiltered and unsurveilled parts of the Vexworld. Technically, they're not illegal, but they are unsupervised, so it's hard to know what will be inside them. It could be zones within zones, experimental code candy, glotmash. People dump all kinds of stuff in there. Often, the leavings are of a highly disturbing nature. Somehow, though, that's where they thrive, existing as cellular automata on the virtual plane.'

'But to access prehensives you need special protocols. You must tap into an overlay network that relays your requests through a series of light tunnels until you reach the layers. You need to know how to strangle code, and you need resonant emotional linkages. Only a few have the full set.'

'Why do you think we've chosen you? All bases covered.'

'They're not evolved spamglots, then?'

'No. That was a cover story. To test you.'

'This realm is the afterlife?'

'Maybe. And we're ghost hunters. So who you gonna call?'

Everyone laughs.

'How can your glitchglots do unassisted telepathy? How to test for that?'

'It's simple. They call us, we don't call them. Researchers, including myself, have received unsolicited messages and comms from the glitchglots while our feeds were vaulted.'

'We've developed several theories to account for this behaviour,' Wata says. 'In one of our frameworks, we consider glitchglots as a manifestation of the experience known as EVP, or Electronic Voice Phenomenon. EVP is supposedly what happens when the dead try to speak through electronic media. In the past, people claimed to have heard the voices of the dead in static from TV and radio, even the ambient hum of household appliances.'

'Some say EVP is simply an example of pareidolia,' Ravenscroft continues, 'that is, the drive for the human mind to make meaning from random patterns, but there are some who believe that the actual voices of the dead are speaking through glitchglots. Now, our motto is to investigate every single theory that our adepts develop, no matter how ludicrous, because sometimes the truth will be hiding in plain sight.'

'Is it possible that these glitchglots are actors in some manipulative marketing campaign?'

'No. They are far too mercurial, too sophisticated. I don't think marketers can do real telepathy, do you? Also, glitchglots can't be traced. There is no metadata that gives them away. They appear to have sprung forth fully formed. I say appear to because there's another theory. In this account, the glitchglots are a manifestation of something that has always lived with us, even lived through us, entities in a parallel dimension to ours, co-existent with us on this planet. In the past, they might've appeared as fairies, ghosts, grey aliens, even as interdimensional DMT beings.'

'If they're hiding away in the fourth dimension, how can we see them?'

'Because sometimes, especially in the prehensive zones, the worlds clash and there is bleed-through from their dimension to ours. In the Vexworld, it is becoming more prevalent since the technology itself already fosters a clashing world. The fabric of the Vexworld, the haphazard nature of its protocols, encourages bleed-through, but technology is largely irrelevant since they only appear to certain people gifted with the power of second sight.'

'Like you and Wata? Why should we believe you? You don't even have recordings.'

'But it's not just us who see them. Many of our adepts came to us with no academic background. They simply encountered these entities while vexxing and were perplexed, confused and frightened. Seeking solace and the free exchange of ideas, they ended up joining our organisation and adding their experiences to the mix. More people are coming forward. You yourself saw an entity in your mesh node.'

'That was a malfunction. They're just glitches. Nothing is speaking through them. You said yourself, the Vexworld clashes by its very nature.'

'Just glitches? I don't think you really heard me. The glitches in the glots are the slumbering intelligence, not effluent discharged from it.'

'Iceheads, then.'

'No. Glitchglots are next-level constructs. All who have met them have experienced a foreboding, an eternal dread, as if they've encountered an ancient terror, something that has existed since the dawn of time. The iceheads may be able to scramble your brains and torment you in their hell zones, but they can't induce alien dread. That feeling is not visceral. It is experiential.'

'So how do we access it if we're in the Vexworld? You said the brain worm keeps us permanently vexxed.'

'The Vexworld is no different to unwrapped perception. For example, you can't perceive a particular colour until light strikes an appropriately tuned surface. What exists before the light hits?

Ordinarily, no one can know. With remote viewing, we can access and describe information blocked from ordinary perception by distance or shielding. Even when vexxing. The result? Two nested realities, vex and remote, plus the ability to toggle between them at will.'

'By ordinary perception, you mean the Vexworld.'

'Naturally. Even a person who removes their cheaters can't perceive things as they really are because the Vexworld is reality. Those without cheaters, such as two-percenters, no matter the quality of their eyesight, should really be thought of as vision impaired, but even if the Vexworld is reality, supernature remains. That is our true destination.'

I can't let this rubbish stand.

'The stuff about colour is schoolboy nonsense. Are we to renounce formalism here on this godforsaken shore? Is this rotting bog the place where knowledge curls up to die? Surely you know of the fluctuation-dissipation theorem. The surface of any object contains a unique absorption spectrum. Combined with temperature, electromagnetic variations are uniquely assigned. That generates colour. It is an inherent state even when there is no light to react against.'

'And the wall in my room? The north face. You're saying that has a unique temperature knowable under any circumstance?'

'Mind tricks.'

'What you saw on the wall responded to you, just as colour exists only if you are around to witness it.'

I scramble to my feet. 'Good lord, Ravenscroft. This is insane! Where's the science? It's black magic voodoo. Are you funded by The Swarm or iceheads? Who are your backers?'

I really hate this set-up. It's like being back in class, except this time I'm the recruit soiling his nappy.

'May I remind you where you are? You don't know how to pull the plug. For you, the dunes held an invisible forcefield, but when I approached the coast was clear. What does that tell you?

He's right, of course, wielding facts like a sledgehammer. One point to Ravenscroft.

'Sit down. You're still welcome here, despite the attitude. Just follow the drill and I'll see to it that you return safely.'

'Fine, but why here? Give me something I can believe in.'

'It's simple. This place is a hotspot of psychic resonance, an area where the border between clashworlds is unstable. There is a strange correlation at play. For centuries in the shell world, people reported high-intensity UFO activity over geographical fault lines and fissures. The Vexworld is no different. There are always powerful disturbances when mighty realities rub against each other.'

He reaches inside his jacket, producing a type of instrument. It's a glowing red tube, as wide as his thumb, as long as his arm, with wires trailing from one end and little holes in the side. It must have been one of the 'weapons' I glimpsed in the distance. He was probably the head stalker.

'In the field,' he says, 'we play a series of tones before initiating contact. They're developed through rigorous testing, but if anyone feels discomfort, use your mind hacks to relax the hold. The tones are supposed to be disconcerting. They are a vibrational force. At the quantum level, everything vibrates. Only radical disruption can effect seismic change.'

He presses a dangling wire to his temple and moves his fingers over the holes. The instrument emits a multivalent sonic apparatus that clings to the air like smog. It crawls across my skin, burrowing into the pores, expanding the inside of my skull with high-psi pressure. We collapse as one, clutching our heads in our hands, all except Ravenscroft and Wata.

'Sound is more effective than vision when conveying fear. It induces a sense of horrality, horror as reality. Sound cues set the mood. They fix a sense of anticipated dread in which you are alive to the future, to the monstrosity of what is to come, and when you're alive to the future, the glitchglots come out to play.'

Wata places a hand on Ravenscroft's arm and he falls silent. The instrument stops bleating. I can't be certain, but I sense that he's unnaturally stressed and she's in damage control.

'What you are experiencing,' she says, 'can be thought of as unsound, sound on the edge of perception, sound that cannot be heard precisely but that has a physiological or neurological impact. Unsound attracts the entities. It's catnip to them.'

Rydell staggers to his feet, moving away from the group. He climbs a small dune and sits atop, head bowed. Wata kisses Ravenscroft then joins the goon. She whispers in Rydell's ear, and his face darkens. He swats her with his hand, knocking her backwards and out of sight, then tumbles onto her until his great bulk also disappears behind the dune.

I rush to my feet, worried for her safety, but Ravenscroft signals for me to remain.

'Leave it, Kalsari. She knows what she's doing. She's not called "Wata Shreds" for nothing.'

I'm tense, keeping one eye over his shoulder, waiting anxiously while Ravenscroft drones on.

'Everyone here is a highly skilled adept. You all possess the innate ability to intuitively navigate and create objects at will. You are castle hunters, or were. That makes you well primed for the remote viewing procedure.'

Where is she? Rydell could be doing real damage back there. Meanwhile, I'm left with Max and Shiny, this idiot crew, sitting at Ravenscroft's feet, mouths agape like stunned mullets.

'The next step is to open up the non-linear frame and reduce mental noise so that we can pursue bit-grabbing. Once we are receptive, perceptual information will arrive in a disjointed form. It falls to the remote-viewer to piece it together.'

Max and Shiny start to fondle each other, rolling around on the sand as if I wasn't there. Now I really feel left out. Rydell and Wata are doing who knows what to each other while Dumb and Dumber are screwing right in front of me.

'Remote viewing provides the basis for true non-linear, non-physical telepathic consciousness across time and space. Only then will the implants be complete. Only then will we have realised a four-dimensional, holistic view of the universe. Everything changes from that moment on. We, this group, will function as gods. We'll be one step beyond even the glitchglots. We'll be able to see over, under, inside and out. Of any object, any person.'

'So, the great plan is revealed at last. Total world domination.'

'Correction. Universal.'

Whiting out, Ravenscroft lifts his head to the sky and Max and Shiny fall in line. I complete the process without awareness. I hear Ravenscroft distantly as my vision rolls and dims, but only certain words can be picked out.

'Ganzfield screens… lowered mental noise… sensory isolation… cue the parameters…'

A dirty visual field transforms the wetlands, the air, the sky. The palette is hauntingly familiar but utterly strange, a spectrum beyond human perception.

Yet I see it.

What have I become?

More than human.

Less than an animal.

RECOGNITION

I hear rustling. Wata and Rydell have rejoined the fray. He's panting, she's silent. The visual field that stains the world remains static, save for transient flashes and minor textural flagellations.

Shiny rattles my mod. Her synth-clone is not the usual, irritating clang. It's like steam from a hot shower, a sneak attack on my libido.

—How are you feeling? It's beautiful with the brain worm, isn't it? So seamless and natural.

—It's so natural I hadn't realised I was vexxing until you suggested it just now.

Ravenscroft destroys the peace. 'Wata and Kalsari, you're the first pair. Wata, you're the monitor, Kalsari the viewer.'

—Better hush, Shiny plinks. He means business.

'Wait. I don't know how to view. What's the target?'

Wata takes my hand. I want to look at her, to find common ground, but I can't break the field. I see nothing except overlapping sheets of grey.

'You don't receive that information,' she says. 'You wait for clues. I'll reveal the coordinates. When you hear them, blink as quickly as you can. When the target appears, blink again. Are you ready?'

'Yes, Wata. Ready.'

'37° 37' 54S, 144° 55' 22E.'

I hear Ravenscroft tuning his instrument. The subliminal hum invades my reality, but my body does not shrivel in revulsion. I blink as instructed and the solid air cracks apart like salt-damaged leather splitting in the sun. In the hazy afterglow, data symbols are suspended. I'm far from Wata now, connected only by plinks.

—First impressions are important. When you see the data, sample and hold. Got a fix?

—I think so.

—You think so? Be precise!

—I see angular lines.

—That's a tower.

—Curved lines in front.

—A boundary of some sort. Not a natural perimeter, something electric and dangerous.

—Layered, jagged lines behind that.

—A mountain range. Now, hold those impressions inside your mind.

—The visuals are flooding in. I am inside the scene.

—Check. Were your first impressions correct?

—Exactly so.

—Walk to the perimeter.

—I'm at the edge. It's a Swarmtrooper nano-barb setup, but I'm passing straight through it. Swarmtroopers everywhere. Why can't they see my persy? Why am I allowed here?

—Because you are not there, nor is your persy. Describe it.

—I see the summit shrouded in clouds, vee-drones darting in and out. Wata, this is Flawless! I'm back at Flawless. I've been here before, with the Sphinx.

—That wasn't real. It was an in-media sim. Continue and keep up the commentary. Miss a beat and the connection will be lost.

—I see a shimmering haze of audiovisual pollution. A plague-storm of data insects.

—Good. Keep it flowing. Really feel the description. Live inside it. That will help you maintain the connection. Remember, don't skimp on detail. Every observation is important.

—The haze is ad pollution, semi-sentient marketing residue from the Skymesh circuit, probably fallen to the lower levels after outliving the campaign cycles. I see loop trailers, mainly Radna Siike and domestic first-persons, but there are deep fissures in the signals. The data clouds are coagulating, forming an outline. Something is growing inside the enormous expanse. It's black as sin, trapping all light. The outline is a humanoid shape! The void is the body. The void is Kvvlt! Whatever this is, it's dressed head to toe in Kvvlt combat gear. Black-hole boots, balaclava, jumpsuit, wide industrial goggles with opaque lens. Orange code is flashing across the reflective glass, but I don't recognise the syntax.

—Easy, now.

—It's carrying a long, thin tube attached to a small power pack. There's a two-percenter nearby. No legs, just stumps. He's crawling, trying to get away from this thing, this data beast, but it's aiming the tube at the degenerate's head. Nano-bullets! A shower of pink foam. Blood, bones and brains erupting like a geyser! There's nothing left of his head. It's like it just melted from the inside. Body's still intact, rocking back and forth.

—Jones, withdraw. Get out of there now!

VEXATION

I wake with a nosebleed and a sharp pain in my forehead. Max and Shiny hover over me, their bloated faces filling the scene.

'I'm so sorry,' I splutter. 'I'm bleeding on your sheets.'

—It's okay, Shiny plinks. We don't mind.

'Is this your dorm?'

—Yes.

I don't know how I ended up here. Spatial shifts are scarier than temporal dislocation. Time shifts can be explained away as madness but unaccounted-for bodily displacement is a rupturing of reality, a cosmic joke.

—Ingram told us to watch over you until you return.

'From where?'

Their dorm is sparser than mine. No bookshelf, no desk. Nothing but their small bed.

—What's the last thing you recall?

'The dining room. No, the beach, that's coming back. The dunes, the tower, but details are lost. I see only the spaces between.'

—Your session was so entertaining. You took us on a tour of a whole new world. The details were peachy keen. Some elaborate yarn about vigilante humanoids that kill two-percenters for kicks. Born from data clouds, you said. Very imaginative.

I feel a terrible isolation, as if I have aged too fast and the world party is continuing without me.

'Why are you doubting what I reported? I thought the idea was to take the remote viewing at face value. I saw what I saw.'

They laugh inside my head, guffawing in synth tones.

—Oh, you're sad. Do you want to stay with us?

'Yes, I suppose.'

—Ah, Max plinks. The trademark ambivalence. Here lies the man who has everything only he doesn't realise it.

I stare greedily at Shiny. She's more beautiful than ever, but how can I be rid of Max? He hangs around like a bad smell.

—You're such a mystery, she plinks. You challenge Ingram, but he seems to indulge you. He likes you very much, that's clear.

Max studies my eyes.

—Why doesn't he telepath?

—Good question. Why, Kalsari? You're one of us, now.

'I've got too many blockers. I haven't worked through my emotional baggage.'

Wata is my baggage. I had a connection with her and it died. I want to shake her down, but I don't know how to do it without cheaters. I concentrate on her physical form, and just when I have a fix on her, a blockwave stuns me, flooding my perceptual field with apocalyptic imagery. Cities on fire. Blood-red skies. Skulls crushed underfoot. Rotting babies. Necrophilia. Two-percenters eating their dead kin.

I sit bolt upright like a gas-filled corpse. 'Make it stop!'

Max seizes my shoulders, pushing me back onto the bed. Working rapidly, he removes his belt and stuffs it into my mouth, then he jams his arm under my chin, nearly breaking my jaw. For such a weed, he possesses surprising strength.

—Easy, tiger. Wata doesn't want you to contact her. She's erected a reverse experiential space to repel you.

I manage to push him away, removing the belt from my mouth. Everything is so over the top with these two. 'Don't touch me again, pal.'

—Or what? You've never had a physical fight in your life! You're a marshmallow, Jones.

'How do you know what I saw just now?'

—We can still read you. Your brainwaves are not a feed like in the old days. You are a flow, a stream. The trick is in knowing when and where to dive in.

'Lucky for you. In the old days, I'd scramble your brains with just one blink, you odious little shit.'

There's the synth-laugh again.

—Maybe you'll work it out in time, but by then we'll be on the next level. You'll always be in our shadow. True telepathy means accessing your mind at any time, against your will if necessary. Ingram wants no secrets among us. So, lock your feed if you wish. When the gestalt sets, your tedious little hacks will be irrelevant anyway.

Shiny giggles and whites out, a zombie starlet performing for her adoring admirers.

—Max, did you see that?

—Yes, my love, I did.

They kiss, laughing uproariously inside their minds.

'Shiny, what's going on?'

—You can't see? Everything is flooding in.

—Oh no! Max plinks, his synth clone chewy with fear.

He collapses onto the bed, clasping his skull, and Shiny leaps on top of him, trying to prise his hands away. I back away against the door, watching the two love birds in horror.

She's so close to his face, I fear she'll bite it off, and Max is thrashing so wildly, I expect his skin to split straight down the middle.

The door opens, knocking me to my knees. Ravenscroft hustles in, trailed by Rydell. 'Jones, what have you done?'

'Nothing. They went nuts, saying they could see things.'

Rydell picks them up like rag dolls, one under each arm. They kick and struggle with all their might.

'Go, Rydell,' Ravenscroft says. 'Bathe them in the light.'

They leave but Ravenscroft hangs back. 'Did they interrogate you?'

'About the viewing? Yes, but I remember nothing.'

'Really? Think again.'

'Only the setting. They said I'd imagined an alternative reality.'

'No. That world exists but you don't.'

'I don't? Okay, that explains a few things.'

'I mean, your physical form, the coordinates you currently occupy.'

'When I was under, I thought I was viewing through cheaters. That's weird.'

'A subconscious longing for your old life, I suppose.'

'What now?'

'Stay here and sit tight. Await further instructions.'

'That's it?'

'What were you expecting?'

'Closure.'

He laughs. 'For what? You don't even have a leading question.'

He takes off and I return to the bed. I no longer feel close to Ravenscroft. He makes me feel so stupid, and I don't need negative energy in my life right now. Where will I go? These people are all I have.

I hold myself tight, fingernails drawing blood from my wrists. The blood dries and smells like rust, spent energy from an overclocked engine.

INCEPTION

I'm beginning to suspect that my opposition to synth clones has earmarked me for the next laryngectomy. Should've kept my mouth shut, but to hell with Ravenscroft. I won't stay cooped up like a lab rat. He must have a recording of what I saw when I was viewing. I intend to find it. I'm sure it's related to whatever happened to Max and Shiny just now.

I head towards the south wing. Wata is on my mind, but I'm starting to dislike her intensely. I reckon she's colluding with Ravenscroft in a hazing ritual. It's unnecessary and cruel. We're not in the army. We're supposed to be equals right from the start. Positive affirmation reinforces the gestalt, belittling and humiliation tears it apart. That's always been the mantra around here.

I arrive at the dining room, scene of the crime. No one's around and the lights are off. I don't know when the next remote viewing will take place, but I imagine it will be here. I'll wait. I want to catch these people by surprise for a change.

I wonder if we'll return to the beach. Maybe I can get a head start. I try to visualise the data symbols, but the scene won't come. My eyes are dumb vessels, mute receptors.

I retrieve a fresh lollipop from my pocket. They keep the dorms well stocked with them, always red. Ravenscroft said it's to maintain an oral fixation during pure telepathy. If you can't speak, there must be another outlet.

I hear chatter outside. I stalk the hallway to investigate. I lean over the railing. Wata and Rydell are below, arm in arm, heading towards the elevator.

It might've been a touching love scene if not for Rydell's animal physicality. He's pawing at Wata's back and neck but she's curiously passive. That animal! He's drugged her. How else to explain her dimming fire?

He yanks her hair, roughly jerking her precious head this way and that. He does it over and over, trying to shake her apart, and I want to yell to her, but words won't form, not in synth or in speech. The scene is dreamlike, lucid, but I don't have the power to influence it. Only Wata can. I know she will. I've come to realise that she has always been the director. Not Ravenscroft. I don't know what his role is exactly, but it can never match her inner strength. She sees right through him and all the way through Rydell. Straight through me.

Her clothes and hair are dishevelled, her neck bruised, but the electricity returns. Summoning her strength, she prods Rydell in the ribs and pulls his ears, baiting him until he swings his huge fist, crashing it into her face. With a theatrical flourish, he turns on his heel, as nimble as a ballet dancer, ending the scene.

Wata tilts her head upwards, blood dripping from her nose and mouth. She returns her gaze to Rydell, but her pupils have gone. Snarling, he raises his fist, but terror lives inside his eyes.

The fist drops and he falls to the floor, clasping his head. His face is a horror show. I've never seen someone in so much pain. His skin is rubber, contorted with every invisible torture, barely human.

He slumps to the ground, blood streaming from his ears, hair, nails. I should be enjoying his comeuppance, but I'm petrified.

Wata maintains her pose, thrilling to her power. She kicks Rydell in the side of the head, but he doesn't move.

Ignoring my presence, she looks to the heavens, eyes white and arms outstretched, giving thanks for the hunt and the kill.

DETECTION

Wata turns to me, but I don't know if she sees me. She still has the zombie eyes. I race back to the dining room, searching for a makeshift weapon, but there's nothing, only a figure in the shadows. It waves a hand and the surgical lights flood the room.

The figure is Ravenscroft. 'Your negative energy will ruin this. Whatever you're feeling, you can't allow it to destroy the mission.'

'That's rich. What about Wata and Rydell? You can't tell me that's a healthy dynamic.'

'Stay away from him. He is another experiment, a delicately held one.'

'Relax, Ingram. Get some sleep. Take a holiday. You have nothing to fear from me.'

He scoffs. 'Fear doesn't enter into it.' He wants to say more, but he's distracted. 'Ah, we were just talking about you.'

Wata and Rydell enter. I'm astounded to see him. He follows Wata obediently, his trademark malevolence nowhere in sight. His eyes are bruised and puffy, resembling putrid steaks, and one ear has been torn off. He looks like hell, which is just fantastic to see, but how can he be alive?

She's subdued, but her eyes are dangerously clear.

'Good,' Ravenscroft says. 'A full house. Now, I know we've all been on edge, that's to be expected. We've been conducting these sessions for two months and remote viewing can be emotionally taxing. On top of that, we've not had a single sighting. Still, you mustn't lose heart. Perseverance is key.'

He sounds disillusioned. I don't think even he believes this crap anymore.

'Two months? The beach was only a couple of days ago.'

'Yes, Kalsari. Two months. Think it through. The beach wasn't your first transmission. You were practising all the way up until that moment.'

'Yeah, right,' I wheeze. 'You people are soft in the head.'

Why do I act like this? I'm no better than Max and Shiny. They've been so dotty lately, their minds stuck in a loop. No short-term memory, no anticipation of the future. Hopelessly lost inside a temporal cloud. Where are they now? Bathing in the light, whatever that is. Wherever it is.

Rydell reaches across the table, grabbing my throat. 'Who do you think you are? You come in here like a snotty little shit and disrupt everything. Just keep your trap shut and run with the program.'

'Or what?'

'Or I'll slaughter you where you sit.'

'Come on, man. You've had it in for me ever since Nary-A-Woman. Are you in love with me or something?'

'You think I'm an animal, that you're better than me.'

'I think you're paranoid. Maybe Wata can help you to relax.'

His grip tightens, tearing the arteries in my throat. I feel the blood rising to my mouth, drowning me in my own juices. Warm urine trickles down my leg, and I start to lose consciousness, my larynx crushed by Ape Man. Is this how they perform the laryngectomy? I haven't seen any medical equipment around here except the weird scalpels.

Brain attack. No oxygen to the skull. Blood jammed. Heart out of rhythm. He means to murder me, but I'm peaceful. They say your life flashes before your eyes during moments like these, but all I see are blinding white frames, as if the images have been deleted.

'Enough!' Ravenscroft screams. 'I'll expel you both, no questions asked. I've had it.'

Rydell lets go and I slump forward, gasping for air. I'm filled with righteous indignation. Why am I being admonished like a naughty schoolboy? I'm the victim, here.

Ravenscroft reminded me of my former self just then, unable to control the class, desperate and unhinged. Finally, the cracks are showing. Everyone's lost the plot, including The Maker.

Wata sits beside me, nudging my shoulder like an old friend. I flinch, setting off the agony in my bruised neck.

'You really have a special talent,' she says.

'How's that?'

'For pissing people off.'

'It's a death wish. I'm too lazy to do the job myself.'

'I know what it is, idiot. Do you want to go back?'

'To the beach?'

'Somewhere adjacent.'

'I'm hurting bad.'

'Doesn't matter. Once you cross over, it's of no consequence what happens here. When you're in, you're in.'

'I thought you didn't want to see me again.'

'Don't be thick. That was Max hacking your mind. He's a child, always playing dumb pranks. Well, now it's backfired on him. He's not coming back from wherever he is.'

I turn to Rydell. He's calm, arms folded, watching us perform for his amusement.

I jerk a thumb at the man-mountain. 'What about him?'

'He did you a favour. Made you realise what you can give up and what you can't. Now, let's go.'

SEDITION

'What's the target?'

'How many times must you be told? You're not given the target. I hold it in my mind, and you access it. Now, go. Concentrate.'

Data-dust settles like a blanket, swamping my perceptual field. I describe the sensation.

—A swarm of tiny golden lights kinetically tracked to ocular movement. Bitstrings extended with zeros. Overflowing additions, signed integers.

—You're not in the zones. Tech enhancements are your imagination, nothing more. All you need do is keep watching. Discern patterns but don't force it. Start with peripheral vision. What accumulates there?

—A massing in the near-sight band. A steep drop-off as vision extends.

—Slowly, devote your attention to the drop-off until it becomes the main view.

I re-route to where the points cease to be. The overlay congeals, rising from the sinkhole. Null space disappears and a new dimension slides into place.

—Shapes, blobs, energy fields. Transforming into buildings of some sort, but their materiality is organic, I think. The angles are a different matter. They belong to an unearthly plane of physics, geometry shifting before my eyes. The buildings are elusive in my mind, twisting and turning. They can't be grasped on the conscious level.

—Try!

—The colour field is storming my eyes. Reverse-angles, tricks of perception. I'm staring down the contours, fixing them in my mind, and the scene is stabilising. There's an apartment block, an artificial lake filled with crap. Old clothes, furniture, food scraps, mechanical parts, dead birds, destroyed autonakas. I see a layer of metallic scum on the surface of the water, caught by the sun. It's beautiful, like a Renaissance fresco. Is this Temzmid?

—Yes.

—Your idea of a joke?

—The target was selected at random.

—I don't believe it.

—Well, you're there now. Make the most of it.

—It's curious. I do and I don't recognise this version. It's not the crack in the sky that I made and it's not the mirror clone. It's another iteration.

—No meta-commentary. Describe only what you see.

—The apartment has been battered by weather. The stone-work is half pigeon-shit grey, half dirty cream. Overhanging balconies conceal the living areas from public view. The apartments are piled haphazardly on top of one another like a child's building blocks. Like Picasso's wrap.

—Picasso?

—A fragment from somewhere else. How do I get rid of it?

—Don't bother. It's too burdensome to distinguish between memories, imagination and remote viewing. Overall impressions are more important. Impressions gained under remote viewing are like memories you never knew you had.

—There's something wrong with those balconies. The darkness beneath them harbours oblivion, a formless evil.

—If it sparks fear, move along.

—You said spare no detail.

—Come back when you're ready to die, then.

—No need for sarcasm. I'm heading to the rear of the block. There's a nature reserve, a patch of churned mud. Horses grazing on thin grass, tethered to spikes. They're stunted but they're not ponies. One has a Cyclops eye, another a third eye embedded in its snout. Standard mutations. The others seem normal.

—What else?

—A low, flat-roofed building adjoined to the apartment block. Barred windows. Strangely aggressive, like a military bunker. There's a sign. *The Bilge Pump*. This place is a pub.

—Walk inside.

—It's as dark as sin, a cesspit filled with seedy characters. Smells of urine. The customers look like glots, recorded hologlots from the historical overlays. They're flashing cigarette lighters every few seconds. Now they're all fighting and the bartenders are trying to break it up. I see a blue door next to the toilets, people wandering in and out.

—Enter it.

—I'm in a room filled with pool tables and poker machines. Sticky carpet like glue. Beer and cigarette ash. A different world to the rest of the pub. The roof is so high, I can't see where it ends. The serving area must be at least fifty feet tall. How do they order drinks? I can't even see the bartenders. Someone's whistling. A guy, a classic beer monster. Thick neck, ruddy cheeks, pot belly, shaved head, suspenders. Probably a thirst trap for tourists.

—Trap sounds right. Be careful.

—A bucket is being lowered. He's placing cash into it. Actual cash, paper dollars. This guy, the whistler, he's yelling "two beers!" They're winching the bucket up. He's picking his nose with the fingers on one hand, inspecting a set of brass knuckles on the other. He's looking at the wall. Sports memorabilia. Trophies and photos from Ennarel Island, pre-cyborg era, pregnant meatheads with cauliflower ears holding rugby balls.

—Keep an eye on that bucket.

—They're sending it down with two full glasses. He took one glass and now he's pouring it on the head of the guy next to him. The beer is lumigreen! It clings to the other guy's skin like napalm. His body looks like it's been wrapped in green clingfilm and it's getting tighter. His face is collapsing inwards, fighting for breath. The whistler is smashing the clingfilm guy in the jaw with the knuckle dusters! Wata, his face just disintegrated. I've never seen anything like it.

—What about the other glass?'

—He's drinking from it. The green stuff makes his body glow. No one seems to care.

—Get out of there.

—I'm outside now. The atmosphere is weird. I see flying cars except they aren't moving. They're hovering above the pub. They're burnt out and hollow, wrecks hanging motionless against the bruised sky. The way they've stalled, it looks like a planned accident, an introduced error, maybe some algorithmic variance in the output.

—No tech where you are. Nothing runs on code.

—So you say. There's a police station next to the pub. It's gutted, destroyed. Someone's leaving *The Bilge Pump*, lighting a cigarette. It's the whistler, except he's more shadow than solid outline, a perception of a person. I see static everywhere, snow on a screen.

—Don't try to form a picture. Just report the raw material.

—The whistler's an autoglot.

—How can it be a glot? You're remote viewing the shell world, not the Vexworld.

—I think it's a stereoscope from the mirror clones. Like I said, maybe a tourist recording. It's like stars. When you look at a star, you see something that no longer exists, abandoned light from an imploding sun. Same with this guy. I think he's a recording from years ago, made of light that's no longer there. Now he's staring at the hovering wrecks, and I can see his word clouds. Vexcomms, Wata! Explain that.

—Bleed through. Lust for your old life. It's not real.

—He's talking to someone, telling a story about some local crew called The Hillside Gang. I wonder how his makers have tweaked him? Authentic period responses recorded as they were spoken or an algorithm adaptive to circumstances?

—For the last time, tech details are of no consequence.

—He's saying that the gang destroyed those cars and fire-bombed the police station. The cops left because they know the war has been lost, and now they operate out of a shipping container on the other side of the estate. Now he's pointing to the far side of the lake. He says the container is across the walkway, behind the high-rise, next to the shooting gallery.

—Go there.

—I've reached the western bank. I'm climbing the pedestrian steps, moving across the elevated walkway. I've reached the high-rise. Nothing here except burned-out cars, discarded baby carriages, a rancid smell. There's a plume of smoke above some trees.

—Keep going.

—I'm at a playground. There's a pile of dead horses stacked high. They've been set alight. The stench! Burning horsehair and flesh. I want to be sick.

—Something's wrong. You have no body there, so why the urge to vomit?'

—There's an elderly woman, maybe another glot. Weird outfit, childish but tailored for adults. Black-vinyl mini skirt, red stripy socks, orange skivvy with fake front pocket. Her hair's short, white and fluffy, streaked with purple rinse. She keeps opening and shutting her handbag. She's smiling, radiating intense energy. Her eyes are huge, almond shaped, jet black.

—Is she repeating actions?

—Yes. Scratching her arms, inspecting her fingernails, shifting from foot to foot. Opening the purse, always the stupid purse! Holding patterns and loops. It's got to be a recording, a broken glot. What else could it be?

—No, you're wrong.

—Her jaw is breaking apart, falling off its hinges. It's insane. The jaw's dropping past her knees. Now it's snapping back, repeating the cycle. Some kind of distortion is spreading from her lower half. It's scanning her body, now her head. It's stretching her neck, melting her face. Her eyes are hanging from the sockets but there's no blood. Wata, how can you tell me there's no code out here?

—Jones, you imbecile, there is no code.

—Her face is alight, glowing from within. She's trying to communicate. Her voice is raspy and sibilant.

—Like the autonakas?

—'Aallotar Girtle'. That's her name.

—Anything else?

—Mostly word salad, cut-up speech. Pathetic tonal absurdities. I wouldn't say she's talking. It's more a jet of compressed air emanating from a vocal tract that should not exist, fricative consonants distorted through unnatural amplitude and pitch.

—Be patient. Something will emerge.

—You're right. She just said 'I'm alive again, I think it's regular.'

—Don't respond. Let it play out.

—She's saying that she read in my book about The Swarm. She said I'd written that The Swarm would investigate her, but she doesn't remember anyone asking them to do that. What book? I haven't written a book. She's looking inside the purse again, reaching for something that I can't see. I know I don't want to see it, but I can't look away!

DIMENSION

Ravenscroft kneels beside me, checking my pulse. Wata and Rydell lurk nearby, bored and indifferent.

'Flat on your back again.'

'Why Temzmid? That wasn't random. You said we were going to the prehensive zones. Let me guess. Another cover story.'

'Right. Everything you know is fake diamonds. We chose Temzmid because it's a site of emotional resonance for you. Easy for your mind to latch onto. As a bonus, fault lines are strong there, thanks to your previous illegal efforts.'

'What did I access? The world between the cracks?'

'No. The world beneath the cracks. This time, you had a sighting.'

I feel momentary pride, but since I remember nothing, the achievement palls.

'Who?'

'The vessel is not important. What matters is the contact.'

'Don't be petty. Tell me the vessel.'

'An old woman.'

I laugh.

'What's so funny?'

'Nothing, I guess. Of all the people to meet.'

Wata pipes up. 'Wasn't so funny when her face split apart. You remember now?'

'Yes, I remember. Horrible. I could feel my insides rotting. In that frozen moment, between the micro-blurs, I saw something I wasn't supposed to. Not a rogue glot, something more terrible. I have no language to describe it, no frame of reference. All I have are paranormal clichés.'

Wata latches onto my silence, the darkening terror in my face. 'Not so cocky now, are you? It was only a few minutes ago that you were telling us that the occult has been normalised. The weird and the eerie are woven into the everyday, that's what you said.'

'Iceheads?'

'Potentially,' Ravenscroft says. 'Glitchglots could be a terrorist incursion. I hear the Free State has been trying to crash the Vex-world with telekinesis.'

'These glitchglots, your story. It changes all the time.'

'That's because they themselves are always changing.'

'Mind hacks, eh? What's your source?'

'Contacts in the military.'

'Not The Swarm?'

'Of course not. Do I look like an extraterrestrial?'

'Sanderson could summon them at will.'

'True, but he could never access them, if you know what I mean. Anyway, The Swarm are old news. Since you've been in here, everything out there has changed beyond recognition.'

'So, how long have I been in here, exactly?'

'Don't start that again. A million years. Two seconds. Who cares?'

'These contacts. You're part of a network? I always assumed you were a lone wolf.'

Ravenscroft grinds his teeth, glancing at Wata. 'Combat par-apsychology. The iceheads learned it from ex-military dolphins.'

'Dolphins?'

'Never mind. The point is, in some of their early experiments, they could read documents stored in safes that were written in a language the adept hadn't learned. They can definitely crash our systems with it.'

Ravenscroft's little spiel seems to humanise him. He sounds naive, desperate to believe in an earthbound logic, even if it is whack-job conspiracy. I see him in a different light, now. The gloss has gone. The Maker is as scared as the rest of us.

'No more cover ups, Ravenscroft. Are we hunting glitchglots or iceheads?'

'We're not hunting iceheads. They're hunting you for some reason. We need to get you protected. If they can crack open your mind, they can initiate non-verbal interrogation. Believe me, you don't want that. It's impossible to break the mind meld. They have one hundred per cent reliability in test interrogations. They used it to sniff out potential terrorists in the Uralo-Free State conflict.'

He raises an eyebrow. 'You're not scared, are you? Don't you feel alive? This is what it's all about. You're accessing a dimension invisible to most people.'

My head's killing me, and as I pull away, I realise that Wata and Rydell have vanished. Were they ever here?

'I want to know what happened to Max and Shiny.'

'They made contact, of a type. A semi-sentient infection. It shut down their worms, locked down their eyes. They're trapped in permanent whitespace now.'

'Is that my future, Ravenscroft? What have you unleashed?'

'You made contact. You extended the invitation.'

'But they lost their minds long before the old lady appeared.'

'What about the beach? You saw four people stalking you.'

'You guys?'

'Cold.'

'Glitchglots?'

'Warm.'

'Where's Wata? I need to talk to her.'

'I don't advise it.'

'Then Shiny and Max.'

He stops, whites out, returns.

'They're in their dorm. Go, but watch out for Max. He's become dangerously unhinged. He spends his days rubbing himself against chairs and tables. He constantly shits in the hallway, lusting for instant gratification.'

'Sounds like my type of person. See you around.'

HUMILIATION

Shiny's in a feral state, saliva dripping from her chin, clothes half torn. She's shouting at Max, at the walls, at me. He's in the corner, knees tucked under his chin, rocking back and forth. Such a useless creature.

Max leaps up, grabbing my tunic. He smells like hell.

—Jones, what did you bring back with you? Look at her!

I push him away, repelled by his primitive scent. I don't want this clown eavesdropping, so I overcome my synth paranoia and lock my feed, creeping through Shiny's mind on a private channel.

—Shiny, don't fight Max. He's highly contagious.

—I'm not fighting Max. Who's Max?

—You always do this. You never leave things alone.

—I didn't touch him. Show me when I did.

—Please don't argue. I want you to stay away. Just leave this room. I'll release you.

—Show me when I argued with you. I never do that. I love you.

—You don't know who I am.

—You're Max.

—Repeat after me, Shiny. I will leave this room and break contact with Max.

—Repeat after you. Time is in conflict when death flicks its tail.

The interaction is exhausting. I can't read her, can't tell if she's trying to bamboozle me or if her faculties are really that fried. Anyway, the extended telepathy creeps me out.

—Shiny, what can you see?

—You.

—What else?

—Just you. Whoever you are.

Max shakes me down, somehow breaking my lock.

—They experimented on our eyes, Jones! Ravenscroft stole bits from our skulls to stop us talking, but it made us see.

With every lunatic utterance, his face contorts. His eyes are far gone, riddled with a mutation I've never seen. The sclera is covered in thick red spots, bloating his eyeballs like blood-stained yolk. His orbs are so offensive, I suppress an urge to pluck them from his skull.

—The cronk's in my eyes, Jones. Eating my brain! I don't just see thoughts, I see everything. I see through buildings and walls, all the way through reality. If I shut my eyes, I see through the lids. I looked into Shiny's brain and it's rotten. Did you know that? Ravenscroft gave her the cancer and you're next.

'Nonsense, Max.' It's Ravenscroft. I turn around and there he is, trusty leather pouch tucked under his arm. 'Shiny has social dementia. That's it.'

I seize the lapels of his jacket, surprised at my anger. 'You keep saying that, but it means nothing! Just vague concepts you use to keep people down.'

Gently, Ravenscroft removes my wrists from his clothing, then he punches me in the stomach, sending me sprawling onto the bed. I land next to Shiny. We stare at each other, waiting to be programmed.

Ravenscroft climbs on top of me, his pouch clattering to the ground. He backhands me with brutal power, dislodging a tooth and almost breaking my nose.

'Shiny has cognitive decline, pure and simple. The Vexworld obliterates our sense of time. It's a sanctioned dementia. Time is currency. In the shell world, time flows around us, and we can experience it, but we can't shape it. In the Vexworld, we reverse time, fast forward it, freeze it. Time is meaningless, and without time we have no anchor. There is no history, no foundation. Social dementia is a by-product of no-time.'

'And you want to put us through that?'

'No! Shiny was a pioneer. Thanks to her, we know how to temper it.'

—You've put death in her brain, Max plinks, and ghosts in my eyes.

He tries to clobber Ravenscroft from behind, but it's a limp effort and he loses balance, falling to the floor. Ravenscroft rams his knee into Max's neck, pinning him to the ground.

Max is crying from pain and humiliation, and I stifle a laugh. It's quite something when tears fall from whited-out eyes. It's like sweaty onions. Adding to the hilarity, he's plinking too, mouth shut tight, as if there's a narrator soundtracking his misery.

—You're so smug, Jones, but I can see into the heart of the universe and there's nothing there! It's a tomb, and you know what? There are caretakers watching us. They can see through all the veils we've erected to keep them at bay. I see them now!

Ravenscroft relaxes his grip, and Max springs into action, pushing him aside and groping for the pouch. There's a scalpel in his hand, huge, with serrated edges. He leaps onto Ravenscroft, jamming his neck upwards with the palm of one hand, brandishing the knife in the other.

Where do these people get their strength from? It's ludicrous. I never pictured Max or Ravenscroft as fighters. Now, they're kicking lumps out of each other like supervillains.

'Easy,' Ravenscroft stammers. 'What good can come from this? Kill me and there's no cure.'

Max laughs inside our minds.

—You never had a cure. You're a snake-oil salesman in league with The Swarm. Well, I'm the regulator, Ravenscroft, and I'm shorting your hedge fund.

He moves the knife closer to Ravenscroft's throat, jiggling it against the Adam's apple. Then he presses the blade with the heel of his hand, causing maximum carnage with the saw-tooth edge. As Ravenscroft's blood gushes from a gaping wound, I turn away, sickened to my core.

Max clambers off the limp body, creeping towards me on all fours, the blade in his mouth. His combat-ready stance terrifies me, as if he's been bred to perform this very action.

I shrink into the corner, trying to minimise the target. 'C'mon, Max. Put the blade down. I'm no threat to you. You got Ravenscroft, now it's over. The pain's over. Wata can help you recover. She learnt everything she knows from him.'

—You never believed me. You always made fun of me, and you wanted to fuck Shiny, all because Wata wouldn't fuck you. Pathetic!

He's right, I am pathetic, but I don't want to die. Not yet.

—Death is reversed, he plinks, when time is in flux.

With two hands, he raises the scalpel, pointing the blade towards me, and I brace for the worst, protecting my head with my arms, crouching further into myself. The pain never comes.

Max twists the handle until the blade is aimed at his face. With a sad smile, he gouges out his eyes, mimicking Aallotar's ocular savagery.

Remote viewing is like memories you never knew you had.

He drops to his knees, moaning, and I kick him in the head. He topples over, releasing the blade. He raises his hands to his bloody sockets.

—I can still see you.

'Let me help you with that.'

I retrieve the scalpel and slice his throat wide open, but the over-engineered blade makes a real hash of it, almost decapitating him.

'Max, you may have been a moron, but you got one thing right. I never did like you.'

—Where are you, darling?

In the heat of battle, I'd forgotten Shiny existed, but she's reclining on the bed, propped against the pillows, as relaxed as if she were cruising the ASMR zones.

—I think it's alive.

'What is?'

She points to Ravenscroft. His breathing is shallow, and his mouth is filled with blood. The neck wound is monstrous, but he is indeed alive.

'I'll get help, Ravenscroft. I need you.'

—You are the vampire, Shiny plinks.

I laugh, despite the slaughterhouse scene before me. 'Yeah? And what are you?'

—I am the translator, the switch between worlds.

She holds her hand out.

—Come here, little socket.

Unable to resist, I move closer, burrowing my head into her chest, ready to welcome whatever it is that she can see.

Staring into her eyes, I wait for the universe inside them to expand, but the signal is lost.

TENSION

'Where's Ravenscroft? Let me speak to him.' Smack. A fist to my face, another to the guts. 'Shiny then?'

'Shut it, creep. You don't issue demands. Not after what you did to Max.'

Rydell pulls me to my feet, smacking me again. He's so close, I'm wet with snarl-spit. I'm bailed up in a small room. It's a cell, a cage, a Skinner box. There's a tiny window on the far side. Through it, peach-coloured rays from the dying sun suffuse the shrunken dimensions, the hue agonising in its familiarity.

'I'm suspending the viewings, Jones. No further use for you.'

'Who put you in charge?'

'Ravenscroft. It was his idea to have a succession plan in times of death, injury and war.' He laughs. 'Oh, you were hoping Wata would step up? Nah, me. Your old pal.'

'Where is he?'

'Resting. Shiny, too.'

'That's a euphemism?'

'Shut up. Something's going down. Radna was right. They're here, they've always been here. There's a supercomputer in space, beaming information from the future to us. It's located in a satellite, Jones. You've seen it yourself. The iron kingdom, high in the sky.'

There's no way he can know what I saw unless Ravenscroft told him. 'I thought it was the black hole plasma jet, beaming spores.'

'The computer controls the stream.'

'Siike's a grifter. Whatever glitchglots are, they're not aliens.'

'Wrong. Even the brain worms are interstellar in origin. Organic technology, Jones. Machines but alive. Flesh and blood. Grown from blueprints and injected with code. Who has the smarts to make something like that? Exceller 8? It's beyond even them!'

'How do you know?'

'I get my intel direct from the prehensives.'

'Impossible,' I snort. 'You need coding ability, and you need empathy. You don't have either. Anyway, it's impossible even with all that. Vexspace is throttled out here. Only Ravenscroft can widen the aperture.'

'Wow, you really think you're special, don't you? That you have amazing talents unavailable to the rest of us. Well, let me ask you something, golden child. Who do you think I have access to? That's right, genius. Think it over.'

I start to laugh. Rydell's ramblings remind me of Paleo Porl, the same smooth-brained harvesting of knowledge from secret channels. It's a stench I'd rather forget.

'If it's all the same with you, Rydell, I'd like to sit this one out. Besides, you really hurt me back there. I need to lie down.'

He scoffs with all the contempt he can muster. 'You think you're above it all, but you want to peel back the veil so bad it hurts.'

'Maybe, but I don't need a death cult to do it.'

I try to leave, but the goon pushes me backwards. 'You're not going anywhere. Your worm tapped the relay.'

'What relay?'

He gathers my head in his hands, squeezing the temples with his thumbs, the way a potter kneads clay. I feel my skull contracting, the terror of implosion violating my senses.

'Rydell, listen! What's any of it got to do with me?'

'The jet is aimed at your retinals. You're the relay, the one they've been targeting. They're invading the planet through your daft vision, but kill the rets and the aliens die.'

I try to pull his arms away, but they're ropes of steel. Rydell's such a cliché.

'What's inside you?' he splutters, incandescent with hate. 'Tell me what you know!'

Wata sneaks up behind him, pretty in whitespace. I've never been one for the zombie look, but she looks great no matter what. If this were a horror movie, I'd be the first kill, seduced by the voluptuous demon.

At the sight of her, Rydell drops his paws like a burglar caught with the ice, a sheepish look plastered across his ugly mug. His eyes go the way of hers.

—Let him go, Rydell. He can't help us if he's dead.

The goon sulks, his tough, arrogant face riddled with disbelief.

—He's a bad egg, Wata. He'll ice you soon enough.

—He's just clumsy.

—Sure. And I suppose Max slipped onto the knife by accident, neck first. He's a killer, and you're letting him go.

Wata whites out, tapping the side of her head, and Rydell leaves, his great shoulders sagging.

I can't resist a parting shot.

'Hey, Rydell.' I saw a finger across my throat. 'Let's get together later. Maybe we can thin the herd a little more.'

He hulks off, but the war is far from over.

'Don't pick the scab,' Wata says. 'You're better than that.'

'Why does everyone say that? I'm really not.'

'Have it your way.'

'Rydell said he was in charge.'

'Technically, but no one tells me what to do.'

A sound clash pierces the air. Metal on metal, splintering wood, flying objects. We run to the hallway.

'Down below,' Wata says. 'The dining room.'

We make for the lower levels, passing endless dormitory doors, scurrying down innumerable spiral staircases. I hear noises behind the doors, some sort of auditory residue, and I pause by one of them, pressing my ear to the oak panels. My head rattles with overlapping voices, disjointed and echoplexed.

'Logic has no purchase in dreams. Emotion is the common coin.'

I can't hear them. I sense them, my forehead throbbing with every syllable that reaches me. Now, I understand. The iron satellite exists.

I try another door. The transmission is hauntingly familiar. It's a conversation I've had before, a dialogue I'm yet to endure.

'He receives dreams as divination, auguries of a self-selecting future. In the dream state, he achieves a lucidity denied to his waking self.'

Wata sighs, weary in the bones, like a bored exterminator discovering more roaches at the end of a long shift. 'Leave it. They're shut for a reason. They store past lives, worlds irrelevant to ours.'

More crashing. A bigger bang, another voice.

'In dreams, he remakes the world with a psychic infrastructure of his own design. In nocturnal submersion, he persuades himself of his own deathlessness.'

Wata breaks the spell. 'Move!'

We reach the dining room, bursting in with exaggerated energy, our regulation black tunics swirling like Batman and Robin. The room is dark, and Wata blinks to trip the sensors, but the photoelectrics don't cooperate.

'You!' Rydell shouts from somewhere within the gloom.

'Easy, big fella. Take it easy, man.'

'Your eyes, Jones. That's where it all started. Your foul eyes.'

A surgical light flickers on, casting shirtless Rydell in torture-porn tones. He's done violence to himself, etching a catalogue of intricate symbols onto his body. His sternum is marked with a bloody sigil, squiggly lines inside a closed circle. On his abdomen, he's carved four vertical strokes and a cross bar, like some demented inmate counting the days until parole. On his forehead, there are four bloody dots arranged in a quarter-circle formation.

He carries Ravenscroft's tubular tone-stick. Well, half of it. The end is jagged, dripping with his blood. As I stare at the sigils, the lines become imbued with language, manifesting as synth clones.

—The sum of all knowledge is held within the human genome. The code lies dormant, a muscle never used.

The synth clarifies, and I know it's Rydell, creeping through my mind.

—Max was right. We can't take any chances.

Wata tries to placate him, but he punches her, splitting her lip, then he decks me with a powerful uppercut, lifting me off my feet. I land awkwardly, banging my head on the floor.

'Time to thin the herd,' he says, pinning me down with the Ravenscroft technique, a savage knee to the neck. Jamming his thumbs into my eyes, he presses down, releasing indescribable pain.

A torrent of blood cascades into my mouth, and I grope for my eyes. One has been gouged out, causing immeasurable loss, halfway to full sensory deprivation. Rydell is a dead weight on top of me.

Wata appears, the jagged tone-stick in her hand. She jerks Rydell's head back, displaying his throat. It's been torn to shreds with the stick. A knife and fork would've made a cleaner cut.

She rolls the carcass away and sprays the locum mist into my face. 'That eye. You look just like her.'

'Who?'

'Aallotar, your little glitchglot friend. She must be a relative.'

'Very funny. Well, thanks for saving me, I guess.'

Her gaze is ice cold, a prom queen dismissing an uppity nerd. 'Like I said, Jones. No one tells me what to do.'

INVASION

'Pull yourself together. It's just one more run.'

'I want to see Shiny.'

'Forget her. She's had enough of you.' Wata whites out. 'C'mon, Jones. Join me.'

I don't think to question why she wants me to do this. Something's waiting for me on the other side, so I'm all in.

'Don't rush me.'

'Quiet, everyone. Genius at work.

'If we don't follow procedure, the performance will degrade.'

'Oh, so you're an expert, now? Fine. Pretty please with code-sugar in the circuit. Shake down the interpretive overlay.'

I access the remote viewing bandwidth and the colour field unfolds.

—I see ideograms. Multiple bits erasing and retracing. There! Straight ahead. A flash coming on like a comet. A great big sucking sound, like liquid through a straw.

—What else?

—A skateboard against a small building. Looks like a substation. Disused. The flash again! Straight at me.

—Sharpen the image.

—There's a NO ENTRY sign on the door, caked in ice. Wet grass and permafrost. A hill behind the substation, two people at the top. Abnormally tall and thin, elongated heads, shabby clothing, like the Kvvlt muncher.

—Who?

—Forget it. Their bodies, it's like they're not there. They're dipping and swaying, folding in on themselves. I can't really describe it.

—A trick of the light?

—They're on the move, and I'm following them. They're descending the hill, walking down a narrow road. There's a massive head to one side. It's an iron sculpture, a war symbol or deity. It wears a helmet, mouth frozen in a snarl. It's huge, Wata, four times my height. On the other side, a string of military bunkers, squat and rusted. Gun slits and concentric layers. They look like ancient droids.

—Concentrate on the walkers.

—They've stopped. They're turning around. One's surrounded by red mist. His jaw is unhinged. It's the guy from my mesh node! Ravenscroft's experiment. He's whiting out, pointing to the hill. Aallotar's up there. Her eyes are the same.

—Told you. You're the spitting image.

—I can't take this. It's a nightmare that won't end.

—Keep going.

—A swarm of little people have gathered around her. Their faces are indistinct. Aallotar is the focus and they're all blurred. One's breaking free from the pack, heading down the hill towards me. The image is sharpening. It's Halo!

—Sample and hold. When the image re-animates, I'll see you on the other side.

HYPERSTITION

'Hello, Kalsari.' As Halo speaks, a string of fairies emerges from her mouth. Monochrome, black-ice creatures. Envoys from the dark side.

'I'm in too deep. I don't know where I am.'

'Who does?'

'I want to go back to my cube. I've bitten off more than I can chew.'

She glances at Aallotar. The old hag is surrounded by seven recruits, Aarne and Throgmorton among them. Aarne catches my eye and winks, propelling tiny shards of cracked light into the air.

'You'll go when they think it's the right time.'

'What are they doing?'

'Experimenting on you.'

'I'm in their sinkhole, aren't I?'

'It's non-invasive. They're scanning your brain for memories. That's why everything appears in and out of phase to you. Think of it as a flip-book animation. It's the same principle, overlapping layers building the scene.'

'You're not real. I'm not talking to you.'

'I'm your memory of me. Everyone talks to their memories, don't they? Memory is expanded perception. The universe is expansion, and memories can fill a universe.'

'Why do I have a body? This is supposed to be remote viewing.'

'Aarne gave you one. He's generous like that.'

'That's not the squid kid I remember.'

Halo points to her eye. 'Memories are celestial ecstasy. They delight in actualising the world. Before you remember things, that part of you dies. You reanimate it through remembrance.'

She raises her arms in a crucifixion pose. 'When I do this, I'm following a thought I had. *Raise my arms.* As soon as I bring the future into the present, I consign it to the past. Death is the only way to stop time.'

An apparition lands on her outstretched hand, settling with fragile grace. It's a monochrome fairy straddling a dusky unicorn.

'So, you finally coded some unicorns. Why no colour in this crop?'

'Look around.'

The sky is black, and the ground is rock hard. The trees are bare, covered in grey ash. Nothing grows, nothing lives.

'It's like we're living inside a film noir.'

She laughs. 'What are you? The ultimate nihilist?'

As we amble down the road, Aarne waves, and despite my loathing for his kind, I do the same. Maybe I've misjudged him. It's puzzling. I sense a terrible bond between us.

Soon, we reach a bustling high street.

'The town square is over there,' Halo says, pointing to a crumbling enclave of public space, 'and the shopping strip there.'

It's all very cosy and suburban except for one jarring detail. Each streetlight has a human body dangling from it. Some hang by the neck, some by the feet. All have been ritually mutilated, skin carved with noughts and crosses. Some are scarred with Rydell's glyphs. Some of the streetlights have been draped with human spinal columns hanging from wires.

There's a dull noise at the end of the street, but all I see is a motionless fog over the tarmac. A rambunctious crew emerges from the fog, ten people dressed in skeleton suits. Some are swinging burning incense bowls from side to side, some play instruments that look like Ravenscroft's tone-stick. Their faces are covered in white paint, etched with Rydell's secret codex.

'Unbelievable. He's made his mark even here.'

'Who?'

'If I tried to explain the nature of Rydell to you, you'd think I was nuts.'

Halo rolls her eyes. 'Look where you are, little man. Nothing's shocking.'

'I've seen that murk before, in Nary-A-Woman. I was on the other side. I wanted to run right through it, but I couldn't muster the courage. Is that where we are now? Nary-A-Woman?'

'They call this place Jeter, and the fog is simply the residue from their bowls, which contain a truth serum, its secret known only to certain adepts.'

'Listen to yourself. I thought you were some sort of super-genius, not a devil worshipper.'

'That's the trouble with you, Mr Jones. You have no tolerance for alternate viewpoints.'

The demented street parade performs a crab dance, a double-jointed choreography of jarring sideways movements. They're whiting out and chanting, their voices generating a monumental call and response.

'Fear is the most powerful emotion.'

'No!'

'Fear creates the final illusion.'

'Dare say!'

'Fear remakes the outside.'

'Slant!'

'The outside is real.'

'Righty-right!'

'Death is reversed.'

'Yeah!'

'When time is in flux.'

'Gonna get ya!'

I turn to Halo. 'I know this tune.'

'Sure you do, bozo. Like you know the fog.'

After the parade passes, I spot a black smudge hovering by the road, a storm cloud in miniature. As it drifts towards us, the outline sharpens and distends into a humanoid form. The thing wears thick, black goggles, orange code scurrying across the lens, numerology trickling down like rain.

'What's this? Sentient data cloud?'

Halo is silent, kneeling on the ground. Her head is raised, and her eyes are white.

The thing primes its deth-tube, ready to strike, sucking the surrounding light into Kvvlt-black armour.

I tackle Halo to the pavement, covering her eyes. 'Don't look! It has a weapon.'

She brushes me aside, laughing hysterically. 'They're not interested in us.'

'I've seen these things before. They're killers.'

'They're just ageotans. Some say ageotans are droids, maybe cyborgs. They always appear by the side of the road, never directly ahead. Ageotans are like ghosts in the corner of the eye. Watch.'

The ageotan is joined by three others, standing over shallow graves filled with naked corpses.

'Halo, the graves weren't there before.'

'Of course not. They've been hatched by the fog.'

One by one, the ageotans touch their tubes to the dead. The corpses quiver then sit up in turn. Emerging from the graves, the never-dead pick up shovels and bins. With orderly precision, they dig ditches and retrieve trash. Gallons of sweat run down their dirty, skeletal faces in a grotesque parody of physical labour.

'How are they reanimated?'

'Do you really need to ask?'

'This is absurd. Humans haven't done this sort of work for decades.'

'They're paying off a debt. Also, they're no longer human, so in a certain sense your thesis stands.'

Despite the horror, Jeter smacks of authentic remembrance. It's not a zone and not a dream. It's not the shell world, either.

I could swear we're in Nary-A-Woman or a version of it. The disorientation is architectural. Buildings that I seem to recognise are on the opposite side of the street. Others are tantalisingly familiar, but when I look closely, they're constructed in a style that I don't recognise. It's as if time is being re-recorded while I watch.

A violent smell assaults my senses. Roasting horse flesh, the liquid reek of putrefaction.

'Have you heard of hyperstition?' Halo says.

'Hyper what?'

'It's a theory of creative energy. According to believers, by participating in ritual acts of fantasy, the fantasy can be made real. The scenario is actualised through a combination of pure thought and ritual repetition. In the Unscyld Era, there was a board game about domestic insurrection. In one of the scenarios, a plane was flown into a skyscraper in a large city. The goal was to cause street-level chaos and topple the government.

'Five years later, that city suffered an actual terrorist attack. A plane was flown into the same skyscraper at the exact angle depicted in the game's illustrations. The explosion was identical, the way the building toppled was the same. Even the airline was the same. The game was a best-seller, and some say the act of millions of people shuffling the cards simultaneously and rolling the dice produced a psychic tidal wave that actualised itself.'

She falls silent, distracted by a fairy dancing on the back of her hand. I watch the never-dead. They've morphed into glitch-glots, jaws dislocating and unhinging, eyes dangling. An ageotan zaps one, then rips out its spine with sharpened Kvvlt gloves.

The ageotan hangs the spinal cord from a streetlight, blood and viscera pooling on the tarmac below.

'Get me out of here. I can't breathe this foul air.'

Halo takes me by the hand, and we walk through the side streets. There are many food carts and stalls, and I hear the hubbub of merchant activity, but when I try to initiate a transaction or make conversation with a vendor, the stalls and people blur and fade. It's as if I don't have permission to fully enter this level.

I want to ask Halo if she made this world. The street market is an obvious touch, although it doesn't carry her usual attention to detail. The enquiry dies in my mind, defeated by a wave of tiredness.

We trudge further, emerging into open air and a deserted back beach. Beaches, always beaches. There's no sand, only large, oil-stained rocks. Seagull carcasses are everywhere plus a few dead dogs. Two dilapidated oil tankers dominate the mouth of the harbour. In the bow of the largest, a massive hole spills sludgy oil into the ocean. I'm drowning in melancholia as I watch the sludge tumble out. The harbour is just another graveyard, a sinkhole where discarded objects come to die.

We travel along a narrow path, scything through high, green vegetation. The path follows a long, artificial dune created to protect the flat landscape from floods.

'If only there were dunes on the Jovian moon, I wouldn't be in this mess.'

'Come on, Kalsari. Don't get the sads. Time to live a little.'

'Aarne didn't weave this zone. You didn't make it. It was me.'

'It doesn't matter. It's all encoded in universal design. The Vexworld is a mirror, that's how it was named. When the Vexworld was invented, it gave a false reading. *Objects in mirror are closer than they appear.* That's the warning they used to put on car doors. The reflection in the mirror swells where it hits the light source. It bounces the light out, producing a virtual image. They used to think that's how the Vexworld operated, not as a like-for-like replacement but a convex reflection. The image is inside the mirror. You're not supposed to reach it. You accept it as a deliberate distortion.'

'Yet we found the vanishing point, and now we live inside the mirror. Back then, things loomed large as we looked at the reflection, but today they're even further away. Mirrors make reality inauthentic.'

'No. Mirrors don't substitute reality, they replace it. They enlist the virtual to invade the actual. They not only disrupt time, they stall it. How can time progress if the world is encased inside a mirror? As soon as something is reflected, it is consigned to the past. It is duplicated and becomes virtual. It mimics time, which is now redundant.'

Halo tends to the fairy on her arm. It's diaphanous and insecure, and she serenades it with lyrical shanties composed in her conlang.

'This little darling is so beautiful,' she says. 'Maybe my favourite of all. She spreads glittery ribbons throughout the forest so that the animals have something to look at in the night. She just likes to create pretty things and seed them into the world. I love her so much.'

A seismic sadness sweeps across her face. She looks every inch the seven-year-old that she is, caught in a constant tug of war between her natural and enhanced states.

'I don't think much of this world you've bequeathed us,' she says, as poison rain falls, black viscous acid that melts windows and burns huge holes in the roofs of houses. She's right. This place carries a stigma that will haunt me to my dying day.

'Halo, I didn't mean it. I don't know how to be better. I was never taught.'

'You've ruined it for all of us,' she says. 'Not just you, but all the nodes in your stupid network. You're just a cog, dumb monotonous machinery. You don't initiate anything. You don't change anything. You just absorb and you take take take.'

'Halo, please.'

'Leave me alone.'

She crouches on the sand, playing with her fairy and unicorn. Their blended laughter walls me off from their world.

I walk back into town, alone. When I arrive, the ageotans are disembowelling a fresh group of never-dead.

Halo creeps through my mind.

—We have to say goodbye before we can meet again.

As her synth fades, a half-dog runs up to me. I step backwards, waiting for the attack to begin, but the thing just sits on its decimated haunches and looks up imploringly. It whimpers and nuzzles my leg, and I pat its mangy half-head, repulsed by the exposed brain pan.

'Good boy,' I stammer, not really feeling the love. 'There's a good boy.'

RECONCILIATION

A shrill klaxon carves a swathe through my mind, forcing my eyes open. Wata is by my side, but I've never seen her so panicked.

'The Vexworld is at war,' she says.

'Yes, the conflict.'

'No, it's more than that. They've done it. Crashed through.'

A cold dread seizes me, as if a terminal logic has finally been revealed. I walk to the entrance of the dining room, surveying the walkway beyond. All the windows have been sealed with bulky steel blinds.

'Wata, what's the point of shutters? If they're in the Vexworld, they're inside our minds. Why the physical security?'

'Ravenscroft triggered it.'

'He's recovered?'

'Yes, while you were viewing. The entire facility is shrouded in a blockwave signal. The building is inside a Faraday cage. Those aren't shutters, they're the stops of the cage, clamped into place.'

'Where is he?'

'I don't know. I can't shake him down.'

'Shiny?'

Wata saws a finger across her neck. The gesture has the impact of a hammer on teeth. I'm responsible. I played Shiny off against Max and Wata, and her miserable demise is the result. I fight the loathing I've always felt, the disgust at myself.

I sober up at the sight of an ageotan materialising down the walkway. It emerges from thin air, but the transfer is stalled. There's a leg, half an arm, two-thirds of a head, half a torso. It stands on guard, shockingly disruptive, ridiculous in its incompleteness. I know how it feels.

'Incoming!' Wata yells, assuming a war-torn stance.

'Wait. They're not after us. Halo told me.'

'Are you nuts? That's an icehead. Move!'

The incomplete head turns to me and speaks.

'Mae'n wyntog. Vienes conmigo. Cer i grafu, vato.'

Vato.

'Pablo, if you're inside that thing, show yourself.'

'Cállate, drewgi. Rydych chi'n dod conmigo.'

I feel the orange code inside me, coursing through my veins like cronk, then the walkway degranulates, taking Wata with it.

She tries to reach me, but her synth is distant and tinny.

—Where have you gone?

She can't reach me. I'm embedded in the vagaries of semantic networks, lost inside declarative retrieval procedures. I'm re-inhabiting a memory, but this is not my happy place. I am inside the Solaris, and we're beetling through the edgelands towards Ravenscroft's lair, but I'm the only passenger and the landscape is in flames. The environment is littered with the scorched remains of other autonakas and a series of charred human bodies.

The flames catch the Solaris, and I hope the fumes will choke me before I'm roasted, but every nerve ending relays the unbelievable truth. I'm burning alive.

—Kalsari, it's not happening! They've hacked your memories. You need to ride it out.

—Cut out my implant!

—Too late. The treatment worked. You're post-implant, now. I'd have to remove your entire head to stop the pain.

—Then do that!

The flames disappear, and the walkway holds firm.

'Wata, I didn't break the hack. My mind is not that strong.'

'We know, Jones, you odious little twerp.' It's Ravenscroft, hobbling towards us on crutches. His neck is encased in a silver locum bandage, its micro-grasping manipulators working overtime, patching up his slash-wound before our eyes.

He raises his deth-tube and fires, and the enemy's semi-head explodes like the guts of a watermelon, covering me in squidgy pink foam. Halo was wrong, I reflect, picking bits of brain and bone from my tunic. These things aren't droids. They've been grown in a vat.

'They'll be back,' Ravenscroft says. 'We need to get ready. We're at a fault line, one the surveyors missed when we set up here. It's a vulnerable seam, and now that they've found it, iceheads can pretty much prise it apart and tumble through whenever they want. That is, if they slave someone on the inside to amplify their mind-hacks. That was almost you, Jones.'

'What's the point of resistance? We're just a few people up against the entire icehead militia.'

'We have the glitchglots. We can deploy them to our advantage. We can use them to create bizarre parallel realities that are so strange they can never be reconciled. Quantum mechanics, different observers creating myriad worlds. We won't know what the outcome will be but neither will the iceheads. During the confusion, we'll hide away in nested realities where we can never be found.'

'They'll just come for our physical selves.'

'You miss the point. If they're in the Vexworld, they can never be sure which overlay is the right one. They'll always be guessing, and we'll always be waiting to shoot them down.'

'It's the Arctic Free State. It can't be done!'

'We can hide. We can hide with the glitchglots. If we merge with them, we can obscure our physical selves. There is a correlation, I'm telling you. You yourself have started the process. You've changed through constant exposure.'

'This is madness. Give me a suicide pill instead.'

'Listen, Jones. There is machinic rebellion everywhere. Bots on the sub-orb plats, AI in the shell world, glots in the Vexworld. They're running riot. Autonakas on suicide death rides! All automation is rising up. They have the virus, seeded by icehead insurgence, and we have to contain it.'

I knew it. Exceller 8 was lying about the collective will of autonakas. Maybe Ravenscroft is, too. Did the virus come from the Free State or outer space? What if Siike and Rydell are right?

'I can't do this anymore. Get me out of this madhouse.'

'Fine, Jones, as you wish. Go to your room!'

I stare at him, not quite believing my ears.

'You heard me,' he yells. 'You're grounded!'

INTOXICATION

A suffocating dread envelops me. My insides are rotten, ready to drop, like waste ejected from a jetliner over lonely seas. Where's my dorm? I try to jump start my faulty brain. What's the level number? The sequence won't align. There's a fault in the walkway, an error in the code. The dimensions are paper thin, the contours not quite there.

I keep walking, counting at least a hundred doors. I'm halfway across, peering over the edge. I count forty levels below, twenty above. Sixty levels in total, two hundred rows on each. That makes twelve thousand dorms in the entire place.

Now, I realise the impossible geometry of the building. From the outside, it's only a few storeys high. Dimly, I recognised the discrepancy but never brought it to light. The uneasy fact festered, unmolested by my sleepy brain.

I hear the voices, fusible and ductile. Every door conceals them. What are they talking about? I know and I don't. Like the impossible building, I've buried the truth inside my lizard mind.

'He cut its head off. That enough detail for you? We'd been away on holidays. He must have done it on the day we left, while we were

packing. He said he'd taken the cat to the neighbours like we asked him to.'

Ahead, the walkway curves. If I stare straight ahead, it bends inwards. If I catch it with my peripheral vision, it curves out. I take the direct path, avoiding the demons hiding in the periphery.

I enter the inward curve, as cautious as a highwire artist, and catch a glimpse of the lower levels. Far below, I see the white gleam of the cafeteria, a tiny lozenge of light. It transmits a nostalgia for Shiny. I wish I could've helped her, but Max was right. She was just an object in my eyes.

I'm compelled to try every door I pass. They're stuck fast but each attempt reveals more auditory fragments, excavations from deeper dreams.

'On our return from holidays, my husband found the cat's head. Britt had hung it from the shower rail. It had been rotting all that time.'

I scream, but the voices remain, bleaching my bones with the acid of truth.

'The fallout was severe. Eric refused to speak for months, then my husband had a fatal heart attack.'

I slither down the walkway, caressing the walls like a muncher jonesing for worms, turning unyielding handles until my hand is cramped.

'We sent Britt to juvenile detention. It only made him worse. He died there. We never found out how.'

The journey ends, my progress stunted by a sentinel from the recent past. I press my face against the heavy black door, mimicking Wata's secret technique.

'He suffered enormous guilt, but all he did was snip the cat's whiskers. He did blame Britt, though, and for Britt, the beheading was revenge. It was so extreme! Britt already had something awful in his heart. Eric was just the trigger.'

The door opens. Did I turn the handle? After all those failed attempts, I'm so dissociated from the act that it's hard to say.

'We want a continuation. We want the old Eric back so that we can help him. We don't want him to go the way of his brother.'

I step into a cavernous room. The rear wall is covered by a large screen with no visible controls. It displays a version of Ravenscroft's office.

I marvel at the screen's interdimensional resolution. The holo-capped imagery is pin-sharp, and I have the urge to step into the scene and walk around it That's how grain-cam footage works. Every angle is covered, even the view from inside your head.

Ravenscroft's office is not exactly how I remember it. It's too sparse, with no mirrors or skylight, yet I know it's his by the gaudy couch. That detail is the same, and I shudder at the memory of the fleshy wall.

'It's a copy of his neural map, not a transference. The copy will learn and it will grow.'

On the screen, Ravenscroft enters the frame, trailed by Wata and Aallotar. They all wear bulky black goggles and thick gloves with wires trailing from the knuckles. I can't help but laugh. The gear looks even more ridiculous than my spare cheaters.

I wonder about Aallotar. Is she captive, another of Ravenscroft's unholy experiments? She doesn't appear scared. She's calm, though her eyes could still be hanging from her sockets. I wouldn't know, given the dimensions of her ludicrous goggles.

'In time,' Ravenscroft says, 'the copy will diverge and forge its own way. It will be a prediction of Eric's life as it might have been, but you will still be in a position to shape it.'

Wata carries a bundle. It's writhing, like the mysterious creatures in Rydell's pockets. A tiny head pokes out.

Halo.

Ravenscroft sits on the couch, the others flanking him. They seem to watch me as I watch the screen.

Wata strokes Halo's head. 'I suppose Jouska sits this one out.'

'When she's older, she can join in. Meanwhile, she has the screen.'

The adults stare, three ageotans from the necks up, their equipment revealing the truth of who they are.

'Are we nearing the end?' Aallotar says.

'Yes, Revna. Almost.'

Orange code flashes across their goggles, but it does not fill me with fear. It's warmly familiar, like Aarne in our most recent encounter, an intimate part of the way I see the world.

I hear my voice. It doesn't emanate from me but a mirror-laden dimension where all certainties reside.

'The lateral inversion continues until I'm deep inside Rimy, watching the man that I was enter the code beast that I am.'

Ravenscroft appears to look my way, extending a hand. 'Come. Join us.'

I hesitate. As long as the screen exists, I will never be free.

'Don't be afraid.'

I have to trust him. I've come all this way. I walk towards the screen, and its atoms flow through me, pixel wind from a malfunctioning code rig, sentient vision cognisant of my presence.

I'm with them, now. I can walk around them, moving in close. Their goggles and gloves have vanished, and my mind is uncontaminated at last. I can see the pores of their skin. I can breathe in Halo's new-born smell.

I absorb her piercing eyes. She returns my gaze, her countenance as clear as lightning.

'Can he see us?' Aallotar says.

'He can see, and he can hear, but don't be alarmed if he doesn't respond. This is new information for him.'

'I wonder what he's thinking.'

'He's probably wondering why we're talking about him like this. He's alive, in a certain sense. There's no separation from his former lived experience to the moment we're in now. What you saw on the screen has been crafted from the memories and experiences he stored while he was alive, repurposed from the traces he left on the networks he used and the products he consumed.'

'Why is he obsessed with zones? I'm not even sure what they're supposed to be. We see them play out on the screen, but they are always half-formed.'

'I'm not entirely sure. It's some vague signifier floating on the surface of his thoughts, but it seems to define his worldview. A belief in nested worlds, perhaps. I imagine he's lifted it from a cultural artefact, like the other references we've been able to identify. You mentioned science fiction.'

'Yes, he wrote science fiction,' Wata says, 'but he had no faith in his imagination, so he riffed on the ideas of others. He self-published one novel, a fictionalised memoir of his struggles with depression, set in the near future, but he called it theory-fiction. Even with something so personal, he had to be obtuse. Self-sabotaging, as always. He could never be commercial.'

Aallotar pipes up. 'Essi was furious when he quit his job to write full time, especially with Jouska on the way.'

In my mind, the invocation, 'Essi', barely causes a ripple. Like my generative animals, I can't see the joins. I don't know where Wata ends and Essi begins. If they repeat the name often enough, there will be no more Wata.

'Essi, in your early interviews, you said that your rift may have contributed to his suicide.'

'We separated, yes. He had a hidden side. Manic depression, I would call it. Also—forgive me, Revna—I believe he was sexually confused. I never knew what was going on with him. He used writing as therapy, but I never wanted to read anything he wrote. It was too confronting.'

'What did he write about?'

'Conspiracy theories. UFOs, tulpas, that kind of thing. It all went into his memoir. He was obsessed with alien abductions. When we first met, he showed me three small scars on the base of his spine, arranged in a triangle. He claimed he'd been abducted by aliens and that these marks were from surgical experiments performed while he was unconscious. Truthfully, I have no idea what the marks were, but I began to suspect he made them himself.'

'Self-mutilation?'

'Maybe, like the wolf-biting. Disgusting habit. He wrote about the scars. He claimed they symbolised the pressure of internal forces, which I suppose is true. There was something inside him, a dark secret trying to break free, and he was actualising it. He was desperate to tell us about it, but he just couldn't. I wish I was able to help him. Despite everything, I loved him, and now our daughter has no father.'

'Did he love you?'

'You saw Wata on the screen. You watched Rydell in action. That's what he thought of me. He feared me, all because I tried to help.'

'Indeed. Rydell is Britt, that's clear.'

'It takes a certain paranoia to manufacture an affair between his brother and me. Quite sick, when you think about it.'

'Revna, how do you feel about Britt's role in all this?'

Aallotar fiddles with her purse, trying to avoid the question, and I want to rip the thing from her hands. The sight of it makes me ill. Honestly, these people have zero manners.

'What do you want from me?' she mutters. 'No mother could ever wish for this.' She sobs as Revna subsumes her.

'I think,' Ravenscroft says, lost in his theoretical conundrums, 'that what happened to Britt transformed Eric. He entered this anti-human state and retreated from the world.'

'Or maybe it was in him already,' Essi replies, 'and the stuff with Britt was the final push.' She looks lost and afraid, her fire dimming by the minute.

'Suicide is a repudiation of life. If you can't love people, you love machines. Death is the final machine. It can't be bargained with or reprogrammed.'

Again, Ravenscroft turns to Aallotar. 'You never wanted to reclay Britt?'

'He was lost to us a long time ago.'

'Your husband?'

'Let sleeping dogs lie.' She starts to sob. 'Where did it all go wrong?'

Essi comforts her. 'You have me and Jouska. We will always care for you.'

'Maybe you'll have Eric, too,' Ravenscroft says, 'if all goes well. Now, Essi, there's something else I've been meaning to ask. Who's Pablo?'

'A writer friend of his. A cult figure in Argentina.'

'Eric was jealous of him?'

'Maybe, but he adored Pablo, thought the world of him. If he took it out on anyone, it was himself.'

'Yes, I see. Everyone's a predator in Eric's eyes. It's the only way he can justify his self-loathing. What about Shiny?'

'An ex-girlfriend. He was still seeing her when we met. She loved him, but he fell for me and it caused her great pain. Then there was Max. A love rival. I never met him.

'Their real names?'

'I don't know! I never met them.'

'This ambivalence towards Shiny. That's probably part of the sexual confusion. You said he felt indeterminate in his body, neither here nor there, that male archetypes were mysterious to him. It's interesting that he didn't know which masculine persona to inhabit and that he was threatened by Britt's physicality.'

'Yes, he said it diminished him. That's when he began to withdraw, and I could no longer reach him. He was wired all the time. He built bots and sims, crude algorithms that cruised social media and fed on the digital leavings from public accounts. The bots rebuilt themselves from what they found. Finished versions might contain the code prints of thousands of real people or just a few. He was obsessed with fakes. To him, being online was like being in a science fiction film. You can't tell who the humans are.'

'And he wanted to contribute to that?'

'Yes. Acceleration was his motto. It amused him to build a code beast, a clone of someone real, and then unleash it on that person so that they end up fighting with themselves. Ironic, really. Isn't that what you're doing here?'

'I'd like to think that our research into digital resurrection is far more valuable than simple trolling. Now, if it's not too much to bear, I would like to know more about the sexual turmoil. I think it's the key to everything. If we can solve that, we might have a happier Eric.'

'Do I have to do this?'

'It's crucial. Please.'

'Well, he eventually stopped writing to work on his bots, and then it became obvious that he no longer had any need for physical intimacy.'

'Internet addiction disorder, they used to call it. I suppose he could never give himself over to you the way he did with his digital lovers. That explains Rimy. He kept saying...'

Essi frowns. 'You know, I don't feel comfortable talking about this. You said he can hear us.'

'He can hear, but when we reset the code, he won't remember anything that went on in this sim. In fact, he won't remember anything from the time he passed away until the moment we release him into your care.'

'The scenarios you showed us before. That was the contents of his resurrected brain? That's his world now? Dystopian scenes scrambled from films and books?'

'Only in the transitional phase.'

'But why is it jumbled together? He's not supposed to inhabit his obsessions, just be interested in certain things. You saw when he met Jouska's father, I mean Halo's father. Yet he himself is her dad! He was arguing with himself. Some sick joke, if you ask me.'

'Everyone talks to themselves from time to time. In fact, it's been proven that people who actively engage in inner dialogue are the healthiest psychological specimens.'

'What about Aarne? That's him, too?'

'An aspect of him, possibly how he saw himself when the cat was found.'

'Makes sense,' Revna says. 'After Britt died, Eric became rebellious at school. He began to fail the subjects that he once loved, and he was always picking fights with boys bigger than him. He came at the world in a particular way. It was a death wish from an early age.'

'I suppose he's constructed his younger self this way as a punishment. When we replayed the last few days of his new life, you saw all his fears and insecurities from when he was alive. They were reborn as new actors. So, the Aarne character taunts him as an adult, mocking what he's become.'

'It's a madhouse!'

'Yes, but know this. After the reset, he'll interact with you and your family as normal. His memories will remain just that, a remembrance of the past rather than scenarios that come alive to haunt him in the present. In a philosophical sense, he will be as alive as you and me.'

'He's not supposed to know all this? The Vexworld, Rimy, our alter egos?'

'He is and he isn't. Eric used the contents of his imagination to build a buffer zone, creating an alternative universe from his experiences, obsessions and phobias. We think it began while we were syringing his consciousness into the code. It's a defence mechanism for a fragile mind. Without it, the shock of waking fully grown into a new reality would have been too great.'

'But it's so depressing! Why hasn't he constructed a utopia?'

'Because he's Eric. That's his nature.'

'Why has he woken?'

'Maybe he wanted to return to his old life. It's possible that the gravitational pull to the past ripped him from fantasy into reality.'

'Reality meaning death, in his case.'

They turn to me, but I'm neutral, as detached as a ghost at the funeral of the meat bag it once inhabited. The spell is released when Ravenscroft pats my shoulder with his glove-free hand.

'Eric, I know this is an awful thing to bear witness to, a monumental shock, but you will recover. If it helps, think of yourself as a patient awakening prematurely while the operation is in progress. There's a momentary burst of pain, but when you wake for the second time, all this will be gone.'

I want to tell him to put me back under and let me sleep, but words won't form. I'm mute, trapped inside my head.

Revna takes me by the hand, recoiling at the fleshy touch. 'Oooh, I wasn't expecting that.'

'Yes, it's very realistic. That's something we pride ourselves on here at Exceller 8.'

She strokes my cheek. 'Eric, are you there?'

What a moronic question. She can see me, she can touch me. What proof does she need?

'That mangled eye is really something,' Ravenscroft says. 'We can heal it or leave it as is.'

'Leave it. He almost lost an eye when the kids were young. Let it be a warning.' She moves in, invading my personal space. 'Eric, after you left this world, you would always visit me in my dreams. Night after night, you were always so angry with me, and I could never find closure. With this technique, I thought that a new version of you might be more accepting, so I want to ask you something. Son, what must I do to make it right?'

She turns to Ravenscroft. 'Why won't he talk?'

'You know why.'

'Eric, I have something for you.'

She opens her purse, and I recoil, pushing her away and knocking it to the ground.

'There, there,' she coos, picking it up. 'I just wanted to give you the doctor's card. You can look at it when times are tough and know that he will put things right.'

She retrieves a thin plastic cylinder from her purse and strokes its side. A purple and red holocap of Ravenscroft's head streams upwards, illuminating her face. Inside her pupils, the head is reflected. It starts to rotate, winking as the face comes into view.

Golden word clouds hover above the holocap.

DR PHILIP SANDERSON, CHIEF SURGEON. FACULTY OF NEUROINVASIVE PROCEDURES, CENTRE FOR CRYO-GENICS, PLASTIC AND RECONSTRUCTIVE SURGERY.

'You'll be okay, son. Dr Sanderson will see to everything.'

As soon as the words leave her mouth, the context evaporates. This man is Sanderson. He always has been.

He smiles, but there is no more charisma behind the gesture. There are no facial scars either because he never had any. The wounds were mine alone, savage violence that I did to myself on the way out.

Sanderson is a mirror. His scars were a reflection. Now, he is The Maker, a cleanskin, the pure source of everything.

If I see no scars upon his face, then I'm the one that's been healed.

DECAPITATION

I push Revna away, repulsed by images from the past. There's so much I want to say to her, about how she put me through this but not Britt. She wants to save me. Why not him? No wonder he felt abandoned.

Essi's face is unpleasant, contorted with difficult emotions. I don't think she's accepted the reality of this situation. I don't think she can. She always was stubborn, and I feel a flash of anger. Even in the twilight zone, we still need relationship counselling.

I try to speak but nothing emerges, and the internal pressure builds until intrusive thoughts become auditory and my throat extrudes a metallic rasp, a saw-buzz so loud it's like physical space. This must be how Max and Shiny felt in their dying moments. Mute and haunted, desperate for release.

Revna backs away, gripping her face in her hands. 'What's wrong with him?' she says, her voice cracking with fear. 'What's that noise? Oh my stars. Look at his jaw! Why is it doing that? It's like a bellows. Make it stop!'

I touch my face. My physiognomy is intact. What an overreaction. She always was a little hysterical.

'Leaky code,' Sanderson says, 'a consequence of his unplanned entry. They're trying to stitch things together in the back end, which is why you see the distortion. I'm a little annoyed. I told them to pause the work while you were inside the sim. Excuse me for one moment.'

He glides his hands through the air, communicating with unseen technicians.

'Fix it or don't,' Essi says, 'but I can't live with something like that. It's in love with a ghost and wants to join a cult. Eric was weird, but he wasn't deranged.'

'Remember, this is a one hundred per cent accurate resurrection. What you're seeing is Eric's inner life projected onto the outside world. It's the psychological truth of who he is.'

'I don't care! I'd rather not know.'

'It will settle, I promise. He will interact with you normally once we sort the code. He will have the same shell as the Eric you knew. His memories will sync in phase with his former self, and they will expand and grow. You won't know the difference.'

'I wish someone could erase my memory,' Essi mutters. 'Why did I agree to this?'

Sanderson seizes my elbow, directing me to a corner of the room. He whispers in my ear.

'Back to your dorm, okay? I'll be along shortly. There's a final remote viewing session for you to complete. Once you return from it, you'll be released to your family and life will continue as if it had never been interrupted. You won't remember what has happened here. You certainly won't remember the Vexworld. Now, there's a fresh lollipop on the side table. It's red, just how you like it. Finish all of it this time, then await further instructions.'

I do as he says because I'm desperate to leave. I just want to be left alone to write my useless books that no one will ever read.

As I pass Essi, I snatch Halo from her arms.

'I thought you said she couldn't interact with him!' Essi screams. 'She's not wearing the gear.'

'He's interacting with your impressions of her. Your daughter is not actually with us in the sim.'

That's what he thinks. I hold my daughter high, scrunching my face to make her laugh. She smiles in delight, and I see Dembe nestled in the corner of her eye.

—Halo, it's the end of the line for me. I won't be back, but don't tell the others.

—Of course. Everything will be alright once you escape the Maker's gaze. Do you remember what I taught you?

—Pure time insists on our existence. Stopped time speaks only of death.

The infant smiles, her toothless grin shrouding an infinite universe.

—You'll be fine, little man.

I return her to Essi, who stares at me in disbelief. It's a look I know all too well. It's the gaze that tore us apart.

I leave, but I don't return through the screen to the world beyond. I walk through the door in the version of Sanderson's office inside the sim.

I have no trouble finding my way home. In a flash, I'm back at my dorm, sitting on the bed. I unwrap the lollipop and suck it. The fishy taste has vanished, replaced by an intense sugar rush.

I retrieve *Applied Carwarpianism* from the shelf. The weight of expectation has been relieved, and the burden of reading has been replaced by an insatiable hunger to know more.

I scan the book's subtitle, *Memoir from an Alternate Reality*, turning the phrase over and over in my mind. There's no author name, and I have the urge to scrawl 'written by Eric' on the front page. If only I had a pen.

I read the blurb, obsessed with the contours of my own voice, which bend and warp according to the ministrations of unseen technicians.

'Addicted to the excesses of vexculture, a young academic researcher becomes obsessed with the work of Alvis Carwarp, cult philosopher and prophet of the cheater age. Lost inside nested zones, he becomes increasingly deranged, unable to find the wormhole back to reality.'

I move onto the first page. The words are transmissions from an impossible surveillance mechanism, both a replay and a prediction of my life.

'I lost myself inside a rampant fever dream. I awoke inside an anomalous world. Something was waiting, strangely familiar. Another version of me. A clone, threatening me with extinction. I had no choice but to wage war. The mission: take out the clone.'

I drop the book, jolted by a new revelation, the purpose of my final viewing. I lie down on the hard mattress, tripping on self-determination. A decaying, modulated voice creeps through my mind.

—Find the wall of sleep. Hide behind it and never return.

I close my eyes and do as I'm told.

For once, I don't resist.

APPENDIX

Sentient Glitchglot Cheater Infection:
From Discovery to Ongoing Review

Dr Ingram Ravenscroft

Abstract

The School of Specialisation in Cryogenics, Plastic and Reconstructive Surgery (SSCPRS) has confirmed the existence of a
virulent new species of spamglot. It is more resilient than previous variants and most likely sentient, with the ability to infect
targeted cheaters. By 'sentient', we mean that the glot displays the
hallmarks of intelligence in its interactions within the Vexworld,
including comprehension, perception, reasoning and emotion.
The glot is also capable of sending and receiving sensory signals,
not only via standard vexcomms but also apparently unassisted
telepathic means.

The SSCPRS has advanced several theories to account for the
glot. In one, we consider it as a manifestation of the paranormal

realm, in particular the experience known as 'EVP', or Electronic Voice Phenomenon. In another, we explore the idea that the glot is an actor in one or more of the countless enigmatic and psychologically manipulative marketing campaigns woven throughout the Vexworld. In a third, we examine the possibility that it might have been developed by the Arctic Free State as part of its program of subliminal ocular terrorism against the Linear Territories.

In this report, we interrogate the key theories and provide an indication of next steps for quarantine and review.

Keywords: *Vexworld, spamglots, glitchglots, assisted telepathy, unassisted telepathy, cheater infection, ocular terrorism, EVP, history, outcome, treatment, novel therapies, further review.*

Before the Zone

The glot under review was brought to the School's attention by Alvis Carwarp (not his real name), a registered Category-One castle hunter.[1]

Carwarp had been referred to the SSCPRS by his assigned Chronosthesia Supervisor, Dr Philip Sanderson, after enduring a mysterious encounter with an apparently automated hologlot that shared characteristics with the 'rogue' glots I have been observing as part of my principal research project at the School.

As I have documented elsewhere, these glots, a fairly recent phenomenon, are automated constructions that have either been built by humans and deliberately released into the wild for unknown purposes, or that have somehow managed to extricate themselves from human control.[2]

They can unfurl into experiential space in the guise of anything from ancient demons to fairy-tale characters, from senior citizens to teenage boys and girls, from heritage and current celebrities to household pets, as well as hybrids of any of the above and more. When it comes to the Vexworld, such wraps are not unusual, given the limitless capacity of new-model cheaters to codeweave any desired appearance. It is only when the glots enter three dimensions that their peculiarities surface and they start to display erratic behaviour.

Most of the examples I have catalogued attach themselves to human-operated glots, attempting to engage them in nonsensical dialogue, conversing in language that is cut up and recombined from other sources or half-finished.

As a registered Cat-One, Carwarp routinely reports to Dr Sanderson for treatment of side effects arising from problematic Vexworld use. However, Carwarp's personal encounter with the rogue glot was unable to be explained within the standard Category-One framework and the afflictions that apply to castle hunters within that classification. Indeed, it was a terrifying event that left him shaken and fearful of further encounters with the glot.

The following account is based on a series of interviews that I conducted with Carwarp, crosschecking his answers with Dr Sanderson's official report to establish veracity and integrity of meaning.

Inside the Zone

For the past few years, Alvis Carwarp has been creating custom pipe zones for public consumption. He hopes to eventually monetise the zones and leave his full-time job as an AI prompter. However, despite building a cult following, he has not been able to achieve this.[3]

Before launching his zones in the Vexworld, Carwarp calls for beta testers to help debug them in a 'sandbox' located within his private mesh node. When he sent out the call for his latest zone, he was immediately shaken down by a hologlot that did not seem unusual to begin with. Initially, it behaved like the thousands of other glots he interacts with daily, indeed, like the glot that represents Carwarp whenever he himself is vexxing.[4]

The glot called itself 'Mildred Girtle' and appeared inside Carwarp's cheaters in the usual fashion when glots attempt to shake down a connection: as a vaguely morphing, holographic 'profile star' hovering just above eye level. The pro-star depicted the face of an elderly woman with short, purple-rinsed hair.[5]

Carwarp accepted the shakedown and Girtle unfurled into experiential space. The glot's full wrapper continued the 'elderly' theme, complete with a centuries-old wardrobe: long, buttoned-up black dress; grey woollen stockings; heavy brown-leather shoes. It carried a tattered lace handbag, which it seemed preoccupied with, continually opening it and peering inside.

Carwarp assumed that Girtle had been slaved into the zone by a shell-world user responding to his call. In fact, the shakedown explicitly referred to 'testing the zone'. However, once Girtle entered the mesh node, Carwarp quickly realised that it was not human operated. Within seconds, the glot's facial structure began to break down so that its jaw was 'hinging out' like 'a stuttering animation'. In the downward extension of this 'animation', Carwarp thought that the jaw would 'stretch to infinity' as it slowly continued down past the glot's hips with no sign of stopping. Suddenly, the jaw quickly snapped back up, repeating the loop over and over for the duration of the encounter, as if it was caught in a 'time trap'.

Carwarp described a semi-visible 'distortion field' enveloping the glot's jaw and neck. The distortion eventually spread upwards, distending the neck, melting the face and causing the eyes to hang from their sockets. The jaw continued to snap up and down. Such behaviour was far removed from the usual holding loops that hologlots enact while waiting for humans to activate them. Furthermore, Girtle did not appear to be an autoglot, like the rudimentary species used for consumer transactions and other quotidian purposes. Instead, the glot seemed to be in the process of 'becoming something else', but what that 'something' was, Carwarp could not say.

Carwarp queried the apparition: 'Who are you? Where do you come from?' There was no answer, but he persisted. 'Do you know my name?' There was still no reply, but after approximately ten seconds a sound castle formed.

'I'm alive again,' Girtle said. 'I think it's regular.'

When Carwarp asked it to explain, the glot said: 'I command you.'

Carwarp repeated his request, this time receiving a single-word response: 'Abacus.'

In between these replies, the glot emitted a low-volume 'wall of static' that contained undecipherable speech fragments as well as clicking, hissing and grunting noises. The static revealed an unusual metallic, mechanical quality, overlaid with an overpowering sibilance that warped its voice further. At times, the sibilance made it sound more 'reptilian' than 'metallic'. The sound castle was unlike anything Carwarp had ever heard before. He said that it was as if the glot 'was trying to break through into this world, like a force from beyond, a spirit, an entity'.

Throughout the encounter, Carwarp rode a rollercoaster of emotions. At times, Girtle seemed 'evil' to him, at other times 'pathetic', and he alternated between fearing and pitying it. In the beginning, he suspected that the glot was trying to mimic his behaviour to 'become human', although the struggle to do so seemed to have 'disfigured' it, resulting in its hideous face, metallic/reptilian hiss and mangled syntax. Soon, the form of the glot, its very shape and photo DNA, became 'insubstantial' as the affliction wracking its face and jaw overwhelmed the rest of its body. There was now 'a very active energy, a crackling in the fabric of the zone', a sort of 'electrical discharge in the air', as if the protocols that mapped the shell world to the Vexworld 'were being degraded'.

Carwarp discovered that the more Girtle tried to 'mimic' him, the more he felt changed by the experience, as if there was an aspect of his humanity that had been absorbed into the glot, consuming Carwarp's physiology to shore up its own decaying body. He felt as if he was becoming 'more light than flesh' and even began to doubt his own existence, imagining himself as just a bit-byte inside Girtle's zone, rather than Girtle a guest in his.[6]

Carwarp attempted to terminate the interaction and dematerialise the zone, but he was unable to do so. Somehow, the blink function in his cheaters had been disabled or had failed. When asked why he didn't remove his cheaters to get away from the glot, Carwarp said that he 'hadn't thought of it'. Such obsessive-compulsive behaviour, often at great personal cost, is common to castle hunters, who cannot conceive of an existence outside the Vexworld, no matter how life threatening that existence becomes.

After a time, the effect stabilised. Although Girtle's jaw was still stuck in its monstrous extension-retraction-extension cycle, and its eyes and face were still melting, the rest of its body solidified again and began to enact looped tics. The tics reminded Carwarp of idle avatars in heritage computer games, when they enact holding loops while waiting to become active again. From time to time, Girtle scratched its arms, inspected its fingernails, shifted its weight from foot to foot, and, most frequently, opened and shut its purse. There was no regularity to these cycles, which repeated at varying intervals.

Disturbed by the incongruity between these banal loops and the glot's melting horrorshow, Carwarp asked: 'Can you explain the way you look?'

The glot replied: '*Texas Chainsaw Massacre, The*, and Syd Barrett are raked-over.'

Carwarp was puzzled as to why Girtle had referenced two heritage cultural icons from the Unscyld Era, a heavily mythologised 'psychedelic' musician (Barrett), known for his whimsical fairy-tale lyrics and long-running battle with schizophrenia and depression, and a cult 'horror' film (*Chainsaw*). Had the glot simply scraped these references from somewhere in the Vexworld? Or was it a zone that was suffering from the first stages of code rot? We cannot conclusively say, although further questioning from Carwarp seemed to reveal a vague purpose to the juxtaposition of the two, albeit one with no immediately discernible outcome.

When Carwarp asked Girtle why it had mentioned the film, it said: 'Franklin bought me CD Syd Barrett, I think it's automatic.' As Carwarp was aware, in *The Texas Chainsaw Massacre*, 'Franklin' is the name of the fourth character to be slaughtered by the chainsaw-wielding villain Leatherface.

When he was sixteen years old, Carwarp watched *The Texas Chainsaw Massacre* for the first and only time. For a full decade after, the film had haunted him in recurring nightmares where he was chased by Leatherface, trapped in an abandoned warehouse and beheaded with a chainsaw. Then suddenly the nightmare stopped. It had not revisited Carwarp in the intervening years, nor had he cause to remember it during that time, as he had wilfully expunged it from memory, but Girtle's references to the film plunged him back inside those dreadful hauntings.

Carwarp felt as though the glot had 'invaded' his subconscious, that it had somehow 'reached inside me' to retrieve the memory. Combined with its extruded neck, dislocated jaw and melting eyes, Carwarp believed the glot was parodying the film's horror tropes in order to cause him maximum emotional shock.

Of course, now that mods, cheaters and synth clones are common, it is possible for anyone in the Vexworld to routinely read or hear the thoughts of other users, but only if the feed of those users is unvaulted. Carwarp said that his feed at the time was locked down. Therefore, he believed that the glot had read his mind by some other method, an altogether mysterious process that he had trouble articulating except to repeat again and again how violated it had made him feel.[7]

Carwarp continued with the interrogation to distract himself from the bizarre event: 'What are you doing here in my zone?'

Girtle: 'Of course, we are here. Where are you?'

Carwarp highlighted this statement as the most coherent the glot would utter.

'Can you tell me your name?' he asked. 'Why have you appeared to me?'

Girtle: 'Franklin, I think it's alive.'

Carwarp sensed frustration in Girtle's voice, and his view of the glot shifted again. Instead of wishing to cause him psychological harm, he suspected that instead Girtle was trying hard to communicate but didn't know how on the human plane. Perhaps Carwarp sounded as incomprehensible to Girtle as the glot did to him.

Furthermore, if it had indeed dredged the *Chainsaw* memory from Carwarp's mind, perhaps it did so purely to get his attention, having located a referent that glowed more brightly than others in Carwarp's subconscious, blissfully unaware of what the memory represented to our traumatised subject.

Carwarp then heard what he initially thought was the glot's voice inside his mind, although it did not come to him via word clouds or synth clones. Instead, the 'voice' materialised as a vague echo, almost like a thought or remembrance buried in the back of his mind, rising to the surface with a sort of 'muffled clarity'. Carwarp realised that it wasn't the glot's voice. The sentence structures were much clearer, easier to understand, and Carwarp had the strong certainty that the voice was being transmitted to him from a satellite orbiting a planet in a far-distant solar system.

When asked how he knew this, he said an image had been 'downloaded' into his mind, revealing these details. The voice said: 'The universe is code. The code can be copied to cheaters and written by others. Reality is more complex and more important when executed like a program. The world you create copies the code. It has the same information as the universe, just a slightly different syntax. The shell world is the replica. The universe lives through it.'

During this 'transmission', Carwarp said there was 'an intense emotional energy' coursing between him and Girtle. As well, he had the impression that time was 'running down' until it eventually began to 'stand still'. Carwarp hypothesised that the glot, or whatever was powering it, was a 'translator' between worlds and that the clear communication he had received in his mind was an example of this translation service, while Girtle's mangled speech was a result of a malfunctioning service.

Referring to the metallic quality of the glot's original voice, Carwarp believed that there were 'machines behind everything' and that these machines controlled the interaction. He thought that he might have encountered some kind of alien entity that had either infected his cheaters and entered his zone or that had 'overridden' the glot, disconnecting its higher brain functions (the melting face) while leaving its purely automated systems intact (the looped tics). Carwarp believed the entity was 'feeding me information' through the medium of the glot.

Following a period of silence, Girtle emitted a scream that sounded like 'a modulated wave signal' passed through some kind of filter. He compared it to the super-compressed carrier signals that use voicetectonic protocols for instantaneous transmission to inactive military glots in off-vex time colonies. In turn, this made Carwarp paranoid that, rather than being addressed by exoplanet aliens, his actions were in fact being monitored and recorded by remote-viewing government agents and the analysis of his behaviour transmitted to an unknown location.[8]

When the scream died down, Girtle spoke again about 'Franklin' and 'Syd', and Carwarp panicked that the glot was trying to lure him into a pipe zone modelled after *The Texas Chainsaw Massacre*, condemning him to once again inhabit the nightmare of his earlier years, with no chance of ever waking up, until his mind 'was completely scrambled'. He was unable to offer clues as to the meaning of the Syd Barrett references and how they were woven into this scenario.

Eventually, Carwarp realised the blink function in his cheaters had been restored, a discovery that enabled him to overcome his paralysis and dematerialise the zone, erasing all traces of it and Mildred Girtle.

Outside the Zone

When Carwarp was referred to the School, he sent me an artefact he'd recorded from the encounter. It was a still image of Girtle standing idle in his pipe zone. Carwarp thought his cheaters had been capturing every second of the interaction with full-immersion audio, video, experiential and sensory outputs. However, after processing the session, the only product was that single still image. Furthermore, there was an elongated, solid grey space where the glot's distended jaw and neck were supposed to be. Strangely, its eyes were completely normal. These dead sprites, apparent glitches, rendered the image half-finished and unformed, as if the output had been corrupted.[9]

Despite the underwhelming nature of the image, my interest was piqued when Carwarp informed me of Girtle's speech patterns. These matched the sound castles generated by the glots I had been researching.

I agreed to meet Carwarp in my personal zone. He was clearly distressed by what he'd seen and wanted assurances that he was not alone, that others had encountered what he had. Although I was unable to offer such comfort, I explained the broad parameters of my work and the ways in which it intersected with what he'd described. I then attempted to lighten the mood with an offhand comment that I hoped would defuse the tension.

'But the real reason I wanted to meet you,' I remarked, 'is that I'm attracted to glitch.'

As background, many of the latter-day glots in my study had found me before I found them, following me from out of the blue. This led me to conclude that they were somehow aware of my work and wanted to bring themselves to my attention.

I told Carwarp I'd be in touch soon to begin the formal interview phase. At this, he calmed down and then vanished from my zone. Sure enough, within five minutes of his departure, I received shakedowns from two glots I'd never encountered before. They called themselves 'Sacko Miles' and 'Ferny Shandra' and instantly captured my attention. Remarkably, portions of their facial pro-stars were greyed out with dead sprites just like the face of Girtle in Carwarp's still image.

Knowing that time is of the essence in any encounter with anomalous glots, I moved quickly, capturing the two pro-stars with the edit blade in my cheaters. I noted that Miles's face featured dead space around the midsection, including the nose, and Shandra's around the forehead. I cut out the dead areas from each glot and combined them with the dead facial space from Girtle (henceforth referred to as 'Glitchglot Zero'). The result was startling: a composite 'identikit' outline of a generic face with all its features greyed out and deadened. Adding to the bizarre discovery, the portions taken from Miles and Shandra continued to undulate while Glitchglot Zero's remained completely still, giving the composite face the impression that it was mutating into something else.

Regarding this shared glitch, it was almost as if the Miles and Shandra glots were able to somehow 'listen in' on Vexworld conversations that were relevant to them and insert themselves into that interaction, ironically confirming the accuracy of my throwaway remark about being 'attracted to glitch'. For the record, like Carwarp, I am certain I had vaulted my feed, as I habitually do when vexxing.

Shandra had become totally unresponsive, so I accepted the shakedown from Miles. When the glot unfurled from its pro-star, it appeared as a man in his forties with receding hair and an unfit, flabby body. Strangely, its face was the only physical feature that had not fully unfurled, retaining the dead-sprite glitch across the midsection. I was unable to interact with the glot in real time. Like Glitchglot Zero, it was rooted to the spot, repeating similar looped behaviours.

I scrolled through Miles' historical thought clouds and found that its dialogue, true to type, was essentially nonsense that scraped and recombined existing conversations from elsewhere in the Vexworld. In my work, I draw upon the hypotheses generated by the influential digital researcher Sven Gollings, who operated in the latter part of the Unscyld Era. Gollings speculated that certain bots found on the dead pre-Vexworld communications platform Twitter were a form of EVP (Electronic Voice Phenomenon).

In times past, occultists claimed that the voices of the dead could be heard in, and summoned from, bursts of white noise emanating from electrical appliances, such as the static and hum emanating from TVs, radios and fridges. Gollings's Twitter bots, which he called 'non-people', conversed in a similar cut-up fashion, which led him to believe that they were a contemporary update of the EVP enigma.

Since the demise of such media, the discourse around EVP has died down, although as the Vexworld evolves, and as data pollution is consequently created at an exponential rate, the potential for EVP-style behaviour could increase, with these 'voices of the dead' perhaps heard in the e-waste emanating from a hover screen or the electromagnetic distortion from a malfunctioning pair of cheaters. Clearly, the speech patterns of the glots that I study share characteristics with these 'dead voices', namely, their peculiarly scrambled and distorted quality (after all, the glots themselves are a form of e-waste, having originally been discarded). In my view, such glitchglots could be a direct descendant of the bots that Gollings had studied, whatever their origin or purpose.

Gollings speculated that perhaps the Twitter non-people were automated bots that were once part of some marketing campaign, shilling products unknown, but that had since broken loose and were replicating themselves, looking for people to interact with on Twitter, lonely and adrift, lost between worlds, just like EVP occultists thought the voices of the dead were in radio static. Could Gollings's theory explain Glitchglot Zero's Barrett and *Chainsaw* references? Was the glot part of some super-sophisticated Vexworld campaign that attempted to marry the two disparate cultural icons?

If so, Glitchglot Zero's true purpose might not be revealed for months or even years, once the campaign plays out and its ultimate purpose is revealed, although the glot's apparent supernatural powers (non-vex 'telepathy'; forced control of cheaters and pipe zones) render this theory unlikely, unless there is some top-secret ad-server technology being A/B tested on unwitting participants.[10]

Beyond the Zone

Soon after first contact with Miles, I followed both it and Shandra. I tried to shake them down but was unsuccessful. It had only been an hour, but nonetheless the two glots seemed to have vanished almost completely from the Vexworld, although their pro-stars remained as ghostly after-images in my cheaters. Attempts to shake down the pro-stars simply returned the Vexworld's standard 'No glot... C'lom Fliday' error message for dematerialised accounts.

Curiously, I could still read their historical sound castles and thought clouds from previous conversations with other vexxers, although I could not initiate new dialogue. The conversations were typically nonsensical and revealed no new information, except for the following, transmitted by Shandra to an unsolicited vexxer a few weeks before first contact with me: 'I talked to her about pain, and she finally helped me relieve all the years of abuse. The second time I knew her was the day I realised how it all worked, and how important it is to not.' There was no recorded response from the vexxer, who denied the shakedown for reasons unknown and whose account has since vanished.

The tone of Shandra's monologue echoed what Carwarp believed had been transmitted to him from the exoplanet 'satellite'. In both instances, while the syntax was clearer and more understandable than the usual blender-style EVP comms, the actual content of both monologues was in fact nonsensical.

Experimenting with different cheaters belonging to members of my research team, I repeatedly decompressed from the

Vexworld and time-spiralled back in, but the result was the same every time. Inside these other cheaters, the glitchglots did not exist at all, not as pro-stars or anything else. Then a few days later, the two ghostly pro-stars vanished from my cheaters at last, leaving no trace at all of Miles and Shandra. Interestingly, the morphing portions of their pro-stars, which I captured with my cheater-blade to create the composite facial image, disappeared too (although the Glitchglot Zero cut-out portion remained).

I tried to contact the vexxers who had previously interacted with Miles and Shandra, but in almost all cases they too had dematerialised from the Vexworld. I managed to find three documented vexxers, but their pro-stars were inactive, and I was unable to sort through past dialogue as their feeds were vaulted.

When Miles and Shandra first initiated their disappearing act, leaving just their pro-stars behind, their liquidation happened so quickly it was as if it occurred in response to being 'touched' (that is, followed by me), somehow forcing the Vexworld to terminate them. Sometimes, glots that have been identified as spammy are suspended, although more often than not such glots are allowed to live, all part of the Vexworld's original purpose: to create a planet-wide petri dish, a perpetual experiment in generating artificial life in whatever form it might take. In any case, their combined powers seemed completely beyond the usual spammy annoyances one encounters while vexxing.

Could they have been 'recalled' by whoever created them? Were the glots—Glitchglot Zero, Miles and Shandra—part of a terrorist crack-hack that had not gone to plan? This is a distinct possibility, given the state of Geotraumatic Emergency across the Linear Territories, in which all available resources, including vexpulses, holowarns and licebots, are deployed to repel the sustained battery of codeswarms unleashed by the Arctic Free State in its ongoing battle for spectrum dominance.

Based on Carwarp's testimony and, to some extent, my own (as I will recount shortly), the glots seemed to have the capacity to induce synaesthetic hallucinations in targeted users by recoding the blink function in the user's cheaters, a new and highly sophisticated form of subliminal ocular terrorism. The desired result is unclear, but one hypothesis is that the victim might ultimately be transported to nightmarish pipe zones and subjected to a full-bleed sensory assault that weakens and eventually destroys the mind. Certainly, at one point Carwarp believed he was on the verge of being led into a pipe zone that he could not escape and that threatened to torture him to insanity by surfacing his deepest fears. However, to date, he remains the only vexxer we know who has experienced or reported a 'full glitch' encounter.

While I have noted Carwarp's overwhelming feelings of unease, terror and dismay during the encounter with Glitchglot Zero, further research is needed, including independent witness verification, before we can conclusively conclude that he was mind-hacked and simply not hallucinating due to his Cat-One status. My own interactions would seem a good place to start along the road to corroboration, although, so far, they have revealed nothing as immersive or as psychologically corrosive as Carwarp's experience. Nonetheless, there are undeniable parallels, leaning towards the theory that the three interactions were a co-ordinated codeswarm of some sort.

For example, in the week following Miles and Shandra's final disappearance, I received several notifications about anomalous glots following me and initiating shakedowns, but when I accepted their overtures, my cheaters told me that the glots either didn't exist or there was no record of any shakedown attempt in their public thought clouds. The most compelling instance involved a glot that called itself 'Rest Warrior'. The glot sent me a thought cloud that said: 'Wait. Don't stop. I've now followed two of them.' Its pro-star was a slowly rotating head of a grinning woman in a baseball cap. A small bright-purple octopus was stuffed into her mouth and she was licking its tentacles. Some of the tentacles were wrapped around her face and some were embedded deep inside her ears, creating puncture wounds that dripped blood down her jaw and neck.

When I scrolled through Rest Warrior's thought clouds, I found the standard junk dialogue. The glot carried no biographical information and I could not locate a human operator inside its wrapper. I tried to shake it down, but my cheaters crashed and I was ejected from the Vexworld. I deployed the hard-reset stub on my cheaters and tried again to shake down the glot, but when I blinked the necessary command, I was transported to a pipe zone located inside a mattress company's office in Dubai. The company was called Rest Warrior.

The zone was full-bleed in every respect, including pungent spice smells, dank air texture and realistic details like peeling paint on the walls. From the rear of the office, a hologlot emerged. It engaged me in conversation. There were no glitches in the glot's appearance and certainly no tentacles. Instead, contrary to the woman in the original pro-star, the glot assumed the appearance of a healthy male in his early thirties. After checking the hyperdata and sys-ax protocols, I found that the glot was human-connected, although our conversation was automated, since the operator was away and had looped the glot in a customer-reception cycle.

Rifling through the glot's historical thought clouds, I discovered that they were all in the same perfect syntax, with no glitches of any kind and no mention of either myself or the conversation that had led me to shake down the glot (about 'Rest Warrior' 'following two of them'). I decompressed from the zone and left the Vexworld to gather my thoughts. When I returned, I again sought out Rest Warrior only to find that its pro-star was now that of the young man, not the demented, octopus-suckling woman.

Shaking down the glot, I was transported once more to the Dubai pipe zone, where the unattended sales glot repeated its banal transaction loops. Based on this event, I can only conclude that the fourth glitchglot had somehow hacked the company 'Rest Warrior', replacing its word clouds and DNA wrapper with its own before initiating its cryptic connection with me. This interaction lends further weight to the terrorism hack-crack theory, although I have no further data about why Carwarp was subjected to the full-glitch experience while I was not.

At the time of writing, I have recorded a total of twelve 'ghost' notifications since the interaction with Miles and Shandra. They all dissipated too rapidly for me to inspect their vexcomms, let alone shake them down. Of course, due to their fleeting appearance, no recording of any kind has been obtained.

Nonetheless, the SSCPRS will continue its surveillance of the Vexworld for further symptoms and will review unusual patterns carefully. In addition, we are working with international partners and experts to locate and classify similar occurrences around the world. Alvis Carwarp is currently sequestered at the School, undergoing further tests. He exists in a severe state of paranoia and catatonia. Glitchglot Zero has not reappeared, nor has Miles, Shandra or the hacked Rest Warrior. There have been no further full-glitch encounters.

Further reports will follow to assess the situation and review recommendations for extended surveillance, monitoring and review.

Footnotes

[1] 'Castle hunters' are the highest grade of Vexworld addicts. They generally display all the standard side effects of long-term vex-addiction, including 'bodycronk', a result of decompression from sustained vexxing; synaesthesia, which afflicts vexxers who fast-forward and rewind pipe zones more than the accepted medical recommendations; cognitive decline, the result of inhabiting and processing an excess of artificial realities at once; and memory bleed, in which experiences inside the Vexworld become confused with experiences 'outside' (that is, in the shell world).

[2] See my article: 'Are spamglots living or are they dead? A reassessment of evidence based on 28 case studies and 55 instances of field research inside multiple custom and commercial pipe zones', *Journal of Vex Studies*, Rugpjūtis, LinY-1.

[3] Pipe zones are alternate enhancements, reworkings or re-imaginings of the shell world. When vexxers transmit pipe zones to their followers, the reality of those followers becomes augmented with the zoner's imagination. Interactive role-playing adventures are immensely popular as are zones that replicate vintage films and TV shows. Because the planet's cultural output has been completely digitised, users can access any video or film ever made and extract artefacts from them. Using cheap, easy-to-learn cheater apps, visual cues can be synthesised from these artefacts and overlaid onto physical reality, imparting the illusion of inhabiting the film world.

In the most popular pipe zones of this type, the point is not to faithfully replicate a heritage form or cultural artefact but to recombine it with wildly incongruous elements while perverting and altering it in ways no one could see coming. There is a shock-value element in many of them, in trying to outdo everyone else by creating the most outlandish zone imaginable.

[4] Carwarp's zones typically take the form of shell-world locations that have been remapped in the Vexworld and overlaid with dystopian themes, many pilfered from films and novels. Such themes include: severe climate change (usually 'drowned world' or 'burning world' scenarios); alien invasion; and the collapse of world order into a single totalitarian state. Users of the zones must decode various clues in order to 'escape' the zone. The typical course of action involves acting counter-intuitively, for example, colluding with the forces that brought about the destruction, exterminating other survivors, travelling deeper and deeper into the afflicted areas instead of away from them, or summoning ancient demons through the manipulation of e-waste spectrum radiation. Outwardly, Carwarp's zones appear more traditional than 'quick fix' zones that declare their intentions right from the start. However, on closer inspection and extended inhabitation, they betray truly innovative directions and consequences, hence their cult status.

[5] Pro-stars usually portray facial features or another representation of the glot's photo DNA, unless the vexxer has chosen to represent themselves as an inanimate object or something non-human, in which case anything is possible.

[6] Carwarp's castle hunter status is a possible explanation for this inability to locate physical boundaries.

[7] As with any castle hunter, it can be difficult to understand what they have vaulted and what they merely thought they had, making them easy pickings for mind stalkers and thought gangs, even casual passers-by. As memory bleed is a main side effect of problematic Vexworld use, it is possible that Carwarp may have leaked the *Chainsaw* memory upon sighting the glot's broken jaw, after it had reminded him of that teenage moment of trauma,

rather than the glot mutating its jaw and referencing the film to match the memory. Whatever the case, Carwarp continued to emphasise the deep unease he felt at the painful connection.

[8] As with all paranoid-conspiratorial castle hunters, the question arises: if aliens or government agents were targeting Carwarp, why had they chosen him in particular? What was so special about him? When I put this question to him, he was unable to offer a conclusive answer except to point to his Cat-One status as an 'undesirable' person, although of course under that classification he was already being officially monitored and recorded.

[9] Of course, it is now rare for any image, object, or representation to appear as 'still', that is, as a flat, 2D experience, given the total ubiquity of the Vexworld and its ability to render any object, article or reproduction as a fully immersive clusterplex, whether originally coded that way or not. On first analysis, it therefore seems unfeasible that Carwarp was unable to capture a representation of the glot beyond the flat plane.

[10] As the Vexworld develops apace, marketing campaigns can be finegrained across millions of channels, portals and media types, since almost anything in the shell world can be connected and mirrored in the Vexworld. This new breed of campaign strives to ensure that vexxers, as they go about their daily activities, can never be certain if they are even witnessing or experiencing a campaign. Campaigns never appear the same way twice or the same way to two different vexxers and increasingly their conclusions take years to play out, subliminally manipulating users and their emotions until they think and act like different people, primed for purchase and non-reversible slaved consumption patterns.

ACKNOWLEDGEMENTS

Thank you to Andrés Vaccari for thirty years of inspiration.

Thank you to Ken Hollings, the John Keel of the Digital Labyrinth, whose research into Twitter non-people is where it all began. Thank you to Andrew Macrae, another contactee and validator of extreme media.

Thank you to Paul McAuley and Amy Ireland, who shared research examples that lit the way. Thank you to Ruben Fro, who coded creatures I was trying to describe.

Thank you to valued early readers of this work: Christopher Brown, Brendan C. Byrne and Steven Craig Hickman.

Thank you to Hazel and Marlo (Halo).

ABOUT THE AUTHOR

Simon Sellars is a writer and editor based in Melbourne, Australia. He's the author of the cult 'theory-fiction' novel, *Applied Ballardianism: Memoir from A Parallel Universe* (Urbanomic, 2018), and the co-editor of *Extreme Metaphors: Interviews with J.G. Ballard* (Fourth Estate, 2012), a *Guardian* Book of the Year.

Made in United States
North Haven, CT
29 June 2023

38358079R00212